# ORCHID CHILD

*Liminal Books*

Liminal Books is an imprint of Between the Lines Publishing. The Liminal Books name and logo are trademarks of Between the Lines Publishing.

Between the Lines Publishing
1769 Lexington Ave N, Ste 286
Roseville, MN 55113
btwnthelines.com

First Published: June 2023

ISBN: (Paperback) 978-1-958901-15-1
ISBN: (Ebook) 978-1-958901-16-8

# ORCHID CHILD

Victoria Costello

This book is dedicated to Brendan, Devin, and Diep,
With all my love

# West Ireland

## July 2002

Across the Atlantic, Kate hears the wagging tongues still dissecting her sudden exit from the lab. Forward motion of any kind used to soothe her, but she finds no comfort in the gentle sway of the high-speed train. Nor does she want the life that begins at its destination, even if her ticket and work permit say otherwise. She is hugging her knees, running the wheel of regret, when the Iarnród Éireann slinks out of a fog bank into bright sunlight performing pirouettes on saturated fields. Her eyes adjust to make out geometric fields dotted by black-faced sheep and whitewashed houses. An azure lake in the shape of a melting snowman. Bands of orange, yellow, and blue fill the sky, and she gulps for air, stunned by the uncanny welcome—not yet aware that breathtaking rainbows are the regular dance partners of Ireland's showers.

"Teague, you've got to see this, Tea—"

She reaches for her nephew but leaves her hand suspended over his bony knees. He's sprawled in the seat with a Yankees bomber jacket covering his head, his legs crisscrossing their shared floor space. She lifts the jacket but can't bear to wake him. Sleeping Teague is an aging cherub in a Raphael painting. Lips slightly parted. The last of his baby fat padding a square jaw. Thick black hair falling in waves to his collar. He'll be drop-dead handsome in two years if she can keep him alive that long. She's acutely aware of the effort he puts into

1

appearing normal. The long, pained pauses before he answers simple questions . . . Are Cheerios okay for breakfast again? Shall I turn up the heat? Maybe this change will be good for him—for them both. She pulls off her shoes and socks, rubs her toes, and vows to make it so.

A conductor ambles down the aisle checking tickets. He shouts something unintelligible, then, "Welcome to Tullamore," before exiting the car. A sign on the platform reads, *"Fáilte romhatchuig Tulach Mhór. Welcome to Tullamore."* Only then does she catch on he's been announcing each station twice since they left Dublin, once in each language. Two people exit, one boards, and they're moving again.

On the platform, a banner with an enormous brown cow announces the annual Tullamore Show later this summer. A fading poster hails the World Sheepdog Trials. No doubt they brought in thousands of sheep as extras for the big day. All this industry reminds Kate why she's here: paid employment; career rehab; distance from a debacle of her own making—far more distance than she'd like. She already misses Phoebe, her aging Siamese, not to mention her view of the UN, an eleven-block commute to the job she loved, and the hours she and Sebastian stole in his Chelsea pied-à-terre.

Her attention returns to a pair of red-faced retirees facing her from across the aisle. Two corks ready to pop, they could be regulars at the annual Callahan Fourth of July barbecue. The man wears a gold-and-burgundy team shirt and reads a tabloid. The pixie-haired woman's nose is in a Maeve Binchy paperback. The back and forth between them is unremitting, as if extended silence would be an affront to one or both.

"Didn't I tell you that arse Bertie's a rotten tool? He said there'd be no cuts. Now all there is is cuts."

"So it is," she says, without looking up from her book. Kate filters out the words while holding on to their lilting brogue: clipped consonants and soft vowels, no line undeserving of a melody, delivered with a seen-it-all, long-suffering tone that brings to mind the grandmother who largely raised her. When she was a child, Gran's voice, flecked with an accent Kate had never, until now, consciously linked to a specific place, felt like a path to hidden treasures. Her curiosity piqued; she pulls a map from her carryon

2

bag. Ireland is 170 miles across, shorter than the distance between Grand Central Station and New Haven. Moving her finger counterclockwise from Belfast to Donegal, south to Galway and Cork, eastward to Dublin, she searches her memory for a city or county that Gran may have called home and comes up empty. Why didn't she ask? Even as a child, she knew the subject was out of bounds. As if it would have been rude to suggest Gran ever lived anywhere other than with them, in a cookie cutter suburb, thirty miles north of the George Washington Bridge.

It was enough to know she was her grandmother's favorite, complete with a private nickname. Only Gran called her Katy Bird. When she went to the library and asked to see one, six-year-old-Katy was startled to learn a katy bird wasn't a real bird. Neither did any appear in made-up stories, or so the librarian said. Undaunted, she conjured her own petite creature with iridescent feathers to match Gran's baby blues, which took off whenever Gran called her by that name.

Pins and needles in her leg pull thirty-one-year-old Kate back to the present, tucked in an economy coach seat on a westerly bound train. She threads her feet under Teague's knees and reclaims some floorspace. As sensation returns to her lower body, she releases her memories of Gran, allowing the scent of talcum powder, an old lady's gnarled fingers looped through a Royal Tara tea cup, the scratchy threads of a wool sweater brushing her cheek. Palming the same cheek, she drops her head on the seatback and feels calmer. Her pupils dilate and the landscape becomes a verdant blur. No wonder there are so many words for green, they need them all here: emerald, pea, sea, lime, jade, olive, sage, mint—it's a veritable *Times* crossword out there.

"*Fáilte romhatchuig Gaillimh*. Welcome to Galway."

Her eyelids lift in time to take in an impossibly quaint cityscape, a crescent bay cuddling its side. The train enters a tunnel, and the scene is gone. She touches Teague's leg. "Sweetheart . . . time to wake up."

Teague jolts awake. Why is Kate's hand on his thigh? She knows he hates to be touched. Or she should. Her face—drooping mouth, wrinkled nose—is the one she makes when she's trying to figure out what a real mom would say.

"We're here!" Like a chirping bird. "How do you feel?"

"I'm good." Shit warmed over is closer to the truth. And where is *here*? Oh right. The train. Before that a plane. *Die Hard II*. Newark Airport. Maureen's house. Sunlight stabs his eyes as a city comes into focus. A seashore butting up against a row of houses painted in primary colors. Whoa, it looks like brown grass growing on that roof. A tiny hotel, pink like cotton candy, cars driving on the wrong side of the road—they must have a law here against boring. The tallest building is a church steeple. Hey, there's a McDonald's, Holiday Inn. It could be Queens or Hoboken, only cleaner with more old stuff mixed in. They're heading into a train station.

"What's the other language on that sign?"

"I think it's called Irish."

"Good guess."

Kate is standing in the aisle reaching for the overhead rack. The train stops short, and she plops down next to him hugging her small suitcase. He takes her closed-mouth smile to mean *please don't freak out*. He doesn't intend to. The meds are doing their job. Keeping him tamped down and propped up at the same time. Safe and sound in the middle. Fine for getting by, not so good if he has something important to do like paint. Sitting around doesn't count as anything. It's fine as long as he doesn't have to chat. Chatting is the worst.

Kate doesn't understand him any better than most people. It's just that she's known him since he was born, and that stuff tends to stick. It's easy enough to love a normal little kid. Even Meghan, his junkie mother, managed that, until she couldn't. At least, that's what Kate said. The point is the good ones don't turn on you when you can't pull it off anymore. Hear that, Maureen? He gets why Maureen couldn't do it. Blood matters and Meghan wasn't her kid. She got stuck with her after she married Meghan's father, Jack, who's dead. He only knows about Jack Callahan because there's a picture of him with his cop badge hanging in the dining room, but nobody ever talks about him. At least he had Gran, his real great grandmother, for a while. Out of all of them, Gran acted most like his mom. Yeah, it's exhausting for him, too.

He didn't even get a chance to move out of Maureen's house into Kate's apartment in the city before Kate got fired, then blacklisted, which is how they ended up coming here. At least that's what he heard Kate say to her friend Joanne. When she asked him if he was up for moving to Ireland, Teague said he was okay with it. She might as well have said Iceland or India or Iran. It can't be any worse than hanging out in Rivervale with crabby old Maureen. Maybe he'll find someone weird enough to be his friend here.

"Ow!" Damn overhead rack.

Kate and Teague walk single file along the train platform into Galway City station. Her instructions are to meet Ryan under a clock suspended from the ceiling of the main waiting area. On the way down the escalator, she spots a stocky fellow beneath the clock holding a sign: DR. KATHERINE JONES written in black Sharpie.

Her first thought: Maybe she should start using her maiden name again. So what if she's published nine research papers under Jones? She wasn't the lead investigator on any of those. The divorce was final two years ago; why not reclaim Katherine Callahan? After a rush of pleasure, she feels oddly naked, and cycles back to the status quo.

Which makes room for her second thought: So . . . this is Professor Quinn. Flesh and blood Ryan bears little resemblance to the buttoned-down academic pictured in his faculty profile. Like a jack popping up out of his box, this Ryan doesn't appear to have run a comb through his thick, curly hair in some time. The beard, faded jeans, and sandals suggest a carpenter more than the well-published clinical and research psychiatrist she knows him to be.

He spots her and waves. "Welcome, Kate! You are called Kate?"

"Yes, please." She shakes his hand. "Thanks for picking us up on a Sunday."

"Not a bother."

A closer look at his ivory-pink complexion settles any doubt about where this man spends his daylight hours. His broad smile strikes her as the real thing. Teague lumbers to her side and she introduces them.

"Here, let me take that." Ryan grabs the larger case. Teague trails after them pulling his own. "Your first time?"

"I presented a paper in Dublin two years ago."

"I was at that conference. I must have missed your panel. Then this is your first proper visit to Ireland."

She doesn't argue his point.

A ten-minute drive through Galway City brings them to the sprawling campus of the National University of Ireland Galway, NUIG. Ryan explains its meteoric growth as a byproduct of the Celtic Tiger economic boom. His psychiatry program, which used to fit into the tiny brick building they just passed, now fills a four-story concrete-and-glass structure commanding the adjoining lot. His brow creases as he points to the new building, suggesting he's embarrassed over their good fortune, a reaction she finds charming.

"Except for the developers lining their pockets, you'd be hard-pressed to find anyone happy about the shabby construction going up around here. Not to mention the housing prices out of control."

By the time they finish their driving tour of campus, the conversation flows easily between them. It helps that his country-boy looks are not her type. That should keep things simple. And it's a relief to have an agreeable research partner. She's had her fair share of the other kind.

At the faculty apartment complex, he leads them to a second-floor unit and hands her the keys. "Take tomorrow to rest and recover. I'll pick you up on Tuesday morning."

Kate makes a 180-degree sweep of the furnished living and dining rooms. "It's lovely," she says, belying her first impression of the place as brutally bland. A near-total absence of color, milquetoast Berber carpet, tan microfiber sofa, glass tables—standard faculty fare. Then again, she can't be choosy.

As Teague wanders out of earshot, she motions for Ryan to step into the hall. "Should I bring him with me on Tuesday?"

"Aye. I'll do his intake interview first thing and we'll take it from there."

Before accepting Ryan's offer, Kate asked if Teague could get treatment at his community mental health clinic. She knew it had a robust teen program specializing in early intervention for cases like Teague's, better than anything she could find for him in New York. Ryan took a look at Teague's clinical records and agreed to it, as long as Kate was prepared to pay out of pocket for his care since she wouldn't be eligible for the national health service.

After spending two weeks in an adolescent psych ward in New York, Teague was unenthused about the prospect of doing more therapy. But, when she made it clear that outpatient treatment would be part of his future wherever they lived, he grunted his consent.

Kate says goodbye to Ryan and re-enters the apartment, where Teague is standing in the hallway between the bedrooms, looking uncertain. "Pick whichever one you like," she says.

"It doesn't matter," he replies with a practiced scowl. "We won't be here long. A month tops."

"Come on, Teague. It won't be that bad."

He shrugs and rolls his suitcase into the smaller bedroom, leaving her the master—and a massive spike in jitters.

Kate forces herself to stay awake until nightfall. She collapses on the surprisingly hard mattress with a thud, hugs the pillow, and brings her knees to her chin. She'd give anything to have Phoebe slide into the small of her back and purr them both to sleep. Good God almighty, who thought coming here was a good idea? She, the single mother of a teenager, no friends or family in the same time zone.

"You know better than anyone I'm not the nurturing type," she told Joanne, her college roommate and one close friend, also a law partner raising three kids with Roger, another lawyer.

Joanne answered with a straight face, "Last I heard, necessity is still the mother of invention."

"I'm serious, Jo, I'm no good at this stuff."

"Good at what stuff? Being alive?"

That ended the conversation and Kate's waffling. Two weeks later, newly unemployed, she swore to her readiness for parenthood before a judge who signed the petition making her Teague's permanent legal guardian.

Now her eyes mist and the neon numbers on the digital clock become a puddle of red. She pulls the sheet to her chin. Voices and footsteps filter up from the parking lot. Teague runs water in the bathroom, pads down the hall, and shuts his door.

It was only yesterday morning, as Manhattan Island shrunk to a sliver in the window of their 747 and Teague settled down with a movie, that she dared breathe a sigh of relief. "Am I done?" she asked Gran in a whisper. Surely, by losing her job and lover and gaining a problem child in one fell swoop, she'd completed her obligations under Gran's Rule of Three. It didn't matter that she no longer believed in it; Gran's Rule had the weight of memory and the ring of natural law, like gravity or magnetism. According to Ellen Callahan, "When two bad things or two good things happen to someone in a short period of time, a third thing of the same nature must occur or that person will be left dangerously unsettled, even haunted." Since her life started to fall apart in June, Kate has had no doubt about the negative nature of her three things. In her darker musings, she sees them as comeuppance for her audacity; or as her mother, Maureen, put it, for wanting too much.

"I hope to God it's nowhere near Belfast."

That was her mother's immediate reaction when Kate told her she was leaning towards accepting a job offer and moving with Teague to a small town in Ireland called Ballymore. They were in the kitchen cleaning up after dinner.

"What on earth does this small-town need with a neuroscientist?" her mother asked incredulously. That *is* still what you do for a living, right?"

"Yup." Kate picked up a tomato sauce encrusted pan and started scrubbing. She hadn't told her mother what really happened at the lab, so Maureen's confusion was understandable. Obviously, Mom suspected there was more to it. Kate kept her eyes on the pan as she continued, "A famous neuroscience study was done in Ballymore in the early nineties. I'll be doing a follow-up study with the same population."

"Hmmm."

Kate then pointed out that Ballymore was located in the Republic of Ireland, reminding her mother that there were two different Irelands. To which, Maureen huffed and said, "I'm well aware of that fact, dear," adding, "they've still got plenty of trouble *over there*. Too much for a boy with Teague's problems."

Kate tried another tack. "Doesn't the fact that both sides of our family came from *over there* count for anything?"

"Your grandparents got here a long time ago," Mom replied, rather nonsensically Kate thought.

Unlike Mom, Dad had relished his Irishness. He marched with his NYPD brethren on Saint Patrick's Day and saved his drinking for Irish pubs. There was the time he brought her along to help sell raffle tickets for the Belfast widows and orphans. Mom had argued with him, saying he should leave her out of it. The stronger memory for Kate is the fun she had exchanging tickets for coins and bills and helping Dad count their haul.

But it was as if the family's past died with him. They were Irish only on Saint Patrick's Day or if the subject of JFK should arise.

As she nods off on her uncomfortable new mattress, Kate thinks again of Gran's Rule and releases a full-throated groan. It will take her much longer to consider the possibility that she misunderstood the nature of the three things that changed her life that summer.

Car engines starting in the underground garage and rain pelting the windows alert Kate to the start of a new day. She wavers, desperate for a few more hours of sleep, but quickly abandons the idea of sleeping in. They need to acclimate. The prospect of coffee gets her out of bed. She's on her feet waiting for a wave of dizziness to pass when a gust of wind blows open a crank window below the slider. Cool air hits her bare skin, and she shivers. Conceding the inconvenient reality that she is more than a brain; she stretches her hands to the ceiling and bends over to touch her toes. More. I want more. More of what? Confidence. Clarity. Joy. Yes, but to what end? When no answer comes, her senses return to homeostasis, meaning they dull. In the process, self-doubt finds an opening and roars back. Who does she think she is taking on a multi-million-dollar study in another country?

Kate's imposter syndrome is atypical, tinged with perfectionism and poisoned by the sexism ruling academic science; more insidious because it hides behind noble motives. As everyone working in academia knows, the system that determines who gets research grants and the status they convey is rotten to its core. Ryan's project is a perfect example. As a family mental health study, it garners zero prestige. A function of it being low-tech, containing no linking up of rare genetic mutations in massive databases, no DNA splicing, just a lot of traipsing back roads for in-person interviews. Bottom line: "women's work." Throw in the fact that interactions with mentally ill patients and their families are notoriously messy, any ambitious young neuroscientist would opt to stay close to her lab bench.

Even though she's both a perpetrator and victim of this rotten system, Kate considers her relationship to science the cleanest commitment she's made in her adult life. It came about while she was an undergrad, when she discovered that the pursuit of hypotheses bested romance, and—no question— God for yielding answers she could count on. To this day, she marvels at the rigor of proofs, the grandeur of cells, and the logic of binary results born of well-defined methods. Buck up, she tells herself. Write a decent paper from whatever results come out of this study and you'll have a clear path back to where you belong. She pulls clothes, toiletries, and shoes from her suitcase and drops everything in or near the closet until she finds her favorite jeans and sweatshirt.

Maybe it's the pattern of holes in the ceiling tiles—eleven by thirteen, diabolical—and walls whiter than chalk making Teague feel like he's a stowaway on the *Challenger*. This place is so clean he wants to cough just to add some microbes of his own. The mattress is made of some kind of outer-space foam, hard as a rock. He didn't expect to miss the lumpy bunk bed he's slept on his whole life. Now he pictures his old room the way he left it a day and a half ago, empty and echoey, and wonders whether his old enemies are staked out in the closet waiting to make the next kid's life miserable.

Teague hasn't told anyone about the voices that have been bugging him for months. Every once in a while, he'll catch a glimpse of one of them; more often he hears them moving around out of sight, trash-talking him. A supersized rodent with a Russian accent he named Ivan, after the middle brother in *The Brothers Karamazov*, tells him he's an ugly piece of shit and the world is a junkyard of toxic trash and nasty people. It's like he is trying to get him to drop out of the human race and join the rat race. No joke.

Larry's a pit bull who talks like a kid and always seems to know when Teague is having a bad day. A few times, Larry told him things weren't going to get any better; he might as well end it. When he learned the word *sadist*, Teague knew who to pin it on. At Walgreens, Larry told him to steal a jumbo bag of Kit Kat bars. When Teague said no, Larry wouldn't leave him alone. Teague put his hands over his ears, yelling, "Fuck you! You're not even real. You're some trash that fell out of my brain." People stared, but what was he supposed to do? Larry just laughed. *You wish, kid. Do it or I'll be up your ass twenty-four seven.*

"What if I do it?"

*I'll give you the rest of the week off.*

Since Larry usually kept his word, Teague grabbed the bag of candy and tore out of there. That's how his klepto career got started. Now it's turned into a habit he can't break.

Whoa, Teague stops himself. He shouldn't be giving Ivan or Larry any airtime. It's like saying, "Come on back, guys, I'm over here!" He wipes his mind clean and fills the empty space with nonsense. *Da, da, da, da, da, zippity, da dooooooooooooooo . . . Da, da, da, da, da, zippity, da dooooooooooooooo.*

He remembers the pendant hanging around his neck and fingers the wizard on its face.

"Gran asked me to keep it until you were older," Kate said when she gave it to him on his sixteenth birthday—a month ago.

"She told me you'd be needing it one day. I'm not sure what she meant by that."

Teague did. To help him fight off enemies like Ivan and Larry. The first time he saw the pendant, he knew it had power. Now he lays it on his forehead and tries to absorb some.

"Teague, are you awake?"

He goes rigid under the covers. How long has Kate been standing in that doorway?

"Yeah. Why?" he asks.

"I thought we could go out for breakfast, then shop for food. If you want, we'll stop at the student bookstore and get you some art supplies. How does that sound?"

"I can't go."

"Why not?"

"I haven't unpacked my books."

Kate's eyes dart to the three unopened boxes lined up against the wall and then back at him. "Aren't you hungry?"

"Yeah. But I'll feel better after I do it."

Her face scrunches up like a sponge. "Fine. So, why don't I help you? It'll go faster."

"All right."

While she gets a knife from the kitchen, he slides out of bed and grabs sweatpants from a pile of clothes he dumped on the floor. Besides the new pendant, nothing matters more to Teague than his books. When they were packing his stuff, Kate suggested he give them away, since they could buy the same books or new ones when they got here. He didn't want to sound like a wuss and say they were his only friends, even though it's true. In the end, he flat-out refused to give any away and she agreed to ship them all. There's an empty bookcase in his room. Plus, a desk he'll never use.

"Shall I do the honor?" She holds the knife over one of the boxes. "Or would you rather?"

"I'll do it."

He slices the tape and pulls open the flaps. The smell gives him an instant high—not just because he sprinkled weed in the pages of *The Hitchhiker's Guide to the Galaxy*. Kate's on her knees by the bookcase with an armful of paperbacks. He holds his breath. Worst case, he'll just have to re-shelve them. She stares at their spines and looks up at him. "I bet you have a system."

Phew. "Yeah. Alphabetical, by author."

"Of course." She smiles and takes down the books she already shelved.

"Except Fyodor."

"Fyodor?" Her head is cocked to the side.

"Alphabetical worked okay when I was just reading sci-fi. They're good but there's no way those guys can sit on the same . . ." He picks up his battered copy of *The Idiot* and fingers the embossed title. He found it on the Metro-North and barely looked up until he got to the end five days later. When the Prince said, "If I had had the power to prevent my own birth, I should certainly never have consented to accept existence under such ridiculous conditions," Teague was blown-away. It was like Fyodor had read his mind across time and space.

"Oh, you mean Dostoyevsky. Well, I'm impressed."

Is she making fun of him?

"What did you think of *The Idiot*? Teague?"

The chance to declare Fyodor's awesomeness knocks down his guard. "It's the best book I ever read."

"I'll take your word on that."

"You mean you never—?"

"Me, no. I took the easiest electives I could get away with. You have to admit, Fyodor is not exactly a beach read."

Wow. He's always thought of Kate as such a brainiac . . . Maybe each human can only be good at one thing because their brain gets stuffed with that one thing, and there's no room left for anything else. He isn't sure what his one thing is yet. Or if he'll even have one.

Lately, his paintings have been, well, boring. The same half-human, half-robot creatures, just different body parts. Philip K. Dick's *Do Androids Dream of Electric Sheep?* got him started drawing humanoids. Now he's cranking them out like he's a copy machine. It must be his new medication keeping the good stuff out of reach. He opens to the page in *Electric Sheep* he marked with a purple sticky, his color for stuff to read when he can't feel a fucking thing and needs something to remind him other humans have survived in this condition.

"So, I left the TV sound off and I sat down at my mood organ, and I experimented. And I finally found a setting for despair. . . . So, I put it on my schedule for twice a month; I think that's a reasonable amount of time to feel hopeless about everything, about staying here on Earth after everyone smarter than you has emigrated. Don't you think?"

Yeah, Dick-man. You better believe it.

13

Kate is on her feet waiting for him to look up from *Electric Sheep*. "That's two shelves done. So, can we leave in a half hour?"

"All right." He puts *Electric Sheep* with the other Dicks and lays out another armful in alphabetical order. . . LeGuin, Rowling, Tolkien. He forces himself not to look up. They're just holes, even if whoever thought them up is out to get him. By the time he's done, bleating hunger pains trample over his paranoia.

Tuesday morning, Kate has a cup of coffee in one hand, a checklist in the other as she paces the apartment. She's preparing for her first day of work and Teague's entry into therapy, along with the massive amount of paperwork required for both. On the kitchen counter she's lined up passports and private health insurance ID cards, her Special Skills Employment Permit, plus Teague's birth certificate and medical records—all of these for the clinic administrator. For Ryan's academic bosses, she's got her vitae, validated medical degrees, and a list of her publications. She puts each stack in its own folder and looks around. What's missing? Hmm. The sky is several shades darker than the last time she looked. From the closet floor, she retrieves two windbreakers, with their tags still attached.

A loud buzzer sounds. She rushes to open the door and finds no one standing there. It takes two more buzzes for her to locate the intercom for the security system.

"Your ride, madame." he says through the speaker.

"We'll be right down."

"Fair warning, it's about to lash buckets out here."

"I noticed. Give us two minutes."

She opens Teague's door, relieved to find him dressed. "Time to go."

Teague grabs a book and exits the room barefoot. She retrieves his flip-flops and slicker and follows him downstairs. Teague stopped wearing shoes six months ago, which became a big problem for him and Mom, then Kate. The principal warned Teague the next time he got caught shoeless on school property he'd be suspended, which of course happened. The explanation Teague gave her after Mom insisted she talk to him was straightforward enough: "I need to feel my feet on the ground, and I can't with shoes on. So, what's the big fucking deal?"

Kate ran down a list for him: glass and other sharp objects, the school's insurance policy, snow. To which he'd rolled his eyes and told her he was sorry, but the shoe thing was nonnegotiable. Soon after, he failed the eighth grade and Mom threw in the towel. He still has to be cajoled into wearing shoes. She doesn't have the energy this morning. Fortunately, it's August, only rain to worry about.

Ryan threads the traffic out of Galway City like a Formula One driver while Kate grips the door handle. She has no idea how two opposing lanes of traffic—tour buses and delivery trucks on top of the morning rush hour—are sharing these narrow roads. Her wariness about getting behind the wheel of a rental car later in the day is now off the charts. After grinding her teeth for the first fifteen minutes of the drive, she shakes her head and grunts.

"That bad?" Ryan asks.

"Not to worry. I'll manage."

"We're taking the scenic route so you can have a look around."

"Wonderful."

"I'm having you on. The M6 is the only road connecting Galway and Ballymore."

"Well, I'm enjoying it so far."

Teague is sitting up in the back seat, his head moving back and forth like a windshield wiper.

She relaxes as the city sprawl gives way to more green space and lighter traffic. They pass single-family stucco homes adjacent to rectangular pastures holding small herds of sheep enclosed by waist-high lines of rocks.

"Is it just gravity holding these rock walls in place?" Kate asks.

"It's called dry stone. Not a speck of mortar. If you study them, you'll notice different patterns. They go according to the original clans."

"Cool." Teague wedges against the back of Ryan's seat.

"Do they still serve a practical purpose or is it just a poetic touch to keep them around?"

15

Ryan's half smile hints at mischievous intent. "And these two things are different how?"

"Sorry, I know nothing about poetry or farming."

"We'll remedy that in no time."

They enter the County of Ballymore, a continuum of older single-story, and newer two-story houses and pastures linked to towns with fairy-tale names. Castleblakeney, Ballinasloe, Glenamaddy, and Horseleap, each comprised of one or two pubs surrounded by storefronts of uncertain purpose. A sign heralds their arrival in Castleplunket.

"What's with all the castles?" Teague asks.

"Our history is one long fight over land, who has it, and who wants it." He glances in the rearview mirror. "With regular cattle raids to keep things lively."

"Awesome."

"How do these old houses stay so white?" she asks.

"The owners wash them with lime every three years, as a rule." He says it with no detectable sarcasm. "You'll still see some of the original thatched, two-room stone cottages with their roofs converted to slate. By the fifties, almost everybody had electricity and running water."

"Not so long ago."

"I suppose not."

They pass a property with the ruins of a cottage standing less than twenty feet from a brick-faced structure with Georgian columns.

"Is there a reason they keep a stone ruin on their lawn?"

"If the owners were to tell you straight, they'd say so they don't disturb the souls of their ancestors resting in those stones."

"Interesting." She isn't sure if he meant it as a joke, but she permits a note of skepticism in her voice.

As if on a time delay, Teague asks, "Are you kidding about the stones?"

"No, not at all."

When they arrive at the clinic—a long, squat building sharing a parking lot with the county hospital—Ryan takes Teague to his office for the intake interview.

"See you at lunch, sweetheart," Kate says in the crowded reception area. Too late, she interprets his frown as *Don't call me that in front of other people.*

Ryan's office is messy—not dirty messy, just cluttered. Files and books in a pile half blocking Teague's view of a framed picture of a girl in a team jersey, a plate with crumbs, and a half-full cup of coffee—which helps Teague relax a teensy bit. There's nothing worse than having to sit across from a shrink in a spotless office. In his experience, that guy or lady is an asshole.

"They sent me your records from New York, so we're not starting from scratch." Ryan opens a file. "But I prefer to hear as much as I can directly from you. I can promise two things. First, I'm not going to put you in a box. You're Teague Callahan, not a list of symptoms. Second, everything you say here is confidential, unless you give me specific permission to share something. The exception is if I think your safety, or someone else's is threatened. Am I clear?"

"Yeah." They all say that. No kid believes it for a second.

"Let's talk about the medication they started you on in the hospital." He looks down at an open file. "You've been on Zyprexa for three weeks. What have you noticed?"

"You mean besides feeling sleepy and hungry all the time?"

"After a few months, I might be able to lower your dosage, so we'll keep an eye on that. Anything else?"

"Well, yeah. Sometimes instead of having a hundred thoughts at a time, I have one or two. That's easier."

Ryan's eyes pop. "That means the medicine is helping your brain process information."

"Will I have to stay on it forever?"

"That's not a given. Recovery is possible when we intervene early, as Kate did with you. I don't rule anything out."

He's never heard a psychiatrist say that before. Just when he's feeling better, Ryan starts the stupid test. He slouches in his chair.

"Do you ever feel like a part of your body isn't attached to you"?

"No."

"Do you ever lose track of time"?

"No."

"Have you ever thought a voice was speaking to you from the radio or TV?"

"No." No way he's admitting that. One, two, four in a set makes six . . . Teague counts the books on the shelf above Ryan's head.

"Do you ever feel like you're being watched?"

He sits up straight and considers the question from a new angle. "If you mean, am I being watched by aliens who look like humans but have more powers than us? Sure, we all are. You've seen The X-Files, right?"

"Yes, I have. The question is, have you had a direct experience like that?"

"Well, maybe not. But I know they're out there."

He writes something down.

Ryan's assistant, Dara, a cheery, athletic type with bouncy curls and the legs of a footballer under her short denim skirt, escorts Kate to her new office, which she's delighted to see has a door. It's three times the size of her old cubicle with a view of the parking lot, a round table with two chairs, a desk, and a large, clunky computer. She leaves the computer dark and digs into a pile of studies Ryan left to help her get up to speed.

First, the prospectus for their study. A target population of 260 families with at least one member diagnosed with schizophrenia within the last three generations. Starting in the 1970s, County Ballymore recorded the highest rate of schizophrenia in Ireland and one of the highest in the world, making Ballymore a famous place name in neuroscience. And while there have been plenty of theories—one laid blame on the 1845 famine that wiped out a third of Ireland's population—the question remains, why was Ballymore hit this hard? And to what degree is the spike still present in 2002?

Teague will receive the same treatment as the teenagers in their study: weekly sessions with Ryan or a staff therapist, group therapy, and medication if he needs it, an issue Kate views as settled but she's eager to hear what Ryan thinks. Medication for children and teenagers showing symptoms of serious mental illness is controversial, putting clinicians like Ryan on the defensive. Anti-psychiatry sentiments have coalesced into a movement of patients resisting any medical interventions after many were harmed by lazy or untrained practitioners who relied excessively on drugs and involuntary hospitalizations. The groups have names like Mad Pride and Voices International. Kate finds their arguments reductive and dangerous. She's grateful not to have been one of their targets.

In comparison to the trench warfare of frontline psychiatry, the years she spent working at her lab bench seem quaint and rarified. Well, that's over. As part of her separation agreement with the university, she surrendered all rights to research she did there, including the experiments she did on her own time in which Sebastian played no part except to downplay their value. She holds her breath as she recalls his barely concealed rage when she balked at that clause—as if she'd betrayed him by not going quietly.

"What if I refuse to sign?"

"Kate, I'm warning you. Playing the victim is not going to get you your next job."

Before their affair, she'd managed to keep the objects of her desire separate from her ambition to alleviate human suffering through science. Her downfall, the thing that had wrecked her grand plan, was the commingling of the two. Commingling ... putting two elements together into one, making the constituent parts more or less homogenous. In this case, definitely less.

In the immediate aftermath, she made a vow that for the next year she would stay away from men, meaning no actual sex. That's not to say she doesn't permit herself small thrills, the way someone steals an occasional bite of dessert while they're on a strict diet. Under this regime, she's allowed to relive certain moments of loveliness without reproach ... The first time he touched her naked breast after a year and a half of propriety in the lab. Their thrilling mix of nerdy shoptalk and pillow patter—"I've never met a woman who can flip from her head to her cunt and back again as fast as you can. I love that about you ..."—as he made her beg before getting to the finale.

Oh shit, her concentration is gone. She shimmies her shoulders and drags her focus back to the document on her desk.

A siren blares, comes closer, then quiets; no doubt an ambulance pulling up to the hospital entrance, a block away. She checks her watch, surprised to find it's nearly one o'clock. The clinic parking is full. Her shoulders ache. She stands, stretches her arms to the ceiling, and rotates her neck. She should go check on Teague and get them both some lunch. A good half of the parenting game, Joanne pointed out to her last month, is sticking to a schedule. How hard can that be?

# West Ireland
## *1920*

Two years back, without telling a soul, not even the man himself, Ellen Mitchell decided she was meant to marry Michael Callahan. He'd just walked in the door of her father's apothecary when a portrait of the two of them standing together, wearing formal clothes, came to her like a waking dream. Ellen was not the kind of person who had visions. When this one showed up out of nowhere, she knew to take it seriously.

She was minding the counter at the time, Da in the back preparing medicines, Mam upstairs in their living quarters. Ellen had been told that one of the Callahan sons would be coming by to pick up a remedy for their mother, Anne, who needed something for her colicky newborn.

"How long has it been going on?" she asked him.

"Coming on a month and a half."

"Then you'll be needing the chamomile," Ellen said to him after Michael finished telling her about the wee one's shrieking at all hours, leaving the family at their wits' end.

"If you say so," he said, eyeing her curiously.

She turned around to face the wall of jars. Although the remedy she would give him could be counted on to bring down the noise level and give her more breaks, Anne Callahan surely faced several more weeks of wailing before anything resembling peace returned to the household.

A sweet fruity aroma filled her nostrils as she scooped the walnut- and pea-size yellow balls into a cloth satchel. "Tell your Mam, I'm sorry for her troubles," she said as she extended her hand with the satchel.

That's when fate seemed to make up its mind—or maybe it was just when Ellen answered the invitation—which set loose the spell that put everything in motion. As she waited for him to take the chamomile, Ellen found herself waylaid in the congealed greens and blues of Michael's eyes. With the two locked in a stare, his heat reached across the counter and caressed her cheek. It was as if each had come upon an unfamiliar creature and felt compelled to linger and study its ways, losing their individual boundaries as time slowed long enough for them to say *aye* or *nay* to what was being offered. After each chose affirmatively, they were lifted together onto an elevated path reserved for the two of them. They followed it to its end and lay their bodies down in a field covered with tall, soft grass offering privacy and the promise of untold delights.

"I thank you," he said, breaking the silence but not their stare as he took the satchel and his fingers brushed hers. Behind him, a low sun reflected off the gold-etched letters in the store window spelling MITCHELL'S APOTHECARY. It didn't matter that they'd known each other for years as neighbors, schoolmates, and parishioners. They had just met anew.

Ellen relived those moments as she and Michael walked to the Callahans' cottage where they were expected for supper. She'd been up since sunrise, helping his family harvest a field of hay. Now, as their shoulders grazed, it bothered her that Michael hadn't said a word since she'd told him her news. Long enough for the clouds of worry shading her full heart to darken.

*Maggots*, she thought, when a neighbor, Tom O'Shea, came out his front door to meet them in the road. "Afternoon, Michael."

"Fine day, isn't it?" Michael offered.

"How's your harvest then?" Tom asked.

"Not too bad, considering the rain."

Tom looked up and down the road before he went on. "Has your father talked to you about the matter I brought to him yesterday?"

"I don't think he has. Do you want—"

Tom raised his hand. "In good time." He tipped his hat to Ellen. "Give my best to Paddy," and he walked back to his cottage.

After several more silent steps, she could wait no longer. "Well then?"

He stopped and met her eyes. "Then we best set a date." His smile filled her with joy. "A child is a blessing," he said unequivocally, and squeezed her hand.

The weight fell from her shoulders and her lungs filled with air. "I don't doubt you, Michael. I only worry what else will happen before we can share our good news."

Midway through the year that would later be called The Terror, simply aspiring to things usually considered parts of normal life felt like stealing. Ellen had become accustomed to feeling afraid some part of every day, trying to chase one or another bogeyman just to get some peace of mind or a night's sleep.

Violent skirmishes happening to the east and south since the 1916 rising in Dublin had set things in motion that could no longer be contained. The fighting now at their doorsteps; it occurred more often, with each rebel attack earning a vengeful reprisal. Crown forces crossing county lines to quell rent boycotts. More locals taking up arms and fighting back. Not choosing a side became harder. Families and neighbors split in their loyalties. As strongly as some supported this latest in a long history of rebellions, others blamed it for making a bad situation worse.

Called Volunteers, the rebels moved around the countryside ambushing squads of the Royal Irish Constabulary, known as RIC. Mind you, the RIC were Irish-born, people they'd grown up with, serving uncomfortably as a national police force under the command of their British occupiers. Ellen's Uncle Killian was one of them. He fought with the English in the Great War and used his connections with the Jacks to become a constable when he returned, which is why most everyone kept their distance from him, his wife, Nora, and their young'uns. Of course, Da didn't shun his own brother. A man had to put food on his table however he could, Da would say, but their relationship grew more strained as the summer wore on. The mercenaries known as the Black and Tans were the newest horror unleashed upon them, brought in by the British to back up their troops and the RIC. The Tans would go through towns randomly killing and burning down homes and stores if the names and hiding places of Volunteers weren't given up. People said they made a habit of shooting into any random stretch of woods they passed to head off an ambush.

Not long ago, Ellen's younger brother, Brendan, had come home from school upset, saying his teacher had been taken away by the RIC on account of teaching them a poem called "The Wearin' o' the Green." When Ellen said it must have been for some other reason, since "Nobody gets arrested over a poem," Brendan recited the lines he and the other boys decided must have sealed their teacher's fate. "Did ye hear the news that's goin' round? / The shamrock is forbid by law to grow on Irish ground!" Ellen had to admit the poem had nothing nice to say about the British, but she'd stuck to her argument, more out of stubbornness than conviction.

# 2002

Teague runs his hand over the smooth stone of a column that's wider than he can wrap his arms around, one of four columns holding up a three-story concrete building at the north end of Old Town Square. It's the tallest building in Ballymore, not counting the castle. A plaque by the entrance says it used to be a jail, then a lunatic asylum—they actually use those words—and now it's The Bank of Ireland with an Italian restaurant off the back alley.

He leaves the square and walks the two blocks called Old Town, where he passes a row of tiny stores, one each for jewelry, hats, cigars, newspapers, and stops in front of a pile of rubble. It's the bones of a house collecting cobwebs, moss, food wrappers. Are they waiting for a ghost family to come home and clean up the mess? Maybe they are. Great zombie Jesus, Ireland is like living in a theme park.

At the crosswalk, he's waiting for the traffic light to change when he spots the turrets of Ballymore Castle jutting over the trees. Yesterday, when he took the castle tour, the guide said the Normans built it in the twelfth century to get a good shot at anyone trying to steal their cattle. He went to the top of the tower to check out the angle it offered on cars driving on the M6. Sure enough, it gave him a perfect shot.

The drugstore is on the edge of Old Town. It looks modern from the street, but behind the register, the wall is stacked with dusty blue and green glass bottles, labeled by hand: *Lupili, Bismuth, Tinct Buchu, Nux Areca, Carryophyl, Eucalyp*. He likes how the syllables roll off his tongue as he whispers their names. Another shelf holds a rusty scale, stone bowls, grinding tools. These people don't throw anything away.

"That's all we've got left of my grand-uncle Paddy's apothecary," the guy behind the counter says, nodding over his shoulder. He's Maureen's age, on the fat side.

"What happened to the rest of it?"

"The Brits burned it down."

His name tag says Sean Mitchell, Chemist.

"Why'd they do that?"

"Retribution, subjugation, call it what you want. We had a wee rebellion going on. I like the feeling of having Paddy looking over my shoulder while I carry on the family business."

Teague drops a pack of gum on the counter and some coins. Sean drops his eyes, then lifts them to meet Teague's. "Are you going to pay for the candy?"

"Oh yeah. I forgot." He pulls the chocolate bar out of his pants pocket and adds a Euro.

Sean raises his eyebrows and blows air like his cheeks are popped balloons.

From a rear pocket, he takes out a pack of batteries. "I don't really need them." He gives the batteries back to Sean while avoiding eye contact. It's like his hand has a mind of its own.

Sean points a finger below the counter. "Since I put in these cameras, I'm seeing a lot more than I'd like to."

"Sorry. I won't do it again." Probably wishful thinking but it can't hurt to say.

Sean's smile isn't the happy kind. At least he didn't bust him.

Teague is retracing his steps through Old Town Square when he catches the sounds blowing past him in the breeze. Words, parts of sentences. Voices without people. Of course, that's not so strange for him but he's never heard these voices before, and, as far as he can tell, they not talking *to him* or *about him*. Which is kind of a relief.

*Traitor . . .*

*I'm the same as you.*

*On your knees . . .*

He stops next to the statue in the center of the square and does a 360-degree turn. The old lunatic asylum is straight ahead. Main Street runs parallel to his right. St. Brendan's is to the left. Maybe that's where the voices are coming from. Except the church steps are empty and the doors are closed.

*You've got the wrong man.*

*Then give me his name.*

When he walks back to the rock wall surrounding the church, more words join up to make whole sentences.

*Not my boy. Leave him be.*

*Nooooooo. Mother of God, tell me it's not so!*

He's pretty sure these voices belong to dead people. Maybe they're talking to each other. Nah, it's more like they're trying to get somebody's attention.

*Do you have anything I can feed my wee ones?*

*Off to the workhouse with you.*

*Take them, please, I won't make it there.*

*Mam!*

A lady carrying a shopping bag in each hand walks by and gives him a friendly smile. Oblivious. Did she really not hear that?

Teague leans against the rock wall and pops a fresh stick of gum in his mouth. Maybe people around here are sick of hearing these voices—the way he feels about Ivan and Larry—so they ignore them, which pisses off the dead people and they talk louder, and to strangers. He gets ten paces away from the wall and the chatter dies down. He backs up and touches a rock and it's like his finger is stuck in an electric outlet. So many voices he can't tell them apart.

He backs off from the wall and makes for Main Street. A block away, the voices fade back into the wind and his breathing slows down until it's normal again. The sidewalk is packed with shoppers, kids out in packs, deliverymen double-parked. He could be walking down Main Street in Rivervale, except for how old everything is here.

His stomach has started making hungry noises. Maybe he'll his skip three o'clock group.

"Don't worry, Ryan will help you fit in," Kate said this morning when he complained about having to go. She can be so clueless.

He spots a juice bar and buys a banana smoothie. He's slurping it, checking out a video store window, when he remembers what Ryan said about souls hanging around the ruins of houses. Maybe it's the same with the rock wall. Then, it's like his thought turned on a switch. The voices start up again. He's curious, so he doesn't try to shut them down. He takes a deep breath and catches glimpses of old timey people and connects them to the voices he's hearing.

*Run, lads, run.*

*I'm hit. Leave me. Go!*

Whoa, there's some seriously bad stuff going on in the square . . . A column of British soldiers busting down the doors of St. Brendan's . . . they drag out a bunch of rebels, line them up against the rock wall, and shoot point blank. Now they're setting fire to the houses and stores . . . Holy shit. People are running into the street and getting shot at.

It feels like he's there with them. Or they're here. He can't tell the difference. Teague holds his breath and the pictures freeze. Leaving him stuck in some kind of void where it's dark with no sound except the blood swishing through his veins, his heart pounding, echoing off his skull. Come on brain. Wake up! He hits his forehead with the palm of his hand. Nothing. He does it again. Ow, damn it. Once more, harder, and finally, some light and sound seep in. Hand-held video cameras, Xbox, E.T. on a bike; the video store window display slowly comes back into focus. A bus pulls up behind him. He whips around, dizzy, and makes out a woman in a headscarf staring at him. He goes into the video store to get away from her and think.

Some quick laps around the store's two aisles calm him down. He's got the four-disc boxed set of Lord of the Rings in his hands when he gets an idea. What if the rocks in the wall held on to the voices and pictures of what happened here the same way silicon chips store data? Silicon comes from quartz crystals and, duh, quartz is a rock. His arms and legs vibrate. The voices stayed around all this time, waiting for someone to tune in at the right frequency. Someone like him. But why?

Teague returns the boxed set to the rack and heads back to the square where two old men are playing chess at a stone table. He sits on a bench across from them and waits for his thoughts to settle down. The pair have finished one game and started another before an answer jells in his head. The ones who died in the massacre won't leave the square because they want witnesses to what happened to them here. Even now. It could be a quantum thing. Like, unless people pay attention, they never existed, and their suffering was for nothing.

Or maybe he's just thinking crazy shit. He's still sorting it out when St. Brendan's bell peals three times. Damn. He's late for group.

# 1920

Even with her feet planted on the dirt floor, Ellen swayed on her stool, her stomach unsettled by the fish-oil lamps and loamy spuds cooking over a peat fire. She may as well have been riding on board a heaving trawler, not sitting next to her sweetheart and his kin by the hearth. How much longer could she keep their secret?

"I just want to live my life." Michael said with a hand shielding his eyes. "In America, if it can't be here."

Drat! He didn't have to say that. He knew she wanted to stay near her family. It was what he wanted, too. Someday farm a lot of their own. They'd heard plenty about people turning on their kind in New York and Philly. Enough to know there was no pot of gold waiting for them across the Atlantic.

Anne stopped pulling bowls from the cupboard and put both hands on her hips. "This isn't a good time to be holding out on your own blood. You best be telling us what you know."

Michael gave Ellen a sideways glance. She nodded, hoping he would do as his mother asked. Months ago, he'd admitted his mixed feelings about the second sight he'd inherited from his father. Ellen had witnessed it in large and small ways since they were young'uns. When he could tell what she was about to say before she said it. The time he found a lost child who came close to drowning in a bog. His warning to Anne about the coming death of her brother, who, she learned a month later, had died that day fighting as a conscript in France.

The gift of sight passed between Callahan men was considered special even in this part of the country where the old ways were still a way of life. Plenty of people made a point of keeping their distance from the good folk, who made it their business to be good to the kindly and plague the nasty. Some of their neighbors still put bowls of fresh milk on their windowsills at night for the benefit of a thirsty visitor who might pass by and slipped a stake under the mattress to ward off a vengeful one, since the fae were known to steer clear of iron.

Because of Michael's troubles, she understood the heavy burden the gift foisted on the ones who carried it. The way he saw and heard things left him open to outside forces, good and bad, and it was sometimes hard for him to tell them apart. In a time when informants were the only class of people more hated than rent collectors, Michael's second sight had on more than one occasion raised suspicions, particularly in other boys his age who were eager to grab hold of the new century and leave the past behind.

"All right. I'll give it a go." As he hung his head and closed his eyes, a thicket of long black hair shielded his face. Ellen turned away and traced his profile from memory: a high forehead giving way to sloping cheeks, the bulb at the end of his nose looking over a strong square chin. The sum of its parts a work of beauty in her eyes.

Minutes went by until he spoke again, and when he did, he sounded older, as if he'd forfeited his youth to reach deep in time. "There's a target sitting on us. But it's much wider than you'd think."

Michael squinted at the fire and twisted his mouth. Ellen's body stiffened. An attack on Ballymore would be a major escalation of the fighting.

"There's a rake of Black and Tans coming our way. They're here for vengeance. I'm seeing bullets flying, buildings alight." He shook his head slowly and stared into the fire.

John, whose second sight had faded as Michael's grew stronger, as was the way of things, pressed his palms together and touched his fingertips to the cleft in his chin. "When, son?"

"A week, maybe two."

"Hey Merlin, how about telling us who's going to get hit? This shite does us no good. Could be Killarney or Dublin for all you know." Colm was warming for a fight. Any goodwill they'd brought back from the harvest seemed to have disappeared with the sweat on their backs.

"That's what I seen." Michael's eyes narrowed. "So, this would be a good time to move anyone, or anything stowed in town before innocent people pay the price."

Colm clenched his jaw and looked away.

When Ellen noticed Michael's curled fists, poised on his thighs like sentries, she permitted herself the tiniest of sighs—not nearly reflecting the size of her disappointment—as she realized this would not be the night they announced their plan to marry. Nor would another better time come soon. The struggle for independence had caught up with their plans for an ordinary life. A simple dream made even more complicated by Michael's gift.

Early on in their courtship, Ellen had railed to her mother about Michael being as good as gone for hours or days at a time, not saying where he'd been when he returned. It left her feeling like she couldn't count on him because whoever he'd answered to came first. To her surprise, Mam had had no sympathy for her. "Shame on you," she said. "Use your head. Why do you think their kind is still with us? When Mother Nature makes a mistake, she leaves that poor creature to waste away." She went on to explain how, according to the old ways, there's always a reason for the gift re-appearing in a lineage. Most of the time, you don't know what it is until much later. She finished by saying Ellen needed to accept Michael as he was or walk away right then."

Ellen knew that was impossible. Fate had given her a choice that day in the store and she said yes. There was no going back. After that talk with Mam, when Michael's second sight tried her patience, she did her best to cleave to her mother's way of looking at it. That is, until her own brush with death, and the unimaginable consequences that came of it, showed her why Michael carried the gift, and why they chose each other as mates for the difficult journey.

Michael sat up straight and eyed his mother. "I just gave you all I got."

"Hmmm." Anne kept ladling stew.

Ellen said a silent prayer . . . Please, let it be enough.

Colm was on his feet. "That's brilliant, Michael. But I don't need your magic to know what's coming. Not after those two RICs got blown to pieces. I heard—"

"Sit down, son." John used the booming baritone he saved for hymns and Bible readings. "There'll be no more talk of payback, or America." The last aimed at Michael. "Colm, your brother is telling us their targets have changed. With the two killed, they'll be wanting to teach us a bigger lesson."

"Lord, protect us." Anne made the sign of the cross.

"Aye." John looked down and picked dirt out from under one fingernail, then another, and held the hand up for inspection.

To Michael, he said, "Rory O'Shea, you remember him, oldest to Tom. He went north a year ago. Yesterday, Tom tells me Rory was one of them done the ambush. Now the lad's hiding on the bog. Tom wants us to know he's sorry about asking the question, but he's hoping we can point him to a safer hideout for Rory—until this blows over."

Ellen remembered Tom asking Michael earlier in the day whether John had raised a certain *matter* with him. Now they knew what he meant. The question put Michael in a dangerous position, but it couldn't be helped. Anne added herbs to the stew. Colm paced. Bile rose in Ellen's throat.

Michael closed his eyes for a minute, then said, "He'll be safe in Cat's Cave."

"At Rathcroghan?"

Michael nodded.

"I'll pass it on to Tom."

Ellen wondered whether he chose Cat's Cave because it was the site of a famous cattle war, and some fierce faeries were known to keep a fort there. Might they help stand guard for Rory O'Shea? She would have to ask him later.

John's features were drawn as tight as fiddle strings and Michael's face offered a mirror image of his father's. Like a rotting smell, their fear soon engulfed Ellen. Everything was happening too fast.

John cleared his throat. "I'm looking to each of you to do what needs to be done and say nothing about this to no one." Michael and Colm turned in different directions while John winked at his two girls and nodded at Ellen.

"There ain't no one and nothing left in town to worry about." Colm again, making a claim for the last word. Ellen wondered where he got his information. For all she knew, he'd already joined the Volunteers. But Colm didn't talk like someone with convictions of either kind. She touched Michael's arm to urge him to stand down. He pulled it into his lap without looking at her.

John looked from one son to the other. "I've had my fill of your bickering, lads. You forget we're one family here. It's time for our supper."

Tessa pushed her little sister off her lap and got up to serve the stew. She returned with two bowls, handing one to her father, the other to Ellen. "Thank you for having me tonight, Mrs. Callahan," Ellen made a point of saying.

"Never mind, dear," Anne replied with a glance over her shoulder. "You baling hay in the hot sun all day, it's the least we can do."

After that, only spoons scraping bowls broke the silence. Lest she draw Anne's attention by not eating, Ellen swallowed wee bits. When she couldn't stomach anymore, she twirled a leaf of cabbage in the broth and pictured the day she still hoped might come ... Michael standing at the altar of Saint Brendan's in his maroon waistcoat. Their eyes meeting as Da led her down the aisle wearing Mam's dress. If the feckin thing still fit. Between her nausea and bulging middle, Ellen felt less like a bride every day. She hung her head, fearing her face might catch fire with shame.

# 2002

Eight kids, counting Teague, are sitting or lying on beat up chairs and sofas in the clinic lounge. He doesn't dare look at any of them above the waist. He can hardly make himself breathe. It's like facing off against a bunch of fighters in a ring. He knows they're checking him out and trading smirky looks. Hanging with the devil in actual hell can't be much worse than this. He'd rather be at the dentist. Or therapy. Oh right, this is therapy. It's like he has no body. He's a pair of eyes floating on the ceiling. Just when he thinks the situation can't get sorrier, two hands land on his shoulders from behind.

"Settle down, guys," Ryan says. "Our group has a new member. Teague is here for a year from New York. I'm sure you'll make him feel welcome. Why don't you go around and introduce yourselves?"

Teague wipes sweat off his face with his tee-shirt.

Two girls, five other boys say their names. Only the last guy looks at him; wow, he even cracks a smile. His name is Liam O'Shea. Teague knows a gamer and a stoner when he sees one, and Liam is both.

Now they're supposed to talk. When no one does, Ryan puts the pressure on. "Do any of you have a situation from last week you'd like to share?"

"I do," a girl named Emer says. "Me mum keeps trying to get me to eat even when I tell her I'm not hungry. I'm sick of it."

A boy laughs and says, "Give it to me, then."

35

"Shove it up your arse!" Emer yells back at him.

"Cut out the cross talk," Ryan says to the boy who started it. "Emer, why do you think your mum is after you like that?"

"Because she doesn't want me to die of starvation."

"It sounds like this has turned into a contest of wills between you and your mum. Do you think you could move away from an all-or-nothing stance?"

"How do I do that?"

"You decide what you will eat and tell her. Then ask her to back off."

"I'll try it."

"Good. Anyone else?"

God, he hopes Ryan doesn't call on people. A kid sitting across from him is sweating and breathing hard. "Are you all right, Niall?" Ryan asks.

"I had to run the last mile to get here on time." He keeps his eyes on the carpet.

"Did you get off the bus too soon?"

"I had no choice. She was evil." He brings his head up.

"Who was evil, Niall?"

"A lady had her knives out for me; I had to get off."

"I understand she felt threatening to you. But is it possible something else could have happened to this lady before she got on the bus, a spiff with her husband, that made her mad?"

"Yeah, I guess."

"Her angry look could have been about that."

Niall shrugs.

"Okay, let's dive into this." Ryan stands in the middle of their circle and gives them each a look. "Every human being gets paranoid sometimes. But for people with your symptoms, it can be harder to pull yourself out of it. So, listen up. There's a simple trick you can use to deal with situations like what happened to Niall. It's got three steps. First, *catch* yourself. As soon as you start feeling scared, stop and take your feelings out of it. Just tell them to wait. You'll let them have their say later. Put your mind in charge. Another word for this is reframing. You put a new frame around your experience by giving it a different meaning. The second step is to *check it*. Step into the shoes of that other person.

What might be causing them to act or look that way? Might they have had gotten fired? Could they have a bellyache? Check out the possibilities and decide which is the most and least likely. The last step is to *change it*, meaning change your response to this person with a different action. Instead of getting off the bus, maybe turn around and replay something good that happened to you recently. Are you with me?"

Ryan makes it sound easy, but at least it's something to do. "Now say it with me . . . Catch it. Check it. Change it." It's like gym class. Whatever. Teague plays the game.

"What do you think, Niall?"

Niall squishes his face like he's thinking hard. "Yeah, she probably didn't even notice me."

"Great. I want you each to try this at least once during the week and we'll talk about how you did next time."

"Anybody else?"

Kiernan pulls both feet up on the edge of the chair, wraps his arms around his shins, and peeks out over his knees. "My asshole voice Arial came back."

"All right, Kiernan, can you look at me?"

He squints up at him.

"First, I have to ask, have you been taking your meds?"

How embarrassing. Teague feels for Kiernan. He's lucky if he can make himself take his Zyprexa every other day.

"Kind of."

"Okay, you've told me before when you take them on schedule, your voices stay away. And like I've told you all, halfway is half-arsed. Was there anything else bothering you when Arial showed up?"

"Not that I know of. I was just sitting on me bed, chilling, listening to music, when he reminds me how God picked me to stop the evil ones. Why am I just sitting on my arse?"

"Did Arial identify who was doing the evil?"

That's an interesting question, Teague thinks, as he considers the possibilities: Al Qaeda, a serial killer, a bully.

"No, I was supposed to know."

"What did you do next?"

"I cranked up the music. Started babbling so I didn't hear him."

"Can I say something?" It's Liam.

"Fine with me," Kiernan says.

Ryan nods. "Go ahead."

"If you hide from him, he's just going to take advantage of you. Like any punk around here would do."

Jeez. Liam sounds in charge. He's a few years older, but it's more than that. Teague wants whatever he's got.

Ryan jumps in. "Liam has his own approach to voices that works for him. There's no right or wrong way to manage your symptoms. Having said that, Kiernan, the first thing I want you to do is get back on schedule with your meds. Okay?"

"Yeah."

Kiernan's just saying that. And Ryan probably knows it, too.

After group, Teague tells Kate he's going to town. He's tired of walking around but he's more tired of people knowing too much about him. Asking about New York like he's the chamber of commerce. They tell him about their uncle or cousin who lives in Staten Island or Albany. Like he should know these people.

He sits on the curb in front of the clinic, hoping no one will bother him. His bare feet on cool cobblestones feel awesome. He wonders how long they've been here. A hundred years? Five hundred? He's just starting to relax when Liam sits down next to him.

"Howya?" Liam says.

"Doing all right." Teague can't help staring. Up close, Liam's eyes have barely any color in them. His pupils are slits. Throw in his albino skin and orange hair, he's got a real Leeloo vibe. Liam is checking him out, too. They're like two magnets about to crash. Maybe because they're the same kind of schizo.

"You got voices?" Liam says it as if he's asking a normal question, like, You new in town?

"Not much anymore." Teague looks away because he needs a break. "What about you?"

"Me and my voices have it all worked out." He gets on his feet and turns his head to the side. "Don't we? Ha! You're right. It's past time for a pint."

To be polite, Teague looks at the empty space next to Liam who's hunched over laughing. He's probably putting him on, but Teague can't be sure. Larry and Ivan never once said something funny to him. Maybe this is what it's like when you make friends with your voices.

"Why did you come here with your aunt?"

"My mom OD'd when I was five and then Gran died. My step-grandmother couldn't handle me anymore. That left Kate. She's all right."

"Hmmm. What label did they give you?" Liam's got his hands on his knees, staring down at him.

"Schizoaffective."

"Put you on Zyprexa?"

"Yeah."

"I tried that shit. Turned me into a robot."

Liam's eyes won't get off him. If he keeps it up, Teague's afraid he'll bust out of his skin like Plastic Man. "Yeah, the side effects suck."

"If you ever want to get away from that shite, I can show you how. We meet up here on Fridays at five and go over to the castle."

"Does Ryan know?"

"He knows me and some guys who used to go to the clinic have our own group."

"Maybe."

"All right. Later."

Liam strolls to the corner. It's not a regular human walk. He slithers from side to side like a snake, making jazzy moves, leaning forward and back, and somehow still going in a straight line. If he practiced every day, Teague could never be that cool.

# 2002

"Why are you looking at me like that?" Teague is slumped in his chair at the dining room table, pencil in hand, working on math problems she gave him an hour ago. He lowers his chin and snarls at her.

"How am I looking at you?"

"Like I'm made of glass, and I might fall off my chair and break into a million pieces."

It's true she's been watching him from the sofa in the living room. She lost track of how long it's been. "I haven't been thinking anything like that about you. In fact, I'm sitting here marveling at how we ended up in this place, together, doing what we're doing."

"You're *marveling*? That's because you're not the one doing shitty algebra problems."

She laughs and gives him what she hopes is a sympathetic look. Until this evening she hadn't stopped to consider their progress in the parent-child department and she's permitting herself to feel a bit of pride about it, if only for the lack of drama. Her job got harder two weeks ago when September arrived, and she insisted they start his homeschooling. While Teague is willing, even happy, to engage with English and history, he hates math with a passion and only tolerates science. Quite the opposite of her school days. The other challenge is finding the right time to get him to do it; when he's able and willing

40

to sit long enough and focus. This requires a near-constant surveillance of his moods, which he's quick to detect and balk at. She doesn't like being his medication police but, given the situation, she has no choice. When she dares ask if he's taken his pill on any given day, he either grunts or tells her to stop harassing him.

"Would you rather I leave you alone to work?" she asks.

"Just go get a life."

"Okay, I'll work on that." She could use the break.

She goes to her bedroom, half of it converted into an office. On the utility table she uses as a desk, the notes and first draft of a memo to Ryan are waiting. After struggling to remember enough basic algebra to get Teague started on tonight's lesson, her brain is fried, MIA for actual work.

She doesn't dare lie down. With her legs stretched out straight on the floor, back against the bed, she returns to taking stock. Who would have thought, she and Teague making their own little family? Well, Gran for one. In the summer between Kate's sophomore and junior years at Yale, Gran had warned her that some version of this arrangement would come to pass. In the intervening years, while Maureen filled the slack, Kate avoided thinking about it. Now, she'd give anything to be able to ask her grandmother for some clarification.

"Katy Bird?" Kate heard Gran call out. It was two a.m. on a Sunday night during a summer home from college. She'd just returned from driving Meghan to Queens for another round of court-ordered rehab. After switching on the hall light, she saw Gran sitting on the sofa in her yellow chenille robe. Teague lying face down by her thigh in his summer PJs.

"She went in," Kate said as she flopped on the creaky chair, they still called Dad's recliner, although he hadn't sat in it for a decade. After a three-hour round trip and a weekend of histrionics while she and Mom tried to persuade, threaten, and ultimately, beg Meghan to give treatment another try, Kate had nothing more to say about her half-sister.

But Gran had plenty to say to her. "Katy Bird, I know you have big plans for your future, as you should. But this child is going to have to figure in them."

41

Gran's declaration came as a jolt. Kate had at least six more years to go, including med school, and it had never occurred to her that she'd be the one to raise Teague.

But what Gran said next shocked her even more.

"Common sense would tell you he's the least likely in his generation to inherit it. When it skipped yours, I thought that might be the end of it. I should have known better. There's no question he has it."

"Has what?" Gran had stoked her worst fear: that Teague was harmed in utero by Meghan's drug use.

"It's nothing bad. You've seen the faraway look in his eyes?"

"Right, when he's daydreaming."

"That's not what he's doing. Teague sees the future, and he hears from people long gone from this earth. Second sight is what our people called it. At his age, he doesn't know it's special. He thinks everyone sees the same way he does."

Gran eyed her for a long minute while she sat dumbstruck.

"You think I've lost my wits."

"I've never once thought that about you," she lied. Of course, Gran knew her better than she knew herself at nineteen.

"The gift can be a terrible burden," Gran said, with her eyes boring into Kate's. "He'll need your help, so it doesn't get the better of him like it did my Michael, and Jack."

Although Kate is no longer avoiding responsibility for Teague, she's still confounded by what Gran told her on that night, eleven years ago. How the unusual ability Gran identified in Teague at the age of five looks a lot like his present difficulty staying tethered to reality. For Kate, the bundle of behaviors she called *second sight* hardly ranks as a gift. More like a scary list of clinical symptoms, with labels like dissociation, flights of fancy, grandiosity. *Sorry, Gran, I can't unknow what I know.*

One last bit from that long ago conversation adds an even stranger cast to Gran's claim as Kate remembers it now. "There's always a reason why it returns when it does," Gran said. "Mind you, there are generations watching."

Who are these unnamed others with a keen interest in Teague's gift? A chill comes over her as she pictures these phantoms as cheerleaders for a sixteen-year-old boy's unraveling. How is this possibly good for him? The notion challenges her view of reality as a material world ruled by natural laws, not one influenced by spirits or messengers from the past or future. It's beyond her ability to sort this out tonight. She stands and stretches. Time to check on his progress with fractions.

Who are these unnamed others with a keen interest in Teague's gift? A chill comes over her as she pictures these phantoms as cheerleaders for a sixteen-year-old boy's unraveling. How is this possibly good for him? The notion challenges her view of reality as a material world ruled by natural laws, not one influenced by spirits or messengers from the past or future. It's beyond her ability to sort this out tonight. She slouches and stretches. Time to check on his progress with fractions.

# 1920

Ellen topped off the lupili, Da's tincture for calming tremors, and mounted the ladder to return it to the highest shelf. A few steps down, she stopped to check the vial of oil canarium, a remedy for skin wounds. When was the last time she filled it? Only traces of its bitter lemon smell remained. She descended the ladder and headed for the storeroom.

"*Máthair Dé!*"

Her mother's sharp tone made Ellen stop in her tracks. The seamstress with a shop two doors down stood opposite Mam at the front counter. Ellen tightened her grip on the vial as she listened.

"Here we thought *that* horror was behind us," the seamstress said.

Mam covered her mouth and the two began to whisper while Ellen pretended to examine jars on the shelf and strained to hear.

"Someone has to see to Maggie," Mam said in a normal voice as she untied her apron.

"I'm coming," Ellen called out after Mam brushed her shoulder without meeting her eyes.

"This is no business for you," her mother yelled, clearly annoyed.

Ellen stood as straight as a board. Just because she was sixteen didn't mean she shouldn't see this awful thing for herself. She was tired of her parents expecting her to act like a grown woman when it suited them and otherwise treating her like a child. Soon enough she'd have to spill her secret and that would put a quick end to it.

Rita Shanahan held the shop door open for her son Martin and waited until his barking cough eased before ushering him in.

"Afternoon, Rita," Da said, and traded places with Ellen by the counter. "Has it been like this since Monday?"

Rita's face shrunk with worry. "You think it's the whooping cough?"

"It could be. The medicine should help calm his lungs down." Da delivered the news in a way that was itself a tonic, at least she hoped it felt that way to Rita.

Ellen went to the back to retrieve the remedy she'd helped him prepare for Martin: a syrup of honey, marshmallow root, thyme, ivy, and elderberry. On the way, she passed Mam putting on her shawl.

"It's Maggie Donlon's place, then?"

"Aye."

"Can I come?"

"Ask Da." Ellen took that to mean Mam would allow it, even if she wasn't happy to have her along.

"I'll catch up to you."

Ellen grabbed the remedies and ran to the counter, trying to hide her impatience as Da examined Martin's throat and instructed Rita on how to give Martin the medicine.

"Can I go then?"

Da frowned and ran a hand over his round pink head. "I can't see what use you'd be there."

"Delia's my friend. I can help her with the young'uns."

He stared past her, his belly pressed against the counter. "All right, then. Stay close to your Mam. You never know what might happen."

She caught up to Mam in the alley where she was harnessing the donkey.

Mother and daughter said next to nothing on their way to the Donlons' cottage. A British landowner by the name of Blake named the townland Blakemore after himself, but most people still called it Ballycarrick, for the place by the big rock. Given Mam's family and the school were there, the Mitchells regularly made the five-mile trip from Ballymore town, where the apothecary had stood on Main Street for three generations, their living quarters above the store. Since they'd begun courting, two years ago now, Ellen went more often to Ballycarrick to visit Michael and his family.

A crowd of people stood on the road in front of the Donlon cottage on Big Rock Road. Maggie, Mam's closest friend, stood at the center with the four youngest Donlon children laid out at her feet like a clump of newborn puppies, a mass of uncombed heads and small bodies in cloth jumpers, hard to tell apart. An iron pot, a basket of potatoes, rocking chair, bedding, and clothes strewn around them. Delia towered over her mother and the other women. She looked scared with her arms wrapped around her middle. Ellen raised a hand to catch her eye, but Delia didn't notice.

A squad of six RICs guarded the cottage. They wore their navy-blue uniforms and circular caps and carried batons and pistols. Uncle Killian stood with them. She saw him and Mam exchange a wary look when they first arrived. Four other constables formed a circle around a mechanical setup Ellen had never seen before. It was made from three tree trunks leaning to a center point, with a fourth, longer log hung crosswise on a chain. Mam had pushed through the crowd and had her arm around Maggie's waist.

When they were girls, Ellen and Delia would gather the young ones on this part of the road and act out the epic death tale known as *The Táin*. Delia would play Queen Maeve, who instigated a battle to show her husband, the king, that she, not he, owned the mightiest bull in the land. To make it so, Maeve sent her army on a raid to steal the brown bull of Ulster, known as the Táin. The battle ended with a matchup between two mighty bulls hers brown, his white. The victorious and defeated warriors alike, along with their beasts, were enshrined at Rathcroghan, a day's walk from Ballycarrick.

The children watched spellbound as Delia threw her body into playing the queen, who used her feminine wiles to enlist the bravest warrior to do her bidding. Now Ellen's ears rang with Delia's challenge to the warriors: "If the mighty Daire himself comes with the bull, I'll give him a portion of the fine Plain of Ai, and a chariot worth thrice seven bondmaids, and my own friendly thighs on top of that!" At that, they would clap and hoot as Delia's Maeve marched off to battle with her sword raised.

The word people used to describe Delia was sassy. Once, when she mouthed off to her father, Frank, he sent her flying. She landed sideways on an iron stoker, leaving a gash and a scar down her chin she never tried to hide. A ginger-haired, green-eyed beauty, Delia used her freakish height to claim her right to associate with her elder peers. None of Delia's sass was showing that day.

A chorus of shouts came from behind the Donlon cottage. Frank Donlon appeared first, with his son Rowan, small for his fourteen years, by his side, and a handful of neighbors following. Colm stood among them, not Michael, to Ellen's relief.

The eyes of every person standing in the road bounced between Frank and his men as they advanced to where the RIC squad guarded the cottage. If looks could kill, those constables would have dropped dead on the spot. Ellen jumped when one brawny fellow standing by the setup pulled on its chain and thrust the sideways log forward and back. He backed off and rubbed his shoulder as if preparing for a hurling match.

The captain of the squad dismounted and went to his men. A civilian wearing a crisp white shirt under his vest and carrying a rifle walked alongside him. Unlike the captain, who ignored the crowd, this fellow snapped his head in all directions like a nervous squirrel. Ellen asked Mam who he was. "Charles Fahey," she said, "rental agent for the Blake tenants." Her tone gave away her scorn for the man. The setup of logs had a name, too. It was a battering ram.

"Charlie, you're a filthy traitor to your people," Frank shouted at Fahey.

Fahey whipped his head around and drew his rifle. "Donlon, you're three months in arrears. I'd keep my mouth shut if I was you."

Frank mumbled and disappeared behind his cottage. After the captain spoke to the man operating the battering ram, he yanked the log back and sent it flying into the front wall—making a loud thud. At the moment of impact, Ellen fell a step backward as if she'd taken the hit on her own body.

"Put some force into it," the captain shouted.

Before the operator could carry out his order, Frank led a band of men and boys from behind the cottage, while another column snaked along the far side of his neighbor's home. The two lines met in front of the Donlons', where they formed a pincer and moved forward, throwing rocks at the constables, who pulled out clubs and charged back at them. At the rear of the throng of attackers Ellen spotted Colm. He hung back in the near distance, watching.

She recognized another of Frank's men as Willie Costelloe, Ballycarrick's master blacksmith, who ran straight for Fahey wielding a metal poker. Her heart beat faster as Costelloe got off two firm whacks on the agent's chest and side. The blows had Fahey bending over and moaning when Uncle Killian stepped in and clubbed Costelloe on the back of his head. He fell to the ground next to Fahey.

A shot rang out from the road. Ellen covered her ears as the captain advanced with his rifle cocked. The attackers scattered. The women and children backed off the road into the field.

"Arrest him," the captain yelled to Killian, who had his boot on Costelloe's neck.

Two more constables came to the road, each dragging a captive. It didn't take long for the squad to go back to work on the battering ram, except there were fewer neighbors left to watch. Ellen put her arm around Delia's waist as much to gird herself as her friend.

"If Da goes on the run, Mam says we'll have to go to the workhouse." Sun glinted off Delia's face as she wiped tears with her sleeve.

"That can't be true," Ellen answered, although she had no way to know. Why would Frank leave his family at a time like this? She pulled Delia closer. A weight pressed on her chest as she pictured Delia entering the mammoth gray building on the outside of town. Landowners in every county had built an identical structure during the famine years to house the poorest of the poor, who entered as a last resort. As Delia quaked, Ellen planted her feet, drawing on the anger rising in her body to stand firm, hoping she might transmit some of her undeserved good fortune to her friend.

Delia squeezed her before she pulled away and went to comfort one of her siblings who'd taken to wailing.

In front of them, each thud of the battering ram sent stone and mortar falling and made Ellen's stomach swirl. She dropped to her knees, covered her face, and flashed on a red fox she'd come upon earlier in the summer on a nearby farm with its front leg ensnared in a trap. She'd hid on the side of the barn and held her breath as the animal thrashed the metal contraption back and forth. When she stirred and the fox sensed her presence, it froze and stared back—as if she'd become the greater threat. With each of them locked in each other's sight, it seemed only right for her to stay and witness the fox's slow death. Before the end came, it let loose a God-awful keen that stabbed her ears.

Now the fox's cry and the rattling chain of the battering ram were joined as one awful squeal mocking Ellen's heroic fantasy. In her mind she'd waved her fist and screamed in protest at the terrible thing she witnessed, when, in reality, she hadn't moved a limb or said a word since Frank's lopsided battle with the RIC began. The rank smell of her own sweat turned her stomach. Bile rose in the back of her throat, and she clutched her waist, trying to keep the sounds and smells away.

Ellen sensed his presence before she opened her eyes to see Michael extend a hand to her and help her to her feet. He looked her over with raised eyebrows.

"I'm all right," she said.

The lines of worry in his face stayed put. "Aye. Have you seen Colm?"

"Earlier."

"There he is," Michael said. Ellen followed his eyeline to the back of the lot behind the Donlons', where Colm stood talking with Uncle Killian. She couldn't imagine what the two of them had to say to each other.

Michael put his arm around Ellen's waist and pulled her back off the road. "You'll go home with your mam, then." It was more a statement than question.

"Aye." She kept her hand on his arm, not wanting to let go.

"I'm supposed to get Colm and bring him home." Michael squeezed her hand as he pulled away. He skirted the battering ram and ran to the back lot, where Colm now stood alone. They appeared to argue before leaving together.

Her attention returned to the Donlons' cottage, where two other constables held a ladder against the side wall with a third man on the roof swinging a pickaxe at the rafters, causing chunks of heather to fall into the cottage. Out of nowhere, Rowan pushed past the men at the foot of the ladder and climbed halfway up.

"No, Rowan, noooooo," Maggie called out to her eldest son. Mam and Delia held her up as the constables pulled the boy down and dragged him to the road—with Rowan kicking and fighting to break free.

"Leave him be, I beg you," Maggie cried, reaching for the boy.

"I'll be all right." Rowan's bugged eyes gave away his terror. The captain signaled for his men to take Rowan into custody. Fahey conferred one last time with the captain, who dismissed his squad, and an eerie quiet came over the handful of Ballycarrick residents left standing in the field across from the Donlon's leveled cottage.

At the time, Ellen didn't fully register the risk the local men had taken by joining Frank in resisting his eviction. Indeed, if one of the women had dared to give shelter to Maggie and the children after they'd been made homeless, their cottage could also have been demolished in retribution. Their lots offered at higher rents to other farmers expected to rebuild the cottages. These were among the terrible things that happened in her grandparents' time during The Great Hunger. For Ellen, it was as if their nightmare—rarely spoken of by Mam and Da and cloaked in shame when they arose—had visited her today to make sure she knew how much worse her lot could have been.

Now, Maggie hung on to Mam like a rag doll. Ellen would have given anything to entwine her arms with theirs, but she kept her distance. Who was she to put herself in the middle of Maggie's troubles? Mam and Maggie belonged to a private club of wives and mothers, the ones who picked up the pieces after their husbands and sons did the fighting. Part of her wanted to join their club, while another, competing voice warned her to run away as fast as she could.

Ellen leaned over the counter and inhaled the sharp odor of flaxseed oil as she told Da about the awful thing the RIC had done to the Donlons' cottage for no good reason. He dropped his cloth and winced, seeming to ignore her as he studied his fanned-out fingers on the wrinkled wood.

"Da?"

He straightened his spine but kept his eyes away from hers. "I'm sorry to say the ones who did it to Frank had their reasons."

Mam entered from the back and started aligning jars on the rear shelves.

Ellen sidled closer to Da. "You mean for his back rent?"

His shoulders sagged. "He's not the only one who's fallen behind."

"Then why?"

Da looked at Mam. His sigh lasted longer than it would have taken for him to tell her the thing he was holding back. To Ellen's eyes, he was asking Mam's permission, which was out of character for him. Did they think her not knowing this awful thing would protect her from harm?

A frown had taken over his face. "Was anyone arrested?"

"Willie Costelloe and Maggie's boy Rowan were the ones I saw."

He shook his head and closed his eyes as he blew air.

"Da?"

"Word's got out Frank's a Volunteer. Now he has no choice but to go on the run. They're meaning to send a message to anyone else thinking of taking up the Republican cause."

Ellen pictured Delia holding her little brother's hand, the two of them trailing behind Maggie carrying the baby while leading the next youngest, entering the high double doors of the workhouses much of the building as Ellen had ever seen. When she looked again at her father, it was as if he carried extra weight in the bags under his eyes.

## 2002

Kate pushes open the heavy plank door of Murphy's pub and steps into a haze of cigarette smoke and fish grease. When her eyes adjust, she spots Ryan standing by the bar and threads her way there, counting ten men for every woman. Raised eyebrows greet her as she crosses the room. Do they all know who she is? She guesses they do.

The array of bric-a-brac covering the walls and ceiling of Publican's Pub is downright bizarre: a pickaxe, top hat, rusted clothes iron, a framed photo of a flop-haired man in a white three-piece suit captioned William Butler Yeats, a hockey-stick-looking thing, helmeted players holding a trophy on a yellowed news page, the Statue of Liberty with a lit torch, a wooden altarpiece with a paint-chipped sculpture of the martyred Jesus . . . a single green wellie hanging from the ceiling.

Behind the wrinkled mahogany bar, an elegant silver-toned Guinness tap looks like part of a church organ. A floor-to-ceiling whiskey library boasts names both familiar and charmingly strange, from Jameson and Bushmills to Teeling, Paddy, Kilbeggan, Michael Collins, even a Tullamore DEW.

She's standing right behind Ryan, but he hasn't noticed her yet.

"That's what she told me right after we finished. I swear on my mother's grave. What's a man supposed to think?" The question, aimed at Ryan, comes from a pudgy, clean-shaven forty-something fellow in khakis and a blue polo shirt.

"I don't blame you for wondering, Derm, but I have no feckin idea what she meant." Ryan delivers his answer with a shrug.

"Is that right? Here I am thinking this kind of thing falls into your line of work."

"Maybe you want to take it to the PP," says the third man.

She waits for their laughter to subside before stepping forward. Ryan touches her elbow and brings her closer.

"Dermot, Jimmy, meet Kate, my new research partner, arrived from New York two months ago."

Having noticed handshakes aren't routinely offered with introductions here, at least not to women, she keeps her hands at her side when she says hello.

"I've got a sister married a guy from Philly. Another one in—"

"Yeah, well, we don't want to go down that road," says Jimmy. "We'll be here all night. How are you liking our town so far?"

"I'm very glad to have made the crossing in this direction."

"We're lucky to get her," says Ryan. "I promised Kate some supper, we better grab seats before Tommy closes the kitchen." He leads her to an empty table in a quieter corner.

"PP?" she asks.

"He means the parish priest. For the average bloke sharing his troubles, my profession comes third—after the bartender and whoever baptized him."

Ryan swears by the fish and chips and that's what she orders.

"Tell me something about Kate Jones I don't know."

"I hate to think what you've heard."

"Just what you've told me."

She doubts that but appreciates him pretending otherwise. Ryan suggested they meet here after a long day at the clinic. She almost begged off, but the combination of her growling stomach and his relentless good cheer convinced her to come.

"Okay, then. My twenties are a bit of a blur. I spent way too much time in the lab. Enough to finish my thesis and ruin a marriage. At least that's what my ex would say."

Ryan's eyebrows go up. "Then you married young?"

"First year of med school until three years ago."

"I beat you there. I was still an undergrad." Ryan's smile fades. "Niamh and I share custody of Sophie, who's thirteen going on twenty-one."

"Well then, you're ahead of me in teen wrangling."

"Teague's a good lad. He's getting on with one or two of his mates from group. Teenagers, even the shy ones, do poorly in isolation. If they didn't want friends as badly as they do, none of them would come near me or the clinic. It's a good thing I grew up on a farm. I've had some practice wrangling."

Tommy brings their fish, which is as good as Ryan promised.

"From farmer's son to psychiatrist? How'd that happen?"

"My mum used to say I was born with a priest's bedside manner. As the youngest of four boys, I spent a fair amount of time trying to cheer her up when she was too sick to get out of bed. She passed away from breast cancer when I was sixteen. I suppose that had something to do with it. I didn't let on about my specialty until it was too late for my father to persuade me to change my mind."

"He didn't appreciate having a shrink in the family?"

Ryan shakes his head. "He never made peace with it. I can't blame him. Given our tendency to sweep everything that you can't eat or drink under the rug. I'm afraid psychiatry suits my tendency to ask rude questions."

She chuckles. This man appears to be her complete opposite— undefended, open-hearted. She's in awe, even if she aspires to neither quality.

"Why brain research?" he asks.

"The usual reasons." She takes another bite, hoping he'll pick up on her cue to drop the subject.

He cocks his head, either ignoring or missing it. "Which was yours?"

She puts down her fork. Only two psychiatry nerds would consider having this conversation in the middle of a crowded pub. Fight or flight? She can't decide.

His chin is on the heel of his hand with the faux-neutral expression that shrinks command at will. "Dr. Quinn, your therapeutic skills are on full display."

His smile hints at mischief.

Kate remains torn. A conversation with a colleague who enjoys solving a dysfunctional family puzzle as much as she does is a rare treat. But not when she's the subject. She leans toward flight, then finds herself caving to his delicate pressure, annoyed at herself. "Well, there was the time I found my father passed out in a pool of water in the basement."

Ryan's animated expression flips to neutral. She tries to shut out the background noise until she hears just the whistle of his breath.

"How old are you when this happens?"

"Maybe seven."

"Okay."

"I'm sitting on Dad's lap in his recliner. It's a lumpy green brocade, embroidered with country scenes—a horse and carriage, ladies with umbrellas, a boy milking a cow—I used to spin out stories about them while Dad watched TV; boxing or baseball."

"On this particular day?"

"There's a Yankees game on. I'm trying to catch the smoke from his cigarette. The rain is coming down hard. A commercial comes on and he puts his cigarette out in the ashtray, slides me off his lap, and says, *Stay put, princess, I have to go down and bail.* I whine. He tells me to keep his seat warm."

She opens her eyes to explain. "Our cellar used to flood whenever it rained for more than a couple of days, and by this point, it had been three or four."

Ryan nods. "Go on."

"After a while, I don't hear his shovel and I worry. I'm halfway down the stairs when I see him lying on the cement floor next to the furnace. The water comes up to my ankle as I run to him."

She falters and opens an eye. Ryan's neutrality appears to have vanished. In its place, she perceives negative judgment. How did she allow this conversation to happen? Has she not spent thousands of dollars in therapy going over the same territory, and to what end? She kicks herself for letting Ryan trick her into going down this rabbit hole. In a pub!

"Take your time."

She holds her breath to steel herself, then inhales and lets it out before picking up where she left off.

"He's not moving. I poke him and beg him to wake up. Nothing. I smell whiskey like he's poured it all over himself. I can't leave him there because he might drown. I'm already drenched. I lie down next to him and put my head on his chest. First, I think just to make sure he's breathing. But he doesn't wake up and I don't know what else to do."

The light in the bar stabs her eyes as she opens them. The chatter has turned into a roar. "I must have fallen asleep."

"It never occurs to you to get your mother?"

"No. Weird, huh?"

"And then?"

She drops back inside the memory. "Mom finds us later. Yes. There's light coming in the window; she's standing over us yelling at Dad. He wakes up and hollers back at her. I cry . . ." She opens her eyes and sits up straight. Why the hell did she voluntarily walk this plank? She examines her hands splayed on the table. "That's all I remember."

Ryan blows air through pursed lips. "He was?"

She understands Ryan wants her professional opinion and it's a relief to let go of the past and offer it. "By then an alcoholic. Probably bipolar. Undiagnosed, of course. When Dad was working a case, he'd stay up for days on end, then come home and drink himself down."

Ryan's eyes are still on her, but his attention seems to have drifted.

"What are you thinking?" she asks him.

"Sorry. The simplistic way we look at self-medication is one of my pet peeves. I'd like to know why a few pints at the end of the day does it for one depressed bloke, but the next fellow can't get by without a line of cocaine."

"You're right, not enough attention is paid to the mechanics of it. But I tend to believe an addict's drug of choice reveals the emotional wound that got them there."

"Leaning a bit Freudian with that aren't you?"

"Until I hear a better explanation." She looks away and recalls the spirit-crushing moment when she came upon Meghan sitting on the bottom bunk heating one of mom's silver spoons over a blow torch. Until then, Kate hadn't known heroin needed to be cooked before it could be injected. When she freaked out and threatened to get Gran or call Mom, Meghan had dared her to try it and she did. It was the most blissful high she could have ever imagined. High enough that she knew never to touch the stuff again. The opposite of Meghan, who ended up selling all of Mom's silver to support her habit.

It's not something she wants to share with Ryan. Neither does she intend to go into her epiphany of last month when she'd confronted her own drug of choice in men like Sebastian. She already feels raw and overexposed. In. A. Pub.

"Thanks for telling me about your father," Ryan says. "I should warn you. You'll run into a lot of that here."

Sorry. A lot of what?"

"Only a tiny minority of the people you'll be interviewing have been diagnosed. You'll have to tiptoe around a lot of stories like the one you just shared with me. Auntie not leaving her room for years. Brother who gets into scrapes and terrorizes his younger siblings. None of it named or treated."

He's just poured gasoline on her worries about the fieldwork she's due to start in a few days.

"Is something wrong?"

"I hope I was clear when we first talked. The clinical side is not my strength. I'm game to do my part with these interviews, but I fear I won't be much better at it than your interns."

"I suspect you'll get up to speed without much trouble."

"Since people hate talking about these things, wouldn't it be less stressful for everyone if we did the interviews by phone?"

His frown says it all. "Less stressful but also misleading or plain wrong. Just imagine you're in the kitchen cooking dinner for the family when you get such a call. Now picture yourself telling the caller the story you just told me."

"Point taken. But now I need you to fill me in on another gaping hole in my education."

"What's that?"

"Hurling? In twenty-five words or less. It's already come up a few times with the interns. And the game remains a mystery to me."

"You need to fill that gap. And I'm not just saying that because it is—or was—my sport." He leans in, looking years younger. "Picture baseball, lacrosse, and field hockey put together, except you've got lads running faster on grass than they do in all those sports put together."

"I see." She sounds skeptical, but it's coming from ignorance.

"The game is over three thousand years old. Here, let me show you." He takes a pen from his jacket pocket and draws lines and dots on a napkin with arrows crossing and doubling back over other lines. "The point is to get the ball across the goal line."

Isn't it always?"

He drops his chin. "Maybe you'll take more to Gaelic football, my daughter's game."

"Hope runs eternal."

58

# 1920

At first, Ellen didn't connect the noise filtering up from the street to the talk at the Callahans' a week ago. She barely noticed the neighs and snorts and boots hitting the ground, three stories below where she slept in the attic. When the noise started to break through it was easy to blame the commotion on drunks stumbling home from the pub, until a staccato wave of commands tore the veil of sleep, and she remembered the conversation she'd been part of with Michael's family. The column of Volunteers who'd ambushed an RIC squad on the road outside town. Fighters known to be local men and boys. Two constables shot dead. The search for those responsible, along with sympathizers and the guns everyone knew to be hidden under their noses.

"Paddy Mitchell, open up!"

She heard murmurs and footsteps from the floor below, where Mam, Da, her brother, and the girls should have been asleep in their beds.

Something heavy—a rifle butt—pounded the shop door. "Mitchell, this is your final warning. We *will* search these premises."

Where was Da? And why were soldiers here?

A stretch of silence ended with the screech of shattered glass. She caught her breath and pictured the shop window with a jagged wound. With it went her last hope that this was a terrible misunderstanding her father could fix with some straight talk. As much as he voiced his hatred of the English in private,

Paddy Mitchell tried to stay publicly neutral. Continuing the tradition of his guild, he offered remedies and hands-on healing to anyone in need, regardless of their birthplace or current loyalties, as his father and grandfather had done before him. She'd heard him tell Mam not to worry because his standing in town would keep them safe. He'd taken a risk when he ran and won as a Sinn Féin MP in the 1918 general election. Maybe that was the reason for this visit. But why would they go after someone who wasn't calling for rebellion?

At the first smell of smoke, she grabbed the bed frame and poked her nose above the sill. The fumes seemed to be coming from outside, although she couldn't be sure they weren't also sneaking up through the floor. She was afraid to call out or run downstairs lest she come face-to-face with the flames — or a Jack soldier. English accents on the street meant the Tans were among those on Main Street. Her heart sped until it was pounding against her ribs. Frozen with indecision, she got down on her knees and sought out her ally, the Druidess, Brigid. She spoke in a whisper.

"Blessed Lady. I don't believe you'd have it end here for me and this new life I'm blessed to carry. If it ain't yet decided, I'm askin' for a wee bit more time here on God's earth. Michael and I have made ourselves a plan. But what I'm askin' ain't as selfish as it might seem. Just the same, I swear, if I get out of here alive, I'll take up your cause and make it mine. I can't say how just yet, but, milady, you have my word on it. Now, I'm counting on you to show me the way."

The choice before her became clear. If she was going to survive, she had to act and trust that Brigid would help her escape the soldiers, fire or no fire. With her gown yanked to her waist, and smoke making her cough, she put her head close to the floor and crawled toward the door. A splinter caught her knee. Feckin floor.

When a crash came from the direction of the stairs, she stopped and held her breath. Someone had knocked a box of remedies from the stack. But who? Another box went down. Halting footsteps. Not knowing if it was friend or foe, she froze.

"Ellen?"

She let out a sigh of relief and a silent thank you to her protectress. "I'm here!"

"Where the bloody hell is that?"

"Keep on straight ahead to the end of the stacks."

As his footsteps came closer, more smoke rushed in from behind her. She made her breaths shallower. "Watch for the tumblers." The sound of falling glass told her he'd made it halfway. "Now, shimmy to your right around Mam's wardrobe."

At last, Michael's hands landed on her shoulders. "There, I've got you." As he pulled her up from the floor and held her close, she tasted salty sweat on his neck. Relief spilled out in sobs.

"You're okay, love. We have to hurry . . . there's a line of Mausers aimed at your front door."

"What do they want?"

"They say Paddy has a stash of rifles up here."

"But it's not true. Everyone knows that."

"Aye. He's holding them off until I get you out of here."

She took his hand and led the way, wishing she understood why the truth wasn't enough to end this madness. On the landing, she stared at empty beds.

"They're safe with your Mam and Colm," Michael said as he scanned the room. "We're supposed to take the back stairs and meet them . . . love?"

As Michael spoke, his mouth moved out of step with his words. An echo rang in her ears. She couldn't sort how he'd known to come here at this late hour?

When his eyes met hers, he grasped her confusion. "I saw your building going up in flames as I lay down to sleep. I brought Colm and got here as fast as I could and warned Paddy the Tans were targeting the shop in tonight's attack. They were coming quick behind us. Colm took your Mam and young'uns s ahead on the donkey cart while I got you—"

"Your information is wrong, Captain." Da's voice from the street. "I'm an MP, not a Volunteer. You'll find nothing but medicines on these premises."

"We've been told otherwise. Now make way—" The rest was garbled.

"Michael, why can't we just let them come up and see for themselves?"

He took a quick breath. "Think about it, love. They already know there's nothing up here. They're sending the message that none of us is safe unless we turn on our own." He winced. "Paddy Mitchell is a big prize for them." His Adam's apple moved up and down as his neck muscles become taut. "And you can bet there'll be some who'll believe the Brits tipped me off, or how did I get here ahead of them?"

She opened her mouth to ask how anyone could think Michael was an informer when shouts and gunfire rang out. He grabbed her hand, and she led the way to a section of wall that when pushed revealed stairs. In the dark kitchen, she lifted floorboards exposing a ladder to the root cellar. From there, they made their way out to the back alley and ran.

In the vestibule of the seamstress's shop, they took cover and had their first look at the scope of the attack. Flames and plumes of smoke rising from several buildings, including Mitchell's Apothecary. A handful of people ran toward the fires, carrying pots and barrels. A shot rang out and a man fell to the ground. Water spilled from his barrel. She covered her mouth to keep from screaming.

A band of Black and Tans midway down Main Street were advancing toward them. But they weren't acting like soldiers. Drunk as skunks, they stumbled and called out to each other, as if to show off as they took seemingly random shots.

Leaning against the seamstress's shop door, she felt lightheaded. Michael's eyes were watery, his face red and soaked with sweat.

"We'll take alleys until we're out of town."

"What about Da?"

When Michael didn't meet her eyes, her throat closed up.

"He'll catch up when he can."

*No, no, no,* she wanted to yell. *We have to go back for him. What if he's hurt?* She covered her face with her hands. It was all she could do not to bolt away and go back for Da.

Michael grabbed her wrists and brought his face close to hers. "If they catch us, they'll think we're on the run for the wrong reason and arrest us. What good would that do?"

They avoided roads by zigzagging across farms, pastures, and bogland.

They walked for hours until she saw moonlight reflected on the River Clare. At the quay, troops guarded a line of currachs. Colm tied up, slumped against a tree. Mam and her siblings huddled together on the ground.

"Something ain't right," Michael whispered. "It makes no sense for them to be rounded up like that."

Nestled next to him on the grassy riverbank, she felt his body stiffen with what she read as shock. They'd been betrayed. But by who and why? Before she could ask, Michael slid his arm around her waist. They crawled up the bank and ran with their heads held low until they reached the bog, where they lay, soaked, and curled in a ball in the loamy turf—until daylight.

# 2002

Teague is in his room in the lunar capsule, his name for their apartment in the faculty complex, trying to draw. Kate made him put plastic on the rug. Not that he has the energy to make a mess. Stupid meds.

He doesn't miss anyone from home except his art teacher, Ms. Lacey. In an old sketchbook, he finds a poem he wrote for her.

I sit down behind a dumpster and declare it my kingdom.

I begin by drawing knights to fight my holy war.

I draw an angel. I give her eyes and tits.

I almost forget that I'm back here because I'm scared of the world.

He didn't want to bail on her class that day. The voice that showed up was a real nasty Tony Soprano type who ambushed him while he was putting the final touches on a skull he'd made from scratch. Mixed media, Ms. Lacey called it. A 3-D cross-section of the human brain. He made the amygdala out of a sliced golf ball. A twig for the stem. Kate told him there were eighty-six billion neurons in the human brain, give or take. He hammered in eighty-six teensy nails, one per billion, and connected them up with dental floss. It was a rough facsimile, but pretty accurate. Close enough to get him in trouble with Tony.

"Hey, kid. What's da matter with you? Don't you know that stuff is classified? Shred it before I shred you." That flipped him out enough to run for his life.

Teague had heard about the plot from a kid in his therapist's waiting room. Aliens posing as psychiatrists so they could hook kids on psychotropic drugs and turn them into robots to do their bidding. He figured Tony had been hired to handle alien security, and now he suspected Teague was on to them. Maybe he was. He'd taken the threat seriously enough to ditch his antidepressant. Didn't tell anybody.

There he was, crouching low to the ground behind the dumpster in the high school parking lot, thinking the aliens must be pretty far along in their plan if they were worried about a kid making a humanoid brain from nails and dental floss. Unfortunately, he'd left class so fast he'd forgotten to destroy it. The next thing he knew, Ms. Lacey was coming up on him, tiptoeing in her tight skirt and high heels around the burgers and beans— yesterday's lunch strewn on the blacktop—holding up his mixed-media brain. If Tony saw Ms. Lacey with it, he might go after her.

He quickly thought through possible defenses and came up with a plan that required carbon-based matter. A day-old burger would do. He held it in his hands, concentrating hard to absorb its beefy nature. Except it stunk and made him gag. That hadn't come up before. He improvised and created an airtight shield in his brain to section off his olfactory bulb from the limbic system. Then he said a spell to put a hologram of Teague in front of the dumpster. That way, he, real Teague, could stay behind the dumpster, invisible.

"Teague, are you okay?" Ms. Lacey's sweet voice calling him.

She was the only person on the planet he still liked talking to. But if he didn't concentrate on the spell, it would break. They would get in a conversation and expose Ms. Lacey to Tony's wrath. He had to keep that from happening.

"This is fantastic work. Do you want to finish it?"

By then it was obvious he was in trouble. Teague out front was shaking, going in and out of form, which meant his spell was unstable. Maybe he'd screwed it up with the airtight shield.

"All right. I'll keep it for you," she said. He waited for her to go back in the building before he cut out for home.

After that, all he could think about was how much it sucked that Ms. Lacey wouldn't make it through the school year. He'd seen it like a silent movie running in his head after Christmas break, when she started wearing her engagement ring. A head-on crash on the thruway would kill her and her fiancé. He'd been racking his brain to figure out what he could do to keep the crash from happening. The problem was, if he told her, she wouldn't believe him. Worse, she'd stop being his friend. All he could do was hope he'd gotten it wrong. If only he believed that. This wasn't his first premonition.

His report card came in Friday's mail. He knew it was there when he heard Maureen say, Jesus, Mary, and Joseph like when she's pissed. Then, at the top of her lungs, "Teague, get down here!" When he got there, she shot him the evil eye. "How does anyone as smart as you get four Fs?" Waving his report card around like a miniature flag. "Do you even go to these classes?"

"I go . . . sometimes."

She huffed and flapped her arms. "All right. Here's what I'm going to do. First thing Monday morning, I'm calling Ms. Lacey." She brought the report card back up to her nose to examine it. "She gave you a C, your best grade. At parents' night she told me how talented she thinks you are. Maybe she can help you fix this mess."

He debated telling Maureen about his premonition, thinking maybe she'd warn Ms. Lacey about getting in the car with her fiancé that weekend. But there was a good chance Maureen wouldn't believe him and she'd just yell at him some more. He had to risk it.

"Um, that won't work."

She did a double take. "Why not?"

"Something bad is going happen to Ms. Lacey. She won't be around on Monday."

Maureen sucked in her cheeks and glared at him. "What a terrible thing to say! Of course, she'll be around. It's only March. That gives you one more quarter to bring your grades up! I know you don't want to repeat the ninth grade."

He'd already been left back once, which totally sucked. But that wasn't what worried him. He should have known not to have leveled with Maureen.

On Monday morning, he was eating cereal when she came into the kitchen holding the newspaper.

"Mary, mother of God . . ."

He kept his nose an inch above the bowl, praying his worst fear hadn't come to pass, while images of the crash took over his brain. Silence. "What?!"

She read it off the front page. "Shortly before midnight on Saturday, Susan Lacey, a popular Rivervale art teacher, and her fiancé, local insurance salesman, Thomas McCann, were involved a head-on collision with a drunk driver going the wrong way on the New York State Thruway. McCann was pronounced dead at the scene."

No, no, no, no, noooooo.

"Lacey was treated for minor injuries and released from the hospital."

Wait. What? He sat up straight. "She's not dead?"

Maureen stared at the paper, then at him, bug-eyed. "No. I mean yes, that's what it says. Such a shame about Tom. His poor mother."

Blood rushed to his head. His body tingled. He'd never been so happy to be half wrong. He got up and ran out the back door. He didn't want to be there when Maureen remembered what he told her on Friday.


He uses a push pin to tack the poem he wrote for Ms. Lacey on the otherwise empty wall of his new room. Then he gets a fresh sketch pad from under the bed, vowing to steer clear of humanoids. He closes his eyes and sweeps Rivervale out of his mind . . . neurons, nails, floss, even Ms. Lacey . . . and invites new shapes and colors to come in.

Whoa, something's happening. He starts by drawing a single stone with charcoal. He adds purple lines. Red specks. He draws more stones and stacks each snug to its neighbor until he has four walls with ivy creeping up one side.

A door and a window on each side of it with shutters, all painted green. A roof made of brown grass; half-way crashed in.

He props the sketch against his knees. At least it's something new.

# 1920

On the night of the Black and Tan attack, Oisin Quinn, a farmer who counted John Callahan as a friend, let Ellen and Michael hide in his barn. The next afternoon Oisin made a trip to town and came back with a torrent of terrible news. The Tans burned down most of Main Street. At least five people were killed, Paddy Mitchell shot while defending his apothecary, two more taken down while they tried to put out the fire.

Oisin allowed them to stay on his property for several days while Michael exchanged messages with John, who warned of rumors claiming Michael had given up Rory O'Shea's hideout in exchange for their freedom. He told them they had no choice; they had to leave Ballymore, and the safest place was America. There was a Callahan cousin in Boston. John sold a pig to secure their passage.

Their journey began by currach on the Shannon River. In Limerick, they boarded a locomotive to Cork City, changing to a smaller gauge for the last leg to reach the port. The people called it Cobh, a Gaelic word for "cove." They kept using that name after the English rechristened it Queensland, in 1849, in honor of Victoria's pomp-filled arrival for a grand tour of her colony, which, to the quiet disgust of many, happened at a time when the Great Hunger was still ravaging the population. Queensland was the point of demarcation printed on the tickets Michael and Ellen held in their hands on the crowded pier as they waited to board their steamer in August of 1920.

The last bit of home Ellen saw from the deck was the spire of Saint Colman's Cathedral looking over the terraced streets of Cobh, like the candle atop a triple-layer cake. A Cork man traveling alone shed tears when he told them Saint Colman's spire was the tallest in Ireland. Two months later, Ellen's tears would fall belatedly as she craned her neck upward, unable to make out the cloud-covered spire of the Empire State Building.

Their Atlantic crossing was by far the worst trial Ellen had ever been through in her young life. Day and night, she held on to Michael lest she lose him, too, as the reality that they had only each other sank in. The unthinkable was a constant presence. Da, dead. Her mother, brother, and sisters run out of Ireland before she could make contact with them and find out where they'd gone. How would she ever find them?

They spent most of their days at sea in the tomb-like quarters below deck—strangers' bodies reeking of illness and desperation; a loathsome gruel for meals; laundry strung overhead; children wailing—until the constant noise and foul air became customary. The cleaner, rain-soaked atmosphere on deck the stranger experience. Years later, when Ellen would hear a child cry in that forlorn pitch, or when she came upon a rotten vegetable in her refrigerator, her stomach would turn, and her legs would grow weak as her body remembered those awful sounds and smells.

Being with child, her stomach as unsettled as the sea, hardly a moment went by when she didn't have a pail in her hands. Everything Ellen knew about having and mothering babies she'd learned from witnessing her mother's five pregnancies. In the days before the attack, she'd seen signs that her mother was again with child. And now it was too late to tell her and Da about her own. She knew the middle months were more forgiving than the first. Since it had been five months since Ellen's courses stopped, she was hopeful that easier times lay ahead for her.

On a day when the waves were calmer and the queasiness in her stomach seemed to have disappeared, she sat on their bunk, pining for fresh air and room to stretch. "Ready to go up?" she asked Michael, who lay behind her against the wall.

He rose to his elbows. "Aye, if you are."

She held on to his arm as they navigated the mass of people who'd had the same idea. The relief of being without nausea gave her the stamina to think beyond her body. They hadn't yet talked about their flight from Ballymore. With a month now passed, her thoughts took her back to that night. She tried to reconstruct the steps Michael had taken from his own bed to her attic, and she tried to account for what he might have said and done before he reached her.

"I'm having a hard time understanding it," she began, with her eyes fixed on the backs of the people walking ahead of them.

"Understanding what?"

"Why you coming for me that night looked wrong to anybody. How those wags came to think you gave up Rory O'Shea?"

"I don't—"

His voice faded as the pain brought her to her knees. "Michael!" She grabbed his arm and he went down with her to break her fall. People backed away. Like a hunter making a first cut of his kill, it was if a blade had torn through her belly. A shallower cramp released a stream of liquid down the insides of her thighs.

His face, taut with alarm, was her entire world. "No, no, no, please, no," she cried out.

Reaching for Mam, finding Michael, she hated him for not being the one she needed and then she hated herself for her weakness.

Something broke in Ellen that day. But she also met a force of will she hadn't known she possessed. It was what enabled her to put her losses in a box. In their place, a stealthy scorekeeper appeared. From then on, she viewed her relationship to fate as a straight barter, no longer a prize or punishment doled out from above. She would keep going forward in exchange for the promise of seeing home again. When their steamer reached the port of New York, the person who gave her legal name as Ellen Mitchell and identified her nationality as British, her race, Irish, had become a wraith of the person she used to be. Shed of any girlish sense of entitlement.

# 2002

Would it kill them to put numbers on their houses? Kate makes a U-turn and drives the same stretch of country road for the third time. On both sides, stucco or cement block homes, the occasional barn, small herds of cows or sheep on narrow lots.

There it is. A ranch-style house set back behind a shoulder-high wall. No number but the name on the back of the truck in the driveway is O'Malley & Sons Concrete. The gate is open; she parks behind the truck. On a scale of one to ten, her nerves are at eleven. One last look at the file.

*Patient (Kiernan) has a history of social anxiety and auditory hallucinations. Older brother (Patrick) has substance abuse disorder and possibly bipolar I. Mother (Eleanor) with a history of double depression. Paternal uncle (Conor) with schizophrenia (hospitalization in 1970), died 1985, cause of death, single-car accident, possible suicide. Paternal grandfather (Eamon) probably depression, alcoholism.*

A capsule description of three generations of misery—par for the course for their study. Kiernan is the only member of the O'Malley family in therapy. He's in the teen group with Teague, who seems enthralled with an older boy in the group named Liam. According to Ryan, Liam heads up the local chapter of Mad Pride, whose members advocate that people having hallucinations should befriend their voices, not medicate them. Her response, "That's the last thing Teague needs . . ." prompted Ryan to suggest she give Teague room to

72

decide for himself since anything you tell a teenager is off-limits will be the thing he insists on doing. She thought back to her own adolescence and conceded the point.

She scans the page with details on the case of Kiernan's great-uncle, William O'Malley, who received his diagnosis of schizophrenia in 1970, the year Ireland undertook a census of its psychiatric hospitals—which became the original source for the finding of Ballymore's high rate of schizophrenia. That marks William as patient zero for this family, one of four hundred from the original survey, making his descendants high-priority interviewees for Ryan's study. Kate's job today is to talk to any adult who can provide information on the presence of symptoms in O'Malley family members born after William. According to the last survey, now four years old, that includes sixteen first- and second-degree relatives.

If Kiernan hadn't opened the front door, she probably wouldn't have gotten as far as the sofa, where she's now sitting opposite a stone-faced Eamon O'Malley in his rocking chair. Her stomach is in knots. She just explained the purpose of her visit and his extended silence is wearing on her nerves. She should have gone right into the interview, but she couldn't make her tongue work. He's still glowering at her.

"Haven't you people done enough damage to this family?"

"I'm not sure what you mean. Please say more?"

He rocks his chair and shakes his head at the same deliberate speed. "The boy had a bright future before you got a hold of him and gave him those happy pills."

"May I ask what specific concerns you have about Kiernan's medication?"

"Besides the fuzzy thinking and his eating enough to feed a family of five? You see that look in his eyes? There's nothing there. His mother took him to that place without me knowing about it."

Too bad she wasn't aware of that. She changes course.

"With Kiernan's family history, Dr. Quinn is acting cautiously. He prescribed a very low-dose antipsychotic that could head off something much worse. Adolescents take it temporarily, and I'm sure Dr. Quinn is monitoring him."

"Don't 'Dr. Quinn' me. I've known Ryan since he was in britches. They gave my brother, Willy, one of your labels, then your pills. He was never the same."

She opens the file and rereads the paragraph on William O'Malley.

"But . . . didn't William show worrisome symptoms when he went into the psychiatric hospital?"

"He just pissed off the wrong people."

"I don't know the details of your brother's medical history or his arrest record if there is one, but it's common for people suffering from schizophrenia to overindulge in alcohol to self-medicate when they're hearing voices or having manic episodes."

Eamon O'Malley's face turns strawberry red. "There you go. Blaming people, jumping to conclusions, labeling them, until they can't have a normal life. Now you've got the whole county riled up. Bringing this up again. Saying we're all daft. I've had enough of this shite. Get out of my house before you piss me off."

Her hands shake as she puts the file in her bag and gets up. She doesn't want to leave without defending the clinic, which sets the stage for her next big mistake.

"I'm very sorry to have upset you, Mr. O'Malley. But wouldn't it be better to deal with some unpleasant side effects rather than risk losing another member of the family before their time?"

"Get the hell out here, lady. Go back to New York where you belong."

She leaves the house without looking back, lest he pile on a nastier comment. The same desire to escape makes her back her car out of the driveway without taking into account the wall at its end. The crunch of metal where her right rear fender encounters concrete stops her heart.

"Oh, no!" Without getting out to look at the damage, she recenters the car in the driveway and backs out again, only to hear the telltale thud of a deflated tire. She pulls over to the nonexistent shoulder. To make matters worse, her cell phone has no signal. Her sole option is to return to the O'Malley's house.

Mrs. O'Malley explains that Eamon's knee replacement makes it impossible for him to help her with the punctured tire, and she doesn't know where Kiernan's gone off to. Kate can use the phone in the kitchen.

Squatting by the rear bumper of Kate's rental car, Ryan pumps the jack to remove her punctured tire.

"I haven't owned a car in a decade," she says.

Ryan frowns and says nothing.

To fill the silence, she briefs him on her interview with Eamon O'Malley, repeating word for word what she said and how Eamon responded. "I was probably too strong. Even if everything I said was true."

"You think?" Ryan winces, still not looking at her. He puts the spare tire on the axel and reattaches the hubcap. Back on his feet, he makes eye contact. "Which was it? Did Yale never bother teaching basic interview protocols or you just skipped that class?"

She opens her mouth to defend herself and stops. "I blew it. I know. You don't have to—" She catches on that she's making it worse. Shit, he's going to make a huge deal out of this one blown interview.

Ryan brushes dirt off his pants and turns toward the O'Malley house. "I better go talk to Eamon. We don't want him pulling Kiernan out of therapy."

"I'm really sorry."

"Meet me at the clinic in an hour." He starts walking away, then stops. "Kate, I think you should do some role-playing before you try another interview. I'll tell Dara to set it up."

"Okay." He may as well have put a dunce cap on her head and sent her to the corner.

On the tedious drive back to the clinic, Kate's thoughts go to the morning she left for med school. A day she came to think of as her private Continental Divide. After that, she never spent more than a weekend under her mother's roof. Two months later, they lost Gran. The day also stands out because of the brief conversation she had at the kitchen table before she left, when Gran shared more about her life than she had in Kate's previous twenty-two years put together.

When she went into the kitchen to say a quick goodbye, Gran had a steaming cup of black coffee and a plate of cinnamon toast waiting. She sat down and gulped the coffee which burned her throat.

"I won't be around to see you become a doctor," Gran began. "There's something you should hear from me before you get started."

Gran's remark had thrown her. She looked no different that morning: fingers misshapen by arthritis, the stoop in her back she blamed on washing floors, the silver braided mane she'd never cut short. Gran eschewed birthdays, but Kate's quick math put her age near ninety.

"You won't be the first healer in this family."

"I won't?"

"My Da, Paddy, had himself an apothecary. He could find a remedy for anything that ailed you."

Gran had never mentioned an apothecary, nor had she ever spoken her father's name aloud.

"Da would say no matter how much medicine you give a child, it won't do him any good unless you minister to the suffering of his elders."

Gran had piqued her nerdy curiosity. "How does that idea work in actual practice?" she asked.

Gran smiled as if she had told a private joke. "You'll know what to do with it when the time comes."

Her answer had disappointed Kate. Like so much about Ellen Callahan, its meaning lay just out of reach. There but not there, like the smallest Russian nesting doll or the rabbit in a magician's hat. When the taxi blew its horn, Kate's hug lasted longer than either of them usually allowed.

Now she wonders, Has the time still not come, Gran? Will it ever?

# 2002

Riding in the passenger seat of Liam's van is like rolling down a hill inside a barrel. It isn't even a road, more like half a New York lane with no pavement. Tall trees on both sides make it hard to tell where they are. The last farmhouse was way back. The rain just stopped leaving the air smelling piney. Hey, there's a rainbow. Not the wimpy kind, this one's more like a bugle call.

"This is where you live?" he asks Liam.

"A wee bit further."

"You and your mom?"

"It's Finn's place. We moved here when I was eleven."

On the road just ahead, two dudes are pulling a wooden cart with a log hanging off the back. Liam veers to avoid them. Branches scratch the side of the van like fingernails on a blackboard.

"Who are they?"

"Some of our members who work on the carpentry crew."

"Members of what?"

"Ballymore grove."

As the seconds tick by, Liam seems to realize that Teague isn't following what he's saying. "You don't . . . ? We're Druids. Finn's our chief."

"You mean he's a real wizard?"

Liam scowls. "I'm not having you on, Teague. On holy days we get hundreds here from all over."

"Oh, it's a church."

"Not like you're thinking."

The front left wheel lands in a deep rut, and the van stalls out.

"Bloody crock." Liam restarts the engine, downshifts, and guns it. It stalls again, and he repeats the process.

Teague sticks his head out the window and comes face to face with one pissed-off red pine. *Hey, sorry, Mrs. Pine.* She's close to the road and hopping mad at them for blowing exhaust in her face. She retaliates by dropping seeds from her cones, waking the Doberman-like nettle bush at her roots. *Okay, okay, we're leaving.*

"I bet you were an altar boy." Liam has a smirk on his face.

"Yeah. What about it?"

He shrugs. "Just saying."

When Maureen volunteered him to Father O'Brien, he was annoyed as hell at first. Until he found out being an altar boy had an upside. Like when he got to wave the incense ball in processions. And when characters in the stained-glass windows started to move and talk to each other and him. Sometimes they'd shoot him a look and make a crack about Father O'Brien's sermon missing the mark, or about Mr. Brady in the back pew being drunk as a skunk. It was as if he was part of a secret society. A mini-god.

The road ends at Liam's farm and Liam parks next to a row of cars and trucks. Up a rise, there's a gate and a wooden sign with a bunch of vertical and horizontal lines like a Scrabble score. Behind the gate there's a house, and, down the hill, a big red barn, with fields as far as you can see.

"All this is yours?"

"Sixty acres."

They walk beyond the barn to a pasture with three sheep, white with black faces and much bigger up close. In another field, he counts six cows. Next to the barn, rows of crops and a scarecrow. It's his old Lego Farm set come to life.

They wander farther down the hill until they reach a massive oak tree, almost as wide as it is tall. *Good afternoon, Teague,* the tree says. More like it sends a *whirr* in his direction. *Thanks*, he says. Not out loud, of course. He can't be the only one having these conversations with trees, but he has enough problems without adding another thing to stuff he does normal humans think are too weird.

"You coming?" Liam is walking back up the hill. Guys with shovels are digging out a clearing. One is in a hole throwing dirt up, two other guys are building a circular mound around the hole with the dirt.

He catches up to Liam. "What are they doing?"

"Our ceremonies happen in that pit."

He pictures a *National Geographic* cover with natives in loincloths dancing around a fire. What does he know about ceremonies in a pit?

They walk to a house with a stone center and modern wings made coming off each side. Behind it, there's a windmill taller than the roofline, and it's turning. "What's the windmill for?"

"We're off the grid. We don't get shite from the state."

The inside of the house is an open space with a cement floor. Rustic sofas and chairs around a woodstove. A kitchen in the far wing. Everything looks homemade.

"This house has been in Finn's family since before the Great Hunger."

"What hunger?"

"You probably heard it called the potato famine."

He shrugs. Liam drops his jaw, like, how can you be this dumb?

"The way Finn tells it, the Brits made a bad situation worse by shipping our grain and beef to their own people, leaving us with nothing."

"So did people around here starve to death?"

"This county was one of the worst hit. More than a million gone by the end." He curls his upper lip. "If they didn't starve, they left for America. Lots of them croaked on the way."

Huh. The voices in the square. Things are starting to make sense. Teague puts his hand on the wall. It's yellow and shiny with sharp ridges, like the moon. "What's this stuff?"

"Hemp with putty on top. Keeps us chilled or toasty warm, depending."

"Hemp?"

Liam nods. Now he's supposed to believe their walls come from the same plant he smokes? He'll Google it later.

"Radiant heat under the floor." Teague looks down while Liam walks ahead. He has to take a dump and he's hoping there's a bathroom somewhere inside. "Um, how do you guys flush the toilet? I mean . . . you know."

Liam rolls his eyes and points beyond the woodstove. "There's one down that hall, and it flushes. We use a reed bed system to get rid of our waste."

"Okay." It's hard to picture how this homemade electricity and plumbing actually works, but Liam seems to know what he's talking about. He comes across different out here, more farmer than hard-core hipster.

On the way back from the bathroom, Teague bumps into an older guy, who stops to look him over. He's a real sight himself, a regular Rumpelstiltskin. His overalls are greasy, no shirt underneath, and he's wearing a leather fringe vest and shin-high boots. His hair is white and wavy and long. He wears it in a mullet with short bangs cut across his forehead. His head is a perfect rectangle with a spiky beard the texture of a bottle bush. His skin is different shades of red and pink like his freckles bled out. His eyes are greenish blue, and they sparkle even in this dim hallway.

"Who's this, then?"

"I'm Teague. Liam's friend."

"Aye. The Yank."

He's not asking, but Teague answers anyway. "Yup. That's me." The guy's eyes won't let him go. "You must be the wizard."

He laughs but doesn't confirm or deny it. "You have a last name, son?"

"Yeah, it's Callahan."

His eyebrows shoot up. "Not Jones?"

"That's my Aunt Kate. She works at the clinic. With Ryan." Teague isn't sure why he's telling him all this. If he's heard Kate's last name, he already knows why they're here.

"Where are your people from?"

"New York."

He frowns and shakes his head. Teague guesses he's done talking.

"Liam's room is all the way to the back and upstairs."

"Okay, thanks."

He stops in the kitchen to check out two girls chattering while they move sticks around big metal tubs. One could be the girl in "Sleeping Beauty," she's got albino skin and silky light-brown hair hanging to her waist. She flashes him a smile. He starts to say hi, but it gets caught in his throat.

"Take a look," she says.

One tub is filled with red liquid, the other green, with cloths immersed in both.

"Is that paint?"

"Plant dye," says Sleeping Beauty, pointing to each tub. "This one is made of beets . . . Here, spinach."

"That's awesome."

"We're making flags for Liam's ceremony," the other girl says. "You coming?"

"Maybe." He still doesn't know what Liam's ceremony is. When Liam invited him, he said it was to show him a computer thing. Liam knows a shitload about code and programming. Teague didn't expect to find a whole compound of people, or a stepdad who's a wizard. But it's not like he has much else to do.

Liam's room looks a lot like Teague's. There's a dresser, a boom box on the floor, and piles of CDs. Nine Lives. Cranberries. U2. Nothing on his wall but a cross, the Celtic kind with knots in a circle. You see them everywhere around here. He's got a fiddle lying in an open case.

"You play that?"

"Since I was six."

Liam is sitting at a desk with two monitors filled with a massive amount of data. This is what he thinks is cool?

"Check it out."

Over his shoulder, Teague scans the two-screen spreadsheet. The header on the first column says Patient ID, just numbers. The next column lists family members: father, mother, grandfather. The one after looks like acronyms. He recognizes one. PE for psychotic episode. It was on his hospital discharge papers. He's getting a bad feeling. "What am I looking at?"

"It's a spreadsheet of everyone around here they've labeled mental."

"How'd you—"

"Duh . . . The clinic computers. Their software is lame." He makes his mouth into a corkscrew. "You don't want to be letting on to your auntie about this."

"What do I have to do with it?"

"You're the one who gave me the password, *eejit*."

"Did not!"

"You did. That night after group when we were fooling around in your aunt's office."

"No way." Then he remembers. Liam on his knees next to his chair with the keyboard at eye level while he logged on to Kate's desktop using her usual password: Teague's initials, TJC, and birth date, 06071987. "You just took it!"

"Give, take, what's the difference? We're on the same side, right?"

Puke comes up the back of his throat. He swallows it. "Who's we?"

"That information is on a need-to-know basis."

Teague is pretty sure he means the guys in Mad Pride. He was wrong about Liam being so different out here.

Liam keeps scrolling. "Hey, you cool with my plan?"

"I guess." He wouldn't say if he wasn't. Why did Liam have to tell him? Now he's sort of in on it whether he likes it or not.

"Why do you care about the study?"

"Because I'm in it, eejit. They've got no right to meddle in our private family business."

Teague backs off a few steps and drops to the floor on his butt.

Liam turns around. "There's nothing to worry about. This operation is rock-solid."

"What makes you sure it will work?"

"Because Ryan will be scared about everybody's information getting out, he'll do what we want."

Teague crawls back to get another look at the screen. "I don't see any names."

"That's because they're on a master file. They use numbers for patient IDs."

"And you have that, too?"

"You better believe it."

"Is Finn in on this?"

"No. At least not yet. But he's got his own reasons for wanting the study shut down. He'll think it's a good thing when he finds out."

Teague scooches back and drops his head to the floor. The dust is an inch thick under Liam's bed, where a long metal thing with a wooden handle catches his eye. "Is that your rifle?"

Liam swivels his chair around. "What are you doing down there?" He looks mad.

"Just asked a question."

"No. It's Finn's. I was practicing taking it apart and cleaning it. Just forget about it, all right?"

"No problem."

"Are you with us?"

This sucks. Kate's the one human being left on this earth who gives a shit about him. And now Liam is trying to turn everybody against her. If she gets fired, where does that leave him? On the other hand, if he rats . . . "I won't give you up for it."

"Thanks, mate. Hey, Finn says it's okay if you want to stay for my initiation ceremony."

"Tonight?"

"Aye. I turn eighteen tomorrow."

"If I knew it was your birthday, I'd have gotten you something."

"Not a bother. When's yours?"

"June seventh."

"What year?"

"Eighty-seven. Why do you want to know?"

"No reason."

Liam goes back to clicking through reams of data while Teague hugs his knees on the floor. Huh. Maybe Druids are into astrology. Whatever. Liam's invitation wasn't just to hang out and play computer games. He wanted to trick him into getting on board with his dumbass hack. Still, Teague is pretty curious about this ceremony they're all talking about.

He stands up. "I have to call my aunt and ask if I can stay."

"Phone's in the kitchen," Liam says, with his eyes still on the screen.

# 2002

At the point in the drive when Kate should keep going east on the M6, she does a U-turn and heads west towards Galway City. "I don't need you or your fucking study."

With the wind on her face, she keeps shame at bay for the next forty-five minutes until she reaches the parking lot of their apartment, where her mood sours again. Teague should be home from Liam's, and she can't face him like this. She puts the car in reverse and drives to the Uni Pub, a drinking hole she visited on a prior Friday night with the interns, only to find the door is locked. A sign says it opens at five. She goes back to her car and flattens the seat back.

The hour before Monday-morning staff meetings was her and Sebastian's favorite time for a rendezvous in Chelsea. The very last time, they'd been lying at arm's length on his bed, enjoying their usual mix of nerdy banter and foreplay, when he picked her up like a sack and set her across his knees. She arched her shoulders in the spirit of play, expecting to roll off and move on to the main event, when he grabbed her butt hard. Was he going to spank her? She wondered. They'd never gone there. Her reaction split in two. The needy little girl craved the hardness of it. The woman cringed and judged herself for wanting it. She ping-ponged between the two while his palm hovered in the air. *Shall I?* he asked. She groaned and said, *yes*. In the seconds after his hand came down, she felt owned and loved; a feeling that lasted until he left, as usual, ten minutes ahead of her to avoid showing up at the lab together.

She rights her car seat. A pair of fresh-faced students pass arm in arm on the sidewalk. Their apparent bliss stings her. She runs her feelings in reverse. He didn't *own* her if she gave herself willingly. Not *put-a-ring-on-it* loved. More like the high that comes from your first sip of mediocre wine. Three glasses later, your taste buds have dulled. The first swallow is all that matters.

Consensual: an act or contract completed with the agreement of both parties involved. Right. A black and white exchange. It *was* that clear between them, wasn't it? The grey parts are starting to haunt her.

For most of the last year and a half, Kate's affair with Sebastian felt like more than enough. A husband, even a regular boyfriend, would have demanded too much from her. Time. Regular meals. A sympathetic ear for his frustrations. Likewise, a cheerleader for victories. Even her ex-husband, who'd had his own affairs on the side to fill any needs she couldn't or wouldn't tackle, felt like a drag on her toward the end. Then what's this cramp in her gut about?

By her third gin and tonic, when a lanky young man takes a stool at the other end of the L-shaped bar, Kate is enjoying a pleasant buzz. He's clearly not an undergrad. She surmises by his arty style—slicked-back dirty blond hair, black turtleneck, green corduroy pants, and a man purse—his field isn't science. After they exchange a sufficient number of fleeting looks to establish mutual interest, she offers a sustained smile and he moves to the stool next to hers, bringing his half-pint with him.

"Looks like it's just the two of us," he says with a goofy smile. He's not Irish; Liverpool is her best guess. "I'm skipping, how about you?" he asks.

"Guilty as charged."

He raises an eyebrow. "American."

"I am. What brings you across the Irish Sea?"

"My PhD in the semiotics of early twentieth-century experimental Irish fiction."

On her blank look, he elaborates. "Flann O'Brien, Aidan Higgins, Joyce, of course."

She has heard of James Joyce. More important at this moment is the fact that his obscure literary specialty places him on the opposite side of campus, far from the psychiatry department to which she's linked.

Archie's student flat is a lower-rent version of her place, with some twenty-something male touches. Unpacked boxes for furniture, an enormous TV on the floor, an overflowing trash bin, food containers and empty bottles on the counters. Smells combining all of the above. Kate keeps her breath shallow as she crosses the living room. Archie goes into a bedroom and emerges with a pipe. "Care for a toke?"

It's been at least five years, but hell, why not? Splayed on a beanbag chair, Kate inhales deeply, proud of herself for not coughing. After three tokes she's more stoned than God knows when. The walls are tipping and swaying. Archie's smiling face elongates first vertically then horizontally. Oh dear. This isn't the same pot she used to smoke. Her eyes focus long enough to make out the fact that Archie's face is connected to the arm extended to help her out of the chair.

On her feet, their hands get to work stripping each other of clothing. Shirts, pants, belt, bra, underwear, and shoes are tossed as they stumble to his bed. Flesh on flesh, groans replace words, until Kate arrives at the destination she's been seeking all afternoon. Total anonymity, bargain-basement pleasure, sans shame. Her lasting impression is that Archie is well endowed and energetic, if a bit clunky. Then again, it may have been her awkwardness flavoring their sex. She's out of practice and overeager.

Archie is sleeping like the baby he is when she wakes up early Saturday morning. Her shoulders and thighs ache from a drunken night's sleep in his twin-size bed. In no mood to chat or bond with him, she lets herself out and walks back to her car. By the time she drives to the apartment, she's relived grades seven through eleven, with all their attendant horrors. She's Katy Callahan, the awkward, too-smart girl with a junkie sister. The one boys ask out because she's easy, who acts like she's above it all but cries as soon as she's alone in her room. She washes her face and looks in on Teague, who's lying atop the bedcovers still in his clothes, snoring lightly.

Under her comforter, the past isn't finished with her. It delivers Rafael, the boy to whom she gave her virginity at age fifteen. They worked the evening shift at ShopRite. Kate, a trainee cashier, Rafael, a stock boy and seventeen-year-old Fonzie lookalike on whom she had a crush. It happened one night at the end of their shift. Before they did it, Rafael lit a joint and offered Kate her first taste of the stuff, which makes the memory a bit fuzzy, but it's etched in her brain regardless. His rough hands yanking off her jeans, the smell of gasoline on the loading dock, her thrill fading to terror someone would take a shortcut behind the store and see them. Penetration was unpleasant but brief. Far worse were the words he spoke. *Tu es muy fea*, he said, over and over, while he fucked her. She knew enough Spanish to understand he was calling her very ugly—*yet not too ugly to fuck.*

Worse, after that first time, she conjured the fantasy they'd begun a grand love affair. Grand enough to do it several more times that summer. Always rough and degrading. Sixteen years later, Kate hates the girl who allowed it to happen to her, who fooled everyone with her stellar grades and ambitions, while she gave her body and her self-respect to any boy-man who might fill the hole in her heart. The same weakness that made her throw everything away for a bargain-basement romance with Sebastian.

She's back in her own bed, sleep out of reach and nausea churning her stomach. Sitting up, she drops her head into her hands. Chirping birds mock her misery. Maybe she just hit bottom. God help her if there's further down to go. That's when she remembers the surprise ending of the Rafael saga. It was Meghan who put an end to it. She found out and told Rafael that her boyfriend, Lou—Teague's biological father—would flatten him if he ever touched her sister again. To Kate, she said, "You can do better than Rafael." It was the closest she ever felt to her half-sister.

# 2002

When Kate doesn't pick up the phone at home or the clinic, Teague gives himself permission to stay late at Liam's. About thirty people show up for the ceremony, including Kiernan from group, Liam's older brother, his uncle, and two cousins. There are some twenty and thirty-something hipsters and gray-haired types, even a few families with little kids. Liam says they're all grove regulars.

After a potluck dinner, everyone except him and the uncle changes into white robes. Finn wears a gold one. Liam's mom, who's a lot younger than Finn and says to call her Morgan, wears a blue robe. Her hair is white with black bangs, and she has big eyes and a swooping nose—pretty, in a witchy way—like Narcissa Malfoy. When the sun sets, Morgan rings a bell, and everyone walks down the hill.

"I'm Denny." A guy around Finn's age with white curly hair and a pug nose has caught up to him. "Would you care to be one of our drummers?" Denny hands him a drum the diameter of a dinner plate with a skin head.

"Cool, thanks. I'm Teague."

"Ah right, the—"

"Yeah, the Yank."

At the pit, Denny shows him the arch he and his crew built from the yew log Joe brought back earlier in the day. Made of two upright poles with the bark stripped off, there's a gate strung between them, everything notched together.

"You won't find any nails," Denny says as Teague inspects the arch. He recognizes the girls' tie-dyed flags hanging from the two poles.

Everyone forms two circles on the dirt mound surrounding the pit. Teague stands between Denny and Kiernan, who tells him he should get ready for something awesome.

Teague likes the wet, squishy ground under his bare feet, but he's shivering in his T-shirt and shorts. Too bad he didn't take one of the robes Morgan offered him. The moon is full and there are thousands of stars. He's got goose bumps on his arms and legs, but that's because he's cold. Finn jumps into the pit, and everyone goes quiet. In his gold robe, with his face painted blue, he looks just like Mel Gibson in *Braveheart*.

"AAH-oo-wen," Finn says.

"AAH-oo-wen," everyone says back.

"Behold spirits of the east, west, north, and south."

Joe brings Finn a lit torch that throws a fierce light and shadows on his face.

"People of the tribe, behold this torch by which I kindle our sacred fire."

The logs crackle and send up flares.

"A blessing I cast upon it and all who are warmed by it. They shall not be slain. They shall not be imprisoned. They shall not be wounded. They shall not be ravaged. They shall not be left bare. Nor will the Gods of our people leave them forgotten."

Liam shows up at the gate with his mom. Finn meets them there.

"Liam, you've sought the Druids, learned much, and passed many tests. Is it your wish to continue?"

"Aye, it is."

"You cross a perilous bridge, the secret path to the Otherworld, followed by the seekers of truth who hear the calling of the sidhe."

Finn opens the gate.

"What's *shee*?" Teague asks Kiernan.

"The fae folk," Kiernan whispers, which doesn't explain anything.

Liam steps through the gate with his mom, now the three of them form a triangle in the pit.

"What do you stand for?" Morgan asks Liam.

"The well of wisdom, the sacred truth."

"What trees do you know?" Finn asks.

"The oak, ash, hazel, pine, hawthorn."

The ceremony goes on like that, more questions and answers from the circles, more prayers. Teague half listens. There's a buzz in his head that's been in the background since he came down the hill but now it's getting louder. Pinpricks in his arms and legs go off like sparklers.

Wait. What!? There's a whole new row of new people sitting above the heads of the grove regulars. They're wearing old-fashioned clothes: flat hats, short pants, vests on the men, scarves covering the ladies' heads. One of them, a big woman with a tiara and a face like a prune, catches his eye and gives him a big smile. Now she's fading. They're all doing that. Coming in and out like, duh, ghosts. Ghosts in the cheap seats. At least they look happy to be there. Not like the voices he heard in town.

In the pit, Morgan holds a chalice. She takes a sip and brings it to Liam's lips. He drinks and passes it to Finn, who does the same and hands it off to Joe. Liam and Finn leave the pit and then it's just Morgan singing. Except she doesn't sound human. More like a bird trilling in a high pitch that keeps going higher and higher until her voice is freaky high enough to break glass. When she finishes, no one talks, and Teague's ears feel different. He hears more. Sounds he didn't notice before. Wind riling the fire . . . snip, snap, whoosh. A barn owl shrieking like an out of tune ukulele.

Then Sleeping Beauty, standing next to Kiernan, starts to hum. Soft at first, then louder, and really loud. Everyone joins in and it's like the ground is shaking from their vibration. The hum flies around the circle, picking up speed until it's everywhere at once. One loud *whir*. He pictures them flying—a massive flock of birds. Diving and sailing over the trees. Now the hum fades and disappears . . . but they're still all connected.

A guy holding an accordion and Liam with his fiddle step forward and play a tune. Everyone knows the song and joins in. Teague picks up the rhythm and goes with it. He's drumming, not thinking, when he hears a conversation.

"He's the one we've been expecting," says a male voice.

"The Yank? Pftt . . . an unlikely choice," a lady answers.

Teague's hand freezes above his drum. Since he's the only Yank, they must be talking about him. Weirder than that though, by the laws of acoustics, he shouldn't be hearing them, or anybody, above the music. So where are they? He scans the faces of everyone in the circle, but all eyes seem to be on Finn. Denny, Kiernan, Sleeping Beauty, everybody singing.

"I have it on good authority," the man says, clear as a bell, "the clan is Callahan; the boy called Teague has come to take care of some unfinished business."

There! He spots the pair of them on the far side of the pit by the oak tree. A dude no more than two feet tall, holding a staff. A lady in a blowy white dress. She doesn't even look human, more like vapor with a face. When the man points his finger in Teague's direction, he darts his eyes away.

Great zombie Jesus. If he's seeing a leprechaun—and he can think of nothing else to call him—Teague knows he's in trouble. As much as he'd like to believe they're both real, it's more likely he hallucinated them because he went off his meds. If he ignores them, maybe they'll go away.

He hits his drum and follows Liam's fiddle back into the rhythm of the song.

"I tell you; he's got it." The man's voice, forceful now, makes the hairs on Teague's neck stand at attention.

"How can you be sure?" the lady asks.

"See the sparks where his hand meets the skin of the drum?"

"Oh, my. Yes!"

Teague drops the drum and watches it roll into the pit where it lands in front of Finn, who shoots him a curious look, then pivots to the oak. Are Teague's eyes deceiving him or did Finn just give those two characters a nod?

The leprechaun puffs up his chest and points his staff at Finn. "There's no question about it, Chief. The lad is one of us. And if you won't deal with him, the fae will have to step in."

The lady in white claps and floats off the ground.

*The fae will do what?*

Finn's eyes lock on Teague's. Then it's like they're at two ends of a tunnel, with rays shooting back and forth. Finn's chest glows as if there's a gas lamp under his ribs. As Teague's chest expands, a feeling of power comes over him. He's had surges before, but they usually throw him off-kilter. This one does the opposite. He feels calm. Grounded. Finn nods and gives him a wink Teague takes to mean something private and important just passed between them.

Then, amazingly fast, everything is over.

People hug and chat and walk up the hill behind Finn and Morgan. Just Teague and Joe are left at the pit. Joe smothers the fire while Teague leans against the arch. His head is roaring, like the surge is still moving through him and he needs to let it settle.

"How's the lad?" Joe stops raking the fire.

Before he can answer, the old lady in the tiara is back, peeking over Joe's shoulder, with her hands cupped to her mouth. *Lovely. Tell him you're lovely.*

What do you creatures want from me? He doesn't say it out loud, but she hears him.

*There, there, Teague. Don't let the Good Folk put you out of sorts. They're just excited to see you. They've done their job by letting Finn know you're here. All you must do now is answer Joe nicely and put one foot ahead of the other. We'll be back to tell you more in due time.*

"Son?" Joe is staring.

*Go ahead*, she says.

"I'm lovely," he says. A word he's never used in his life.

"Glad to hear it." Joe picks up a full bucket and sprinkles water on the smoldering embers.

He gets home around two in the morning surprised Kate's not there. Maybe she got herself a boyfriend.

When he wakes up, it's still night out. Or it's night again and Kate is calling him for dinner.

"Teague, did you hear me? It's on the table."

"I'm coming!"

He thinks back to last night. A bunch of people dressed up as wizards and witches held a ceremony for Liam's birthday. Some ghosts came. One was an old lady with a tiara who seemed nice. A leprechaun and his girlfriend showed up and started talking about him like they knew his whole life story. Then Finn zapped him, and the little people cut out. No harm done. He's not sure why, but he feels pretty good, and his head is clear.

In the living room, Kate's lying on the sofa in her pajamas with a pillow covering her face.

"Are you sick?"

"No. I'm fine."

Could have fooled him. She's not usually like this. Actually, she's never like this. It's cool if she doesn't want to tell him what's up. There's an open pizza box on the table with steam rising from it.

"Is that dinner?"

"Yes, just help yourself." She sits up. "I ordered your favorite toppings. Mushrooms, olives, and pepperoni, right?"

"Yup." He piles six slices on a paper plate. "Are you having any?"

She squeezes her face like it's a wet sponge. "Not right now. Save me a couple slices for later."

"Okay." He takes the full plate back to his room.

An hour later, he's on the floor with his sketch pad when she sticks her head in the door.

"I'm going to bed early. Are you okay?"

"Better than you."

She does a half-assed laugh, starts to shut the door, then comes in. "You know what? You're right." She sits at the end of his bed. "I blew it at work, and I've been feeling sorry for myself."

"Don't you like your job?"

94

"I don't like being bad at it." She blows out air and pulls her hair into a ponytail on top of her head. "The problem is I'm more suited to benchwork."

Teague flashes on Kate's lab, her fancy electron microscope, the wall of mounted cages. "You mean those mice?"

"Well, yes. Since our genes are eighty-five percent the same as theirs, I do, or did, all my research on mice."

"What's the point of it?"

She wrinkles her nose and looks up at the ceiling. "I was trying to find out why, when bad things happen, some mice, like some people, do okay, while others . . ."

"Lose their shit?"

"That's one way to put it. Let's say a hundred years ago people lived through a famine, which was common enough for us to study it in a lot of places, including here."

"Wait. How do you dissect something that happened a hundred years ago?"

"Well, we already know starvation can change how a gene is expressed without changing its core DNA. That's called an epigenetic change. What we don't know is how that alteration affects later generations. Do all offspring inherit it or only some? Is there another gene that protects the heartier ones? That's what I'm investigating. Or I was."

"But how do you do that?"

"Now you're asking about methods. If I have a suspect mutation, I breed an experimental group of mice with that genetic profile, and I kept the same number of normal specimens as a control group."

"What did you find out?"

"Someone ahead of me already established that undernourished mice don't lick their babies the way new mothers usually do. My results showed that the daughters and granddaughters of those mice don't lick their babies either. Even when they had enough to eat. Exciting, no?"

"Yeah. Kind of." He almost says, *Yeah, Dr. Frankenstein,* but that would be mean. His stomach feels pukey. The same thing happened when he was at her lab. He felt sorry for the mice. Not all of them. Some seemed okay. They were playing on the wheel, hanging out with their buddies at the spigot. But others looked miserable, standing alone in the corner shaking, not eating or playing. It turns out that was the whole point of it. Then Kate could figure out what made them like that and fix it—or not.

"Okay, that's it for me," she says. "Sleep well."

"Later."

While she's brushing her teeth, Kate remembers the deadly serious look on Teague's face as he stared at the cages that day. Afterwards, she was surprised and a bit disappointed that he didn't ask questions. In fact, he complained about the lab having no windows and left to walk around Times Square. She figured the science was too strange for him—as it was for many of her colleagues, including Sebastian, who called epigenetics the Wild West of neuroscience, and made clear to Kate that she should do those experiments strictly on her own time, albeit in the laboratory with his name on it.

To pass the time on those long nights and weekends, she would picture herself the sheriff in a lawless Laredo. She'd arrange for half of Laredo's furry residents to be born with the shorter form of the serotonin gene that made them reactive in the face of challenges. In the parlance of researchers, they were the orchids, prone to dysfunction. When faced with the stressful choice of which lever to push to get their next drink of syrupy water, orchids sat and trembled with indecision. Their luckier peers, her control group, born with a longer form of the same gene, were hearty like dandelions—a group with which she wholly identified. Dandelions drank and worked and played, as if shielded against life's slings and arrows. They might not have been the happiest specimens, but they stayed alive and got stuff done.

With her last experiment on maternal licking behavior, she'd gotten close to the point where she could publish her results—when everything blew up.

# New York City
## November 1920

It was still dark when Ellen and Michael left Five Points to walk the seven miles uptown to Carnegie Hall, hoping they'd get a seat. Only to find a line already snaking around the block. Someone said over seventy thousand had turned out for him last week at Fenway Park. They heard a cop tell his partner "the Chief" was on track to raise over $5 million for the cause before his US tour ended.

When, at last, the fedora-wearing Éamon de Valera, much younger than Ellen expected, strode to the lectern adorned with the tricolors, she and Michael rose to their feet, clapping and cheering, until de Valera quieted the crowd and began his speech.

"I've come to America as the official head of the Republic established by the will of the Irish people in accordance with the principle of self-determination," de Valera proclaimed. The floor shook from the thunderous applause and a thrill went up her spine.

"The pious wish of every Irish heart today is the same spirit that drove America's war for independence in 1776," he went on to say. "Like America's forefathers, today in Ireland we fight for complete and absolute freedom and separation from England. The only banner under which our freedom can be won at the present time is the Republican banner. This is our time to win freedom."

De Valera was the statesman of their dreams and they hung on his every word. He'd traveled to New York to lobby for recognition of an independent Irish state by the US government and raise money. Then his Republican Volunteers could keep up the fight. De Valera thanked his audience in advance for doing their part with the hard-earned coins they dropped in the baskets making their way up and down the rows.

But Éamon de Valera was more than a statesman for the people gathered in Carnegie Hall that day. For Michael, he represented the land he would never plant or harvest. To Ellen, de Valera became a stand-in for her father. By the time the great man left the stage, she'd given up trying to stop her tears.

They walked south on a gas-lamp-lit Seventh Avenue, which had turned into a frigid wind tunnel by dusk, Ellen's shawl a weak barrier. She linked arms with Michael, but he seemed far away. Instead of the awe she'd felt earlier in the day upon seeing the skyscrapers of Midtown for the first time, now their unreal size made her feel small and alone. Living around so many who looked and sounded like them brought little comfort. Each new report of the rising violence at home became the only topic of conversation at church, in the shops, or waiting their turn to use the outhouse.

As they crossed Fifth Avenue, Michael pulled away from her and walked three steps ahead. She stopped and waited for him to turn around. "You going to tell me what's bothering you?" When he didn't answer, she took his hand and led him to a patch of grass between the avenues with a fountain and young trees. A sign identified it as Madison Square Park. On the bench, he hung his head. Unable to see his face, her attention went to the immense triangle-shaped building across the street. She'd heard people talk about it, but this was her first close look at the Flatiron. Truly, the strangest and least friendly manmade structure she'd ever seen. A cold blast added to her feeling of dread.

"There's a letter from Da," Michael finally said.

His twisted features made her more afraid. Instead of following her first impulse to be angry with him for not telling her about the letter sooner, she bit her tongue and gave him time. Clomping hooves and neighs on Madison Avenue provided a steady drumbeat. The occasional sputter of an automobile rattled her.

"He had reason to believe revenge was coming, so they packed up and moved to Kerry with Colm and the girls. My Uncle Thomas took them in."

"How terrible." She paused, confused. "I thought the Black & Tans arrested Colm. How did he get out so soon?"

He lifted his head and looked her in the eye. "Da didn't say."

"Michael . . ."

"I don't know what to make of it. At least they're all safe. And it doesn't change anything for us."

"What else did he say?"

"He said we should be careful about who we tell our name or where we come from."

She catches her breath and squeezes his arm tighter. "Has it really come to this?"

She didn't expect an answer from him, and he didn't offer one. They sat on the bench in silence until the wind became fierce and she couldn't feel her cheeks or fingers. Their walk back to the tenement felt twice as long as the morning journey to Carnegie Hall, the news from John Callahan making each step harder. Still, she refused to let go of the hope that she might someday go home—if only for a visit. It was what kept her going.

# 2002

Disgusted with herself over Archie and the botched interview with Eamon O'Malley, Kate moped all weekend. She spent Monday in bed replaying the twenty-minutes she spent with Eamon backward and forward, trying to figure out how she could have avoided stepping on quite so many land mines. The answer comes to her on Tuesday morning while searching for a space in the nearly full clinic parking lot: She should have let the man rant. His complaints weren't even off base. She'd been emotionally insensitive and culturally ignorant. Humility is her goal for the day.

She walks straight to her office without stopping for coffee in the break room, relieved when she doesn't run into Ryan. She wants to organize her thoughts about the interview before facing him. At her desk, she pushes all the usual buttons on her computer and waits for the screen to light up. She's wondering what's wrong when her door opens.

"Good. You're here." He pokes his head in but doesn't wait for an invitation before taking a seat at the table. She lets the cramp in her belly subside before joining him.

"I'm sorry I didn't make it in yesterday."

Without asking how she's feeling this morning, he scratches his beard and looks straight ahead. When he tilts his head toward her, his face is flushed. "For

Christ's sake, Kate, a grad student? Why not a lorry driver or the postman? At least then I wouldn't have to hear about it."

She opens her mouth to speak and stops. He heard. Of course, he heard, you nitwit. It's the first time she's seen him this angry. The flat tire was more annoyance. This is scarier. He cracks his knuckles. Her throat tightens and she turns to stare out the window. Muffled voices filter in from the hallway. He clears his throat and she's forced to give him her full attention.

"Listen, Kate, what you do in your free time is your own business unless it connects in any way to the university. As you know, our study is already up against negative public opinion.

The betrayal in his voice is hard to hear. "I . . . I—I have no excuse. I'm . . . sorry. I don't want to resign but if you need me to—"

His hard, glazed look suggests he's already lined up her replacement. The awkwardness continues as he sniffs and holds his breath. Her body goes rigid. She waits for the ax to fall and wills her panic away. Getting fired twice in one year would be an absolute disaster. If she loses this job, she can kiss her career goodbye.

"You must realize I'm not the only one who knows about the nasty business between you and Sebastian Souza."

She's vaguely aware of rocking in her chair, but it's as if she's looking down at herself from ten thousand feet. According to her mother, Kate's rocking habit began in infancy and never stopped. She does it unconsciously in bed, with or without another person present. She's even caught herself doing it in business meetings, mortified if she fears a colleague has noticed. Now she grabs the seat and rearranges her face. He's still talking, apparently oblivious to her movements.

". . . it makes me wonder what kind of game you're playing here."

She leans against the seatback, willing her state of alarm to tamp down— a feat akin to squeezing her size-eight body into a size-four dress. The downside of this exercise is the hollowed-out sensation it leaves from her neck down, which creates its own problems. Wires get crossed; perceptions go awry. Like the blue pinstripes on Ryan's shirt now pulsating. His eyebrows moving as if in wave.

"Frankly, Kate, I don't have the luxury of firing you."

The harshness in his voice causes a seconds-long delay in her catching his meaning. He doesn't have the luxury of what?

"Believe it or not, an even bigger problem has fallen on my lap. And I need your help." He produces a folded sheet of paper from his pocket and lays it flat on the table. In large block letters, written with a Sharpie, she reads:

> YOUR COMPUTERS HAVE BEEN HACKED.
> PATIENT FILES ARE IN OUR POSSESSION.
> STOP THE BALLYMORE FAMILY STUDY IMMEDIATELY OR
> WE WILL POST THEIR IDENTITIES & DIAGNOSES ONLINE
> FOR THE WORLD TO SEE.
> DON'T BELIEVE US? HERE'S A SAMPLE:
> TEAGUE CALLAHAN. MALE. DOB 06/07/1987. NEW YORK
> CITY. DIAGNOSIS: SCHIZOAFFECTIVE DISORDER WITH
> AUDIO HALLUCINATIONS AND PARANOID TENDENCIES.
> MOTHER OPIOID ADDICTION, FATAL OD.

"Teague! Oh my God." She turns around to look at her monitor, which is still dark. "Is that why—?"

"Aye, they'll be down for at least the rest of this week while we deal with this."

How did they get Teague's diagnosis? This is her fault. It must be. She reads the rest of the note:

> A COPY OF THIS WARNING HAS BEEN SENT TO THE
> COUNTY HEALTH DEPARTMENT AND THE BALLYMORE
> NEWS. GIVE US YOUR ANSWER BY POSTING A NOTE WITH
> THE WORD FREE WHERE YOU FOUND THIS ONE. IF IT'S
> NOT THERE BY NEXT MONDAY, WE'LL TAKE THAT AS A
> NO. DON'T UNDERESTIMATE US. YOU AND YOUR
> PATIENTS WILL REGRET IT.
>
> SIGNED, THE DEFENDERS

"You got this when?"

"Yesterday morning. It was taped to the front door. Fortunately, I had a seven-a.m. session, so I saw it first. Besides me, only you and Dara know, among staff. The local Gardaí have been here and started an investigation." He rolls his eyes and picks up the note as if he needs to look again to believe it. "This is a copy of their note. The Gardaí kept the original to look for fingerprints or God knows what." He shrugs and shakes his head.

"Oh, Ryan. You should have called me."

He winces and says nothing.

"How will we know if and when the hackers post any patient data online?"

He shrugs. "I'm sure as hell not going to sit around surfing the net to find out. We've got our full roster of regular clients, and you have two interviews scheduled for this week. I'd like you to take Dara with you on this next round."

The mere mention of her next set of interviews revives the horror of her terrible performance with Eamon O'Malley. But he's right. She's better off with a partner for the time being.

"If the hacker posts anything, we'll hear about it soon enough. Meanwhile, a guard by the name of Conor Rafferty will be here to interview any staff who have access to the clinic computer network, including you."

"Of course."

"I'm obliged to give the county health director a full report." He rolls his eyes. "Today."

"God. What a mess."

"Aye. Meanwhile, Kate, I think it would be better if you and Teague leave faculty housing and move into something here in town."

Her cheeks warm. Is this his ham-fisted way of trying to keep her chaste? Who does he think he is? She swallows her pride when she remembers that not only is he her boss; he knows everything.

"I asked Dara to check the local listings, and she's found a two-bedroom rental within walking distance. Is that all right with you?"

"Sure. I'll go talk to her."

He starts to get up.

"Ryan?"

He halts.

"I'm going to take you up on the offer you made on Friday."

His brow creases. "Remind me."

"You suggested I do some role-playing before my next interviews."

"Aye. Since Dara does the training, I'll let her know and you two can set up a time." He leaves without pleasantries.

Dara gives her the business card of a realtor named Bill Hogan, who, she says, handles most of the rentals in town. Kate thanks her and after a bit of small talk works up the nerve to ask Dara about the gossip spreading about her on campus. Dara is glad to oblige. Among other things, Kate is now known as the "ginger *beor*" — slut — "who got the boot from her lab in NYC because she slept with the boss." She's also "the right little dinger who comes across like a gobshite with a massive brain." According to Archie, she's "quite the mot after a good lashing." The latest talk is that Ryan's under pressure to put her on the next flight back to New York. It's about what she expected.

Eight clinic staff members assemble in the conference room to talk with Guard Rafferty. In addition to Kate and Dara, there are two staff therapists, the clinic receptionist, and three counseling interns. Rafferty begins by explaining that stealing computer files from the county health department is a crime, one the gardai´ take very seriously. He'll do the initial investigation on the clinic cyberattack. Depending on what he finds, he may call in someone from the Cybercrime Unit in Dublin to assist, all of which Kate finds reassuring.

She groans silently when he says they should change their passwords on computers or cell phones that they use personally or professionally. She hasn't changed hers since she first started using the internet, which, when forced to look back, she realizes was four years ago, in 1998.

It gets worse. They're obliged to account for their whereabouts for the last seven days and nights, including their computer use for the same period. She wonders if he'll ask for corroboration. In which case, she'll have to call Archie, whose last name she doesn't know.

Rafferty conducts his individual interviews in a smaller room down the hall. He doesn't say why he does them elsewhere and one at a time, but from having watched every episode of *Law & Order*, Kate guesses it's so guilty parties can't coordinate their stories.

After an hour, Rafferty has talked to two people. The group's small talk has petered out and she regrets not bringing work. Dara is reading a Chief Inspector Wexford mystery called *The Babes in the Wood*.

She sits and stews. What on earth has Teague gotten himself into? Or is he just a victim in this? She needs to talk to him. And not just about the hack. In a few days, they'll be moving to their new flat in town. She rented it on the phone this morning after Dara gave her the description. Clearly, Ryan hopes her new residence, in walking distance to the clinic, will keep her from screwing around with any more NUIG grad students. Great work on that vow, Kate.

A memory intervenes . . . Minutes after she and Teague walked into the faculty apartment, he said it didn't matter which bedroom he chose since they'd be leaving *in a month tops*. And here they are, exactly a month later, about to move into a new flat. Coincidence? Maybe. What else could it be? She's about to dispense with the thought when she remembers Maureen going on about Teague's art teacher having been in a car accident and how upset he was about it. As if he had known it would happen and should have warned her. Kate hadn't had the patience to ask her mother for details and now she can't piece it together.

The door opens and Rafferty enters alone. He scans his list. Kate bites her tongue to keep from asking if she can go next.

"Dr. Katherine Jones."

*Oh, thank goodness.* "Right here."

They enter a room containing two armchairs facing each other, the requisite tissue box on a side table, and a potted plant by the window. Given her association of this setting with psychotherapy, it feels more than a little odd to share it with this barrel-chested older man in a uniform almost identical to those of the NYPD. Dark-blue pants, snugly buttoned jacket, round cap with a black vinyl visor, and a radio. They differ in the four-pointed brass star with Celtic symbols and the words Garda Síochána above his pocket, the absence of a gun on his belt.

"Dr. Jones, what is your relationship with Teague Callahan?"

"I'm his aunt and legal guardian. His mother is, or was, my half-sister, Meghan. She died ten years ago from a heroin overdose."

"His father?"

"Lou Giordano, her dealer, a resident of Fishkill Correctional Facility for another five years." It's an effort not to add her usual *scumbag* when she says Lou's name.

He pauses as if to consider this motley set of facts and scribbles a note. "I understand from Ryan that Teague's was the confidential information provided on the hacker's note. Do you have any idea why?"

"No. But I'm guessing it's because he's linked to me, and the hacker knows I'm co-lead investigator of the study, which he's opposed to."

"Teague is also a patient here, is that right?"

"Yes, he's in individual therapy and part of the teen group. Sometimes he uses the art therapy room."

"Why is that?"

"Why does he go to the art therapy room or what's his diagnosis?" No doubt he recognizes her dodge. As uncomfortable as she is sharing any more of Teague's clinical information, Rafferty's stern look convinces her she better. "He has schizoaffective disorder."

Rafferty's expression is blank.

"It's on the schizophrenia spectrum, but his symptoms are in remission."

"Thank you." He makes a note and eyes her. "How would you describe your relationship with your nephew?"

"It's fine. I mean, it's getting better. I've only been his guardian since June. Of course, I've known him since he was born. But I was away from home a lot." She stops when the point of his question dawns on her. "To be honest, I haven't considered the possibility I think you're getting to."

"I'm looking at everybody connected to the clinic, starting with any individual with a motive."

"Then I guess you will want to talk to Teague because I can't imagine he would—"

"Have him here tomorrow morning at ten."

"Okay."

He takes two printed sheets from his binder. "This is a copy of the form for you to record your whereabouts going back seven days. Bring them back filled out tomorrow."

"Is that it?"

"For now. I have your contact information." He writes a long note.

Her nervousness, more on Teague's behalf than her own, keeps her talking. "You know we're an NYPD family."

"Is that right?" He stops writing.

"My dad."

"If you don't mind my asking, what was his name and where did he serve?"

"Jack Callahan. The Bronx."

"Is he retired?"

"He passed away."

"Sorry to hear that. How long ago?"

"He died in the line of duty in 1973."

"You have my sympathy. I've got an uncle and a cousin on the force there. One retired. The other still active."

"A small world."

He makes eye contact for the first time. "Not that long ago, New York felt closer than Dublin to people living here in the west. I doubt you'd find a single household in Ballymore without kin in America."

"Really?" More ignorance on her part.

Rafferty keeps writing in his binder. "We'll see you in the morning, dear," he says with a quick glance.

His *dear* is an unexpected, reassuring touch, but she's still uneasy as she walks to Ryan's office. Everything Kate knows about hacking comes from movies or the occasional malware scare at the university—incidents that would make the IT department frantic, while irritating the faculty and staff. The perpetrators, who never seemed to get caught, were hard to take seriously when they used aliases like DefCon and WarLock and gave their worms cutesy names like à la Love Bug and Melissa, as if they were teenage crushes, not viruses meant to take down the Pentagon or Microsoft.

107

It's a good bet the clinic hacker is the same sort of pimply-faced adolescent. A socially awkward boy with a computer for a best friend who spends his days and nights locked in his bedroom hacking away. They have several of the type in the Ballymore Family Study population. The clinic data breach could turn into a hideous public humiliation for over two hundred local victims, Teague among them. And if that happens, their study will be history.

She stops at Dara's desk, who looks up from her screen. "Did you call Bill Hogan?"

"Yes, it's all done. Thanks for finding it. We move in this weekend."

"You didn't want to take a look first?"

"No need. It sounds adequate for our needs." She nods at Ryan's closed door. "Is he in?"

Dara wets her lips and lets out a sigh. "He's still at the hospital with the big boss."

"Oh. I wonder how that conversation is going."

"I'd put it somewhere between telling your dad you've totaled his car and showing up for confession after missing a decade."

"Ouch. I'll leave him a message."

Dara's phone buzzes and she pivots her chair to pick it up.

Kate is writing her note on the corner of Dara's desk when she notices the latest issue of the *Journal of Neuroscience* atop a pile of mail in Ryan's box. She picks it up and peruses the table of contents. No. It. Can't. Be. The second of three featured studies in the table of contents: Sebastian Souza, lead author . . . "The Epigenetics of Famine." *What the—!?*

Dara is turned away, talking animatedly. Kate leaves the note for Ryan and hugs the journal to her chest. The clinic's labyrinthine hallways seem more convoluted than ever on the way to her office. At her desk she opens to the article page. There she finds her methods, her results, and her analyses, under his name, along with the names of everyone else on her old team—except hers. *That fucking bastard.* He had this in the works when he fired her. He used his connections with the journal editorial board to get it fast-tracked. She grips the edge of her desk and boomerangs back to the state she was in three months ago; demeaned, and heartbroken, after Sebastian told her she had to resign.

When, in the space of ten excruciating minutes, the question of which was worse—losing her lover or the job she loved—had sorted itself out in real time.

"I'm trying to tell you it's over between us," Sebastian blurted out from his desk chair. "It has to be. With the kids still at home. And my father-in-law the fucking editor in chief of the only journal that matters."

Like a flailing boxer, Kate had thrown a useless counterpunch. "If we have to, we can end our relationship. Just be colleagues again."

He rolled his eyes skyward. "That's just not possible."

His voice—the deep, authoritative tone he used as Dr. Neuron on his hit PBS television series—rang thin and forced. He deepened it to deliver the knockout punch and spoke slowly as if addressing a non-English speaker. "You. Have. To. Resign. Today. She won't accept anything less."

Even if she could have brought herself to protest, say this wasn't necessary, question how he could destroy everything they'd built together, the Mojave Desert in her throat made speech impossible. Their affair had lived only in their imaginations until two years before. Why couldn't they end it and go back to how it had been when she was a postdoc, Sebastian her dream mentor. The work was all that mattered. Except it would have taken both of them to have wanted that and only that.

His lips curled at the corners of his mouth. "Come on, Kate. Surely, you've gotten as much out of this relationship as I have. Maybe more."

*Surely . . . what?*

"HR will bring the paperwork to your desk." He spoke in a monotone. "Please keep this to yourself. I need to control the staff messaging."

As if the entire lab and much of the faculty didn't already know what was going on. In their tiny corner of academia, gossip moved at a breakneck speed: affairs, impending divorces, maternity leaves, suspicions of faked results; it was all grist for the mill. She splashed cold water on her face in the restroom and the truth hit her like a squall: posing as a Hillary, she'd been exposed as a Monica. She was no better than that deluded, oversexed intern, who could at least blame the whole episode on her youth. It took every ounce of willpower she possessed to retrace her steps through the lab where every colleague hard at work reinforced her failure.

A "voluntary termination" agreement from Human Resources was waiting for her in her cubicle. A clause titled Rights to Research spelled out the stunning fact that she would leave with zero rights to the work she'd done in the university's laboratory. It all belonged to Sebastian, even if he'd played no role in it. Three years of her best work, gone, just like that. She'd told him about the epigenetics experiments she'd been doing in only the most general terms. He'd opined that the whole line of research had no valid scientific basis, and she should stop wasting her, meaning his, time. Her mistake: duly logging her results on the lab server.

Joanne was the only person she'd told the whole sordid story. How she caved and signed the agreement along with a nondisclosure statement in exchange for a year's salary and a $25,000 "bonus." Despite these missteps, Joanne told her they had a good shot at nailing him and the university with a sexual harassment lawsuit. But Kate nixed it, fearing the controversy would only ruin her reputation in the tiny world of academic neuroscience. Which happened anyway.

By the time Kate leaves by way of the clinic's rear door, the day's crises have multiplied exponentially, and she feels totally disoriented, like the sole survivor of a tornado tiptoeing through unfamiliar debris. Where did she park? It seems like days, not hours, since she arrived for work. She finally finds her car in a rear section of the lot near the M6 where she has no memory of putting it. Now, where are her keys? She's still fishing in her purse when a grim-faced, overweight woman in tight jeans and a sweatshirt, approaches from the bus stop. The woman averts her eyes, but Kate can't help but stare. Trailing a few feet behind her is a rail-thin, glum-faced pubescent girl wearing pink leggings and a sparkling pink bomber jacket. Kate doesn't have to work hard to guess the girl's diagnosis. Anorexia is a cross-cultural phenomenon. Watching the mother hold the clinic door open for her dawdling daughter, a forced smile on her face, Kate feels an intense bond with this woman who couldn't be more unlike her. Except for the fact that they're both dealing with an intractable mental illness in a teenager, making them members of an exclusive club that no parent willingly joined.

She tips her handbag over until its contents, including her keys, spill on the pavement.

Behind the steering wheel her arms and head feel too leaden to drive. She turns over the engine, lets it run for a minute, and switches it off. The scent of a greasy burger wrapper reaches her from the back seat. She rolls down the window, takes an exaggerated breath, and blows it out. As she stares through the windshield, the sight of castle turrets in the near distance only adds to the feeling that her life has taken a surreal turn.

When she wakes the next morning, Kate is sharing her bed with an empty wine bottle, half a sandwich, and the neuroscience journal open to the title page of her stolen experiment. The clock says ten something. Which means it's five something in New York. Fortunately, Joanne is an early riser. She picks up the phone next to her bed.

"This is fabulous," her friend says in a deadpan voice.

"Are you being sarcastic?"

"No, not at all. What an idiot. If he'd just given you proper credit, it wouldn't be such a clear case of retaliation. He's just doubled our odds of winning. Are you ready to go to court?"

"You mean for sexual harassment?" She's embarrassed to say the words aloud.

"Yes, but now we can add intellectual property theft. I'll get Roger on that and draft something with the partner who does employment law. Hang in there, Kate; it won't be quick, but we have a good shot at getting you what you're due."

"My credit?"

"Yes, of course, your credit. But I think we should go for quadruple the money they gave you in that measly severance. Am I right to assume you don't want your old job back?"

Kate's heart thumps like a base drum. Her old job. Sebastian. Laredo. Would she go back to that life if given the chance?

"Kate?"

"Yes, I mean no. I don't want it back."

She hung up and stared at the phone. What she said was true. Although shocking to hear herself say aloud. But what does she really want? For today, she'd be happy if she manages to do her job without pissing anyone off.

# 2002

Teague likes the new flat in town a lot better than the lunar capsule. It's more his style, old and shabby, so he doesn't have to worry about getting it dirty. They moved in last weekend. Kate bought shelves at the used furniture store for his books. They even got a TV. The kitchen is where he paints.

He's mixing tempera: one part powder, three parts egg yolk, three parts distilled water. He loves saying the pigment names out loud . . . "Phthalo blue, caput mortuum, Hansa yellow, alizarin crimson, burnt umber, oxide of chromium, viridian." Yowee. He feels rich.

Since he's out of canvas, he's using a broken door someone put out with their trash bins. He gives it a coat of white primer and sets it on a chair to dry.

Here comes the best part: before he picks up the brush, when he closes his eyes to see what wants to be painted. Instead of the usual way he thinks, all his thoughts getting backed up like cars in rush hour, when he's painting and things are working, his brain slows down. A new thought slides into place next to the one that's most like it. Or it backs off and waits its turn. When a feeling breaks through, it acts like a wave, bringing a new thought or image. Since there's no regular order, it doesn't matter which comes first, or how long each one lasts, because time goes in every direction.

Like right now . . . A dolphin breaks the surface of the water and hangs in the air, squeaking and cackling. He's never seen a dolphin in person. He'll

113

have to go off what he remembers from Animal Planet. Teague shakes out his hands and starts with the ocean.

He's into it, not thinking, when he smells something burning. It's probably coming from outside. After a while, it's still there. He gets up to check. Nothing looks wrong. His dirty dishes are piled in the sink. Half a cold pizza in the oven. He has no trouble believing there are ghost smells in their kitchen, just like there are ghost voices and faces hanging around this town.

He's mixing the phthalo blue when he flashes on Finn in his gold robe standing in front of the fire at Liam's initiation. Then he remembers the yew branches burning, giving off a sweet, musty scent. The same smell! He hasn't seen Finn in person since that night, but it's like they're tethered. When he wakes up in the morning, he sees his face. Sometimes, like now, he knows Finn is watching him.

"Did you make that?" Kiernan's finger hovers an inch over the dolphin's nose.

"Careful, I still have to varnish it."

"I didn't know you were an artist."

"I usually don't paint such sappy stuff."

"It's not sappy."

His chest gets bigger. It's weird to get a compliment on his painting from anyone other than Kate and Ms. Lacey.

"Do you have any minerals in here?" Kiernan's head is in the refrigerator.

"Take whatever you want."

They bring two bottles into the living room.

"I came to get you," Kiernan says after he chugs his. "Liam says the action's going to start at half four."

"What are you talking about?"

"Come on. I'll tell you on the way."

The bus lets them off at a traffic circle outside of Castlerea, where a bunch of people, including some familiar faces from the grove, are standing on the side of the road holding handmade signs: *Hands Off Fairy Hill. Save Sacred Sites.*

Some drivers honk and wave. One guy hangs out his window and gives them the finger.

On the grass, a bulldozer is parked in front of a thick wood. A guy with a hard hat stands next to two uniformed guards. A sign on a pole says Hogan Development Corporation. Shit, there's Rafferty, the cop Kate made him talk to yesterday about Liam's hack. He's with a bald guy in a suit. On the other side of the bulldozer, a student type has a video camera pointed at Finn, who's talking to a girl with a microphone.

"Hey, let's go watch," Kiernan says.

"There's a good reason why no one's tried to build on this stretch of land," Finn tells the reporter. "The people of this county would be wise not to destroy their heritage."

Finn gives Teague and Kiernan a wink.

"Are you saying the fairies will take vengeance on any developer who messes with their hill?" the reporter asks with a nod at the bald man.

Finn tilts his head to the side and raises his eyebrows. "I know no such thing to be true. The members of Ballymore grove are here today to ask the good people of Castlerea to weigh the value of our common heritage against the dubious benefits of putting twenty poorly built condos on this piece of land. Let's put it this way, Bill Hogan's proven he's better at making deals than houses." Finn looks over at Rafferty, and the guy with him who must be Bill Hogan, with a smirk on his face, and they're giving him the same look back.

"Thank you, Mr. Mitchell."

"You're welcome, Deidre . . . Lohan, is it? Dave's daughter?"

"That's right."

"I'm sure your dad's proud of you."

She blushes and tells the cameraman to follow her. She goes to Hogan who gives her a big fake smile when she puts the microphone in his face. He's shaking his head and pointing to the woods as he talks when Teague stops paying attention. Liam has joined their huddle along with Finn, Joe, and Denny.

"Should we get underway, Chief?" Denny asks Finn.

Finn nods and looks over his shoulder at the road. To Joe, he says, "Can you sort them?"

"Aye," Joe says, and he heads to the sign-holding protestors.

"You need to stand clear," he says to Teague. "You, too, Kiernan. The last thing I need is Eamon getting riled at me. Take the signs and let folks driving by know why we're doing this. Liam you go with them."

"No way. I'm staying here with you," Liam protests.

Finn gives him a dirty look. "Not after what you pulled."

Liam kicks the dirt and huffs off in the direction of the woods. Teague guesses Finn is pissed off at Liam about the hack, which he must have just heard about. That means he wasn't in on it.

The guy in the hardhat powers on his bulldozer. After that, it's like everyone is doing a dance. Teague and Kiernan trade places with two of the sign holders, who follow Finn to the bulldozer where they drop to the ground and link arms, eight in all.

Rafferty walks over to where they're sitting and yells something at Finn, who talks back to him. The two of them don't seem all that pissed at each other, more like they've done this before and they're just going through the motions. Rafferty's reciting something. The eight grove members act like they're listening, but, when he's done talking, nobody moves. Rafferty calls the two uniformed gardaí. They lift each sitter by their elbows and lead them to a van that's shown up to take them away. The reporter and cameraman trail along and film everything. Nobody resists or yells. One gray-haired guy puts a fist in the air while they usher him to the van. After it takes off with the sitters and the gardaí, Rafferty and the bald guy leave, and the video crew after that. The bulldozer starts moving toward the trees. Teague and Kiernan help carry the signs and put them in the boot of a grove member's car.

"Let's get out of here," Kiernan says.

They're at the traffic circle, about to cross, when Liam catches up to them.

"Hey, hold on. Teague, what you say to Rafferty yesterday?"

"Nothing about you."

"Yeah? What about your aunt's computer?"

"I told him I mess around with it sometimes. I didn't get into the whole password thing since you stole it off of me. I said I don't need it because she leaves it on all the time. That part's not true either but how would he know?"

"Who are they looking at for it?"

"Don't know. But you should figure Rafferty's going to want to talk to you, too."

"Not if he can't find me."

"Where ya gonna go?"

Liam gives him one of those need-to-know looks.

"Well, keep me out of it, all right?" Teague pleads. "Nothing about using Kate's computer or getting her password from me."

"What do you think I am, an eejit?"

He lets that slide. "And do me a favor, don't post anything you stole without letting me know first."

"I'll be sure to give you a heads-up if I move on that."

"What's a fairy hill?" he asks Kiernan when they're at the bus stop.

"It's a mound of dirt with a tree or two on it. Sometimes a cave underneath. It's like their home base or fort, a halfway point between this world and the next one. You'd have to be brainless to mess with one of them."

"What'll happen when that guy runs his bulldozer over the fairy hill?"

"It's not like a bomb goes off. Although it could. More like he'll never have another good day in his life, if you know what I mean.

"Wow. Yeah."

# 2002

Kate pads across the living room in her pajamas and slippers thinking only of her first sip of coffee. Teague is on his belly watching *The Simpsons*. She fills the coffeemaker and assesses their kitchen. It's cute in a seventies, thrift-store kind of way: chipped black-and-white ceramic counters, yellow painted cupboards, linoleum floor with a repeating pattern resembling a Calder mobile.

She brings her coffee to the sofa and immediately picks up the journal she left there. The summation is far too generic. The results they left out would have made a stronger case. She tosses it across the room. "Fuck!"

Teague turns his head. "What's with you?"

"Nothing." It comes out louder than she intended. He stares and waits for her to say something else.

"Okay. A really shitty thing happened."

He mutes the sound and sits up. "What?"

She tells him about Sebastian stealing her experiment.

"What a dickhead."

"You've got that right." His clear judgment lifts her spirits. "Joanne and Roger are looking into what we can do about it. Legally."

"I hope they slay him." He turns away as if lost in thought, then whips his head back. "Hey, I just thought of something cool."

"Okay."

"At your old job you were just doing stuff to those mice, right?"

"Right. Why do you ask?"

"Well, now we're your mice. Me and Kiernan and the guys." His face lights up as if he finds the idea fascinating. He watches her gulp coffee.

"Well . . ." She's not sure she likes where he's going with this.

"I'm not saying you engineered us. More like you made an experiment out of who we already are."

"To some extent, that's true."

He rolls over and unmutes the sound while she wonders why she's still dismissing the Ballymore Family Study as second-class work. What would it mean if she fully invested in the messy humans in their study population? She hates to think she's holding out because she's still beholden to the rotten system that produced Sebastian and his ilk.

Her thoughts skip to another uncomfortable truth. As long as she allows men like Sebastian to tug on her heart, jeopardizing her career in the process, she's no better than one of her mice running the wheel. Happy to keep going with no end in sight. Whereas an available man might require . . . what . . . she can't quite say. She's never invested in anyone long enough to find out. Ergo, she'd rather be miserable than surprised. Unless she steps off her wheel.

# 2002

"So, are the files corrupted?" Kate asks Ryan. He's at his desk, hunched over the damage assessment he just received from the county IT team.

"No. Thank the Lord." He has the dazed look of someone who's been working underground. "They found evidence of entry and extraction but no corruption of the actual files. At least not yet."

"What do you mean *not yet*?" She sits opposite him.

"The hacker may have planted malware."

"Planted what?"

"It's some sort of trojan horse that could hurt us at a later date." He shakes his head and pushes the report aside. Seemingly eager to get off the subject, he reaches for the top file in a color-coded stack. "These are the original therapy notes for the digitized summaries.

I—"

His intercom rings. He picks up the phone, listens, and checks his watch, "Oh shite! I'm on my way."

"What happened?"

"Sophie's team plays Ballymore today. I've got to go." He's on his feet.

"Of course. We can reschedule."

He grabs his jacket from behind the door. "Why don't you come along? We can talk more on the way."

"You're sure? I don't want to intrude."

"Not a bother. You'll be expected to cheer at the right plays."

"I'll mimic you."

Ryan drives as fast as humanly possible through the crush of afternoon traffic on the M6, which is to say they move along at a tortoise's pace. "With luck, we'll get there by the second quarter. Sophie's a goalie, so she's always on the field."

"Who just called to remind you?"

"Oh, that was Niamh."

He tilts his head and glances at her. "It's an old habit. Probably not a good one. My schedule was a major point of contention in our marriage."

"How often do you see Sophie?"

"It feels like I give her every shred of time or energy I have left at the end of the day." He sighs. "Now that I'm single, I'm getting worse at time management. The best I can do is every other weekend and when I can make it to one of her matches."

He's embarrassed. Kate is sympathetic, even relieved. Apparently, neither of them is in any shape for a relationship.

A sour frown takes over his face. "Shite!" They're behind a lumbering cement mixer. He cranes his neck out the window. "Nothing I can do it about." He clenches his jaw and turns to her. "Let's get back to the patient files."

"Can you catch me up on your process?"

"Sure." As if a switch has been flicked on, he straightens his back, takes a breath, and speaks in an animated tone. "So far, I compared the older clinic files to our cases from the last five years, plus what we've collected so far for our study."

She recognizes the state he's in: he's come up with an insight he's dying to share with someone who will understand its scientific significance. "And?"

"Either something is out of whack, or we're looking at some surprising trends."

"Say more."

"The good news is there's much less full-blown schizophrenia in the last five years compared to earlier years. But that doesn't account for these other spikes."

"What are you seeing?"

"Virtually everything else is way up. Major depression. Attention disorders. Kid-on-kid violence, which we diagnose as a conduct or antisocial disorder. OCD. The increases in a single generation are up a hundred and fifty percent. What's going on?"

A shot of adrenalin goes through her. "Tell me what you think."

"There's a real possibility Ballymore's collective genetic vulnerability for schizophrenia is producing a wider range of disorders, including several never linked to it before, and they're showing up at younger ages. When I tracked several individuals into their late twenties, these lesser conditions appear to predict something more serious, including schizophrenia, opioid addiction, even suicide."

"You realize you're going against accepted science on multiple scores."

"Aye. I do." He scratches his beard and squints at her. "What bothers me more is when a mother comes in worried sick about her kid's behavior. I see she's on to something, but my hands are tied because I can't stick him in the right box. Instead of just patronizing her, telling her 'boys will be boys,' I should be getting that kid into therapy, early, and trying to lower the level of conflict at home.

"Sure, there's the danger I'm following my own bias, but I think there's something worth looking at here." He pulls onto the shoulder, more like he invents one, and turns onto a side road. "We're almost there." There's a sports field dead ahead.

"You know, Ryan, I'm the last one who should pooh-pooh your hypothesis just because you're coloring outside the lines. And I'm happy to help you pursue it. But I'm a little worried about what might happen when word gets out that we're charting increases in every psychiatric disorder known to science right here in Ballymore. They'll all chip in and buy me a ticket home."

Ryan turns into the car park and finds a spot. "Hopefully, it won't come to that." His smile is high wattage, and their eye contact runs into overtime.

She twirls a chunk of her hair.

A roar from the field draws his attention and they're off.

When they reach the bleachers, the cheers have grown to a fever pitch. Most of it is for the red and golds—Ballymore's team—whose players are advancing rapidly toward the goal line of their green-and-black-clad Galway opponents.

"There she is," Ryan says, pointing to the Galway goalie. Sophie's blond ponytail flies in the air as she leaps from side to side, psyching out who will make the kick.

"Hold the line, Soph!" Ryan yells. She does just that, landing with the ball secure under her belly. "Brilliant!"

Sophie gives her father a big smile. Upon noticing Kate standing next to him, she tilts her head to the side—establishing her territorial claim. Kate likes her already.

The next two quarters fly by with constant motion on the field and nonstop encouragement from Ryan, who stays on his feet the whole time. The match ends with a victory for Sophie's team, capped with flags raised and trophies awarded.

"What does GAA stand for?" she asks while they wait for Sophie to join them afterward.

"The Gaelic Athletic Association sponsors football and hurling. But not just sports, they also champion the Irish language and music. Before independence, GAA was a base for the resistance. Let's just say they never missed a chance to sabotage the occupiers."

"Hi, Daddy."

"There's my star." He wraps her in his arms and kisses the top of her head. Sophie gives her a once-over.

"This is Kate. She's working on my study."

"That was a great catch you made, Sophie," Kate says.

"Which one?" she asks, dead serious.

"The catch that ended the second quarter was pretty spectacular."

She savors the praise, then asks, "Do you have kids?"

"I have Teague. He's sixteen." It's the first time she's answered the question without elaborating. It feels good.

"What does he play?"

"At the moment, he paints and games."

"I'm thirteen."

"I would have guessed at least fifteen."

"Who wants pizza?" Ryan asks.

"I do," Sophie says.

"Kate?"

"If you could drop me off at the clinic, I have to get home and feed Teague."

Later, in bed, she puts down her romance novel, a guilty pleasure she picked up from Gran, distracted by thoughts of Ryan and Sophie. Even with the divorce, their father-daughter bond is strong and sweet; she felt high just watching the love flow. In no time, she's standing with Dad on the grassy shore of the lake where their family went in the summer, on the day she wore her new blue-and-pink polka-dot swimsuit and he nearly made her drown in the deep end.

As he squatted to give last-minute instructions, she followed the trail of freckles across his cheeks.

"Remember . . . bring your head up for a breath, down for a stroke."

"Got it!" She shook out her hands and dropped them to her side, mimicking how she'd seen Olympic swimmers get ready for the starting gun. Dad turned her around and she faced the water. She stole a glance at Mom to make sure she was watching from her beach chair on the grass. She was looking, but not smiling.

Her pride at being Dad's prize pupil had puffed her up to try this shore-to-shore test at the deep end, where kids her age weren't even allowed. He caught her looking at the Adults Only sign. "Katy, it doesn't matter which end you're at when you swim like I taught you."

With a one, two, three, he tossed her in the air . . . and kaboom, she was underwater. She opened her eyes and a school of minnows darted away to make room. She kicked her way to the surface and got down to business . . .

timing her breaths and strokes just like he taught her. Her confidence grew with each small forward advance. She thought only of the next stroke and the next. She was a sea creature, returned at last to her natural habitat.

"That a girl!" she heard him say.

She made the mistake of turning back to look at him and his small size startled her. Both sides of the lake were far away. Dwelling too long on the thought, she neglected to tread water and swallowed a mouthful as she sank. A scarier thought stole her last bit of confidence: what if Dad didn't jump in to save her?

She bobbed back up, but another mouthful garbled her cry for help. Her coughing and struggle for breath tired her and she dropped down to where the water was colder and darker. As she drifted, she wondered why she couldn't make her legs kick. She knew she'd soon run out of breath, but she held on to the certainty that Dad was on his way. When an arm grabbed hold of her chest, she felt a rush of relief, only to be disappointed when she came face-to-face with the teenage lifeguard.

They drove home in the peak afternoon heat, she and Meghan sitting thigh-to-thigh in the back seat with muddy inner tubes laid across their laps while Mom and Dad fought in the front seat. Dad insisting Katy was fine out there. Mom going on about him ruining their day. Why can't he control himself?

Dad stayed away for the rest of the day and night. In the morning, Kate was relieved to see him asleep on the sofa, but any respite from worry was outweighed by her seven-year-old certainty that it was a temporary lull in a forever war.


Kate hugs her pillow and thinks again about Ryan and Sophie. He isn't a perfect father, just a decent guy who somehow manages to convey unconditional love for his adoring daughter. She tries to picture her and Teague having the same kind of bond. Her worst fear is that she's incapable of it. On the other hand, there's some evidence she, and they, are getting better. That cute thing he said about him and his buddies being *her mice*. He's making friends. Perhaps she's doing something right. Surely, better than Mom did with her.

For whatever reason, they never bonded as mother and daughter. After Dad died, Mom jumped at the chance to go back to work at the hospital. Kate used to wonder why Mom chose evening shifts when she could have worked mornings. With Meghan a teenager, the job of mothering seven-year-old Kate fell to Gran, making Mom the absentee parent. Kate abruptly stops her train of thought when it occurs to her that she and Mom had shared a disinclination to mothering. If she'd been born a generation later, Maureen could have chosen to live child-free—the life choice Kate always assumed she would make. It's strange to find herself commiserating with her mother as if they were just two women freely making choices, devoid of the emotional baggage each still carries and blames on the other.

# 2002

Teague's legs ache from crouching in the castle tower, where he's hiding out with Liam, Kiernan, and a set of twins, Cormac and Rowan, he just met. They're waiting for the elderly guide to finish his last tour and lock up. Once they have the place to themselves, they'll descend to the courtyard and start the Mad Pride meeting, Teague's first.

"All's clear," shouts Liam. "The old coot's gone."

The five race down the stone stairs, pushing each other and laughing as they go. In the courtyard they build a fire with kindling they brought with them. Sitting in a tight circle, they warm their hands over the flames.

"Well done, lads," says Cormac. He's a Harry Potter look-alike with round-frame glasses and short bangs who talks like an old man. Rowan is a messy version of Cormac with bald spots where he did a bad job cutting his own hair. It gives him a deranged look. Since he doesn't say much, it's hard to tell whether Rowan is or isn't deranged. Both used to be patients at the clinic, and Teague's pretty sure they're on the same spectrum as him.

"Hey, mates," Liam says, "Teague is here to check us out. Of course, you can tell he's not from around here. But he's one of us, right Teague?"

"Yeah, I guess."

"I don't want to put you on the spot, man, but if you want to tell us anything . . . Someone else can go, first. Kiernan, what's up with Arial?"

"Like shite on a shingle." The guys laugh.

"Are you back on your meds?" Cormac asks.

"Not really."

"What's Arial saying now?" Liam asks.

"He's still banging on about how I should be crusading against evil."

Cormac scratches his head. "Did you ever say you wanted to be one of his crusaders?"

"I might have back when I had a messiah complex going. I never talked to the Big Man myself, but Arial told me it was God who chose me, and I believed him."

"Are you sure he wasn't tricking you about that to get you in trouble?" Cormac asks.

Kiernan drops his head in his hands. "I don't know. Maybe. I was sick of my life, it felt awesome to be picked for something."

"More than awesome. It's noble." Liam surprises Teague with that one. "Look at the blokes who act like they're doing good in the world, who go around destroying it every day. They poison the water. Build a highway through the Hill of Tara. Then they turn around and call us certifiable."

"Yeah, but what if I don't want to do what he tells me?"

Cormac gets on all fours close to Kiernan. "Can you give us an example?"

"The other day me and me Dad were watching Mr. Houlihan from the bank when he was at our neighbor's front door. Dad said he was there to evict him. Arial told me I should go slash Houlihan's tires."

"Ah ha!" Liam stands up. "Arial makes a reasonable suggestion. But you still need to be in charge."

"How do you mean?"

"Did they evict the family?"

"No, it was just a warning."

"Tell Arial you'll think about it. Then weigh your pros and cons. If Houlihan goes through with the eviction and you're ready to act, go ahead and slash his tires. It'll be a bother to him. But a lot less than getting evicted. Might make him think twice when someone else falls behind."

"What if I don't want to do it?"

"Then you thank Arial for the suggestion but let him know you're going to choose the time and place. All right?"

Kiernan thinks about it and says okay.

"You got anything, Teague?"

"Yeah. I'm sick of the shitty side effects I get from my meds, and I don't like how they interfere with my painting. I'm gonna chuck them." He pulls the bottle from his pocket and rolls it back and forth in his hands.

"That's wicked!" Liam is the first to give him a high five. The others follow.

"If you want, you can throw them in the fire," Ronan says.

"All right." Teague leans over the fire and empties the bottle. He's been off and on them for a couple of weeks. But this feels final.

Cormac talks about Lionel, a voice in his TV. "He's not nasty," he says, as if he's defending a real friend.

"Then what's the problem?" Kiernan wants to know.

"He just won't shut up. He talks about dumb stuff all the time."

"Like what?"

"Every hour, on the hour, he asks me if it's gonna rain. I tell him since it rains every feckin day there's no reason to talk about it. Then he does it again."

That sounds like it would be annoying, but nothing compared to Larry and Ivan.

"I've been trying to train him," Cormac says.

Everyone wants to hear about that.

"I worked out a deal where if he keeps his mouth shut for an hour, I talk to him for five minutes, but if he messes up, I don't."

"Is it working?" Kiernan asks.

"Yeah, sometimes two or three hours go by without him bothering me."

"That's brilliant!" Kiernan gives Cormac a high five.

When everyone is done having their say, they stamp out the fire and take turns giving each other boosts to climb over the wall. Liam's the tallest; he goes last. The water in the moat is up to their knees and muddy, fun to wade through. They crawl up on the grass and part ways at the M6. Teague heads home thinking his life is finally getting good.

# New York City

*July 4, 1927*

Bursts of red, white, and blue fell behind Lady Liberty's torch drawing oohs and aahs from the crowd swelling Battery Park. Ellen, Michael, and the girls got there at midday. In the hours since, they've played, picnicked and napped. Michael joined some men for horseshoes. The girls found playmates for games of tag and jump rope. At last, the fireworks show was in full swing with a band playing patriotic music.

"Pick me up, please, Da. I want to see!" Meggie crawled halfway up Michael's leg before he lifted her over his shoulders.

"That's not fair," Annie yelled, jumping up and down to get a look before the next firework went off.

"Come here." Ellen helped Annie climb on top of a trash bin.

"I'm higher than you," she said, needling her sister. Standing, she towered over them. The next burst of red flares reminded Ellen of her favorite flower, peonies.

The band launched into a new song, and people around them began to sing along, "My Country 'tis of Thee . . . Sweet Land of Liberty . . ."

At the second verse, Michael grabbed her arm. "Is that—?"

Their eyes met in shared surprise. "Aye. It's the same tune."

His jaw dropped. It baffled her too. After all the years the Americans spent fighting the British, why would they pick "God Save the King" as their song?

130

The show went on with blasts of colored flares taking on different shapes—falling stars, a weeping willow, a spiral twist—each bringing its own deafening blast. After the umpteenth explosion, Ellen's head throbbed. She covered her ears but the memories she'd kept locked in her body had already made their escape. The thud of the battering ram. The spray of gunshots that felled Da. The fox's keen. Flames gobbling up Main Street. When the fireworks came to an end, she let out a sigh of relief and found an empty patch of grass where she dropped to her knees. Michael joined her with the girls who were bubbling with excitement. She nodded toward the fountain and Michael took them there, giving Ellen a minute to herself.

The night air remained sultry as throngs of people moved from the park onto the streets of Lower Manhattan. Since they were in no hurry to return to their sweltering apartment, they lingered for another hour. She and Michael sat on the edge of the fountain as Annie and Meg lifted their skirts and waded into the water. She hoped their laughter would chase away her unbidden memories. But they lingered, too.

Michael lit a cigarette and turned to watch people passing. She fastened on his profile.

His skin had weathered, but his features were still strong. Even though she no longer felt the flutter in her chest when she looked at him, a sense of pride for his beauty still sat quietly with her. Even in the prime of her youth, the word *handsome* had more often been used to describe Ellen's features. And while another woman might have been pained by the contrast with her own husband, jealousy had never visited Ellen on Michael's behalf. Now she wished she could wallow in such trivialities and chase away her other disturbing thoughts, but they stood their ground. She would have to let them spill out and risk ruining their day.

"Why is it . . ." she began, and faltered, waiting for his eyes to meet hers before she went on. "Why is it this hard to let in a wee bit of happiness?"

His brow creased with what she read as wary impatience. "Say what you're meaning to say, love."

"All of us here together on this pretty night, it should be enough." Her voice wavered, chased by tears.

His jowls slackened. Creases took over his forehead. "It won't ever be enough," he said in a steady voice. "Not for us. We already lost too much." He nodded at the girls. "No reason why we shouldn't hope for them."

He held on to her gaze. It was one of the rare times when he opened the window to his deepest self wide enough for her to feed off his light. In their silent exchange, he stripped her of a craving that no longer served them. Her longing for home had become a ball and chain. By letting it go, the ground they tilled would become more fallow, richer for what they'd given up.

At first, letting go of that familiar weight left Ellen feeling unmoored. But, over time, she filled the void with a kind of peace, although, to be honest, on some days it felt more like a fragile cease fire. She prayed nightly that the seeds she and Michael sowed in borrowed soil would take root. Like every farmer, she knew seeds could fail under the best conditions. Non-natives had to be that much stronger … and luckier.

A stubborn and practical woman, Ellen vowed to bend those odds.

# 2002

Teague heads down the alley behind Main Street on his way to the loading dock behind Murphy's Pub where he's supposed to meet a guy. The tip came from Liam. Off his meds, Teague feels jumpy. This new scoring territory, way different than Rivervale, only adds to his unease. The guy he's meeting, Brian, is in his twenties and has a limp. This could be him coming down the alley. He's dragging his foot.

"Hey, you Brian?"

He stops and squints. "Who's asking?"

"Teague. Liam's a friend."

Maybe his accent is throwing him. Brian takes his time looking him over before he reaches into his pocket and pulls out a baggie.

"Ten euros."

"Okay. Thanks." Brian takes his money and walks away.

The only reason he has the cash is because he sold his dolphin painting to a lady in the square. When he got home, Kate asked what happened to it. He told her and she flipped out.

"Not the dolphin!"

"Jeez. I'll paint you another one just like it." He was surprised at the fuss she made. That dolphin was the most cheerful thing he's ever painted. That's probably why it sold in five minutes.

He rolls two joints and smokes one before he leaves the alley. He hopes it'll relax him. Ryan calls this self-medicating. Yeah, well, it's better than going cold turkey. It's a crappy trade-off. Off his meds he's more awake, but sleep is a bitch. His brain is crazy crowded with thoughts. Most of them he could live without. Even if some are worth having and wouldn't have made it through his Zyprexa wall. Since he told the guys he's quitting, he feels obligated to stick it out. Getting control of his voices would be worth a few shitty weeks. So far, he's feeling more okay than not, but he can tell things are going in the wrong direction.

Aaaah. That's better. It's like a vacuum sucked all the dust bunnies from his head. When his high settles, he cuts over to Main and heads south, to the newer part of town. He's crossing the supermarket parking lot when he hears him. *Hey, boy. Teague! Wait up.*

FUCK! There's his brown-and-white ass and tail behind a car. Teague ducks through the sliding glass doors and heads down the dairy aisle. He's fast-walking, about to turn the corner, when Larry cuts him off and shows a mouthful of canine teeth. Before he can get away, he's got his paws on his chest, tongue licking his face.

*Buddy, where've you been? You know how long it took me to find you? You deserted me. What kind of dog owner are you, anyway?*

"Get lost, I'm not your owner. You don't scare me anymore. Things are different here."

*You wish!* Larry comes at him with his teeth bared.

In his hurry to get away, Teague doesn't look behind him and falls backward onto a pyramid of soda bottles. There's a crash, glass breaking, soda spilling. Bottles are on top of him and rolling on the floor. The bite on his arm is bleeding and Larry is laughing at him. He yells back, "You're a fake dog. And I'm done with you." He doesn't have time to consider how Larry could have bit him if he's fake. He's on his ass and can't get up.

"Lad, are you all right?" Someone's pulling him to his feet.

"Watch out for the dog!"

"What dog?" It's a bald guy in a white apron streaked with blood. His name tag says John Feeley, Head Butcher. John looks pissed off and worried, but, as it drags on, more pissed than worried. Then Teague remembers Larry, probably hiding in the next aisle, waiting for him to try a getaway.

"I'm all right. Let me go." He breaks free of John and tears out of there.

He's half walking, half running to old town when he notices the blood drops on his shirt. There's no time to worry about it because there's Larry sitting on the bench in front of Murphy's. There he is again, coming out of the laundromat. And again, waiting at the crosswalk. Teague hops off the curb and weaves between cars, trying to get ahead of him.

Through the drugstore window, he sees a line of customers, Sean Mitchell behind the counter. No way he can deal with all those people. He needs a place to hide and clear his head. There's another door next to the one for Mitchell's Drugs. Locked, of course.

"How about it, Archangel Michael, can you help me out?" He leans in with his shoulder and gives the door a heave. Then he's face down on a tile floor. "Hey, thanks, Mike." He kicks the door shut and rolls onto his back. The crystals on the ceiling lamp make spooky shadows fall on the walls and floor. Shadows are shapeshifters. Usually, they mean nothing. But not always. Like that time with Gran and Mr. Malone.

"Why does it follow him everywhere?" he remembers asking Gran about the shadow that trailed her friend. They were sitting under the willow tree in the backyard when Mr. Malone came by with a bag of apples from his tree. He and Gran spent a while telling jokes and teasing each other the way they always did. It was when Mr. Malone got out of his chair and walked away that Teague noticed how the shadow stayed with him even in the shade, where shadows weren't supposed to show.

Gran's smile disappeared when he told her what he'd seen. "It could be my friend's time to meet his maker."

"You mean die?"

She nodded.

"Should I tell him?"

"No, that's not your job."

"Then why did I see it?"

135

Gran said he'd have to figure that out for himself when he got older. In the meantime, if he was worried about someone, the best he could do was pray for them. Since he didn't know how to pray, at least not in any way that worked, he asked for Gran's advice. She said he should just come right out and ask God for what he needed, act as if God loved him and would listen. But if that was too hard, she said, he could pick an ally to ask God on his behalf.

"Do you have one?" he asked.

"I do. Her name is Brigid."

That's when he picked Michael the archangel for his ally.

Voices from the street scare him back to the present, lying on the tile floor feeling pretty strung out. He gets on his knees, then stands, and goes up a flight of stairs. On the landing there's an unmarked door. Should he knock? He imagines the conversation . . . *Sorry to bother you, but a dog is chasing me, and I need a place to hide.* Never mind. Another floor up, he pulls open a smaller door. Six steep stairs and he's in a pitch-dark attic. This will work. He just needs to rest. He slides across the floor and runs into a pile of boxes. Ow! One crashes down on his back. He keeps going until he hits something big and stops. The last thing he remembers is his cheek landing on a blanket of dust.

Is he back in his old room? He turns over and pushes against the floor until he's on all fours. With his spine straight a ceiling gets in his way. "Damn." This isn't his old room. And his brain isn't working right. Things come back slowly. The alley behind Murphy's. Weed. Running into Larry and a bunch of bottles at the supermarket. Bites in his arm. Tearing up Main Street to get away from Larry. The drug store. Breaking in next door. Crawling into the attic. All of it in fucking Ireland.

Something tickles his nose. Is that smoke!? He can't tell where it's coming from, but there's smoke sneaking in from somewhere. He coughs. "Hey, somebody . . . there's a fire up here . . . help!" *Michael, where the hell are you?* He better quit screwing around and get out of there. He's on his knees, pushing things out of the way. Where's that door? He knows it's somewhere nearby or how else did he get in here? Are those footsteps? There's a light moving around. It lands on his face. He can't see a thing.

"Who's there?" An old woman's voice.

"My name is Teague. I'm sorry but can you help me get out of here? Hurry, please, there's a fire up here."

"You wait right there. I'll call somebody."

"Sure . . . just leave me here to die of smoke inhalation," he says, but she's gone. More smoke . . . he coughs . . . Michael, please. He can't keep his head up . . . What's that scratching? Maybe a rat. As long as it's a real one. He's on a raft sailing on white-capped waves. Please, make the floor stop moving.

"Teague?" A man's voice.

"Yeah!"

"Stay where you are. Is anyone with you?"

Oh, fuck . . . not him again. But, hey, if it's a choice between staying put and burning to death or getting hauled into an Irish jail, he'd better go with Rafferty. "No. I'm by myself. What about the fire?"

"There's no fire, son. Just stay put until I get to you."

He's straight enough to know he's in a shitload of trouble.

# New York City
## 1932

*No Irish Need Apply.* Unlike Michael, Ellen took no offense at the signs hung at work sites in lower Manhattan. Times were as hard as she'd ever seen and naturally the ones who got here before them thought they should get any jobs that were to be had. But she wasn't the one lining up at dawn, routinely turned away because of his name or accent. Ellen got cleaning jobs and took in sewing and laundry but they depended on Michael's earnings to eat and pay rent. When they ran out of money for food, she and the girls stood with him on soup lines alongside men in thread-worn suits who, word had it, had once been bankers and stockbrokers. Everyone appeared to be in the same bad way as they were, making things a wee bit better and worse at the same time.

Michael's prospects and their lives brightened in March of thirty-two, when he was hired to work on the IND Eighth Avenue subway line, a massive project that required digging under two existing tracks. After a cave-in that took several workers' lives, Michael got hired as a digger for the section at Fifty-Ninth Street and Columbus Circle. The work lasted nearly a year, his longest stretch. Which made the harder times that followed worse for him, and terrible for her, as the dark forces that had always been attracted to his light found a way to steal it outright. The drink gave them their way in.

On this December night, she cooked a thin stew of onions, cabbage, and leeks. She bought a loaf of day-old bread. That should have made it a good night. Where was he? At nine o'clock, the girls couldn't wait any longer for their supper and bedtime. Eventually, she fell asleep next to them.

Sometime before dawn, she heard the door unlock and his barking cough as he walked to the stove a few feet from their bed. She opened her eyes and watched as he removed the lid and spooned cold stew into his mouth. His clumsy movements told her he'd drunk too much ale. She wasn't sure if she was angrier about the money he'd spent or his lateness. She didn't want to start a fight and she couldn't trust herself not to; she pretended to be asleep. He hadn't had work for over a month, and they were facing calamity if their luck didn't change soon.

He sat in a chair out of her sight. After a long silence she heard what she thought was coughing, but soon realized were his ragged sobs. This coming from a man she'd seen shed tears only twice, for each of the children they'd lost since Meg's birth three years ago. Feeling the depth of his pain, she got up and sat next to him on the floor. She couldn't let him suffer alone for what he believed was his personal failure to provide for them. She wrapped her blanket around his legs and sat on the floor. He stroked her hair. After a while she started to nod off.

"Come to bed?" she asked him.

"You go ahead, love. I can't face my dreams tonight. I haven't drunk enough to keep them at bay."

She knew the nightmare he feared the most as if it was her own. It came more often now that he didn't have hard labor to exhaust him. He'd wake up beside her gagging as if he were drowning. In the dream men with shielded faces and long arms held him under water.

When she asked him if he thought he was being given a look at his own death, he frowned and shook his head. Didn't she know second sight didn't work that way? Ellen knew, but she couldn't help wondering whether this wasn't an exception to the rule.

After that brutal winter, their prayers were answered when a Callahan cousin in Boston helped Michael get hired as a fireman on the Erie Railroad. His line made three trips a week from Philly to Boston with a dozen stops in between. Michael's experience on the subway stood him in good stead as a reliable laborer willing to do backbreaking work. Shifts lasted thirty-six hours. Benefits included free train tickets and life insurance. It was the most secure they'd been since leaving home.

They enjoyed two uneventful years with Michael working on the railroad until an incident on the job revived Ellen's fears. Two men who identified themselves as brethren from home approached Michael while he smoked a cigarette on a promontory over the Hudson River at the Newburgh station. A younger man asked for a light and stepped closer. His older companion introduced himself as an O'Shea and went on to say that if not for Michael, his brother Tom's son, Rory, would still be walking on this earth. If the train engineer hadn't sounded his whistle and called Michael back on board, that could have been the end of him.

After he told her what happened, neither of them spoke of his old nightmare but she knew it was top of mind for him, too. Both asking themselves the same question: was the incident at the station the fulfillment of Michael's premonition—or just a preview of worse to come?

# 2002

"Possession of cannabis is a crime in Ireland, same as it is in New York." Rafferty says. He keeps his eyes parked on Teague before turning deliberately to look at her, as if she, too, is guilty of said crime. Rafferty brought Teague directly from the Mitchell's attic to the clinic and had the receptionist ask Kate to join them. He's still filling her in on Teague's multiple offenses.

Is this when she's supposed to apologize for being such a lousy parent? Better not, she decides. "I understand," she says instead. They're not debating Teague's guilt, given the evidence on display—a bag of green buds, rolling papers, a joint—laid out like a banquet centerpiece on the conference room table.

Teague's chin is on his chest while his stringy hair fashions a barricade against her prying eyes. There's a bandage on his upper arm. The wound, not serious, Rafferty told her, came from his collision with a display of glass bottles, an incident reported to the gardai' by the store manager. After they got a separate call about an intruder in the attic of a private residence on Main Street.

"Breaking and entering is another serious offense," Rafferty says. "Nora Mitchell, who's going on ninety, climbed a ladder and found him hiding in the attic, talking nonsense." Rafferty's frown seems devoid of sympathy for Teague. "Gave her quite a fright."

Kate suspects he's trying to get her on his side and pit the two of them against the perp across the table.

"Teague, what were you doing in that poor woman's attic?"

He seems startled by her question. He rounds his shoulders and squirms, turning his head side to side as if looking for a way out, or a pursuer. His eyes blink repeatedly. "He scared me."

"Who scared you?"

"Larry, the shit."

"Is that someone you know?"

"Larry's a mean dog."

Teague's pathos dissolves her anger. It also points her to recent signs she missed. The broken sentences and long silences. Eyes on the ground. Up at all hours. He's been heading for another break for at least a couple of weeks. She needs to get him some time with Ryan today. That assumes Rafferty doesn't plan on taking him in. Over her dead body will he do that. Kate pulls her shoulders back as Rafferty keeps talking.

"We don't have much trouble in Ballymore, but your boy seems to be looking for it with all the wrong people."

As if Teague is some kind of juvenile delinquent. "Mr. Rafferty, Officer, I'm afraid Teague has gone off his medication. Paranoia is one of the symptoms."

Teague shoots her a look of alarm, like she's just disclosed a state secret.

Rafferty closes his pad. Clearly, he doesn't want to delve into the mental health dimension of Teague's crimes. Another thing he has in common with cops back home.

"Dr. Jones . . . Kate, you're new in town. Consider this a warning. You need to rein in your nephew. This can't happen again."

"I'm very sorry and I can assure you it won't. Thank you."

He stands and puts the evidence in a large zipper bag, then waits for Teague to look up. "You need to stay away from this stuff for your own good."

"Yeah, I just figured that out, too."

To Kate, he says, "You can thank Sean and Nora Mitchell for not pressing housebreaking charges."

"We'll do that."

He tips his cap before leaving.

Teague has his feet on the seat, his arms wrapped around his knees, and his head buried, as if he's expecting to be punished. That's the last thing on Kate's mind.

"Teague, honey . . . I'm sorry."

He lifts his chin. "What about?"

"I should have noticed you were having a hard time. We could have avoided this. I want you to see Ryan as soon as he can fit you in. Hopefully today."

"All right."

"Good."

She's halfway out of her chair when another thought gives her pause. "There is one new rule I need you to follow."

His face collapses.

"You're not to go anywhere near Liam or Finn. No more visits to their compound."

"Why?"

"Ryan says the gardaí suspect Liam hacked our computers, possibly with Finn's involvement. I'm not saying you had anything to do with it. But I don't want anyone to think you did because you associate with them. Can I trust you on this?"

He wrinkles his forehead and averts his eyes.

"Teague?"

"Finn wasn't in on it."

"How do you know that?"

"He's a Druid."

"I see. Is that all you know about the hack? That Finn isn't in on it?"

He hides his head again. An answer of sorts. She won't get anything else out of him when he's like this. Maybe she doesn't want to hear any more about it right now.

"Stay put while I see about Ryan's schedule."

Dara tells her Ryan's session with a client has thirty minutes to go. She asks to be put on his schedule and tells Teague to wait for her in the group room. The extent of her plan is to get out of the building and breathe fresh air. On the sidewalk, she passes a pair of neighbors exchanging pleasantries and feels a tightness in her chest. Only then does she connect some of her disorientation to homesickness. Not for any particular person, it's more the familiarity of her old life she's missing.

She crosses the M6 and thinks of her daily walk down Lexington Avenue to the lab: the produce delivery man shooting the breeze with the corner grocer; curbside vendors arranging their knockoff designer bags and scarves on tables; summer tourists stopping mid-sidewalk to gawk at skyscrapers, even the piles of stinky white trash bags adorning the corners of each block like gargoyles seem endearing . . . Enough, you're getting pathetic, she admonishes herself as she turns into a maze of residential streets lined with duplexes like hers. She's never gone in this direction away from town.

After walking the perimeter of a manicured park and a football field with a practice underway, she finds herself facing the medieval castle Teague and Kiernan are so fond of. No wonder, she thinks as she surveys its turreted tower, moat, and drawbridge.

An unpaved trail takes her into a dense tract of woods where she stops to examine a strange tree. It seems to have multiple trunks sewn together, like a village unto itself. As she walks on, the exotic flora becomes background to the troubling evidence accumulating in her logical mind. Why didn't she put it together sooner? Apparently, denial is a language best understood backwards. She doesn't need to look further back than three months, to her Fourth of July visit to Mom's.

First, she heard Teague's loud footsteps, then his voice ricocheting through the house and out into the hot, sticky night, "Da dadadadadadaaaaaaah . . ." She raced downstairs bleary-eyed. Teague was in his boxer briefs, marching in loops around the living room. She hugged the wall as he passed in front of her waving an imaginary baton, lifting each knee in sync to the music playing nowhere but inside his head.

"Teague, what are you doing?"

He made an abrupt turn and shouted at her over his shoulder, "I'm playing atonally."

As far as she knew, he didn't play any instruments. She headed him off. "Please, stop. You'll wake everyone."

With an eye roll he pushed past her. "Remember, the wand chooses the wizard." In the kitchen, a glint off the streetlight affords him a possessed air. "Did you know I can make myself invisible?"

Her hand shook as she reached out to him. "Come to bed. This is too much."

He stepped back. "Honestly, woman, you call yourself our mother?"

"Is that you, Teague talking? Do you want me to answer you?"

"Since you've asked, I'd say your job is to find the real parts. I have to put out a lot of nonsense to protect the truer things."

"Protect them from what?"

He gave her an incredulous scowl. "Do I really need to explain everything to you?"

Her stomach sank. He plodded downstairs to the rec room. Pulsing bangs, *boom baba boom baba boom*, reverberated to the roof.

Kate flopped on a stool and lay her head on the counter. What was she supposed to do now? At fifteen, Teague was six feet tall. She couldn't wrestle him to the ground and carry him up to bed. The throb in her forehead took on a life of its own.

"Kate, what the hell's going on down there?" Her mother's yell was the perfect mate to Teague's drumming. The light went on in the Donovans' kitchen.

"I'm dealing with it." Kate's voice cracked. "Go back to bed."

"I told you he's getting worse." Maureen's helpful commentary before her bedroom door slammed shut. Kate covered her ears.

She should have called it months ago. The truth is she saw it and chose to avoid coming to the conclusion that was obvious to Maureen, a nurse, even if Kate, the neuroscientist in the family wasn't willing to admit it. "Yes, he's odd," she concurred with her mother on more than one occasion. "But he could still grow out of it," she remembers saying. That, too, was bullshit. Now the question gnawing at her is not *does he have it?* More like, *can she slow it down?*

Suddenly tired, she stops in a clearing and leans against a fallen tree. Its trunk is damp and cool to her thighs while sunlight warms her bare arms. Enough with the blame, she tells herself, and lets her thoughts roam. The conventional view in psychiatry sees a diagnosis of schizophrenia as a life sentence. She's aware of some outlying research suggesting that slowing it down may be possible. It depends, those studies say, on how far the patient has progressed on the schizophrenia spectrum, which, in turn, is contingent on their particular *genetic load*; meaning, how far along on the spectrum any of their first and second degree relatives may have gone. Damn, that puts her smack in another minefield.

Although the risk for schizophrenia in the general population is less than two percent, for any child of Meghan's, it jumps to twelve percent. The genetic contribution of Teague's father, Lou, a doper, would be relatively minor, she reasons. Most likely his genes conferred a vulnerability to depression. No help there.

Meghan viewed doctors, especially psychiatrists, as the enemy, so they never got a clinician's explanation for her violent mood swings and progressively weird behavior. Then, of course, Meghan was only twenty-six when she overdosed, an age that suddenly seems so young to Kate—from the vantage point of thirty-one.

She wraps her arms around her chest and leans down at the waist, head over knees. A wave of nausea comes and goes. Sitting up straight again, she sucks air in and pushes it out while bargaining with the part of herself she's put in charge of keeping disruptive memories at bay. The one hunting her now she'll typically do anything to avoid. Work. Sex. Wine. None currently available. And so here it comes . . . The morning when Meghan's unraveling became clear to fifteen-year-old Kate.

Her sister's bunk was empty and there was no sign of her downstairs. Until the singing from downstairs wafted up to the kitchen . . . Billie Jean is not my lover . . . and Kate found her on a ladder in the rec room pushing a paint roller. Previously a dull white, the walls were covered with alternating stripes of red, yellow, and blue. The linoleum floor was a Jackson Pollock painting.

"Meghan! What are you doing?" She had to wave her arms to get Meghan to notice her and take off the headphones.

"What do you think?"

"Well, it's colorful. Can't you sleep?" She was already playing doctor.

"I've been wanting to do this for ages. I just used whatever paints we had left in the garage." She beamed an oblivious smile.

"Well, I've got to go to work." Her shift at Tastee Freeze was due to start in a half hour. But that wasn't what sped her on her way. It was the inevitable explosion when Mom came downstairs and discovered Meghan's project. Why bother? She figured the damage was done.

The puzzle pieces fall all too neatly into place. Dad. Meghan. Teague. Before now, she consumed the research through the eyes of a neuroscientist, not those of a worried mother. If she's going to help Teague, and not let him repeat Meghan's wasted life, she'll have to figure out how to be a parent and a scientist at the same time.

After she gives Ryan a summary of Teague's episode in town, there's a long stretch of silence while he stares straight ahead, then tilts his chair back and eyes the ceiling. She takes deep breaths to slow her palpitating heart. Cool air pumps in through a vent in the wall behind her. At last, he leans forward and scours the open page of his appointment book. "I can see him at six."

"Great, thanks." It's only two. She starts to get up.

"Sit a minute." Ryan puts his tongue in his cheek while keeping his eyes on her, to the point where she's relieved when he pushes his tortoise-shell glasses to the top of his head and rubs his eyes. "How are you holding up?"

"Aside from feeling like an inept parent and a useless mental health professional, I'm fine."

He tilts his head to the side and waits for a proper answer.

"Tell me honestly," she says. "Do you think Teague has crossed the line into full-blown schizophrenia?"

With his elbows on the desk, he levels his gaze at her. "It's obvious he's gone off his meds. That, combined with the cannabis, caused this break. It's his second, which means he's inched closer to the edge. I still don't see any point in labeling him if we can pull him back."

"And you think we can?"

"I do." He clasps his hands and tents his index fingers. "He acted out of paranoia. I'm suggesting we don't have to pathologize everything he does or says that strays from what we define as normal. Even a visual or auditory hallucination can be a neutral experience."

"Is it selfish of me to want my kid to be normal?"

He drops his chin and looks up at her. "Of course not. All I'm saying is there's no point in alienating him if we can help him manage his perceptions. I'll see Teague twice a week until he stabilizes."

"Perfect." She should get up and take Teague home. Her legs won't move. "Is there anything else?"

"No. I'm okay."

His raised eyebrows shoot down that lie. He leans back in his chair while she squirms.

"All right. I'm afraid I've developed unrealistic expectations for Teague. I catch myself thinking somehow, miraculously, he'll be the one out of a hundred who defies the odds and comes out of this an Einstein despite the half-assed parenting he's had all his life—and he's still getting from me."

"You're jumping way ahead of where we are here. Having expectations that Teague will come out of this a productive citizen is not the same as being in denial. If I gave him an IQ test, which I don't recommend, my guess is he'd land in the top ten percent. Nothing is preordained."

"I know he's smart. It's his sensitivity that terrifies me."

The seconds tick by. Ryan wets his lips. "Teague's sensitivity is also what will save him if we can help him manage it." The intercom buzzes. "Dr. Quinn . . . I'll be right there." To her, "They need me to sign a prescription. I'll be right back."

She exhales and does a head roll. He's right. She should slow down and give Teague a chance to turn it around. He's her precious orchid child, doing what orchids do when they're under extreme stress. They withdraw and get lost in mazes of their own making. As a certifiable dandelion, she let her assumption that anybody can and should be able to bounce back from life's hard knocks obscure what she knows to be true. For Teague, the jury is still out. Like any orchid his age, he can still go either way. Now is what matters. Not the past.

Ryan returns to his chair behind the desk.

"I should get going," she says.

"Hang on. There's something else we need to talk about."

More? He flips the pages of a yellow pad. "It seems our hacker sent a copy of his warning note to the editor of the *Ballymore News* who called me this morning for a comment. I told him the gardai' are investigating and no patient data has been exposed, at least not yet. Unfortunately, he says he's obliged to report it."

"Oh, God, no. You mean he's putting the note with Teague's diagnosis in the paper?"

"We're the only ones who know that was Teague's patient record in the note. But yes, it's regrettable."

Disastrous is more like it. She imagines Teague's horror if sees it in print. She vaguely hears Ryan say something else about the county health director. "I managed to get us on the schedule of the next county council meeting to plead our case to keep the study going." He opens his calendar. "That's Wednesday, a week from today, at six o'clock."

"God help us." Kate's voice is a whisper.

Ryan puts down his pad and meets her gaze. "Aye. We'll need all the help we can get."

The *Ballymore News* is spread across their kitchen table, displaying the headline "Ballymore Mental Health Clinic Hacked: Patient Files at Risk" on its front page. After scanning the lengthy article, Kate is relieved to find it doesn't include the text of the hacker's note. It does describe it, including the fact that the hacker revealed a single patient's confidential information as proof that clinic files had indeed been stolen. Teague enters the kitchen and grunts a sleepy hey at her. She smiles and watches him collect his bowl and spoon, along with a milk carton and a box of Cheerios. She lifts the paper to make room for him and waits until he's swallowed a few spoons of cereal before she shows him the front page.

"Sweetheart, is the Finn Mitchell in these pictures the same person you know?"

Teague's shrug is an obvious dodge.

"He's described as 'the Ballymore-born IRA veteran who spent fifteen years in the Old Bailey and took up Druidism upon his return to the county.'" One photo is a blurry black and white snapshot of a young man wearing a felt beret and holding a rifle. In the other, much crisper photo, he's older, wearing overalls in front of a windmill.

"This fellow doesn't look like a modern-day Merlin to me," she says.

"No offense, but how would you know?"

"Good point."

"Did he say anything?"

She reads, "When asked about the hack, Mitchell commented, I don't know shite about computers, but it doesn't surprise me that some folks in this county are tired of being guinea pigs in these studies. Where has it gotten them? Young people should learn the old ways. Not be taking happy pills."

"Yeah, that sounds like him." Teague holds up the bowl to slurp the milk.

She sits back and re-reads the article, then stands with the folded paper under her arm. "I'll be working at home today. Do you have any plans?"

"Yeah, me and Kiernan are meeting at the castle."

"All right, Sweetheart. Have fun." In the bedroom, she deletes the 1500-word presentation she slaved over for the council meeting and starts from scratch with a blank screen. She's never felt this unprepared.

# New York City
## 1935

A loud knock raised her from Annie's sickbed but a figure blocked her path to the door. As details filled in, she recognized him—or his wraith. Michael's eyes looked vacant. There were bruises on his face and his shirt and pants were dripping wet. They stood within an arm's length of each other until whoever was on the other side of the door took to pounding and Michael disappeared.

A sweating, red-faced officer of the NYPD stood in the hall. "Are you Mrs. Michael Callahan?"

"Aye."

"I'm sorry, ma'am. There's been an accident."

She grabbed the door jamb. The officer's lips moved while she studied every speck of his stout nose and ruddy cheeks. Annie's hacking reached her from the kitchen. His mouth stopped.

"What do I do now?" she asked.

He sniffed and looked at a pad. "The railroad will transport your husband's body to McMurray's Funeral Home."

She shut the door. Her body seized and she toppled.

"Mamma, what's wrong?" Meg pulled at her blouse. "Are you sick like Annie? Mamma, it's all right. Isn't it?"

She brought Meg to her bosom and fought back sobs.

From the moment she heard the officer utter the words, Ellen's grief rode her like an invisible beast, clawing at her back, stealing her balance. With the girls needing her to comfort them, she was forced to save her tears for late at night, and then cut short the sobs trying to scale her throat. It wasn't fair, she whispered when they were out of hearing range. As if fairness had anything to do with it.

What she meant was that Michael wasn't only her husband. They had shared a soul. She wasn't sure she had one without him. She was pumping water behind their building when this thought came to her. She gasped and let go of the pump handle. The air around her became still and weighted with a sense of dread.

"Get on with it or move out of the way," a woman behind her called out.

She carried the full pail up five flights, trying not to slosh water. With each step, she wrestled her grief, seeking more thoughts like the one that had surprised her at the water pump, anything that might help her find another way of being in the world. What came to her was harsh but undoubtedly true. With Michael steeped in spirit, she hadn't cultivated her own. She and Brigid hadn't spoken in a very long time. By relying on his access to their ancestors and the world beyond, she'd hid from the possibility that she was no longer a believer. Now it fell to her to reconnect to that part of herself and be the conduit for her girls and the new life she was carrying. She sat on the stairs to allow a sob to come when she thought about the conversation she and Michael had had only a week ago, when she'd told him that she was again with child. He'd yearned for a boy, and she'd assured him this child would fulfill his wish.

She brought the pail into the kitchen, where she would clean her hands and body, then the dirty dishes, and lastly their clothes. As she soaped and rinsed her arms in the child-size metal tub, she wondered, were his ancestors prepared to escort his soul to the community of kin far from where they lived now? She needed to ask them formally, in prayer, which she vowed to do that night. Her responsibility was to arrange a proper burial of his body in this, their borrowed country. It helped to have this one important task to do to honor him.

In the narthex of Saint Bernadette's Church, Father Dowling spoke in a whisper after she asked him about Michael's funeral mass.

"I'm not comfortable with the circumstances surrounding Michael's death," he said.

Her shock at his response made her unsteady on her feet. She grabbed the waist-high urn of holy water. As if this same priest hadn't married them and baptized their daughters.

"I'm sorry, but you'll need to find another parish for the burial mass."

She refused to flinch or release him from her stare. No doubt he thought shame would do the rest. He was wrong. Not for a minute did she believe he took his own life.

"What you heard just ain't true," she told her priest, allowing anger to creep into her voice. "Michael was a good, believing man who would never take the easy way out." After a long pause when Dowling appeared to weigh how much of a fuss she'd make if he said no against the reactions of certain other parishioners should he give in, he agreed to perform the mass.

In the hours leading up to the service, she found herself mulling the meaning of the word she would never say out loud. Was having an inkling of your fate and not fighting it the same as choosing to die by your own hand? She'd felt helpless as she'd watched Michael's strength wane over the past months, despite their better fortunes. It was as if he'd held on past his human capacity, and a crucial part of him had already slipped away. She'd tried not to resent him for it, but it was there like a nagging pain in her belly. Still, it was no one else's business.

She spent their savings, forty dollars, on two adjoining plots at Saint Raymond's Cemetery in the Bronx. Buying the pair seemed odd, even foolish at first, given she was just thirty-two years old and had no other money to her name. But after the funeral director explained that two plots cost only five dollars more, and that by purchasing it she could reserve the ground next to his grave, she'd gone ahead and bought both. Having it made her feel closer to Michael.

The coroner declared his death an accidental drowning, a judgment Ellen found false on its face. Last Christmas, they'd taken the train to Boston to visit a Callahan cousin. At the Newburgh station, she'd seen the steep cliffs lining both sides of the Hudson. In the weeks after she buried him, Ellen had to contend with waves of grief and morning sickness compounded by hurtful things said by her neighbors just loud enough for her to hear. "She was always ragging on him." "They found his body in the Hudson, now we're supposed to believe he fell in." "Coward. He'll burn in hell." "He was always hiding something. They say he was a peeper. He got what he deserved."

While these busybodies went around with their loose lips, Ellen kept her head high and wished they would soon meet their own wretched fates. She knew the worst slings at Michael stemmed from troubles back home. Twelve years had passed since the last battles of the civil war had been fought on Irish soil; fifteen since the war of independence had made them refugees. The Republicans had branded him an informer on the night they fled Ballymore—accusing him of trading the location of Rory O'Shea's hideout in the cave at Rathcroghan for his and Ellen's safe passage out of Ballymore—but they'd waited to mete out justice for his supposed crime until it suited them. Until now. Their actions should have been enough for Ellen to part ways with the Republican cause forever. But she was no fool. She blamed the English for twelve hundred years of subjugation of her people and for turning brother against brother. She'd never pledged her allegiance to any particular army or political party. Her loyalty belonged to the land and her ancestors buried there.

Now, alone in New York City with two daughters and another baby on the way, she would have to protect her children from the enemy closest to them. In the fall of 1935, the most immediate threat to their survival was hunger.

# 2002

With the Ballymore County Council meeting due to start in an hour, Kate flicks on the bathroom light, hoping to be pleasantly surprised by the state of her face. Meh. Not great, but not too bad. New creases sprout around her eyes like eager young branches enjoying a wet spring. Her frown lines fractionally deeper than they were a decade ago. No sign of gray in her hair. Her chin is still firm. She pulls her hair into an updo, pins it, and raises the hand mirror to check her profile. Kate doesn't need anyone to tell her beauty will never be her currency.

This realization came last spring, on the day she posed with Sebastian next to their new fMRI machine for the cover of the alumni magazine. Prepping for the shoot, the photographer's assistant eyed Kate before asking if she minded having gel applied to her hair " to give it definition." After working on her head for twenty minutes, which included a curling iron, the girl suggested "a bit of cover and color," referring to her toolkit of liquids and powders meant to "tone down" her "shiny nose"—which Kate took to mean her too-big nose—shadow and liner "to make her eyes pop," a demure pink lipstick, and the final touch: a pair of fake horn-rimmed glasses.

All told, the assistant spent forty-five minutes making her camera ready—thirty minutes longer than Kate typically stands in front of the mirror on any given morning. There was no denying the woman's stunning

155

handiwork. Kate's shoulder-length auburn hair fell in frizz-free ringlets, her pale, freckled complexion, and indelicate features masked, her cheeks had new contours where before there'd been none. She looked airbrushed and, well, glamorous—in a Brainiac Barbie sort of way.

Now she continues her amateur efforts to achieve something similar. At least tame her hair and cover her freckles. The upside to having plain-Jane looks, Kate has recently decided, is the promise she'll be spared the distress beautiful women experience when their youthful symmetry devolves to sags and all that dewy skin takes on the texture of sandpaper.

She had a different attitude a few years ago, when she aspired to beauty, as if a basic fact of nature could be changed with sufficient time and money.

The vast majority of twenty-something females qualify as beautiful as a function of their youth. All a woman has to do is look at a ten-year-old photo of herself to see how relative it all is. So much wasted angst.

She kicks off her heels and returns to the bedroom. Sticky notes filled with study titles and scrawled reminders to herself dot the wall above the desk; a crumb trail of her working hypotheses on the possible routes taken by mental disorders as they travel through families. She pulls up her sagging pantyhose and stares until the squares become neurons, extending their dendrites into the great unknown in a valiant struggle to connect with like-minded cells.

What is she missing? You'll know when the time comes, Gran once told her.

Could saving the study and understanding Gran's meaning be as simple as admitting her ignorance and asking the people of Ballymore how they'd like their stories to be told? Good or bad, it's their legacy. First, they'd have to buy into the study as a worthy use of their time and trouble. Her usual approach with civilians is to talk about how their participation will help advance medicine and bring health benefits for them and their children — in the future. That won't cut it here.

Besides the council members, Ryan told her to expect a crowd of skeptical locals. Everyone who wants to will have time to speak their piece. She shudders at the thought. Without a vote of confidence from a majority of the five council members, their study will continue its current death spiral, forcing her and

Teague to go home. When she invited him to the meeting, he rolled his eyes and said he had other plans. She has no idea where he is at this hour. Do most parents know the whereabouts of their teenage children on any given late afternoon?

In the kitchen, she reheats the dregs of her morning coffee and brings her cup to the living room. It's a stretch to call it that. Their new apartment came semi-furnished with two beds, an ugly orange sofa, one fraying wing chair, and the wooden crate where she puts her cup. It's enough to meet their needs for another ten months. Maybe less if this meeting goes poorly.

She's leaning back on the sofa, rehearsing her remarks one last time, when the phone rings. She lets it go to the answering machine until she hears Mom's voice, "Kate, are you there? It's meeeeeee."

It's the singsong she reverts to after she decides the tension has worn off from their last exchange.

"Hi. Is everything all right?"

"Connie and I are fine. You don't think I'd forget your birthday, do you?"

"No, of course not."

"Thirty-two! I can hardly believe it's been that long since you scared us to death by showing up a month early."

She loves this story. How Dad turned on the siren to get her to the Bronx through morning rush hour. In her mother's thinking, the same prematurity was somehow linked to Kate's early graduation from high school.

"Thanks for remembering, Mom. Sorry, I have to leave for a meeting in a minute. Can I write you a letter?"

"Promise?"

"Yes, I promise."

"Let me talk to Teague?"

"He's out with a friend."

"Oh! How nice. Before you hang up, I got a call from Ireland yesterday. An Irish fellow by the name of Rafferty. With his accent, I didn't catch everything."

"What did he want?"

"That's the odd part. He said he just wanted to confirm your date of birth and address. I thought maybe he needed me as an emergency contact for you. Then we chatted about other things. The old neighborhood in the Bronx. His family in New Jersey. He was very nice."

"Well, that's . . . odd. But don't worry about it. This is a very small town. They have their ways of doing things."

She returns to the sofa with her head spinning. Why would Rafferty call Mom? Was there a problem with her Special Skills Work Permit? Ryan had had to pull strings to rush it through. That wouldn't be a police matter, would it? She's at a loss for an explanation. But if she doesn't hurry, she'll be late for the council meeting. And that would make an already bad situation worse.

# New York City
## 1935

Ellen spent the afternoon walking the Bowery in search of piecework with little to show for it. The November sun hung low in the sky, the shops dark, she gave up for the day. On the fifth floor, out of breath, her thighs screaming, she waited for the girls to catch up.

"Mama, I can't," Meg whined, her slumped form visible on the fourth-floor landing.

"Annie, take your sister's hand. I'm not coming back down."

At the door to apartment 5E, the flat they'd shared for the last seven years with the Mulcahy family, she couldn't believe her eyes. Her one good dress, two blankets, the girls' jumpers, a pair of rag dolls she'd made for them, her box of letters and trinkets, their wedding photo—strewn across the floor. It was impossible not to think of the Donlons' eviction: standing with Delia and the young'uns on Big Rock Road, Maggie in Mam's arms, their cottage falling to pieces. *Please, no, not here, not now*, so soon after she lost him.

"Who put my doll out here, Mama?" Annie wanted to know. Meg picked it up and hugged it to her chest.

"It has to be a mistake," Ellen said. Her hand shook as she put the key in the lock. Before she could turn the handle, the door opened. Instead of Ionna Mulcahy, who should have been home, Mr. Daley stepped into the hallway. A

159

big, rude man under any circumstances, the sneer on his face let Ellen know she hadn't seen the worst of him. His bulk blocked her view inside but behind him she heard footsteps and Ionna shushing her children.

"I've got no room for traitors in this building," Daley said, and he handed her the cloth sack containing Michael's belongings the medical examiner had brought her two months ago.

"This ain't right," she said. With her throat closing up, she had to shout to get the words out. "It's the seventeenth of the month and my rent is paid!"

Daley shrugged and shook his head. She leaned in the doorway and pointed to the kitchen. "Those are my table and chairs. My cross on the wall."

He didn't turn around. "Mrs. Mulcahy says she put everything of yours out here." He looked down at the floor. "It's your word against hers and between the two of you, well . . . I want you out of this building." He must have gotten wind of what happened to Michael in Newburgh and had come to his own conclusions, helped along by others in the building.

Meg whimpered and grabbed hold of Ellen's skirt. Annie's eyes appeared unable to open wide enough to understand what was happening.

"But where will I go?"

Daley blew air from his cheeks and pushed a loose strand of thin black hair off his sweaty forehead. He hooked his thumbs into the waistband of his pants and shifted his weight to fill the doorway. "That ain't my problem."

A sharp twinge in her belly drew her hand to the baby, who'd become even more precious to her over the past month. The pain subsided but it was enough to make her see what had to be done. "Come on, girls. Help me pick up our things."

They traveled by subway to the Bronx, where she knew many Irish had moved after leaving Five Points. For three nights, the mother superior of the parish linked to the cemetery where she'd lain Michael to rest allowed them to sleep in a storage room. Ellen looked for maid's work with live-in quarters but found none, leaving her no choice but to rent a room in a boarding house. She found occasional day work but would often have to leave the girls on their own. The one saving grace of the new situation was their closeness to Michael's grave. They went several times a week, in all seasons, and as they sat beside his headstone, Ellen made it a practice for each of them to address him directly when speaking about their day to day lives or sharing pleasant memories. Eventually, as she honed her ability to quiet her mind, her communication with Michael went both ways, allowing her to reach out to him when she needed his help. When blood rushed to her head, making her slightly dizzy, she knew he was trying to contact her. Then her vision and hearing would stretch to receive his message. Without his body tying him in knots, Michael shared much more with her now than he did when he was alive. She worried that this new closeness would be temporary, a brief stop on his heavenly journey, and then he'd be truly gone.

One cold, gray afternoon while the girls chased each other up and down rows of headstones, she felt his presence and sat by his grave to wait for his message. It came and brought her comfort but also a steep challenge.

*Love, take heart. The burdens on you are heavy, but your worst trials are behind you. You were proud of my gift, but you never rightly valued your own strength. You've always been the foundation of this family. Two more generations will need your guidance before you're done. There are many from our lineage on this side helping you. And don't fret about me. I'll never leave you again.*

# 2002

When Kate enters the clinic lobby, Ryan is leaning over the receptionist's counter, pen in hand. He sees her and drops it. "You look . . ."

"Prim? Professorial? It's the heels." It's also her below-the-knee navy-blue skirt and matching jacket, pale-pink blouse, and hair pinned in the tightest bun she's ever twined. Nothing, she hopes, to offend anyone. Kate crosses the lobby, empty except for one woman reading a paperback.

"I was going to say you look *grand*." Ryan rips a prescription from the pad and hands it to the receptionist.

"Oh, thanks," Kate says, embarrassed.

"Are you ready for this?" Ryan asks as he steers his car out of the clinic parking lot for the short drive to the Ballymore County Center.

"I'll say yes if it makes you feel better."

"By the way, I hear Finn Mitchell will be there tonight."

She groans. "Tell me, who *is* this guy?"

"He lives on the old Mitchell family property, north of town. He gets a pass on most things he does because of the badge of honor he wears for planting an IRA bomb in London in '39."

"Wouldn't he have been very young in 1939?"

"Teenagers did a lot of the fighting in the old IRA. Finn used his heroic past to gain followers as a Druid. It was part of the pagan revival that happened in the seventies and now he's recognized as a leader, at least around here."

With a grin and a shrug, he adds, "Stranger things have happened."

"Not where I'm from they don't. So, is Finn Mitchell related to the Mitchells who own the drugstore?"

"There are a fair number of Mitchells in Ballymore. But you can assume that any two people with the same surname living around here are related by blood, even if they're distant relatives. In this case, it's well known that the Mitchells on Main Street are not on speaking terms with Finn. Although I couldn't tell you the reason."

"Thanks. I'll consider myself briefed."

"Finn and his wife, I think her name is Morgan, keep to themselves, other than leading their flock and the occasional protest. I hear he's become something of a prophet."

"Wonderful. Every study needs a seer."

He gives her a deadpan look. "Chin up. Remain calm. Keep your hair on."

"Fine. No more wizard jokes."

"Listen, about tonight. I'll go first and deal with the hack. Then I'll introduce you. Keep your part short and sweet."

Does he not think she's prepared? She swallows her annoyance and asks, "Shouldn't I talk about the study?"

"Aye, but why don't you start with a small personal disclosure."

"I've never done anything like that . . . I mean, in public."

With a smile, he says, "How about in private? Have a think about it."

They enter a modern two-story building. The earth-toned circular council chamber, a bowl configuration of ascending seats, has council members seated around a table at its base, creating an intimate, participatory environment. Ryan and Kate take their places in the front row facing the council.

The chamber is three-quarters full when the council chairman, Jim Lynch, gavels the meeting open. Thirty-five minutes later, his tie is loosened, and his sleeves are rolled up. He thanks the budget director for her monthly report before declaring, "That brings our regular business to an end."

"About bloody time!" The yell comes from a man in an upper row, eliciting a ripple of laughter.

"Thank you all for your patience. It's now time to hear from Dr. Ryan

Quinn, who, as most of you know, is the medical director of the Ballymore County Mental Health Clinic. He has with him Dr. Katherine Jones, who is . . ." he checks his notes, "co-lead investigator of the Ballymore Family Study."

A smattering of boos and hisses erupt. Kate flattens the wrinkles in her skirt. Ryan gets up.

"Had enough of this shite."

"Why don't they just leave us be?"

"Who okayed this nonsense? Should fire the lot of them."

"Enough of that," says an elderly female voice.

Kate turns her head to see an eighty-something woman rise from her seat and point an arthritic finger toward a row of young men in the back. "Sean Murphy, I know your mum didn't raise you to be that rude." Her voice is thin but firm. She crosses her arms.

Ryan leans down and whispers. "That's Mrs. Clayton, maths teacher to me and half the room."

When another young man from the same row yells, "Maybe they deserve it," Mrs. Clayton doesn't miss a beat. "I'm talking to you too, Kenny Brennan. I don't care what you're mad about. There's no excuse for bad behavior." She goes full schoolmarm and glances around the chamber as if to make sure the rest of her class hears her. "Now how about you each wait your turn to talk."

Murmurs and chuckles follow. Ryan nods at Kate and she follows him to the stage.

Lynch pounds his gavel, and the crowd settles down. "As I was saying, we're going to hear from Dr. Quinn and Dr. Jones. There will be plenty of time for questions and comments after their presentation."

Ryan scans the audience. "Good evening, friends and neighbors."

He draws a few nods and polite smiles from the stone-faced crowd.

"As many of you are aware, about two weeks ago, a hacker gained access to our clinic computers. That's the same as a thief breaking in and stealing something of value from your home. If you have any information about who might be responsible, please speak to Guard Rafferty. You can find him in the back row."

Most heads turn and settle on Rafferty, who stands up and looks around the room.

One man in the second row doesn't turn around. Finn Mitchell. Ryan pointed him out on the way in and she recognizes him from his picture in the paper. His long white hair is cut in an unusual style, short bangs across his temple, muttonchop sideburns, and a Viking beard. He's wearing a blue work shirt topped with a leather vest. With the timeline Ryan gave her and his weathered face, she guesses Finn is in his mid-seventies. Their eyes meet and a chill goes through her. She catches her breath and looks away.

"We've just finished an upgrade of the clinic's cybersecurity. Our new software is the best available. The vendor tells me we're on par with MI5, whatever that's worth."

His comment generates scattered laughs.

"If you'll bear with me, I'd like to explain changes we've made to our data collection and storage set up."

There are groans and eye rolls.

"I promise to keep it short. When you agree to be part of this study and give us your personal information, it goes into our database anonymously. There isn't a shred of identifying data that stays attached to your name. That's because we're only interested in community-wide results. Your private information stays in your master clinic file, which doesn't go near the study files."

A woman raises her hand.

"Hello, Deirdre."

"Ryan, if what you're saying is true, how did this thief get ahold of the patient's name and private information the newspaper says he put in the warning letter pasted on your door?"

"It's not clear yet how the hacker got his hands on that particular new patient file."

Kate's throat tightens. Because Ryan called him back and managed to convince the newspaper editor not to print the hacker's note, only the two of them and the editor know that Teague is the new patient whose name and diagnosis were revealed.

"Deirdre, we're looking into that breach. We know the hacker hasn't posted anything online about that individual or any of our existing patients."

"You mean, not yet," Deirdre mumbles as she sits down. Murmurs go through the crowd.

Ryan's eyes dart around the room. "I can assure you that our security upgrade has given us an even stronger firewall to keep that from happening."

Looking at the newly furrowed brows in the audience, Kate wonders if Ryan's explanation of why they shouldn't worry hasn't made them worry more.

"I want you to know that even before this study is completed, it will bring tangible benefits to our community. We've been given a dedicated pot of money from our funders in Dublin and Washington, DC, which we've set aside to cover treatment for any study participants and family members who want to take advantage of it as a supplement to their regular health benefits."

Frightfully aware that she is up next, Kate's hands are shaking. Hopefully no one will notice, and some words will come out of her mouth.

"Now I'd like to introduce a lady we've been lucky enough to snare from one of the most respected research centers in New York. She's whip-smart, although I try not to hold that against her."

He leaves out the part about her being fired by that *respected research center*.

"She's still learning her way around our roads and acclimating to the things that might make us seem peculiar to a transplanted New Yorker, but she and her nephew are adapting well, and I know she will be a huge asset to the clinic and to our patients. It's my pleasure to give you Dr. Katherine Jones, who won't mind a bit if you call her Kate."

There's silence in the chamber. She adjusts the microphone. "Thank you for coming tonight. And for welcoming my nephew and me to your town."

She glances at Ryan, whose smile gives her confidence a slight boost.

"For the people who've signed up or are considering signing up for our study, I want to acknowledge right off the bat that this is a big ask. I've seen the same disorders many of you are dealing with in my own family and—"

The skepticism bordering on hostility on the faces of a middle-aged couple sitting in the front row stops her midsentence. She grabs the podium and stares down at her pumps. *One thousand one, one thousand two . . .* People stir in their seats. She picks up her head and forces a smile, but her train of thought is lost. She reaches for a standby.

"I can say one thing for sure. Doing nothing, pretending the person you love isn't suffering when you see it with your own eyes, isn't the answer. There are new, promising treatments available and better medications coming into the pipeline. By sharing your family histories, you can help us get closer to the day when these afflictions are under control."

She's flailing. A murmur goes through the audience. Shit. Why is he standing?

"What it is it, Finn?" Jim Lynch asks.

Everyone shifts in their seats to get a look at him.

"Pardon my going out of turn." He glances over his shoulder at Mrs. Clayton.

"Jim, I'm sorry to say, this nice lady is wasting our time and hers. Are we just supposed to take their word for it that they've fixed their computers? They say we shouldn't worry about our private information getting out on the internet? Why take that risk? From what I've heard, even her own boy hasn't been helped by what she's come here to offer our children."

Kate's jaw drops. How dare he invoke Teague's misadventure to justify his bullshit!

"I, for one, say, no thanks. They had their chance with this study. As some of you know, I've been against it from the start."

"All right, Finn, that's enough."

He tilts his head and remains standing as if deciding whether to follow Lynch's instructions. He sits.

"We'll take a five-minute recess." Lynch turns off the microphone and huddles with his fellow council members.

Kate steps down from the podium. She and Ryan are left to stand awkwardly on stage. The audience murmur rises to a roar. Perspiration soaks her blouse. Oh, God . . . Why did she even try talking about herself, her family? It's unprofessional . . . She should have stuck to her own rules.

"Dr. Jones. Dr. Quinn." Jim Lynch addresses them from the council members' half circle while they remain standing at the podium. The room goes silent. Blood rushes to her forehead, making her dizzy.

"Enough of us share Finn's concerns that we see no point in continuing this discussion tonight. The council is giving you thirty days to show us why your study should continue. You have a fair amount of convincing to do. Until next month's meeting, that will be all." He gavels the meeting over.

She grabs the edge of the podium. Ryan's expression is impenetrable. Most likely, he's thinking she just tanked his project. Ryan leaves the stage without saying a word to her or anyone else. She follows him and catches Finn's eye on her way down the stairs. Is that a smirk on his face? Who does he think he is? He knows nothing about her or their study. Writing off the entire mental health profession like that. He thinks he's won. But she's not giving up so easy.

# New York City
## 1935

With Michael's life cut short and Ellen's suspicions about who'd done it, she took John Callahan's warning to heart, vowing to steer clear of anyone who sounded too much like home. That made her encounter on the Upper East Side in December even more astonishing. She'd just crossed Lexington Avenue on Sixty-First when a Laundress Wanted sign in the window of a brownstone drew her to the servants' entrance. She hoped against hope it might be her lucky day.

A tall woman in a maid's cap and apron opened the door and eyed her up and down. "What would you be wanting?"

Her light brogue ignited a tremor of fear. "I'm a seamstress and I can launder as good as anybody you'll find for the job."

The woman squinted and wrinkled her forehead. Her mouth dropped opened. Ellen put a hand on her belly. Was she showing already?

"Ellen Mitchell?"

Then it was her turn to stare. The woman's heart-shaped face and ginger hair seemed familiar. But many from home shared the same features.

"Don't you remember me?" The woman tilted her head to the side, enough to reveal the scar that ran from her ear along her jawbone.

"Delia. Am I dreaming?"

"If you are, then I am, too. Imagine a Mitchell from Ballymore showing up at my door."

"I'm a Callahan now."

"I'm glad you married him! I always liked your Michael. He was solid. Not like Colm. That boy was always after me. I told him he had to get rid of the chip on his shoulder before I'd consider him for a beau. I had such a mouth." Delia cackled.

"You're a sight for sore eyes," Ellen said. As she entered the well-appointed kitchen, she gave herself a moment to relish Delia's picture of Michael alive and well. "How long have you been in New York?"

"Since they shipped me out of the workhouse, fourteen years ago. Mam died right away from the typhus. I never knew for sure . . ." the timbre of her voice wavered, ". . . what happened to the wee ones after they separated us." She picked up her chin. "You're the first person from home I've met here. My Danny came from Donegal."

The two of them sat by the scullery sink and talked for hours while Delia washed and Ellen dried the pots and dishes, each cracking open the curtain on the events of her life since they'd last seen each other. Ellen offered a guarded version of her departure from Ballymore and a fuller account of the years that followed. She shared her pride at Michael landing his railroad job while describing his death as accidental.

With similar reserve, Delia shared few details of her first lonely years of servitude and regaled her with the six happy years she'd had with Danny. Tears fell when she talked about losing him three years before to a subway construction accident when she was still mourning the wee one they'd lost to TB, leaving a daughter, Maggie, now eight, to give Delia a reason to go on.

"I'm sorry I can't take your troubles away," Ellen said as she stared into her teacup and considered asking Delia about something that had been dogging her. The warmth in her old friend's eyes gave her the courage she needed.

"Why is it," she began, then stumbled, unable to find the right words, afraid of sounding like a disbeliever.

Delia leaned forward. "You want to know why we're sitting here drinking tea, and not your Michael or my Danny? How it is that Maggie's still breathing air with no sister by her side?"

"I know it's wrong to second guess God's plan, but the question keeps going around my head and it just won't stop."

Delia snorts. "It's good you didn't put it to your priest. He wouldn't have had an answer in his old bag of tricks, at least not a good one." Delia's grin made her scar turn a darker shade of pink. Lines formed half-moons round her mouth.

"After losing the baby and putting Danny in the ground next to her, I got down on my knees and told Brigid straight out, if she expected me to go on, she had to tell me why. As clear as I'm talking to you now, the Good Lady gave me a good answer."

Ellen held her tongue as Delia's eyelids fluttered. It lifted her heart to hear the name of her old ally spoken aloud. While the seconds ticked by, it seemed Delia had floated away. When their eyes met again, Ellen's arms and legs tingled, as if her skin had become porous and she'd absorbed some of Delia's vigor.

"Brigid told me there's just one or two of us in each bloodline given the strength to extract the life force from such terrible sorrows and help the others carry on. When a special soul comes to us, we're meant to recognize the gift in that child or husband and give them what they need to let the gift take hold. When they leave us, we have no choice but to thank God for whatever time we had with them."

"But what if their gift wasn't yet put to use?"

Delia cradled her chin with her palm. "You're worried that you didn't do enough to protect him from the dark forces while he lived?"

"Aye," Ellen said, as shame turned her body first hot, then leaden.

Delia took her time before speaking again. When their eyes met, hers had a new hardness. "That supposes you know more than those watching us from the other world about what a useful life looks like."

Ellen shut her eyes and saw Mam's face, as if her mother agreed with Delia's reprimand. Also to let Ellen know she'd had something to do with this reunion.

Delia touched her knee. "Don't be fooled by the simplicity of it. There's nothing simple about fate. It makes no sense to fight it either. Our grief might tempt us to take things into our own hands when we're meant to bear our trials because they serve a greater purpose. I confess I've looked at trains coming toward me with that thought in mind, and I might have done it if I didn't believe with all my heart what Brigid told me." Delia looked down at her lap and took a slow, deep breath. Ellen closed her eyes and pictured Michael leaving for the railroad trip that would seal his fate. When she opened her eyes again, Delia's expression was deadly serious. "Given everything I know about you and Michael, here's what I think," Delia began, startling Ellen with the deeper register of her voice. "You're meant to hold up the two ends of your lineage. On no account, can you allow a break."

Ellen caught her breath and lay a hand on her heart, knowing Delia's message had come directly from Michael.

Delia put in a good word with the lady of the house and got Ellen hired at a salary of two dollars a week, her first regular income since Michael's death.

Four months after their reunion, Delia was with her in the laundry room when Ellen's birth pains started. After a short labor and one last racking push, the midwife Delia had brought to help her gave Ellen a terrible fright when she held the baby beyond her view and shouted, "Mary, Mother of God."

Delia echoed the midwife's sentiment. "Dear, you've been blessed!"

When she saw the caul covering her baby, Ellen was speechless. Delia encouraged her to understand this rare happening as a sign that the gift of Michael's lineage would continue in his son. The midwife removed the placenta and put it in a bowl for safekeeping. She washed the baby and placed him on Ellen's chest, pink and clean. His eyes were bottomless. Ellen felt more joy than she believed possible.

Delia looked on. "You've heard what the Connemara fishermen's wives say about caul-bearing babies?"

"Please tell me."

"They say a newborn baby covered by his mother's sack will be forever safe from drowning, just as he was in the womb."

"So it is," Ellen said. She took Delia's tale as a promise from Brigid that she would protect her son from his father's fate.

She named him John, after Michael's father, though he went by Jack. Even before he could form words, Jack's second sight manifested, along with his volatile nature. Yelps of glee followed by terror-filled waking nightmares, the emotional seesaw tempering her joy with dread. She worried that she lacked the strength and wisdom to steer him away from the dark forces that had weakened his father. And because she knew the unhealed wounds of her people were certain to find them wherever they lived, she feared even more the harm that might come to him from the progeny of the men who'd pushed Michael to his death.

For Jack's sake, she asked Brigid to give her the courage to hope again. She didn't yet have the perspective to see that her steely endurance, if used too often, would harden into a brittle veneer that made it more difficult to believe in a future. Neither would she have had any way of knowing that calcified grief could be embodied in her descendants, just as she'd been the involuntary recipient of her forebearers' suffering. For Ellen any such inklings would have to wait until she received the bittersweet knowledge of old age.

# 2002

"Would you care to join me at my Uncle Marty and Aunt Fiona's farm in Ballycarrick this weekend?" Ryan asks the question with one foot in the door to her office. "I've been going there all my life. They have a barn full of Kerry cows and plenty of room. It'll give us a chance to plot our next moves."

She's thrown when he doesn't say a word about her mediocre performance of the night before. After she spent hours preparing a defense.

"That sounds great."

"Feel free to invite Teague to come along."

When she extends Ryan's invitation, Teague is skeptical. "Where is this place?"

"The townland is called Ballycarrick. We'll stay at the Quinn Dairy. It's a working farm that belongs to Ryan's uncle, Marty Quinn."

"I'm not going with you and Ryan to look at cows." He's scraping paint off his fingers with the butter knife.

She resists reminding him there's turpentine for that purpose under the sink. "Can I trust you home alone for two days?"

"Yeah."

"Promise you'll stay away from Liam?"

He rolls his eyes in that exaggerated way teens do when they want to express maximum scorn.

174

"What will you do all weekend?"

"Paint. Game. Read. Meet up with Kiernan. Get pizza."

"You could work on your quadratic equation worksheet."

"All right."

"Remember, we've run out of warnings."

"About what?"

"Let's start with buying illegal drugs and trespassing."

He scowls. "How stupid do you think I am?"

"I've never thought you were stupid, sweetheart. Maybe too smart for your own good."

"Fine."

She finishes her coffee and puts her hand on his shoulder. "Ryan and I are getting an early start. I'll call you tonight."

"Have fun," he says, craning his neck to give her one of his ironic grins.


Ryan turns onto a gravel road and swerves to avoid a truck-sized puddle. In a single balletic move, he downshifts and maneuvers the car out of sodden grass and back on the road.

She releases a breath. "Well done."

"I know that ditch by heart and believe me we don't want to be stuck in it."

She goes back to wondering about the sleeping arrangements for the weekend, which is silly since nothing is going to happen.

Earlier in the ride, Ryan characterized her performance last night as "a good try" and left it at that. He doesn't dwell on things, a trait that she finds both refreshing and untrustworthy.

"He's still out with his cows," Aunt Fiona says. They're drinking tea in the Quinn's cozy living room, sitting on a floral brocade sofa. A gleaming fireplace mantle and several pieces of heavy wooden furniture give off an aged, lemony scent. Two parakeets chirp in a cage in the corner.

"He's always back by half eleven." Fiona's feet barely reach the floor in her rocking chair. She has a slight stoop, a solid middle, and coiled white hair.

Family photos cover every surface. Fiona picks up a framed picture of an athlete and hands it to Kate. She recognizes the beefy teenager as Ryan holding a helmet and a stick while trying to look serious.

"Ready for a hurling match, are you?"

His eyebrows shoot up. "Very good."

"The stick gave it away."

He reaches for one with a preteen girl in a team uniform. "Here is Sophie."

Her thick honey-blonde hair and broad cheeks are all Ryan.

"A sweet one, she is," Fiona says. "It's too bad Niamh took my favorite niece off to Galway. I hardly see the girl anymore."

Ryan gives Fiona a sympathetic look. "Don't blame Niamh. It's my fault. I'll get her here soon."

"I've heard that before, Ryan Quinn."

Aunt Fiona is not having it. How awkward. Here she is accepting this woman's hospitality for the weekend when Fiona would much rather be entertaining her grandniece.

"I promise," he tells her.

Kate recalls their conversation on the way to Sophie's game. Her relief that he'd taken himself off the dating market, at least that's how she heard it. Simple is good. Then why did she just imagine his ample body on top of hers?

"I'll bring Kate's bag to the back bedroom and leave mine here in the closet until it's time to pull out the sofa bed," Ryan says from the front hall.

"Not a bother, dear," Fiona answers. She gives Kate a polite smile. "How is your nephew liking it here?"

"Much better than I dared hope." She doesn't say, despite his two run-ins with the gardai', which no doubt Fiona has heard about through the grapevine.

Ryan parts a curtain at the front window. "It's clearing up nicely. If you're up to it, Kate, I'll give you a tour of the neighborhood."

Their first stop is a long, cinderblock structure with a red tin roof and boarded-up windows. "Ballycarrick National School, Built 1906" is etched above a shuttered door.

"This was it for Ballycarrick. All ages in one room. Boys and girls separate. Most went barefoot year-round."

She pictures those shoeless children in the present chilly rain. Teague still walking barefoot wherever he can get away with it.

The largest property in the neighborhood is hidden by a high, gated wall with a brass sign that reads Blakemore. "The Blakes were the original landholders who leased these lots to tenant farmers."

She peeks at a well-kept Georgian-style manor house set far back from the gate. "Are there any Blakes living here now?"

"I doubt it. Most of the English landowners left after independence. The new government made easy loans to the farmers so they could buy their lots. Usually, the land stayed in the same families with one son taking over. Others started small businesses in town or went off to America. Now they head to Galway or Dublin for uni or a job."

"I think I understand why your houses have no numbers."

"I can't wait to hear this."

"There's no need for them. If anybody moves away, there's always one left on the farm or a neighbor who can speak to their whereabouts."

"You're not far off."

She's thinking about the unfamiliar faces she routinely encountered in her apartment building elevator in New York when pea-sized raindrops start falling. A brisk wind blows the drops sideways in sheets. In no time, her head, sweater, and pants are soaked.

"Um, do you think Marty might be done with his cows by now?"

With wet hair stuck to his forehead, he gives her a teasing smile. "I imagine he is by now. Do you want to head back?"

She lets her feet do the talking.


Fiona has set the dinner table with a lace cloth and the good China. Crystal serving dishes hold baked potatoes and mixed peas and carrots. Kate spears the bloody slab of steak on her plate and swallows a bite. It goes down like savory butter. "My god, this is delicious."

Marty's grin expands his cheeks. "I gamble you don't find beef this fresh in New York."

"Kate's people are Irish, but she doesn't know which county they hail from."

After being asked this question several times, she's embarrassed by her ignorance.

Marty lays his fork and knife on his plate. "Jones isn't the family name then?"

"No. I'm divorced. My maiden name is Callahan."

"Is that right?" Marty's eyes dart to Fiona. He retrieves his fork and swallows a gravy-soaked piece of potato. "We had Callahans here in Ballycarrick."

Fiona's lowered chin telegraphs her wariness at this turn in the conversation.

Marty doesn't skip a beat. "What were your grandparents' full names if you don't mind saying?"

"Not at all. My grandfather was Michael, but I never met him. My grandmother, Ellen, lived with us until she died in her eighties. Her maiden name was Mitchell. That's all I know. Oh, and once, she told me her father, Paddy, I think that was his name, had an apothecary."

"So, it is." Marty nods at Fiona.

"Oh, my Lord."

Kate looks for help from Ryan, who's squinting at Marty.

"Aye. It's the same then," Marty says.

"What's the same?" Kate asks.

Marty's somber gaze shifts from Fiona to Ryan and then to her.

"Some Callahans lived just up the road. My parents knew them. I was around ten when it happened, but it came up many times after . . . considering it was such a . . ."

*Such a what*, she wonders, hanging on his every word.

Marty pats his thin layer of hair and takes his time. "The way I heard it, they had to leave Ballymore in a hurry after the Tans did their killing and set the town alight during the Terror. According to the ones who took their side, like my Uncle Oisin who hid them in his barn, Michael had the second sight, and that's how he knew to go rescue his sweetheart from the burning attic above her father's apothecary before the shooting started. A few didn't buy that story."

As Kate ogles Marty, he seems to grasp that she's not filling in the parts he's left out.

"This was during our war for independence."

"But why did they have to leave in such a hurry?"

Forks and knives rest on plates. The parakeet hops from its swing to the cage floor and back on the swing. Fiona sighs audibly.

"There was talk that Michael informed on a Volunteer, an O'Shea son it was—you went by their place to get here—and, in return, the Brits let him get his girl out of the Mitchell attic before they burned the building down. I don't know if it's true, but there were plenty who thought so."

With each new detail worse than the one before, Kate's forehead throbs.

"Nobody who lived in Ballymore back then ever forgot what happened on that night. I heard it in bits and pieces. How they dragged the O'Shea lad from Rathcroghan and shot him dead in front of his family. Paddy Mitchell killed defending the store. His pregnant wife, that would be your great-grandmother, took the younger children to Scotland, where she had family. Her boy, Finn, came back as a teenager and joined the IRA. Spent a long time in prison in England. People say he was never right after."

"Yes. I know about Finn Mitchell," she says.

"Are there still Callahans living around here?" Ryan asks.

"Their cottage is still standing. But the family scattered with the talk about Michael, since it put them at risk." Marty's face twists, seeming to show his disapproval.

"Would anyone care for a second helping?" Fiona asks, homing in on her husband. He nods and purses his lips.

"People here have long memories, but that doesn't mean they want to talk about those times and what they had to do to survive. That puts people like the two of you in a bind. Despite the fact you have a good reason for asking your questions. And I might have just muddied the waters."

She trades a glance with Ryan, whose jaw is locked in place.

Marty's eyes go to the ceiling, where they linger. When he speaks again, his tone has softened. "On the other side of the coin, there could be a good thing come out of it for you."

"I'm lost," Kate says.

"I'm sorry, dear. What I'm trying to say is, the way it's been, people think of you as a nosy outsider. But if you're one of us by blood, as you say, twice over, that's no longer the case, is it? Then we've got a fight in the family. You just need to make sure you're tough enough to hold up your end of it."

*Tough enough?* None of this feels real. Kate leans back, aware of the three of them waiting for her to say something.

"Are you all right?" Ryan asks.

She sets her knuckles on her thighs and presses down, taking small breaths through her nose. "Yes. It might take me a while to process all this, but thank you, Marty, for breaking it to me as gently as possible."

Fiona clears the table and brings out a lemon curd sponge cake with tea. Kate nibbles at hers while contending with waves of unfamiliar feelings.

She appreciates Fiona keeping an iron grip on the conversation over dessert, not allowing it to verge further afield than tomorrow's weather and Sophie's football season. When Fiona pulls out a Quinn family photo album to prove to Ryan that his daughter is the spitting image of her sister when she was in her teens, Kate bids them good night.

She crawls under the covers, relieved to be alone. Drained but wide awake, she tracks the crown molding on the ceiling and racks her brain for anything Gran may have said that might hold more meaning after what she's heard tonight. One word comes to mind. *Queenstown*. The name of the port of disembarkation on Gran and Michael's ship manifest. She learned it not from Gran, but from the database at the Ellis Island Museum, where Dad took them. Nothing else from Gran's lips—except her warning about Teague. *There's always a reason why it comes back when it does. There are generations waiting and watching.* Kate wonders what these emissaries might be trying to tell her. She can hardly believe she's asking the question. But she is.

Having discovered that she's literally walking on the same ground where her grandparents lived, loved, and fought off enemies for the first two decades of their lives, the notion of having ancestors loses its fairy-tale quality and becomes a physical sensation. A pull, seducing her like a newly made bed or fresh-baked bread. She pictures Ellen and Michael stepping out of the art deco frame on Gran's dresser and appearing in front of the Callahan cottage as if to greet her. But then the saccharine scene dissolves and leaves behind a scent of danger, as if she's entertaining another illicit desire, like missing Dad. Her grandparents vanish as suddenly as they appeared.

# The Bronx, New York
## 1950

Ellen took her wedding photo from its frame and ran her finger over its surface, as if by touch she could restore the bittersweet feelings she and Michael had embraced that day. Kneeling at the altar as two and rising to their feet forever bonded as one in the eyes of God. Walking down the aisle past empty pews where their families should have been sitting to share their joy. From Saint Bernadette's they went to a photographer's studio on the Bowery and had this portrait taken—the same image of them she'd seen in a waking dream when Michael walked into the apothecary that long ago day.

Thirty years later, she wasn't wishing she'd made other choices. Her sole regret was that she hadn't relished each day they had together. She put the photo back in its frame and set it on her dresser. She caught her wistful look in the mirror and cringed. Surely hers was a wish shared by other widows who'd outlived their husbands by an unreasonable number of years. And what good did it do any of them?

"Ma!" Jack yelled from the kitchen.

"Hold your horses."

Ellen sighed. On his wedding day, Michael was two years older than Jack on this day when he would graduate from one of the finest Jesuit high schools in New York. Michael would have beamed with pride for this son. She finished buttoning her blouse and saw a forty-nine-year-old woman whose hair contained more gray than chestnut brown and a face with sags and creases earned from hard work and worry. It was her job to make sure Jack felt Michael's pride in his absence.

Only to arrive in the kitchen and find Jack in his T-shirt, pacing, his red curls standing on end. The cap and gown she'd ironed were still hanging on the door with his good shirt.

"Why aren't you dressed? They'll be here any minute."

"We can't go. It's—"

"Nonsense! How dare you say such a thing. After all the Saint Bart's fathers have done for us. What's gotten into you?"

"I have a . . . bad feeling about it."

Ellen put her hand on the counter for support. They rarely spoke of such things anymore. "Just tell me, son."

He covered his face with his hands and slid to the floor. "I'm hearing a lady screaming. Tire skids. A terrible thud—"

A knock at the door stopped him. She met Jack's frantic eyes and made a decision she'd always regret.

"I hope to God it's just your nerves talking. Nothing more. But we're going. Now finish dressing. And comb that hair."

He squinted but said nothing as he took the gown and shirt off their hangers and went in the bathroom.

She opened the door to her eldest daughter.

"You wouldn't believe the traffic from Penn Station. Peter says it's the Yankee game." Annie kissed both her cheeks and looked over her shoulder. "Where's Jack?"

"He's combing his hair."

Her shy granddaughter, Clare, followed Anne and skirted Ellen's kiss.

"Granny," the younger one, Rita, squealed and leapt into her arms. Ellen let the child's high spirits lift her own.

"Did you enjoy the train ride?"

"I got Cracker Jacks!"

"Rita, get down, you'll mess up Granny's dress. We should wait downstairs. Peter's holding the cab."

Rita sat on Ellen's lap, with Annie, Clare, and Jack squeezed next to them in the back of the cab, with Peter up front. Maybe he told the cabbie they were in a big hurry, or the driver took it upon himself to speed on Grand Concourse. Ellen had been about to ask him to slow down when he made a sharp turn onto 192nd Street. It's possible Rita pulled the handle at that moment, but more likely her weight landed on it, causing the door to fly open and taking the poor child with it. The cabbie skidded to a stop. Annie screamed. The car behind them managed to swerve and miss the child but the next car did not. The thud was unmistakable. Little Rita lay silent under the car as the ambulance arrived. She died on the way to the hospital.

One of the many terrible images from that day that would haunt Ellen was Jack's face as he registered the horror of the thing he'd foreseen but hadn't been able to stop—because she hadn't let him. When Jack's first child was born, he told his mother he wanted to name her Rita. Ellen begged him not to, so they chose Meghan. When Meghan's mother drove into a tree, leaving Jack a widower and a single father while still in the police academy, Ellen couldn't shake the feeling that the curse had followed them anyway. She thought the same thing when Meghan, in her teens, became a magnet for trouble. It was her fault. Fate's way of punishing her for not honoring her boy's gift. She would never make that mistake again.

# 2002

After a quiet breakfast with Marty and Fiona, Ryan and Kate return to the place where the rain chased them home the day before and keep walking. An ambivalent sun peeks through a thick layer of gray. Kate slips off her windbreaker and ties it around her waist. Ryan says he wants to show her something, and she appreciates his not needing to fill the silence as they walk.

Fifteen minutes later, they reach a remote part of the neighborhood where abandoned cottages and ruins outnumber intact houses. In front of one such property, Ryan rests his hand on a low iron gate attached to a cinder block wall. Behind it, a narrow lot is overgrown with waist-high weeds. Farther back, a stone building is missing half its roof. "This is the old Callahan cottage."

"You mean . . ."

"The house where Michael Callahan lived with his family before he and Ellen left for America." He pushes open the gate. "Shall we?"

"Aren't we trespassing?"

"I may be. Arguably, you're not."

She pulls her shoulders up and back. "I'm not sure about that. But okay."

By the time they slice through the tall grass and arrive at the front door, oddly painted a fresh coat of green, her jeans are soggy. Both windows beside the door are shuttered and the walls are covered with ivy. In the back, a shutter hangs by a single hinge. Ryan nods at the window, as if to say she should look

185

first. She's still uneasy about being there but the desire to see inside wins out.

The stone is cold and damp to her touch. She pulls the broken shutter aside and stands on her toes to peer into a ten-by-twenty single room with sunlight streaming through the missing roof. There are stools by a giant hearth, a large cupboard, cobwebs, layers of dust and dirt. It's a stage set missing its cast, which, to her amazement, she promptly supplies: A young Ellen Mitchell sitting with Michael and his parents by the hearth, a pot steaming over a peat fire. Snippets of talk about a wedding, rebellion, America. Love and strife filling the room in equal measure.

She steps back and bumps into Ryan. He holds on to her elbow. "It's like they're still there," she says. She doesn't dare describe what she's just seen and heard, already sure she imagined it.

"You have a connection to them," he says, as if that explains her sudden ability to conjure people and conversations out of thin air.

That evening, Ryan parks on a block of dark shops in Ballycarrick. The sole lit sign is for Kenny's Pub. A sandwich board announces live music at 9:30 p.m. The pub is empty save for a young couple—the girl wears tight jeans and a sequined sweater with western boots, her partner has a cowboy hat—perhaps early arrivals for the music. Ryan carries two mugs of draught Guinness to a booth in the back.

"Your grandmother said nothing to you about why they emigrated?"

"Not a word. I have sketchy memories of she and Dad having tense conversations about the Troubles, but that's all."

Frustrated she can't retrieve any other clues about a conversation that may or may not have happened in her presence, she massages her temples, then stiffens.

"What is it?" he asks.

"If Teague is a third-generation descendant of Ballymore and he's on the schizophrenia spectrum, then he belongs in our study population."

"That's true."

"Don't you see the problem? If he's in it, I'm studying my own genes. It's a conflict."

Ryan puts down his mug. "Is that really the first thing you think about after all you've heard?"

"Why shouldn't it be?"

"Your link to our study subjects is unusual, but it's nothing we can't handle with anonymous interviews and DNA samples."

She averts her eyes and squirms, unable to find a comfortable position on the bench.

"You just found out you're in your ancestral home. Don't you find that extraordinary?"

Her shoulder blades meet the back of the booth. "I should be happy to hear about a scandal in a part of my family I knew nothing about?"

"Not necessarily." He furrows his brow and mirrors her move to the back of the booth.

She feels dizzy, as if looking out over the edge of a cliff. Her confusion spills out before she can stop it. "There were parts of Gran's life I knew not to ask her about. Nothing before she and Michael arrived in New York. Why they left Ireland. Or what happened to the rest of her family."

"Kate, I'm not criticizing you."

"To your Uncle Marty, my grandparents are just neighbors he heard stories about as a child. Then, in one sitting, he fills in these major gaps in their lives, things I never knew and wondered about. And then he accuses Michael of this terrible thing. I mean . . . I don't know. It's . . ."

"Go on."

"Gran's approval meant more to me than anyone else's because I never doubted her love for me, and I knew . . . or believed . . . she'd crossed an ocean to make a better life for us. Now I find out she had no choice."

"What does that change for you?"

The naysayer in her says it changes nothing. This is all ancient history; it has nothing to do with her. She's here to do a job and that's it. But that doesn't account for the weight on her chest. She must have held Gran's wedding portrait a dozen times—without asking a single question about their lives before or after they married.

Ryan clears his throat and she's almost surprised he's still there. The lack of judgment on his face allows her to spill more.

"Maybe the rumor about Michael isn't even true. But if this town hadn't expelled my grandparents, none of us would have been born. Not Dad, Meghan, me, or Teague. It's all . . ."

"Extraordinary?"

His awe is palpable. She wishes she could share it. "I'm sorry, but nothing I've learned this weekend makes me feel like I have any special claim to this place." A competing part of her argues the opposite, but those feelings are too unruly for her to handle, so she tamps them down.

His brow takes on lines as if he's studying a strange species.

"Maybe it's an American thing," she says. "Clearly, it's different for you. In fact, I envy the way you all just expect to belong to the ground under your feet. But I've never had that feeling anywhere, and I don't expect to." She falls back and crosses her arms.

He turns to his side as if he's studying the initials previous patrons have carved in the booth's side panel. She downs the rest of her Guinness and surveys the now-crowded bar. A three-person band is setting up in a front corner. The fiddler plucks strings with the fiddle to his ear. An accordionist expands and shrinks his instrument in his lap. A woman takes apart her wooden flute, blows air, and wipes it clean.

When she turns back to him, Ryan is observing her intently. "I see it's different for you," he says. "But that doesn't mean you're incapable or undeserving of the experience."

The same whiff of danger she felt when she let her private thoughts go too far down this road last night, and again moments ago, makes a return visit.

The fiddler picks up the mic and introduces his band mates, saving her from having to answer him. When the musicians pause to confer, she dives for safer ground, hating herself for doing it. "Shouldn't we plot our next moves for the study?"

Ryan squints at her as his Adam's apple moves up and down. "Aye. We should." In a duller voice, he tells her about Ronny, a former patient, who has agreed to speak on behalf of the clinic at the next council meeting. Ronny will talk about his depression, how it crushed him as a teenager, led to a suicide attempt, and the treatment that enabled him to go to college and take on a job as a junior banker in Dublin.

"That should help."

"It might."

The music gives them both an out. But when the first set is over, Ryan wastes no time picking up where they left off—before she changed the subject. As he leans in and makes intense eye contact, her chest tightens, and she tries to suppress her fear.

"There's something that occurred to me last night when Marty was talking about your great-grandfather, Paddy, the apothecary."

She hears *great-grandfather* and misses the rest of his sentence. "I'm sorry, what about Paddy?"

"You know the building Teague broke into?"

"Yes. The flat above the drugstore."

"They rebuilt Mitchell's Drugs on the same site where the apothecary burned down."

"Oh. My. God. The attic where Gran hid until Michael rescued her on the night of the attack is the same place Teague broke into two weeks ago?"

Ryan nods and puts his elbows on the table. "I wouldn't normally share this, but given the things going on, I better. In our last session, Teague filled in more details of what happened to him in the Mitchells' attic. He said he smelled smoke and became convinced there was a fire in the building. He told Nora Mitchell about it and repeated the same thing to Rafferty."

"I didn't know that. How bizarre." She pictures Teague cowering in the Mitchells' dark attic thinking the building was on fire. Then Gran in his place, eighty years earlier, in a real fire.

Ryan's worried expression pulls her back to the present. A clarity of purpose comes to her. She must do a better job of protecting Teague. And that means letting Ryan in on another secret.

"A long time ago, Gran told me that Teague had what she called second sight. He was five at the time. She described it as a gift he'd inherited from his Callahan lineage, including my grandfather, Michael, and my father, Jack. Apparently, they both had it. Gran warned me that as a bearer of this gift,

Teague would be vulnerable to dark forces. I wasn't sure what she meant by that. But since I found her whole premise implausible, I didn't think very hard about it."

"Go on."

"I only remembered our conversation after Teague's symptoms started getting worse last summer. It still made no sense to me. But now I'm beginning to think she may have been on to something. Maybe what's happening to him now is more than a progression of his schizo-affective disorder—if that's even the right diagnosis. Maybe Teague really did sense what Gran went through in that attic. And it led him up there. Would you call that second sight?"

Ryan nods. "Yes, I would have to call it that."

His quick assent tumbles her thoughts forward. "But why would he get that particular message?"

"I suspect Teague, maybe both of you, needed to hear it, or something else that it will lead you to."

She catches her breath. If Ryan is right, she's intrigued, but it also scares her. If he's wrong, she's just plain scared, since the prospect of not having an explanation for what's happening to Teague—and, as of yesterday with her vision at the Callahan cottage, her too—is even spookier. She vows to remove the guardrails from her usual thought process. Since Teague is at the center of these unexplained events, none of it is theoretical, and time is running out. He's already had a second psychotic break. That certainly fits Gran's warning about dark forces. She can't let him go over the cliff. At least she's not dealing with all this alone.

"Okay. I'll go there," she says, eliciting a slight smile from Ryan. "If second sight exists, and Teague has it, what's the link between his *gift* and his worsening symptoms?

Ryan nods. But instead of answering her, he studies his tented fingers.

"Ryan?"

"Aye." When he looks up, there's a new vulnerability in his eyes. "Your question leads to a larger mystery." He cocks his head to the side as if he's asking permission.

"Go ahead."

"With all the disadvantages schizophrenia conveys on the person who has it, including a lower reproductive rate and a higher rate of suicide, why has it held steady at one percent in our species since *Homo erectus* set out of Africa?"

"Don't tell me you're a closet evolutionary biologist?"

"It's more of a sideline."

"All right then, why hasn't schizophrenia gone the way of the woolly mammoth?" She can't believe she just asked that question, but the sparkle in his eyes seems to be disarming her.

"The theory that makes the most sense to me allows for the possibility that these voices and visions held value for the affected person's community."

"What sort of value?"

"Indigenous cultures had and still have shamans and medicine men whose visions are prophetic or healing for their tribes. These same figures are hiding in plain sight in Western traditions. Merlin was a Druid who advised King Arthur on matters of war and marriage. Pliny and Julius Caesar wrote of Druid priests who divined the right times for Celtic warriors to attack or retreat from their Roman enemies. We can walk five miles to Rathcroghan and stand on a Celtic sacred site."

"Wait. Are we discussing mental illness or religion?"

"Neither. I'm talking about divergent minds who perceive things the rest of us don't." He takes a breath. "The Celts called it second sight. In our profession, we throw it all under the label of psychosis. Or we assign patients different positions on a spectrum of abnormality." He stops talking and makes intense eye contact, as if he's waiting for her response.

The old Kate would have dismissed Ryan's line of thought as dangerous pseudoscience. But after three months in Ballymore, she's unable to do that. "I admit, it's intriguing. But I worry. Aren't you getting close to romanticizing mental illness?"

"I'm not saying every person with schizophrenia can turn on their higher perceptions at will and produce something of value. But if we want to know why it and other divergent mental states are still part of the human condition, we must consider the possibility that their unique perceptions have been adaptive at different points in human history. Why not again?" He sits back

191

and sighs. "Have I lost you?"

"Not entirely, but I am confused."

"Say more."

"What makes one hallucination good, or even, as you say, useful, and another one harmful? Teague broke into the Mitchells' attic because he was running away from an imaginary dog named Larry who was persecuting him. So how does a kid like Teague tell the difference between these voices?"

"I admit, It's trial and error. Voices can have negative, positive, or even neutral content. The more patients understand themselves, their own past trauma, even the ancestral wounds they carry, the easier it is for them to discern what they're hearing and seeing. I try to give them the tools they need to recognize when they're projecting or being paranoid."

"I think I get what you're saying."

"I've struggled with these questions for decades. I'm giving you my working theories, which I almost never share with colleagues."

"You are dragging me out of my comfort zone."

"Comfort zones have their place. As long as they don't become prisons."

She sucks in her cheeks and blows out air. Even if Ryan theory remains fuzzy to her ears, her relationship with Teague depends on her taking his experiences—and the meaning he gives them—seriously. Still, she can't help but run Ryan's analysis through the filter of her training. What exactly are these spectral things Teague sees and hears? From what part of his brain do they come? Unless . . . they originate in some other immaterial source? Or in a different time? She shudders at the distance she's allowed her thinking to drift from known knowns.

Ryan isn't done yet. "Most of my adolescent patients stick with treatment just to find a mate. But then they need to learn how to communicate with this other human being. And that becomes the work of therapy."

"Teague has made huge progress on that score. My mother said he never had kids over at home. Now he's got friends. Whatever you're doing, it's helping him. You're the Baryshnikov of adolescent therapists."

Ryan's cheeks flush as he runs both hands through his hair, which has grown longer since she first laid eyes on him at the Galway City train station.

"What is it?"

A hint of a smile. "The Irish don't wear praise lightly."

"Well, you'll just have to suffer because I'm not taking it back."

God, she's missed these nerdy discussions, which tend to happen spontaneously when two or more brain researchers gather in one place. However, she's never allowed herself to veer so far afield. Neither can she deny there's something more than intellectual stimulation going on between them. Apparently, she's not alone in this realization. After an electric moment of silent eye contact, Ryan rests his hand on hers. Their fingers nestle together easily on the table, as if it out of habit.

She leaves her hand there, picks up her beer with the other, and finishes it.

Ryan downs his and grabs both empty mugs. "How about another?"

"Please." She's light-headed as she watches him walk to the bar and fall into easy conversation with a gaggle of customers. She's startled to recognize one of them. Rafferty in plain clothes, drinking alone at the other end of the bar, his eyes on Ryan. Coincidence? Probably. Like she told Mom, it's a very small town.

Ryan returns with a smile on his face, and, for the moment, she's happy to release everything she can't put in a neat cubbyhole and let the music take her away. With her hands under her thighs, she feels supported by the bench and the man sitting opposite her. Gentleness is the quality that defines Ryan, but she's beginning to see more of the strength behind it. In fact, they're inextricable. It takes courage to let people see your softer side. She should know, since she rarely does it. This man seems to have no guile. He cares. Ferociously. Lucky her, it seems now she's one of the people he cares about. What would it be like to be with him? Her pulse speeds up. How long could she tolerate such naked caring?

# Rivervale, New York
## 1973

The conversation in the Callahan kitchen stopped as soon as Ellen's hand met the swing door. That, with the envelope stuffed with cash on the table and Shane visiting Jack at two in the morning, were enough to raise her maternal alarm bells.

"Don't mind me. Just heating a cuppa milk to help an old lady get to sleep."

"It's all right, Ma. Shane came by to drop off the donations for Belfast."

She took a carton of milk from the refrigerator, poured some in a pan, and turned on the burner. "How's little Shane . . . what is he now, two?"

"Just turned three," Shane answered. "Hasn't said a word. He's got Sheila worried."

"Tell her not to fret. He doesn't talk because he has two sisters ahead of him. Jack did the same thing." She sprinkled cocoa powder in the milk and stirred it.

"I didn't think of that. Well, it's time for me to head home."

"Tomorrow by noon." Jack said.

"See you then." Shane guzzled his beer and left by the kitchen door.

His tires kicked up gravel as he backed out the driveway. Ellen brought her steaming mug to the table, aware of Jack following her movements. She took a sip and nodded at the envelope on the counter. "Not hard to see what you two are up to."

"It's a good tally this month for the families."

"Jack, please don't take me for a fool. Shane doesn't drive over here at this hour for widows and children."

He kept his eyes on the envelope. "Ma. You're imagining problems that don't exist."

"What worries me more than what you're doing, is why you're doing it."

Jack's face reddened as his jaw clenched.

"It's clear as day you're trying to atone for something your father didn't do. That was a smear made against him by whoever did the informing. By carrying on like this, you're giving weight to the lie and dishonoring his memory."

"This has nothing to do with what happened back then. I'm doing what any decent man would do to help fight a just cause."

She lifted her hand. "You don't have to convince me who's right and wrong there. I've seen the injustice with my own eyes."

The resentment in Jack's firmly set jaw was all too familiar to her. She saw it as the natural byproduct of a boy coming of age without a father to show him how to separate rage that does him no good from the righteous anger he needs for his manhood.

She had to risk his wrath. "It'll be the guns that bring you down." It was like talking to a stone wall, the same impenetrable fortress she'd seen in the faces of her countrymen who'd made the choice Jack had. "It's always the guns," she added, though she knew he wasn't listening. Her desperation grew. "From here, it can look like a simple choice between good and evil. But when people have been fighting as long as they've been at it, some lose track of who the real enemy is. They turn on each other. And it won't just be you taking the risk. You'll put the whole family in danger."

The look on her boy's face took her breath away. It was as if she were his worst enemy. She saw his fingers tighten on the bottle, and sensed there would be no stopping the fury rising in him, nothing she could say or do. She kept her eyes open as he lifted it over his head and flung it against the wall behind her.

She made herself not flinch as the pieces spilled onto the floor.

A minute went by while each took stock of the other. Ellen's heart ached for him.

He covered his face with his hands and rocked back and forth on the stool. "I'm sorry, you know I'd never hurt you."

"I know that." As always, she forgave him too quick. Mothers and sons can never be sure where one starts and the other stops, although men don't seem to understand and are forever taking out their confusion about it on their wives and daughters.

"Ma, I know what I'm doing here. Please say nothing about this to Maureen."

"I've said my piece."

It's always the guns, Ellen thought, as she sat alone in her room later. Her heartbeat quickened as her thoughts slid fifty years back to the fighting she and Michael fled in Ballymore. They studiously followed news of the uprising that came to a head two years later with the creation of a republic made up of the island's lower twenty-six counties. They continued to watch, horrified, as differences over a treaty with the British spawned waves of violence that erupted into an even bloodier civil war.

After the Republic of Ireland became an independent free state in 1949, Ellen, like many in the world-wide Irish diaspora, held to the belief that the Irish dead—and by extension the living—would not rest in peace until the six counties to the north were reunited with the lower twenty-six under one flag. Her American son had even become one of their foot soldiers. The dead want what they want. Even an ocean away there was no denying them.

# 2002

When Kate steps out of Ryan's car on Sunday afternoon, it's as if her vision goes from black and white to color. The stringy yellow blossoms hanging from the witch hazel tree in the front yard sparkle against the whitewashed front wall. Mrs. Jolisk's flower boxes bloom with violet and pink pansies. Her neighbor calls down from an open window, "Kate. I brought Teague some of my *babcia* this morning. He told me it was the most delicious bread he ever ate. Such a handsome boy."

"Thank you. I hope he saved me a piece."

She opens her front door, and her mood is killed by the drabness of their living room. No color to speak of save the grotesque orange sofa she inherited. The sober Celtic cross Teague hung on the wall. "It's not religious, just cool," he'd assured her when she asked about it. The space cries out for a personal touch, evidence that she, Kate Jones . . . No, Kate Callahan, lives here. Bright pillows or a throw rug at the very least. Interior decoration is another skill she's never given its due.

"Teague, are you home?"

"In here."

On his bed a serving plate that's not hers is covered with crumbs. He's on the floor, head on a pillow, a book propped on his chest. "How were the cows?"

"They were brown and white and quite large. I see you didn't starve,

197

thanks to Mrs. . . ."

"Raff's mom makes awesome bread."

"I heard. Hey, there's something we need to do, and I thought now would be a good time. Are you game to walk to town?"

"I guess."

"Come on, I'll explain on the way."

They cross the M6 to Main Street.

"Where are we going?"

"We're paying a visit to Sean and Nora Mitchell."

He stops short on the sidewalk and looks at her pleadingly. "I'm not exactly their favorite person."

"I promised Rafferty we would thank them for not pressing charges. But there's another reason we need to see them."

He looks skeptical. "Like what?"

"Let's sit for a minute."

As they cross Old Town Square, Teague wonders if the ragged voices are still around. From their bench in the triangle park across from Saint Brendan's, he hears only murmurs, a word here and there, much calmer than last time. Maybe they're more chill because they've gotten to know him.

"I found out something pretty amazing from Ryan's Uncle Marty and I want to tell you about it."

"Oh yeah?"

"It turns out Ballymore is where Gran and Michael were born and lived until they left for America."

"No fucking way."

"That's what I thought at first. But it's true."

There's a major traffic jam in his brain. "I don't get it. Is that why we came here?"

"Absolutely not. I had no idea when I took this job that we had any family ties to this part of Ireland. The study is happening here for epidemiological reasons. It's a coincidence that Gran and Michael also came from this county."

"Yeah right."

"Call it a coincidence or not, there's a whole science of probability we could use to assess factors that would decrease or increase the odds of something like this happening. Factors like us having Irish ancestors and there being a history of mental illness in our first-degree relatives." He rolls his eyes. "Which happens to be the subject of my research—"

"Okay, okay. So, if Gran and Michael came from here, does that mean we have relatives here?"

"Ryan's Uncle Marty didn't know of any Callahans in Ballymore, although I saw their old cottage. It's on the same road as the Quinn dairy, very run-down and abandoned. But there are some of Gran's family, the Mitchells, still living here. They own the drugstore that used to belong to Gran's father, Paddy."

"Those people? I heard about a Paddy Mitchell from Sean, the chemist! Whoa, so that Paddy was my...?"

"Great-great-grandfather. And that's why we're going to see Sean and Nora."

Teague feels a little spooked being back at the Mitchells' front door. The same door he broke into before he passed out in their attic. Kate rings a bell and Sean comes down the stairs. "Hello," he says, looking at Kate quizzically. "What can I do for you?"

"I think you've met my nephew, Teague."

Sean does a double take. "I sure have."

"Hi." What if Sean tells Kate about the stuff he stole? Or tried to steal. Why did he agree to come here?

"Can we come in and speak with you . . . and your mother?"

"What is this about?"

"Teague owes you an apology and we wanted to deliver it in person."

"All right, then. Let's go upstairs."

They enter the apartment through the door he skipped last time. It's an old-fashioned living room with high ceilings and antique-y furniture. "I'll let Mom know we have visitors. Please sit."

Nora comes in the room with a *what the hell are you people doing in my house* look on her face. They sit and Nora rocks in her chair, staring at Teague.

"You're the boy in my attic."

"That's one reason why we've come," Kate says.

"I'm sorry about breaking in and scaring you like that."

"You sure did," Nora huffs.

No one talks and his skin itches all over.

"We're grateful you didn't press charges. You can rest assured that Teague learned his lesson."

She didn't have to say that, like he's eight years old. Whatever. Let's just get this part over with, Teague thinks.

Sean clears his throat. "We had no reason to go any further with it after the gardai' got him out of the attic." He levels a nasty look at Teague, which he figures also covers his shoplifting.

Kate, too, hopes they've made sufficient apologies to be able to move on. "Thank you for understanding, Sean." She's groveling and tongue-tied. Sean is probably in his sixties, which would make Nora close to ninety, give or take. It's not clear how mentally sharp she is. The woman keeps her cards close. *If they throw us out, it'll be no big loss.* She didn't even know they had any relatives in the county before yesterday.

"There's more," she says and waits several seconds until she feels calmer. Both Mitchells are staring at her intently. "My grandmother, Teague's great-grandmother, was Ellen Mitchell. Paddy's daughter. Which I believe means we're related."

Sean and his mother trade a look of surprise; Nora's is tinged with alarm. Sean leans back in his chair. "Is that why you've come to stay in Ballymore?"

"No, I was hired to work on a study at the Ballymore Mental Health Clinic. I only found out that my grandparents emigrated from here in the last few days. Dr. Quinn's uncle, Marty, told me the story of the British attack that killed Paddy and burned down the apothecary. Gran never mentioned it and—"

"Then Michael Callahan is your grandfather?" Nora's voice is icy, her eyes piercing as she looks from Kate to Teague and back at Kate.

"Yes, although I never met him. He died young—"

"I know. Killian told me about him drowning." Nora again.

"Paddy was my father Killian's brother," Sean explains.

Teague has taken it upon himself to get up and peruse the framed photos lining the mantle. He takes one down and brings it to Nora. "Who's this?"

She takes eyeglasses from her sweater pocket and props them on her nose. "That's Paddy and Ellen in the old shop." Teague's mouth drops open. He brings the photo to Kate with a wide grin.

"It's Gran all right, younger than I've ever seen her in a photo." In fuzzy black and white, she's standing behind a counter with a man that Kate gathers is her father, Paddy. "What year would this have been taken?"

"That would have been around nineteen seventeen or eighteen," Sean says after getting up to look. "Right, Mom?"

"I suppose." Nora's face is clouded. She looks down into her lap. "Paddy's wife took the young'uns and cleared out after the attack. Killian was the only Mitchell able to rebuild the store. He gave up his RIC to do it." She shakes her head. "Nobody treated him right."

"I'm sorry to bring up a sad memory."

Teague's gaze bounces between them. To Sean he says, "Are you related to Finn Mitchell?"

Sean ignores the question and addresses Kate. "The way we heard it, my father was doing his duty as a constable when Michael Callahan told him where to find one of Volunteers who did the ambush."

In the awkward silence that follows, Kate uneasily digests the fact that Sean and Nora believe Michael revealed the O'Shea boy's location to Killian Mitchell, and, by doing so, became a collaborator, resulting in the boy's execution. Since hearing the story forty-eight hours ago, she's been clinging to the possibility that the gossip about Michael was unfounded. But then Sean and Nora would have heard it from the horse's mouth, their father and husband, respectively. Her enthusiasm about this reunion is dampening.

"Uncle Paddy and my father took different sides in the war for independence," Sean says. "That happened a fair amount back then. It still brings up hard feelings."

"I'm just beginning to understand."

"I never knew Paddy's boy, Finn," Nora adds. "He came back and took what wasn't his." She makes the target of her grudge clear by the firm set in her jaw. Kate is thankful it's Finn and not them.

She recalls Ryan telling her that the downtown Mitchells weren't on speaking terms with Finn although he didn't know why. It appears she may have stumbled on the reason. How strange. It's as if these things happened yesterday. Not eighty years ago. It's hard to keep track of who did what to whom, with each side of the family having its own legacy of lives cut short, betrayal, and stolen property—with right and wrong changing depending on who's telling the story. Only then does it dawn on her that if the ex-IRA hero, current Chief Druid Finn Mitchell is a younger brother of Gran's—one she may not even have known about but a sibling nonetheless—that makes Finn Kate's Grand Uncle. How bizarre.

"We never knew him, though we heard he was quite the Fenian." Sean looks at his mother, who nods.

To Kate he says, "By my reckoning, you and I are second cousins, once removed."

"That sounds right." Kate feels drained and unsure of their welcome after all that's been revealed. "Well, we should go. Thanks for seeing us. I hope we can do it again. I mean, if you'd like."

"That would be grand," he says, surprising her on their way out.

This parrying with ghosts isn't over yet, she thinks wearily as they retrace their steps up Main Street. She's reminded of Marty's *if you're tough enough to hold up your end of it* comment. How much more of this will there be? She shivers at the thought of more scenes like tonight's.

"How about Italian?" she asks Teague when they reach Old Town Square. A lit sign in front of the Bank of Ireland points to Mateo's Brasserie in the rear alley.

"Sure."

They're the first to be seated for dinner.

"That was weird," he says after they order. His eyes are open wide, his expression more vulnerable than he usually allows.

"Yes. It was quite a roller coaster. What struck you the most?"

"It's like everyone around here knows everything about everybody else but they all act like they've got these big secrets. Then if you spill the beans and say what's true, they get mad at you."

She laughs. "I know it can feel that way. But I don't think Sean and Nora were mad at you. Well, maybe Nora was." She pauses to make sure he doesn't look worried, relieved that he seems more intrigued than upset. "A lot of this history is still very painful for them. Then the Troubles rubbed salt in their old wounds. It's just easier not to bring it up."

"That works fine when you know what you're not talking about. But then we come along and screw up their game."

"You're right. That's exactly what we've done. But I don't see any other option, now that the cat's out of the bag. Do you?"

"Nope. It's too late now." His grin is classic wiser than his years Teague.

# Rivervale, New York
## 1974

Ellen's soap opera drowned out the officers coming and going. Neither did she hear Maureen's cries until her daughter-in-law stood at her bedroom door, choking back sobs.

"It's Jack!"

"Sit." She got to her feet and led Maureen to her easy chair. She didn't need to hear any more to understand the worst had happened. With one hand on the bedpost, the other on Maureen's shoulder, she squelched the urge to scream.

"It was four in the morning . . . This morning . . ." Maureen's voice was a creaky fan as she parroted the official story, more to convince herself, Ellen suspected, than to share it. "They stopped for coffee. Shane stayed in the car . . . Jack went in . . . two punks . . . shots to his face and chest."

Still, each new detail struck Ellen with the force of a fist. She wished she could have covered her ears. Maureen's gruesome litany ended when her sobs returned in force. Ellen took refuge on the bed and waited.

When Maureen looked up, her face and the crisp white collar of her nurse uniform were blackened from the streams of mascara down her cheeks. Ellen had never seen Maureen do more than shed silent tears. Not even at her mother's funeral had she made a sound. She'd always been the sensible

204

counterweight to Jack's volatility. The poor dear would need all her strength now.

"How am I going to tell the kids?"

"Tell them straight. Their daddy is a hero."

Maureen nodded and took a breath as if she'd just reclaimed the part of her that knew what was expected of an NYPD wife at a time like this. She was, after all, also a cop's daughter.

At the window, Ellen watched Maureen back her car out of the driveway, flinching as she pictured the moment when Meghan and Katy heard the terrible news. She gripped the windowsill and eyed the things in this room she could call her own. The maple bed and dresser the Murphys had let her keep when her time as their housekeeper had ended. The bedspread she'd crocheted before arthritis stole that simple pleasure from her. The white plastic portable TV Jack had bought, its antennae flopping in opposite directions. The frayed, braided rug where he'd played with his toy soldiers.

Another scream rose to her throat and died there. Through watery eyes, she saw Michael, dressed for the railroad in a long-sleeve blue cloth shirt, heavy trousers with suspenders, a red-checked bandana tied around his neck, his brow already lined with sweat at dawn. She'd lifted his lunch pail and, for a few seconds, each of them had kept a hand on it. If she keeps coughing, buy another bottle of the medicine. I get my pay next week, he said, before he left apartment 5E. She'd been too afraid for Annie to sense the danger Michael faced on that trip. Not that she could have prevented it. With certain things, only the timing kept you guessing. Or was that just how it looked four decades later?

She couldn't have imagined a worse pain than she'd felt after losing Michael. Now she knew better. For a woman to survive her child, no matter their age or yours, any comparison was a travesty.

She fell on the bed and clutched the spread, girding herself. Were there people capable of meeting each new loss in their lives with a clean slate? She was not one of them. In fact, she'd softened. Her sorrows had been soothed by Delia's friendship, then Jack's ascension in the NYPD and the seventeen years she'd shared this house with him and Maureen and the grandchildren, who still brightened her every day. Only to come to this.

Her head weighed too much to lift from the bed. Every breath had become a chore. Through the curtains, she saw the remains of this terrible day hurtling toward nightfall. The hiss of the radiator mocked her as a chill seized her body. She should have been at death's door to welcome her boy. Her survival struck her as a disgrace. She reviewed her options: a fall down the stairs, the bottle of sleeping pills in her drawer, the five o'clock commuter train, Jack's off-duty revolver in the garage. She pictured and discarded each method. Who would find her? Would Brigid forgive her selfishness? She dodged each question, knowing if she gave any their due, the part of her that had survived the last six decades would reassert its will and put this weak imposter to shame. She buried her face and withdrew from life as much as any physical body could manage on its own.

She was twelve or thirteen, working alongside Da, when a young farmer brought in his wife for healing. She'd been bedridden for over a month with fever and a rasping cough. The farmer feared it might be TB. His mother blamed her daughter-in-law's depleted state on simple carelessness. By forgetting to put a pail of clean water outside their door at night for the banshees to wash their babies, she'd insulted them, leaving the family no choice but to put her out on the bog to face fairy justice.

Da told him the fae operated in a different sphere than he and other healers did, but their purpose was often the same. The way Da saw it, he was there to help people retrieve pieces of themselves they'd lost. The medicine he gave the man's wife came from a seaweed called carrageen . . . known to the world as Irish moss . . . Ellen helped him harvest it the previous summer. Da told the farmer's wife that the seaweed would help her fend off the TB and regain her strength if she was willing to do her part and set the intention to mend her body and mind. The next time Ellen saw the woman, she was in the store buying castor oil for her mother-in-law's constipation, looking much like her old self.

Like the farmer's wife, Ellen faced a choice. If she elected to finish this life, she had to let the grief nipping at her heels take possession of her body and soul. The weight of too many insufficiently mourned losses made the choice much harder. Fear kept her face buried in the covers until a firm pressure came to rest on her shoulder as a briny odor filled the room. Da had opened a channel for her to do what needed to be done in a place she knew well. His presence gave her the strength to make the journey.

When her feet sank into fine wet sand, she knew she was home. Her eyes opened to take in every shade of green, gray, and blue in the patchwork of grasses and boulders lining the sloping mountain above Trá an Dóilin beach. Salt and brine rode the cool breeze and filled her lungs, opening and cleansing her airways in a way she'd forgotten. She stood in the cove they traveled to each August to collect the red-bodied seaweed, known as Carrageen Moss, that flowered like peony on the rocks lining the intertidal shore.

Da sat at a distance as she waded into a shallow pool and squatted among the rocks. A wave grabbed her from behind and carried her away from shore. She thrashed and gasped for air and the roaring riptide laughed, reminding her that she'd surrendered her will for good cause. She stopped fighting and gave herself over to the force of the ocean.

Down was up and up was down as she tumbled in the waves. Rocks on the seafloor gouged her thighs, rib cage, and shoulders. Salt entered her open wounds, leaving behind a sting that reverberated like the swells of a harp . . . short, hard, metallic, clear, rushing, drifting, flowing, blurred, crystalline, faint . . . removing dead tissue and purging her grief. Her old sorrows melded with the fresh cuts on her body; forming an unwieldy burden she gave over to the sea. Raw and cleansed, she turned on her stomach and let the next wave carry her, like a seal, back to shore. She slept on the sand, her body covered with seaweed.

She woke in her maple-frame bed. A shallow breath brought a stinging memory of her fresh-torn skin. On the exhale she felt lighter—relieved to have chosen.

She heard Maureen's car pulling in the driveway, doors opening and closing, footsteps on the stairs. At her dresser, she opened the top drawer to fetch her hairpins and gasped. Jack's pendant lay neatly in its coiled chain.

How could it have gotten there? She took it out and gripped it tightly in her palm.

Forty-five years ago, the medical examiner had delivered the pendant on its chain along with Michael's clothes, wallet, and wedding band. On Jack's twelfth birthday, she passed it on to him and, as far as she knew, he hadn't taken it off since. Why was it in her drawer? He would have had to put it there in the last twenty-four hours. She heard her granddaughter's cries from the next room and moved the pendant to the wooden box where she kept her letters.

In the hall, she knocked. "Katy Bird, can I come in?"

The crying stopped and Katy opened the door. Clumps of soaked curly hair stuck to her freckled cheeks. Her small frame shook as another cry fought its way up. Ellen wrapped her in her arms and brought her to the bed, where she stroked her hair and held her close.

"There, there. A terrible thing happened to your daddy. There's no shame in crying."

As Katy's sobs erupted in fits and starts, Ellen closed her eyes and asked Michael to come. It had been years since she'd called on him. She feared he was long gone, or she'd lost the ability to hear him. Now she wanted his reassurance that he'd would be there to welcome their son, Jack to the afterlife.

While Ellen waited for Michael to make his presence known, Katy pulled her limbs free and stood up. "I'm going to climb my tree now," she said, referring to the tall birch tree in their back yard.

"That's a good idea, Katy Bird." Ellen stayed where she was, sitting on her granddaughter's bunk bed, with her eyes closed. She sat for several minutes, emptying her mind, silently calling Michael. When the old sensations started, the heaviness in her forehead, a slight dizziness, she felt hopeful. Then he spoke.

*I'm here love. I bear witness to the pain you and our granddaughter feel today. Know that your suffering has a purpose. You've done everything asked of you. But you're not finished yet. Another gifted male child will be born in your eightieth year. His burden will be much heavier than mine or Jack's because his times will be even more fearful of those who perceive light and darkness with no filters. If you teach him like you did Jack, he'll come of age with his power strong and clear enough to complete the healing of our lineage from the future. Then each of us will have made good on the agreements we took on when we chose our bodies. And you can come home to me.*

Ellen heard Michael's voice clearly, as if he'd been in the room speaking to her, yet his message baffled her. Why hadn't he reassured her that he'd been the one to greet his son in the next world? She took deep breaths as she replayed Michael's words. Just when she'd been sure she'd failed Jack as a mother, Michael told her she should do the same with another gifted child of their blood still to be born. Wearier than ever, she picked herself up and went downstairs to help Maureen with dinner.

# 2002

Teague and Kiernan hitch a ride to the grove with a guy from Denny's crew who's going early to help set up for Samhain. When they arrive, Kiernan goes with him to build the bonfire. Teague asks Morgan where he can find Finn and she directs him to the barn.

He cracks open the door and hears Finn's voice: "You had no business taking it out of here."

"Like I told you, I was just cleaning it." That's Liam.

"It's not yours to clean."

"I'm tired of you treating me like a thick boyo."

"Only when you need to be put in your place."

"Fuck this shite."

"We'll do more target practice after Samhain."

"I could give a wit."

Teague backs away as Liam pushes the barn door open. "Hey," he says to Liam, feeling awkward, like he shouldn't be there.

Liam scowls and brushes past him.

Teague enters the barn and catches a glimpse of Finn putting the rifle in a mounted case. Finn cocks his head to acknowledge his presence but neither of them speak as he moves away from the gun case and fills a pail with water, pouring it into a trough. A cow lumbers over to drink and Finn moves to the next pen. Teague sits on a bale of hay.

"How are you, lad?"

"Okay, I guess."

"That's doesn't sound very convincing."

Teague had planned to tell Finn what was bothering him but now he's chickening out. The part of him that's sure of their connection is nowhere to be found.

"You know one of my jobs as chief of this grove is to listen to peoples' problems and help them find their paths. You're no different. But it's up to you."

"Yeah. Well. A bad thing happened."

Finn drops the pail and leans against a post. "Tell me more."

"An old enemy of mine found me over here and got me in trouble."

"What does this fellow do or say to you?"

"He acts like he owns me. He's always trash-talking me. He tells me to steal stuff. And scares me half to death."

"I see." Finn drops his head back and rubs his hands over his face. "Have you had others bother you like that?"

"I did back home. One told me my brain was broken and I might as well off myself."

Finn sniffs and puts both hands in the air as if to say *stop*. "First of all, these are not your friends. Liam and I are not of the same mind about how best to handle this type of threat." He blows out air and walks closer. Then he leans down until he's at Teague's eye level. "Lad, I'm going to give it to you straight. The way you and I are different from other people gives us advantages, but we can also screw up worse. That's why we need to be careful not to let our enemies in too close because they can turn us into people we don't want to be."

"How do we stop that from happening?"

"That's where it gets tricky. When we try to outrun them or, in my case, drown our sorrows with drink, it's like giving them a free pass. The same goes for your cannabis."

"Do you hear voices like mine?"

"I used to. So I know what it's like. If you ever hear a voice telling you to hurt yourself, I want you to come to me, or Ryan, or that aunt of yours. Don't try to handle it on your own. Because you can't. Not yet. Is that a deal?"

"Yeah."

He sighs. "If you decide you want to practice the Druid ways, there are things we can teach you that will make you stronger."

"I want to learn them."

"Good, it's settled. I have more work to do in here. Why don't you go catch up with Liam."

When he doesn't find Liam in the house, Teague goes to the field where Denny is putting the final touches on the bonfire and Joe and Kiernan are hanging the Ballymore grove flag over the pit. Nobody has seen Liam.

"We start drumming at nine sharp," Denny says. "That gives you a half hour."

"I'll be there." Except he still needs to get his robe from Morgan and put on paint, then retrieve his drum from the music closet. He breaks into a run and heads for the lower ridge.

"You can't stand the sight of me? Well, I feckin hate you more."

Whoa. From Teague's hiding place behind a tree, Liam looks like he's fighting an invisible opponent. Yelling. Punching the air. He falls to the ground and rolls over. On his knees, he crawls, looking this way and that. "You stay away from what's mine."

Teague's stomach is twisting from the weirdness of what he's seeing and hearing. He steps out from behind the tree and stands in full view no more than fifteen feet from Liam, but it's as if Liam doesn't see him.

Liam backs up and drops to his knees, hiding his head in his arms. Teague feels like a mean god watching Liam suffer, not lifting a finger to help. But he knows when he's hallucinating and someone asks what's wrong, it sends him deeper into it. Like that time Kate found him hiding in the closet and he had to send out a different Teague to tell her he was fine. Liam told the guys at their last Mad Pride meeting that he's got his voices under control. Obviously, that was a big fat lie.

What's that gurgling sound? Teague can hardly believe it. Liam is lying on his side, bawling like a little kid. "I wanna die." Liam coughs and cries at the same time.

This sucks so bad. Teague can't watch any more. He moves back up the ridge and sits on a log. He doesn't want to leave Liam alone but neither does he have a clue what to do to help him.

It's been quiet for a few minutes when the smell of weed reaches him. He stands and spots Liam leaning against a tree, smoking a joint. Shit. Something bad is going to happen. Teague knows it like he knows his own name. If only he could stop the movie playing in his head. Super bright lights. Screams, a siren. A trail of blood on a white cloth turning black. His pendant on the ground. What's he supposed to do? Rat on Liam? And say what? It's like the two of them are on a runaway train and there's nothing he can do to stop it. He runs back up the hill towards the pit at top speed.

## 2002

Rafferty steps aside as Kate sticks her head out the door to look up and
down the street for Teague.

"He should be back any minute. I gave him money for a Halloween
costume, but that was hours ago."

Rafferty wipes his feet on the mat and removes his cap as he enters. She's
embarrassed to greet him in grungy sweats.

He settles on the sofa. "It's you I need to talk to."

"Oh." She takes the armchair. "Is this about the hack?"

"No. I'm here on another matter." He pulls out his pad. "If you recall,
when we exchanged pleasantries after our first interview, you mentioned your
father's police service and his death in the line of duty, and I told you I had an
uncle retired from the Forty-Sixth Precinct."

"Yes. I remember." She scooches back in the chair as a feeling of dread
comes over her.

"The uncle I mentioned to you, Kevin Rafferty, gave me contradictory
information about what you and I talked about. If you'll permit me, I'd like to
go over it again."

"I don't understand. Why would something that happened in New York
in the seventies concern you here in Ireland, in 2002?"

"It may have bearing on a local case we're investigating."

"You've lost me."

"Kate. What do you remember about your father's death?"

Shock at his question puts her in a noiseless vacuum. She wishes she could stay there. She hears the ticking clock in the bathroom and Mrs. Jolisk calling her son for dinner, "*Pornala callacia!*" Rafferty's gaze has a bellicose quality she hadn't noticed before.

"I'm sorry for the question," he says, but he doesn't take it back.

"What do I remember? I was eight years old. My mother decided I shouldn't go to the funeral. My half-sister Meghan, who was thirteen, went with Mom, and my grandmother stayed home with me."

She doesn't mention Mom telling Gran that Dad's coffin would be closed because of the "condition of his body." Or that she declined the Pipes and Drums because she didn't want the fuss. Rafferty seems to be watching for her every twitch. Trying to discern whether she's telling the truth. Why on earth would she lie about this?

"We have reason to suspect there wasn't a body."

She snaps her shoulders back and takes a full minute to answer. "Why would you say that?"

Frown lines skew his face. "Kevin found several irregularities in the case file."

She swallows the bile in her throat. "I'm sure you're about to tell me what they were."

"If you'll permit me." He glances at his pad. "They filed his death as an unsolved case less than a month after it happened. A detailed medical examiner's report was missing. Only his top-line conclusions were in the file. And the funeral home was a known mafia-controlled business, later exposed as receiving payoffs from certain parties in your father's precinct."

Her hand goes to her neck to scratch it but the itch spreads to her chest and belly. "What are you…" She can't get the question out. He doesn't seem to need it.

"An old-timer in the Forty-Sixth told Kevin he suspected the missing pieces in your father's file had to do with a federal indictment for IRA gunrunning that was under seal at the time. The precinct kept it very close and never let it go to internal affairs. Bits leaked out after they charged his partner, Shane Geraghty, with shipping illegal weapons and as an accessory to attempted murder."

She flashes on kind, gregarious Uncle Shane, who would come by the house in uniform most afternoons to drive in with Dad for their swing shift. On weekends he came in Bermuda shorts with his wife and kids. "The attempted murder of who?"

"A longshoreman who flipped in the gunrunning investigation suffered a serious injury in a suspicious accident before Geraghty's trial."

She gets up and clutches the back of the chair. "I'm not listening to any more of this." Thoughts rush in faster than she can dispense with them. "Even if what you're saying is true, which I don't believe for a second, why are you telling me?"

"We think Jack Callahan may have come to Ireland after he faked his death."

*Faked his death.* Rafferty's expression is placid.

"As I told you, there's another case that might connect to him, or his new identity."

Is this related to her conversation with Marty Quinn? She didn't ask him to keep it confidential only because she didn't think she had to. Rafferty's stare feels like a blow torch on her. "Are you saying this because you heard through the grapevine that my grandparents are from here? I learned that exactly a week ago."

"Kate, I've known about your grandparents' connection to Ballymore for over a month. All I need to know from you is whether you've been in contact with your father?"

She scoffs and takes a step backward. "You mean my dead father? No, I haven't." Her body goes rigid. She takes a rickety breath and forces herself to circle the chair and sit down. His shiny black boots reflect the light of the ceiling lamp.

"I'm sorry I've upset you. But there's an open case."

She clenches her jaw and lifts her head to meet his gaze. "And what about this case links it to . . . my family?"

Rafferty clasps his hands together and studies them. When he lifts his head, a feeling of dread envelopes her.

"The Sligo gardai' have asked for our assistance on an investigation into the death by poison of a local spiritual leader. The case has turned into a murder investigation, with Finn Mitchell as a suspect."

She drops her chin and rotates her head while trying to tamp down her panic. She crosses her arms. "When you speak about this murder victim being a *spiritual leader*, I take it you don't mean he was a member of the clergy?"

"No, ma'am. Like Finn, he called himself a Druid."

Rafferty puts his pad in a jacket pocket and stands. "Why don't you think about what I've told you and call me if you'd like to talk again." He hands her a card. "I'll be back in touch if I receive more information."

Kneeling on all fours in her bed, she beats the mattress with balled fists until her arms ache and she's out of breath. It's not true. Rafferty is just a bad cop covering his ass. It doesn't take long for cracks to appear in her wall of certainty . . . The medical examiner's report was missing . . . I have reason to suspect . . . a mafia-controlled business.

What if Dad had no choice? What if a long prison sentence was his alternative? No. No. No. She goes back to pounding the bed. When her energy is spent, the sheet is soaked with sweat and tears. Ordinary noises: Mrs. Jolisk's vacuum cleaner, erratic grunts from water pipes—sound ominous. She touches her cheek, startled to feel warm, damp flesh. The surprise not that her skin is wet but that it belongs to her. She pulls the sheet and bedspread over her head and pleads for mercy and time.

Leaving her body behind, she slips into an in-between state, not fully awake or asleep, and enters a chapel. Like her, the chapel is suspended in space. She discovered her ability to go there as a child when she missed her father more than she could bear. In this private purgatory, she transformed the act of waiting for him into a devotional ritual.

Now the little girl she once was lays on her usual pew, surrounded by fourteen stained-glass windows representing the stations of the cross. The windows hang in rectangles of space where walls should be. A Latin chant thrums, voiced by an unseen chorus. She contorts her body and stretches her neck to study each station. Her purpose is to put herself in each scene—to bear witness.

At the tenth station she's distressed by the Romans making him take off his clothes before nailing him up on the cross. That was mean of them.

Some relief comes at the fourteenth station, where Jesus's body is taken down so the women can anoint him with aloe and myrrh, then cover his battered body with linens.

Her favorite teacher, Sister Evangeline, appears at the end of the pew and reminds her that dying in that awful way was what Jesus had been born to do, the act itself a prophecy fulfilled. His reward, Sister explains, was to leave earth and reunite with his father, who happened to be God. In that way, Jesus could become whole again. Kate has heard the lines hundreds of times before.

This is wrong. Instead of telling her to pray hard and then she, too, can leave and go to heaven where her father will be waiting, the Sister just sighs and turns toward the altar.

"Sister Evangeline? Sister?" the girl pleads. Sister's lips move again but only to chant.

From her bed, the chapel and the girl appear far away. She feels stings in her arms and legs, like being pricked with needles. She rolls onto her back, opens her eyes, quickly closing them, grasping for the pew.

A long car horn, followed by three short honks, creates interference. Damn it!

"Hang on, you eejit, I'm coming." Mrs. Jolisk's son. Footfalls thud down the stairs. Car doors slam.

Kate uses all her will to return to the chapel, where fragments of the dream linger long enough for her to see the girl's face is contorted, her cheeks wet and blotchy. She knows the cause of her distress. Just as she understood Sister Evangeline's silence. But that doesn't mean she's ready to let go of the old desire. Her dream to go and be with him. She wouldn't be Kate without it. She and the girl are still of one mind on this.

A sharp pain in her groin brings her back to her bedroom, in 2002, in Ireland. Her head spins as she pulls herself up to a sitting position. Deep breaths slowly dull the pain in her lower torso. She puts her feet flat on the floor and straightens her spine, breathing slowly in and out until no trace of the girl or the chapel remain.

She stands and waits for balance to return and walks into the hallway.

"Teague! Are you here?" Her voice is strained and scratchy.

In Teague's room, there's no sign he's been back. Sitting on his bed, she collects her thoughts. He was excited about going into town to buy a costume. He and Kiernan had plans to meet up later for Halloween.

In the kitchen, she pours a glass of cranberry juice, and spots an orange flyer under the table. "All Are Welcome at the Ballymore Grove for a Samhain Eve Ceremony," it says, with the date and time, October 30 at 9:00 p.m. Tonight. There's a drawing of a people dressed in robes standing in a circle around a bonfire. Teague and Kiernan must already be there or on their way.

As she sits and drinks the juice, Rafferty's claim echoes in her ears. *We have reason to suspect there was no body.* She pictures her mother dressed in the pleated black dress with a cinched belt she wore to Dad's funeral. "It's better this way," she said to Kate and Gran on the sofa, as she put on lipstick in front of the hall mirror. Meghan, who was waiting in the car, had just honked the horn. Mom yelled through the screen door that she was coming.

The only other thing Kate remembers from that day and night is the ache that tore through her belly as she lay sleepless on the top bunk while voices of mourners filtered up from the living room. It was as if a Swiss Army knife had flipped open in her gut. Her remedy back then had been to wait until they left and sneak into the kitchen where she grabbed several slices of Wonder Bread. With the crust trimmed off, she rolled each slice into a ball and swallowed it whole, savoring the sweetness as it slid down her throat. She repeated the process with a second and third slice and waited for sleep to take over. Between the ages of eight and thirteen, she gained ten extra pounds because of her secret night eating. Her mother ribbed her about it. Now, she drops her head over her knees and breathes into her belly. It's like her experience of loss has its own language—with her gut as its designated spokesperson.

She bolts upright in the chair. Why not call Mom right now and ask her what she thinks? She puts her hand on the receiver, then removes it. Maureen Callahan knowing anything about something this illegal is beyond the pale. Or is it?

"I still feel bad about not reaching out to Sheila after . . . what happened to you," she heard Mom say to a man standing with them at Gran's burial in the Bronx. He was in his fifties and wore a flat cap.

"Kate, you remember Dad's partner, Shane."

"Yes. Of course," she said, although she barely recognized him.

"Katy, you're grown up," Shane said. He kissed her cheek and looked at the ground before turning back to Mom. "You shouldn't worry, Maureen. You had your own problems. Ellen's letters were a big comfort to me."

Mom seemed startled. "She wrote to you?"

A broad smile lit up Shane's face. "That she did. She'd come up with things Jack and I did back in high school. Remind me of the old days." His features collapsed and he looked at the ground. "It's all behind us now." Shane tipped his cap before walking away. "Take care, both of you."

"What was that about?" Kate asked her mother.

"Just some foolish business Shane got himself mixed up with." After meeting Kate's eyes, she added, "Your father had nothing to do with it, thank God."

Kate waited, openmouthed, for more.

With a cluck of her tongue, Mom finally conceded some sketchy details. "They let Shane out after three years. I felt bad about not being in touch with his wife Sheila after his arrest. It went on for months, in the papers and TV news. I had my hands full with you kids. I didn't pay much attention. The precinct captain told us to send anyone asking questions to him. Like me or Sheila would ever talk to a reporter!"

"What would a reporter want to know from you?"

"I suppose they thought Shane being Jack's partner, and the two of them growing up together, Shane would have told Jack what he was up to."

That's all Maureen ever said about it, Kate is pretty sure. Which means she was in the dark. Or she did an expert job of pretending. Unlikely. Mom was not one to hide her feelings.

Gran, however, was a different story. If she'd been privy to an NYPD cover-up meant to protect Dad, she would have taken the secret to her grave—along with all the other things she apparently kept from her favorite granddaughter.

Wait. Why is she buying into Rafferty's story? He's just a small-town cop covering his ass. She shouldn't dignify any of it. She waits for some adrenalin to propel her out of her chair. She needs to clean up and go look for Teague.

In the bathroom mirror, her eyes are red and swollen. There's snot crusted under her nose. She runs the tap and bathes her face in handfuls of cold water. When she looks again, there's nothing to disguise her fear.

A Halloween eve ceremony seems innocent enough. Then why does it feel like Teague is in danger? Maybe because Rafferty just theorized that her father is not only alive, but he also fled multiple charges in New York and escaped to live here under the false identity of Finn Mitchell. A man who just might be involved in the murder of a fellow Druid in Sligo.

If it's true, how would Finn respond if his secrets were exposed? Especially if the imposter's daughter, or grandson, were to spill his secret. Stop! Things like this don't happen in real life.

If only she could wipe it from her mind. As each thought begets another doubt, strength drains from her legs. She sits on the toilet and fixates on the pale green floor tiles. But there, too, Finn Mitchell's angry, condescending face comes into focus. The way he looked at her in the council meeting. She recoils and it fades, replaced by her father's face as she remembers him from twenty-two years ago, dressed for his shift, kissing the top of her head on his way out the door.

Her chest aches, like her heart is made of Silly Putty, stretched to the breaking point. The faces of her father and Finn Mitchell, who may or may not be the same man, converge in her mind's eye and she gags. No. It's not possible. She wants only to go back to bed and forget she heard any of this nonsense. But she can't. Not when Teague is likely with Finn right now.

She stands up straight and recovers her breath, waiting for her eyes to focus on the hands of the clock. 9:20. She needs to get to that Halloween ceremony and make sure Teague is safe. She can't let herself think beyond that.

# 2002

Kate stands on Ryan's front steps, shivering from a brisk wind. She knocks on his door and zips up her flimsy windbreaker, thinking she should have worn a proper coat. Just like she should have called Ryan before coming over. But then the whole story would have come tumbling out and Ryan would have told her it's preposterous. Since it probably is. But there's nothing she can do about it now. She needs his help to find Finn's compound. No doubt that's where her Druid-besotted nephew is tonight.

"Aye. I know where it is." Ryan scratches his beard and steps back to let her in. This is her first time seeing his house and it's much as she expected. A two-story stucco house with its first floor dominated by a rustic woodstove now burning down to embers, the smell of smoke lingering. Denim-blue cushions on a wood-framed couch and matching chairs. A padded rocker under an arched reading lamp, an open book on the ottoman. A Celtic cross hanging on the wall.

The surprise is his serious collection of antique timepieces intermingling with books on the shelves lining his living room. The standouts include an ornate carved mahogany grandfather with pendulum and chimes, a glass-enclosed skeleton with brass gears, and a clockface of Roman numerals encased in green marble and adorned with gilt cherubs, alongside all manner of workaday clocks likely taken from the walls and worktables of local tradesmen.

A quiet symphony of ticks and tocks creates a busy but restful din.

Ryan's flannel pajamas remind her of the late hour. "I'm sorry to disturb your peaceful evening."

"It's all right, Kate. I'm just trying to understand why you're this worried."

"Can I fill you in on the way?"

"Sure, just give me ten minutes to change."


In the car, she shares her concern that Teague is at Finn's compound after she forbade him. And her larger worry that Liam has pressured him into doing a criminal act of more hacking or posting the stolen files online. "Why haven't they arrested Liam yet?"

"Rafferty told me Liam didn't admit to anything, and there isn't enough evidence to charge him. Finn and Morgan won't allow the gardai' to search their home and they can't take Liam's computer without a warrant. It takes time for the internet provider to trace the web traffic, if they can do it at all. All that leaves the investigation in limbo."

"Meaning it will remain unsolved. Like most hacks."

"Maybe. I'm afraid Liam has already achieved his goal by putting our study in jeopardy."

They drive up a long unpaved hill in pitch dark to Finn's place. Cars fill one side of the road at the top. They need to back up a quarter mile to park.

"This must the place to be on Halloween," he says, as he grabs a flashlight from the glove compartment.

"I gather we're supposed to call it *Sam-han*," she shouts from outside the car as she pushes through the brush. Two other late arrivals approach from farther down the hill. Their white robes stand out in the light of the full moon.

The man of the couple flashes a big smile. "Good evening, folks."

"Is this where the *Sam-han* ceremony is?" Kate asks them.

"Yes, and what a night we're given!" The man cranes his neck to admire a panorama of stars.

Kate and Ryan follow the pair up the hill.

"I'm afraid we'll stick out in this crowd," he says with a smile.

"Hopefully, no one will notice us, and we'll just grab Teague and get of here. I appreciate your coming. I don't even know for sure that he's here."

"It's all right. I've been meaning to get a look at this place."

At the top of the hill, an arrow points down a grassy hill. Drumming and chants waft from the same direction.

"What's that sweet smell?"

He sniffs. "Alfalfa hay. They must keep dairy cows in the barn."

They take the lit path past the barn and around an enormous tree. On the other side of it she gets her first glimpse of upward of sixty people assembled around a bonfire. They're arranged in two circular bands around a large pit with the fire at its center. As flames shoot up, her eye goes to a flag strung between two poles with an image of a capped and bearded man in a robe holding a staff. "Let's find Teague," she says, as a shot of adrenalin moves through her.

With his height advantage, Ryan spots him and Kiernan sitting in the pit before she does.

"Can we get closer?"

When they reach the edge of the pit, she's taken aback to see Teague in a white robe with his face painted, beating a drum, and looking, well, happy. Her relief fades after she gets a look at Finn. He's wearing a gold robe with a matching hat, orating in Irish. A Druid chief in full regalia, who may or may not be her father. She lingers on his face, superimposing Dad's there. Hard with the war paint, or whatever it is, on top of the beard and strange hair, plus, the distance between them. She's both repelled and mesmerized by the reverence displayed by his followers as he leads them in a call and response chant.

"What do you think?" Ryan asks, startling her.

She wants to tell him, but where would she begin? More than that, how crazy is she willing to sound? She hugs her chest. "Given where Teague is located, I think we have to wait until this is over."

They retrace their steps to the big tree where there's a bench. As their shoulders and thighs touch, a shiver runs up her spine. Ryan leans over and picks up a handful of acorns. He pops off their tops like bottle caps and kneads the bare nuts between his palms. She picks up a few of her own. Their smooth hardness invites rolling. "They're like worry beads," she says.

"Or a rosary."

She has little experience with either, but she can't imagine anyone else she'd rather have at her side right now, even though she feels guilty about withholding what she's learned from Rafferty. The drums and chanting become white noise, lulling her into a half sleep, which must go on for a while because she's startled when she sees people walking toward them.

"Shall we go retrieve your nephew?"

"Yes, let's hurry."

They weave single file through groups of barefoot Druids milling, chatting, hugging. No one seems eager to leave.

Teague is still in the pit, talking with Kiernan. When he sees them, he waves. His smile is uncharacteristically broad.

"Teague, what are you doing here?" she yells.

"Drumming and stuff. What are *you* doing here?"

"Don't be cute." At least he's safe. "Let's go."

"Kiernan, do you need a ride?" Ryan asks.

"No, I'm staying over. I'll see you around, Teague."

"Later."

They're walking away from the crowd when she remembers Teague's pendant. "Sweetheart, are you wearing the necklace Gran gave you?"

"I always wear it."

"Can I see it?"

"Why?"

"I'll give it right back. I promise."

"I don't like to take it off." His chin trembles as he hesitates before pulling the chain over his head.

She extends her open hand. "I'll be right back," she says after taking it from him. At the edge of the pit, she holds the chain up with the pendant's face and the image on the flag side by side at eye level. As she suspected, they're identical.

Ryan and Teague catch up to her. "Have you shown this to Finn?" she asks Teague.

"No. Why?"

"Hang on a minute." She scans the stragglers around the pit and spots him talking with a gaggle of his followers on the slope near the barn.

"I need to talk to Finn."

Feeling tongue-tied in his presence, Kate lingers behind a couple with whom he's engrossed in conversation—until he notices her and stops talking.

"Finn, can I have a word, in private?"

"Say whatever you need to say right here."

His refusal to grant her a moment alone only adds to her resolve. "Okay. Since we've never been properly introduced, let me start. My full name is Katherine Callahan Jones. I used to be called Katy. But since college, I've gone by Kate."

Finn's eyes narrow. She continues her soliloquy. "I was born in the Bronx in 1970. You know my nephew, Teague. I guess his last name didn't pique your curiosity."

Finn locks his jaw as if determined to say nothing. His eyes are slits. There's a hand on the small of her back. Ryan and Teague flank her.

"Dr. Jones," Finn begins in a derisive tone. "I don't know what you're talking about. And from what I've heard, you don't either."

"What are you doing?" Teague asks. He looks stricken.

Ryan grabs her arm and pulls her back two steps. "Is this necessary? Your issue with Teague coming tonight is not Finn's problem. Is it?" She doesn't blame Ryan for thinking she's lost her mind, but it's too late to explain. This would be the logical point to call it quits. If she could summon logic.

"I've gone this far. I can't stop now." She pulls her arm from Ryan's grip.

When she turns around to face him again, there's a blue-robed woman with shoulder-length white hair at Finn's side. Her piercing glare does the work of an X-ray. She recalls Teague's description of Liam's mom as "witchy."

"Are you Morgan?"

"I am."

"I have business with your . . ." Kate can't get the word out.

The two trade a look, hers questioning, Finn's scornful. He makes a quarter turn to leave.

"Wait!" Kate extends her hand with the pendant.

"That's enough. We're done here." Finn says with nary a backward glance, but there's a flinch in his cheek before his irritated expression turns to thinly veiled shock. His eyes widen and move to her face.

"May I?" He extends his open palm.

She hands over the pendant. "Gran gave it to Teague before she died."

He flinches again, and quickly turns away as he examines it. After several seconds he looks back at her. "A cheap souvenir is all it is." He's holding the pendant by its chain, but she can't make her arms work and it drops. Teague bumps her shoulder as he lunges for it.

Seeing only Finn's back, she shouts, "No, please," and takes two strides past Teague.

A thunderous bang comes from behind them. All around Kate there's movement and noise. People on the periphery scream and scatter.

Finn looks beyond her, shouts, "Liam, you damn fool!" and drops to the ground next to Teague, who lies crumpled. Finn turns him on his back. Is that blood on his robe? Finn puts one hand on top of the other and pushes down on the spot where it's trickling out of Teague's midsection.

She gets to her knees and crawls around Finn making sure Teague can see her. Teague grits his teeth and moans. His eyelids flutter. "What . . . happened?"

She lays her hand on his cheek. "There was a shot. It must have hit you." His eyelids drop. "Teague, don't! It's going to be all right, I promise."

Ryan squats between her and Finn and starts cutting strips of Teague's robe with a penknife. He reaches under Teague's back and wraps a strip around his middle.

She suppresses a scream as the bloody splotch grows larger on Teague's robe. "Sweetheart, please keep your eyes open . . . . I'm right here."

"Come on lad, stay with me, it's not your time yet!" Finn yells.

Kate turns to see Finn's eyes boring down on Teague's face, as if willing him not to give up. She finds herself fighting the voice telling her this *could be* her father. She rejects the idea that she even wants it to be true and pulls her gaze away from Finn to give all her attention back to Teague.

Finn throws a set of keys on the ground next to Ryan's knee. "You've got to get him to the hospital. Use the white van parked in front of the gate."

Ryan pockets the keys. "Aye."

Finn looks over his shoulder. "Come give Ryan a hand." Two men and Kiernan step forward to help. She gets on her feet and backs off to give them room. It's as if Finn has flipped into first responder mode, an oddly familiar sight.

Ryan wraps one more strip around Teague's chest and ties a knot. Finn rises and steps back to give the other men room to squat. Ryan puts his hands under Teague's shoulders and waits for the others to get their hands under the rest of him.

"Okay, ready? Up we go." They lift him and move in unison toward the hill as she trots behind. Her heartbeat thuds like a jackhammer between her ears. *Please, please . . . let him be okay.*

# 2002

What's going on? Why is Kate saying those things to Finn?

His pendant is lying in the mud. He hears thunder or is fireworks? His side stings, like a hot wire under his skin. Wet, warm liquid on his stomach, trickling down his thigh. His face is squished in the grass. He can't breathe.

"Liam, you damn fool!" Finn's voice.

Teague lays his palms flat and pushes down. But he can't move. There's a knife stuck in his gut. Fuck, it hurts. Hands are turning him over, pushing down on his stomach. Finn's eyes, so green. The hot wire again, slinking through him like a snake. Stinging his thigh, leg, now his butt.

"Teague. Oh, my God." Kate's mouth trying to scream.

"What . . . happened?" His own voice sounds far away.

"You were shot . . . You'll be all right, I promise," she says.

No, I won't. Can't you see?

Ryan is tearing his robe. So many faces. He can't feel his body anymore. Relief.

"Lad, stay with me, it's not your time yet!" Finn yells.

How does he know that?

Voices jumbled together. They're carrying him like he's a sack of potatoes. He goes in and out of feeling pain.

He's in Liam's van and it's moving. Kate's face over him. She's crying because she thinks he's dead. Dead can't be any worse than this. You all do whatever you want . . . I'm out of here.

Every . . . thing . . . slows . . . way . . . way . . . down . . . Let . . . go . . . go . . . go . . . it's . . . not . . . worth . . . it . . . nothing . . . but . . . black.

He's not in the van anymore. He's left his body behind. Everything feels lighter up here. Wait. Where is here? No familiar landmarks. Not day or night, some hazy in-between. Clouds of color flitting around, some close enough to touch—if he had a hand. Everything is calm here. Him, too. He moves along like he's the driver of this person named Teague, not a passenger riding in the back seat.

Wait. If he's not in Teague's body, can he still be the driver?

"Of course, you can, dear. You're the same soul no matter what vehicle you travel in."

The old lady with the tiara! At least it's her face, the same voice. She has no body, just a wisp of light around her face.

"What's your name?" he asks.

"I was last called Anne. Suffice to say we're kin. You're the spitting image of my Michael." She smiles. "Didn't I tell you I'd be back?"

"Yeah, but you didn't say I'd have to die first. Not that I mind. I like it here."

"Don't get too comfortable, son. You may be just passing through. That decision hasn't been made yet."

"Oh yeah? Who's going to make it?"

"Oh, it'll be you, with a little help from a certain person who can help you fix what ails you."

None of this is said out loud. That's not how it works here.

"Here he is, now. Teague. Good evening, Mr. Mitchell."

"Thank you, Mrs. Callahan. I can take it from here."

Just like that, Anne disappears, and a new guy, bald, with a belly like a kickball, wearing a long apron, shows up. He smells like the stuff Maureen uses to polish furniture.

"You can call me Paddy. Come along, lad. We have to talk."

231

Quicker than he can say *all right*, they're in a place that looks familiar. He's seen those shelves and bottles before. The scale, too, except it's not rusty. He's the one who was in the photo with Gran. "You're Paddy from the drugstore!"

"Aye, I am. Please take a seat. We have a decision to make."

Teague spins on the stool and watches the jars fly by like he's on a carousel.

"I'm here to help clear obstacles out of your way," he hears Paddy say.

He grabs ahold of the counter. "What obstacles?"

"I think you know."

"You mean my voices."

He nods. "You've been the target of unsavory messengers."

"Yeah. Larry's a total drag."

"True. But it's not just the outsiders you have to watch out for. Already, at your tender age, you've loved and lost people dear to you. Meghan was a beautiful but fragile soul. Your Gran, my darling Ellen, recognized your gift. She shared her excitement with me when she arrived."

"Gran is here?"

"She was but has since returned. Don't worry. You two will meet again. That, I can promise you."

Teague has his doubts about a promise made by a dead person in heaven. But it's a nice thought.

"Because of your losses, you've armored your heart and come close to snuffing out your light."

"I know about my armor."

"But you also have the power to dispense with it."

"What makes you think I can do that?"

"Because of your nature. And because you've come to this place at this time."

Listening to Paddy talk makes Teague feel more alive than ever, which is strange, since they're both dead.

Paddy looks to each side, then back at him. "I'm sure you've seen the displays in museums, I think the word I'm looking for is *diorama*?"

"You mean the scenes of cavemen and extinct animals?"

"Exactly. I want you to picture each of your ancestor's lives as a single moment captured in a diorama. For simplicity's sake, let's call them boxes. My grandmother's hunger lives inside my father's box. My father's stolen language echoes in my box. The blood I spilled on Main Street lines my daughter's box . . . on and on it goes."

Woozy, Teague puts his head in his hands.

"Don't despair, lad. There is more to our lineage than sorrow. Deeper in the past, we were powerful warriors, poets, and diviners."

"You mean wizards?"

"Each had different talents, but they used their powers to help people live well on this land. The battle between the dark and light forces goes on inside and outside each of us. Take Liam, he's lost his way, but I think you would agree there's still good in that young man."

"He was my friend . . . before tonight."

"And he could be again. Teague, you're fortunate to have a circle of love around you right now. The one you call Finn could be an important helper to you."

"He was a total shit to Kate tonight."

"Yes, he was. But there's a reason why you've all become entangled again. Remember, light is stronger than darkness."

"How do you know that?"

"Because light is life. Wouldn't you rather be on the side of creation?"

"Well, if you put it that way."

"When you create a new chapter in the story of your people, you not only heal yourself, but you also help those who came before you. You all suffer from the same wound, which festers as each generation fails to face it head on."

"How can something I say or do right help all these dead people from a hundred years ago?"

Paddy twists his mouth like a pretzel. "Good question. Let's say you re-enter your body with the intention of telling the story of what happened to you today in whatever medium you choose. You can be sure that one of your ancestors is seeing and feeling that story in his own time as a powerful premonition."

"No shit?" In a weird way, Paddy makes sense. Until Teague follows his thoughts a few steps further and gets waylaid again. "But what good does it do him, I mean, he's back there and I'm here?"

"Imagine this ancestor and his family are suffering through the Great Hunger. Or the poor fellow is facing a firing squad. Only one thing helps a man's soul, whatever his fortune might be, and that's hope. If not for his own lot in life, then for his children or grandchildren. Hope is one of the threads connecting you and your ancestors through time. You can't see it. But it's there, occupying every cell of your body."

"You mean like it's in my DNA?"

Paddy smiles like he's got a secret. "That's one word for it."

Teague is having a hard time processing what Paddy is telling him. He closes his eyes, and the words transform into bits of light that move around until they form a perfect snowflake. When it's complete, a new thought crystallizes for him: the things that happen to us don't arrive with meanings. We give them meaning when we put them together in a story or a painting.

The problem is Teague's not sure he's up to the job of creating anything new. He opens his eyes and finds Paddy with his chin down, looking up at him over the top of his glasses.

"Sometimes I just want to hide," Teague confesses.

Paddy puts one hand on each of Teague's shoulders. "Your modern medicines and healers can help if you let them. Until you're stronger."

"You mean I shouldn't ditch my meds?"

"They're for your protection. You'll know when the time comes if it's all right for you to go without. Now you must decide what you're going to do."

"Is this my last chance?"

"For this lifetime, yes. There will be other opportunities, but you've come such a long way as Teague. Maybe you ought to give him this victory."

"Yeah. He kind of deserves it. Can I ask you something?"

"Ask away."

"Did I have to get shot to learn all this?"

He laughs. "Let's just say you signed up for certain things before your birth. Your soul badly wants this lesson." Paddy's smile fills his round face. It's the last thing Teague sees before he finds himself on the ceiling of a room filled with bright lights that make him squint. There's his body again, on a table. He looks like crap. Skin as white as the floor tiles, blue lips, maybe dead. But then why are there still five people working on him? Machines beeping and flashing numbers. An IV pole is attached to his arm. A tube down his throat.

"BP down to fifty. Body temp is sixty and dropping," a woman reads off one machine. "H-six is below seventy gl." A guy with gray sideburns has a scalpel in his hand. "Get me blood," he shouts.

"He's type O," says the woman holding a clipboard.

"Go!" the surgeon tells her, and she hightails it out the double doors.

The hole in his midsection is the size of a quarter and there's still blood oozing out, black not red. "I'm going for a midline."

Yikes, the surgeon is cutting a vertical line down his stomach. Strange, Teague doesn't feel a thing. He puts his finger in there, like he's fishing around for something. Maybe the bullet. Holy shit. This looks like it'll take a while. Teague has seen enough. Where's Kate? He needs to find her.

# 2002

According to the clock on the windowless wall, it's 5:45 a.m. Besides Ryan and Kate, an elderly man is waiting for word on his wife, who, like Teague, is in surgery, in her case, after suffering a major heart attack. Sadly, it's her second this year. There are no secrets in the Ballymore Trauma Center's family waiting room.

Aside from the fact that he's still alive, the news from Teague's trauma team has been terrifying. The bullet entered below his lung and did not exit. He bled a lot and arrived in full hemorrhagic shock. He needed a transfusion before they could perform a laparotomy. Since Teague is type O and Kate is B, she couldn't donate. Ryan is O, so he did. A half hour ago they were told Teague was stable enough for surgery and now all they can do is wait.

Which means she can no longer put off telling Ryan the truth, including Rafferty's theories tagging Finn as a gunrunner, possibly a murderer, and maybe her father, although who the hell knows since the man went to great lengths to deny it last night. The story spills out of her while Ryan alternates between looking astonished and furious.

Ryan's eyes are still fixed on the opposite wall . . . if she didn't know better, she'd think he's studying the poster listing six signs of stroke. He's still holding the box of apple juice a nurse gave him to rehydrate. While she doesn't expect an atta girl, his extended silence and grim face are making her nervous.

236

At last, Ryan massages his neck and turns to her. His cheeks are pink, almost red.

"If you had told me this at my house, I would never have agreed to drive you to Finn's place." His taut neck muscles belie his calm tone.

"Maybe that's why I didn't tell you."

"God damn it, Kate." He stands and crosses the room. While he paces, he looks at the floor, the ceiling, the bulletin board; anywhere but her face. Back in his chair, he scratches his beard and rolls his neck.

She forces herself to meet his eyes.

"I did not sign up to be your lackey," he says with anger boiling over, his voice getting louder with every word. "This is where I live. Where my daughter lives. Where I intend to stay. You don't seem to understand the kind of relationships that sustain people in a town like this. Even with our feuds and secrets, there's something deeper, and you don't get to sail in here and mess with it . . . or me."

"The hospital cafeteria on the first floor is now serving breakfast," intones a female voice over the PA system.

Kate uses the few-second interval to find the words she saved up for this moment. "I should have told you. But I was confused and scared. It felt too crazy to say out loud to anyone. I didn't think you'd believe me. Why would you?"

"Why would I?" He shakes his head. The overhead light reflects off the sheen on his forehead and cheeks. "Let's get this straight. If we're friends, which I thought we were, wouldn't I help you get to the bottom of it? You don't need to have everything tied up in a neat package before you tell me what's going on, not when it's this important. Haven't I earned just a wee bit of your trust these past months?" He looks away from her in defeat.

It's as if she's gagged, her body bolted to the chair. She forces herself upright and nearly shouts, "Yes, you have earned it!" He snaps to attention. Her voice lowers. "Several times over." A sob sneaks up her throat and tears start to fall down her cheeks. "I'm the one who's not trustworthy." She drops her chin to hide from him, but he grabs her arms and lifts her until their faces are inches apart.

"You're a flawed human being like the rest of us."

With that, her defenses dissolve. A *cawing* escapes from her mouth and her head drops to her knees. She pictures Teague bleeding on the ground and cries harder. Ryan's hands knead her shoulders while she cries it out. When she pulls herself up and opens her eyes, his calm is the only thing keeping her from falling apart again. "Thank you for being here."

He nods. She looks up at the clock: 7:45, her throat catches. She rubs her thighs with her knuckles and meets his eyes. Is no news good or bad? Better not to ask.

"Ryan, do you believe in God?"

He meets her gaze. "Actually, I do."

"Well, I don't, but I'm not going to let that stop me. Will you pray with me?"

"Yes, of course." He takes her hand and leans forward in his chair. She does the same and closes her eyes.

Except . . . where to begin? Her first impulse is to return to where she left off as a practicing Catholic, not long after her confirmation. The words to Hail Mary come back effortlessly, but they feel as empty now as they did when she was fifteen and declared herself an atheist.

She goes instead to the night last summer when she saw but refused to acknowledge the unmistakable signs of Teague's disintegration. Their strange interaction as he trooped through her mother's house leading an invisible band. How, when she tried to stop him, he refused, reciting the then unfamiliar line from *Harry Potter*: "The wand chooses the wizard." Leaving her baffled, then distraught when he added, "Honestly, woman, you call yourself our mother?"

"Teague, help me out here," she finally said. "Do you want me to answer you?"

And then the response that left her feeling wholly depressed and useless.

"Since you asked. I'd say your job is to find the real parts. I have to put out a lot of nonsense to protect the truer things."

"Protect them from what?" she shouted as he walked away.

Now she can answer her own question. As Teague's mother, it's her job to protect him from anyone who would dismiss his perceptions as madness or mistake his sensitivity for weakness.

Sitting in the hard plastic chair, holding on to Ryan's hand, Kate meets her worst fear. That she's missed the chance to love and be loved by Teague. She rejects the idea and tries to still her thoughts. Clarity arrives: She needs to find her own words and speak to God, or whoever might be nearby and acting in his name. She's startled when a feminine voice promptly tells her to stop wasting time. God is not waiting on her; it's Teague she needs to talk to. She tries to focus her mind by picturing her precious boy at his most intact, those dreamy eyes hinting at wisdom beyond his years.

*Teague, please hang on. I've failed you. I know that. But if it's not too late, I'm asking you to give me another chance. Give us another chance. I love you so much. Damn. How is it possible I never said those words out loud to you? Please don't go. I want to be your mom. I can't imagine going on without you. I don't want to.*

Tears fall down her cheeks and she feels connected to him for the first time since they got to the hospital. *I'm waiting right here for you, Sweetheart.*

"Katherine Jones, please come to the main reception desk on the first floor."

Ryan and Kate jump from their seats in unison. In the elevator, he takes her hand, and she squeezes his. When the doors slide open to reveal the hulking back of Guard Rafferty standing by the front desk, her stomach turns. They walk with him to a quartet of cushioned chairs. Visitors trickle in with bouquets of flowers. White-jacketed physicians, blue- and green-uniformed staff come and go.

Rafferty's got his pad out. He sits on the edge of his seat and makes eye contact with her. "I'm very sorry to hear what happened to Teague. They say he's in surgery." His tone is sympathetic but firm.

"Who told you?"

"The hospital is obliged to notify the gardai´ when a victim of violence is brought to the ER. We're required to look it into it."

"I see. Well, Finn and I were arguing when the gun went off. I believe I was the intended target. I mean, assuming Liam was the shooter."

Rafferty takes a moment to respond. "Liam was taken into custody this morning. He'll be placed on a twenty-one-day involuntary hold at the mental hospital in Galway. In two weeks, there will be a tribunal to determine his state of mind at the time of the shooting. Teague will likely be called to testify."

Ryan clears his throat. "You make it sound as if it's still an open question whether Liam was the shooter."

"There's an argument for reasonable doubt, since no one at the grove was willing to say they saw Liam with the gun. We're speculating that the weapon he used was the recently used ArmaLite AR-15 we found on a bale of hay in the barn. That rifle was a favorite of the Provisional IRA. I wouldn't be a bit surprised if Finn, or, if I'm right, Jack Callahan, shipped it here himself. Either way, according to the deadline in the Good Friday Agreement, it should have been turned in to us a year ago with all the other weapons in private hands on both sides of the border.

"I'm sorry. I can't think about all this right now," Kate says, letting annoyance show in her dismissive tone. Rafferty seems to take offense.

"Kate, I wish you hadn't taken it upon yourself to share with Finn what I told you in confidence. This is an ongoing investigation."

She bites her tongue and looks out the picture window at inky clouds blocking the morning sun. Rafferty is upset that she's ruined his murder investigation and she doesn't give a damn.

"If I can speak, Con."

"Go right ahead."

Con? She should have guessed they've been on a team together, or they go to the same church, or they're related by marriage; perhaps all three.

"Kate shouldn't have confronted Finn in such a public way. But she was upset, and I can assure you, since I was there, she only brought up her personal stake in the situation, not any of this other crime you're investigating."

"The problem is it could all be tied together."

When Rafferty turns to her, his pique is more pronounced. "I shared my suspicions about your father so you could tell me anything that might shake loose Finn's involvement in my murder case. Or clear up the suspicion hanging over him because people saw him and the murder victim as rivals in this Druid business."

"Then your evidence against Finn comes down to his presumed motive?" Ryan asks the question that's been rattling around her mind.

"The two men had a rocky history."

"How do you even know this other Druid was murdered?" she asks.

"An autopsy showed he swallowed a poisonous amount of crushed yew needles. The dead man had no yew growing on his farm, but Finn's land does. Besides that, his wife is known to cultivate herbs and offer her services as a healer. We're still checking Finn's alibi."

Ryan leans forward. "If you're right, how would Finn's false identity come into it?"

"In my experience, a man who's capable of conspiring to fake his own death to evade prison wouldn't have a problem committing a murder if anybody got between him and his freedom."

Enough about Finn! Kate wants nothing to with that man, whoever he is. She's halfway to her feet, but Rafferty has more to say.

"Jack Callahan's gunrunning twenty-five years ago is not my concern. We've put that behind us. But if this is him posing as Finn Mitchell and he thinks his secret is out, he's going to assume we know or we're close to knowing anything else he's hiding."

He's spelling out the same fear that compelled her to go to Finn's Halloween ceremony last night. Now she pictures her father in uniform; the wink he always gave her before leaving the house. Mom's standard *Don't be a hero*, covering her daily bone-crushing worry for his safety.

Rafferty goes on. "It's possible Finn is who he says he is. With the time that's passed, there's no Mitchell family member who can verify his identity; no one willing to say he isn't Finn."

To tune him out and slow her palpitating heart, she tracks a pair of nurses chatting casually as they walk from the elevator to the cafeteria.

"Kate, after what you said to Finn last night, my guess is if you two are father and daughter, you'll find out soon enough. And I'd appreciate hearing about any developments on that score."

"I'm sorry but Teague will be out of surgery any minute."

He stands. "I'll keep him in my prayers. You can expect to hear from me tomorrow."

An hour later, Teague's surgeon, still in his green scrubs, enters the waiting room.

"He's a lucky lad. The single bullet tore a lot of tissue but missed his inferior vena cava, liver, and esophagus. It's lodged in the muscles of his posterior stomach wall, and for now, that's where we're going to leave it."

Anatomy, her first class in med school, comes back to help her visualize just how lucky a lad he is. "Thank you."

"You're welcome." He blinks his bloodshot eyes. "He's in recovery, not awake yet. Give him another forty-five minutes and you can talk to him." He leaves them alone in the waiting room.

"Oh my God," she covers her mouth. Ryan's eyes widen and meet hers. They embrace and hold each other. The profound certainty that her prayer was heard and answered is not completely unfamiliar to Kate. It's just been a long, long time.

Teague is sleeping when she gets to his room. His face is scrubbed clean of mud and grass stains. Tucked behind his ears, his hair needs a wash. An IV attached to the back of his hand. Digital screens monitoring his vitals. A hospital gown and blanket hide the bandages covering his new scar. With her hands on the side rail, she watches his chest rise and fall. She could stand there all day and night and bear witness to his aliveness.

She lifts her eyes and notices a clump of metal on the bedside table. How can it be here? None of them retrieved it from the ground. That leaves Finn, who must have come and gone from this room without their noticing. She picks up the pendant and squeezes it in the palm of her hand. Who is this man and what does he want from them? Teague's cheek twitches and she lets the question go. It's taken her way too long to realize how much she loves this boy.

"Dad or Finn or whoever the hell you are," she says, as she looks out the window, "if you're not dead and buried in the Bronx, unless you're willing to own up to who you are, you're dead to us." It hurts to think such a thing, but there's comfort in knowing she has her priorities straight.

Another twitch and Teague's eyes blink open. He squints at her and wets his lips.

"Hi, sweetheart. It's over. You're all right." She wraps her fingers around his wrist and delights at the thump, thump, thump of his pulse.

His grimace softens and becomes a typical Teague half smile. He drifts back to sleep, and she settles in a chair to watch him for another half hour. When she's sure he's all right, she leans forward in the chair and allows exhaustion to consume every part of her body. It's a cleansing of sorts. When she sits up, she feels energized. As if by God or whoever's grace, she's not too late after all. On her way out, she stops at the nurses' station. "Did an older man come to Teague's room overnight?" She addresses the question to a young nurse, who checks her log and says, "I've been here since half ten and I haven't seen anyone other than staff go in there before or after Teague came out of surgery."

A middle-aged nurse standing at the circular desk looks up from her clipboard. "Only patient families are permitted on the critical care floor. You're his first visitor."

"Thank you for taking such good care of him," she says to the nurses.

Alone in the elevator, she speaks directly to the man who may or may not be her father, and Teague's grandfather. She conjures him as a blank, nameless silhouette and says, "Have it your way. Just leave us alone."

# Rivervale, New York,
## 1974

The official story sounded plausible enough to Ellen. Jack left Shane in the squad car and interrupted a robbery in progress. Two assailants pistol-whipped the owner, took his cash, and gunned Jack down before fleeing through a rear door. Jack died at the scene. Bronx detectives had no leads.

"I see," was all she said when Maureen finished relating the account of Jack's death the NYPD had given her.

Ellen's decision to stay home with Katy on the day of Jack's funeral surprised her daughter-in-law. "I prefer to grieve for my son in private," she said and left it at that.

Jack's brothers on the force and their wives tended generously to Ellen, Maureen, and the children. They visited often, brought food, and invited them to holiday celebrations. A much-diminished version of their lives went on as before. From Ellen's perspective, shared with no one living, it didn't matter what Jack might have done or not done. He was lost to her.

She had the satisfaction of witnessing the seeds she and Michael had planted take root and become viable in the strongest of their grandchildren and great grandchildren. Although she wouldn't live to see them flower, she had no doubt they would.

It was her understanding of loss that changed the most. She recalled Delia

244

warning about thinking she knew more than Brigid. She came to see that a life cut short was not the waste it might have seemed at the time, because each person mattered in the scheme of things. It was her own grief, rather, her fear it might break her, that had given her that false impression. Each of them was a link in the chain of a lineage and a people. Michael knew he had gone as far as he could in this life. She chose to trust that Jack's choices were as right as his father's had been.

# 2002

Teague is home, sitting up in bed with a wet canvas propped against his knees. There's a palette on his arm, and a trail of brown and green paint spots across his sheet. Ignore it, Kate tells herself. His wound is mending, he's back on his meds, and he seems content. That's more than enough for today.

"Oh, I like that," she says, leaning over the canvas. His work in progress is a beautifully rendered tree with several peculiarities. A face embedded in the trunk. Branches evolving into humanlike arms. A Darwinian *March of Progress* with a surrealist bent. "It's intriguing."

He gives her a side-eye as if judging her sincerity before offering a grin.

"Keep up the good work. Can I have first dibs on this one?"

"All right."

His eyes linger on her.

"What?"

"Did you know I almost died during surgery? I mean, I could have gone either way. Paddy was the one who told me I had to choose. I heard what you said . . . about giving us another chance."

Kate's legs wobble. She makes space to sit on the edge of his bed. "That's amazing, sweetheart. And you heard me right. I'm glad you decided to come back." She wants to make the next move, but it feels like a risk. Even as an infant, Teague eschewed touch. If anyone tried to hug him, he went rigid and

246

put his arms at his side like a little soldier. Oh hell, if not now, when? She risks it. He doesn't flinch.

"In case you didn't hear me say it during surgery. I love you."

"Yeah, I know." He looks down at the canvas with the corners of his mouth rising.

"Just yell if you need anything. The doctor said you shouldn't put pressure on your stitches."

"All right." He picks up his palette and brush.

Ryan arrived ten minutes earlier to talk about the presentation they're supposed to give at the next council meeting—scheduled for tomorrow night. She walks into the living room to find a five-alarm frown on his face.

"What's wrong?"

"They cancelled the meeting."

"Why?" She sits next to him on the couch where he's slouched with his lower lip jutted out, staring straight ahead.

"According to Jim Lynch's letter, it's postponed because of what he called a recent 'disturbance involving members of the study team' and because of the 'heated atmosphere in the county.'"

"Right. I'll get us coffee."

Almost losing Teague has given her more perspective on what qualifies as a life-and-death matter and what doesn't. She's become more philosophical about the fate of their study—but not defeatist.

She puts Ryan's cup on the crate at his knees. His face is slack and twitchy, not at all his usual calm self. This must be Ryan hitting bottom, taking this turn of events as his personal failure. She'd probably do the same thing if the study was her baby. And it isn't yet. Why not? she wonders. He's blinking and moving his eyes around the room. His gloom is palpable.

"Care to say where you've been?"

"Just thanking the Lord neither of my parents is here to see how far I've fallen."

"It's not a done deal yet. Things could still go our way."

His expression is noncommittal. "I know this pales in comparison to what you and Teague have just been through. It's just that I've been trying to launch this study for five years. I hate to see it go down like this."

"I understand. I really do. When we get the opportunity, we'll just have to make a better case for it."

He pushes his fists into the cushion. "At least no patient information has been posted since the last meeting."

To Kate, the hack seems like ancient history. "Perhaps the good people of Ballymore will give you credit for falling on your sword and asking nicely for a second chance."

"That's not how it works here. But we'll try, assuming anyone listens."

Two days later, Kate walks into Ryan's office, which she notices is more cluttered than usual. Mountains of journals, files, CDs, a whiteboard with rows of ID numbers and diagnosis codes. The stress is clearly taking a toll on him. He is ghostly white. New bags under his eyes. She moves a pile of antiques catalogues from one chair and sits.

He's looking over the report she just gave him compiling diagnoses gathered by interns in the last round of family interviews—before work stopped.

"It's good," he says without looking up.

"Can I ask you a question?"

"Shoot."

"I'll let that pass." She pauses and grins. When he doesn't reciprocate with a smile, she wonders if she should come back another time. She plows ahead, eager to get his take on the idea that came to her last night when she couldn't sleep, and she found herself stewing about what was missing from the study. A new component that might make it her baby as much as his.

"What is it, Kate?" he asks with an edge of impatience in his voice.

"I'm wondering how hard it would be to add a qualitative analysis of parenting and social supports for the kids in the study who are in treatment."

He looks up startled. "Are my ears deceiving me, or is Ms. Hard Science advocating for a social scientist to join the team?"

"You act like I'm suggesting we hire a Druid."

He finally cracks a smile. He leans back in his chair and puts his feet on the desk. After a minute of silence, "We would need a sociologist with clinical experience to set up the criteria and controls. It might be tough to keep it double-blind with our small sample size."

"You mean since clinic therapists treating study subjects couldn't also be the ones to interview them?"

"Right. Although we could hire separate interns for that."

Good. If he's problem-solving, that means he's warming to her idea.

"I'd have to rearrange the funds, and I suppose we could put together a control group from other health departments." He shakes his head and adopts a frown. "I'm not sure we want our mums and dads to think we're judging their parenting skills. It could backfire. They could take their kids out of therapy."

"I understand your worry. But there's an enormous potential upside."

"I'm all ears."

"I've read two new studies from Sweden that could guide us in how to begin discreetly with a few families and then scale up if all goes well. In their experiments, they compared toddlers in two groups of twenty, with short and long serotonin transporter genes, tracking how each fared when raised in supportive versus chaotic households."

"Are you talking about the folks doing child sensitivity research?"

"Yes. Otherwise known as the orchid-dandelion hypothesis. Their initial results are fascinating."

"And let me guess . . . not what they predicted?"

"Not at all. The orchids, kids who should have performed the worst on every measure, when given one nurturing parent figure did better than the dandelions, the ones with the good gene. And they even did better than the dandelions raised in stable households. With our test population, we could look at the preteen and teen versions of the same hypothesis."

"Hmmm." He tilts his chair back and stares at the ceiling. He takes his time making eye contact. "I had a feeling you were going there. It's such new territory."

"What's new is combining observation with treatment. The early intervention and family counseling you're already doing is a perfect way to document the impact of services with different families."

He leans back in his chair and looks out the window at the packed clinic parking lot. She connects the butterflies in her stomach to versions of this conversation she had not long ago with Sebastian. Her trying to convince him epigenetics was valid science. Except here she was adding the orchid child hypothesis on top of it. As usual, Ryan cloaks his thoughts in a neutral mask. She projects his thought process as she watches him.

He massages his neck. He's torn.

He scrunches his face as if he's just downed a glass of sour milk. There could be a prestigious publication, even a prize, in the offing if we do this right.

He examines the ceiling tiles. They could run him out of town. Ostracize Sophie.

We could attract high-quality therapists. Our patients would reap the benefits.

Bingo, the clincher. He swivels his chair back around to face her, his face still neutral.

"It's promising. Write it up and include the Swedish results." His forehead furrows. "Of course, that assumes they ever let us finish this study."

"We might as well think positive."

He does a double take. "Right, Ms. Sunshine. Excuse me while I get used to this side of you."

# 2002

Teague follows Kate and Ryan through the metal detector at the entrance of the Galway court building. A man in uniform shows them where they're to wait until he's called.

Teague can't sit still. He makes loops up and down the marble hallway while his stomach does somersaults. "What are they going to ask me?" he asks Kate and Ryan as he passes them for the sixth time.

"Sit." Ryan nods at the space on the bench next to him. "The panel is going to want to hear what you saw and heard from Liam the day you were shot. They'll ask you to describe his mental state."

"Why? I'm not his doctor. You are."

"I've given them an affidavit with my previous diagnosis. But you're in a better position to know how he was behaving in the hours and days before the shooting."

"Why don't they just ask him?"

"Liam's situation is complicated. He's eighteen now and he faces adult consequences. If he's deemed incapacitated due a mental disorder, he'll be required to return to treatment, unless . . ."

"Unless what?"

"Unless, out of pride, he chooses to fight that finding, and then the case would go to a criminal court, where he'd be found guilty of 'assault causing

251

serious harm' and go to jail."

"That would be terrible . . . for everybody," says Kate.

And he'd be the biggest rat in the world.

The courtroom door opens. The officer says, "Teague Callahan? Please come in."

It's not like a TV courtroom. No judge or witness stand. Just three people, two men and a lady, sitting behind a table. Liam is at another table with a woman. In a dozen rows of chairs off to the side, he sees Rafferty and another guard. Morgan and Liam's uncle have their own row. Kate and Ryan in another. The man who fetched him leads Teague to a chair in front of the three people.

Teague's throat tightens. He hopes he can make words come out.

The lady on the panel talks first. "Thank you, Teague, for coming today. We're not here to put Liam O'Shea on trial for any crime. Our purpose is to establish his mental capacity on the day of the shooting. Our first question to you then is how would you describe Liam's behavior on October 30, 2002?"

Teague glances at Liam whose stare back is super intense, like he's shooting him all over again.

"He seemed jumpy and mad. But I wasn't around him very long that day."

"Where were you when you saw him?"

"The first time, I was going in the barn when he was leaving."

"Did you hear or see anything unusual?"

He looks over at Ryan, who gives him a nod. He's just supposed to tell the truth? He considers doing a spell to disappear. It probably won't work in this bulletproof place. "He was arguing with Finn about a gun. Finn's gun. He didn't have permission to use it, that's why Finn chewed him out for taking it out of the case."

Teague doesn't dare look anywhere but straight ahead at the panel. They whisper to each other. The woman talks again.

"Teague, do you understand the word *hallucination*?"

"Yeah."

"From your direct experience with Liam, have you ever witnessed him experiencing an auditory or visual hallucination?"

This sucks so bad. He finally made real friends and now he's going to lose them all. Liam already hates him. If he tells, he doubts Kiernan and the twins will ever speak to him again. He finds Kate, who looks like she's got the second-worst stomachache in the world. Her squished-up face makes it clear she knows how bad this feels to him.

"Yeah, I have," he says.

"Can you be more specific?"

*Jesus fucking Christ. Doesn't this lady know anything?* "I saw him waving his arms and yelling at someone who wasn't there. Then he was crouching down and hiding from them."

"How can you be certain that was a hallucination?" one of the men on the panel asks.

"Because I've had them. If they're mean voices, and most of them are, you're afraid they might kill you. Even though they never do. At least, I don't think they do. They're more like your worst nightmare, but they can happen anytime. I'd still be having them if I wasn't back on my medication."

"In your opinion was Liam's hallucination a factor in the shooting?"

"I can't say for sure. I don't think he meant to shoot me. He was probably just being paranoid."

"Eejit! You don't know anything about me, you wimpy Yank!" Liam's face is tied up in a freaky sneer. "Nobody gets away with calling me mental."

Teague wants to crawl under the table and never come out. He closes his eyes and pretends he's in his old bunk bed.


Kate sighs and grabs Ryan's hand as they watch the officer take Liam out of the room. She goes to Teague and gives him a hug. "You did the right thing, sweetheart."

"Yeah, even if it sucks."

She keeps an arm around his shoulders, which he allows. In fact, he leans into her side, shaking, as they walk toward the exit where Ryan is talking to Morgan. Kate braces. This is the first time she's been in Morgan's presence since the night of the shooting.

"Thank you, Teague," Morgan says, and touches his cheek. "It took courage to say what you did."

Teague is mute. Kate holds him tighter.

"How are you healing?" Morgan looks down at Teague's belly.

He cracks a smile. "I'm good now."

"I'm glad to hear that." Her body language exudes relief. Kate is touched.

To Ryan, Morgan says, "To think, Liam would risk going to jail rather than let anyone know he has a mental illness."

"A treatable illness," Kate says without thinking. She catches Morgan's wince and worries she came across as harsh or judgmental. "I'm sorry you're going through this," Kate adds. "I understand how hard it is."

"Thank you. I know you do." Their eyes lock.

"I think the panel has plenty of evidence to establish Liam's diminished capacity," Ryan says. "I doubt they'll keep him more than a month if he commits to outpatient treatment. Then he's welcome to return to the clinic."

# 2002

On Saturday night, Kate and Teague are sharing their kitchen table with Ryan, eating a pork loin cooked by Kate.

Ryan swallows his last forkful of dinner and puts his napkin on the table. "That was grand."

"Is there anymore?" Teague asks.

From a pan on the stove, she serves him the last piece of pork and two potatoes. The doorbell rings. "Oh no. Who could that be?" She goes to the door.

Jesus Christ. Rafferty is the last person she wants to see, although Finn Mitchell would be a close second after the fool she made of herself at Halloween. "Come in," she says to Rafferty.

"Pardon the intrusion. How's your boy doing?"

"He's much better." In fact, she's almost had to tie him down to keep him home and stationary. His stitches don't come out for another week.

"I have a few more questions for you. There's been a development in the Sligo case."

Teague puts down his fork as Ryan gets up to join Kate and Rafferty in the living room.

"Finn's alibi has fallen apart," he hears Rafferty tell them. "A witness who saw him at the victim's farm the day of the poisoning has come forward."

"And who is this witness?" Ryan asks.

255

"He's a real estate developer . . ."

The bald guy at the fairy hill action? Teague wonders as Rafferty keeps talking.

". . . called Bill Hogan. His company was in the process of buying the dead man's property, which had fallen into foreclosure."

That's him. Finn said his name to the reporter and Hogan Development Corporation was the name of the company on the sign.

"As I told you at the hospital," he hears Kate say, "I have no more blood tie to Finn Mitchell than you do."

"I know that's what he told you," Rafferty answers. "The truth might be different."

"It's also possible I'll never know."

"Finn has been gone for two weeks. Morgan says she hasn't heard from him. I don't tend to believe that's true either."

"Again, what does this have to do with me?"

"Has he contacted you?"

"No, and I don't expect to hear from him."

"Please let me know immediately if he does."

"Is there anything else?"

"That's all for now."

Holy shit. Teague's heart speeds up. He needs to warn Finn.

"It never ends," he hears Kate say after the door shuts.

Kate and Ryan are sitting on the sofa looking glum when Teague walks by them on the way to his room. He has a plan, but he can't tell them because they'll try to stop him.

He remembers the name of the town where Kate went with Ryan and saw the wrecked Callahan cottage. She said it wasn't far from the dairy farm that belongs to Ryan's Uncle Marty. He's guessing that's where Finn is hiding out. He puts on his bomber jacket and opens his bedroom window.

*Ow! Fuck.* The jump yanked his stitches. At least it's just one floor.

"Can you take me to Ballycarrick?" he asks the driver who pulls over for him over on the entrance to the M6.

"I could. What are you planning on doing over there?"

"Visiting family," he says in what he hopes is a casual tone. He's used to people around here being nosy after they hear his accent.

"Get in."

"What's your name, son?"

"Teague Callahan."

"We've got a few of your people around here."

"Yeah. I know."

He's relieved not to have to make small talk since the driver blabs enough for the two of them. The weather. Ballymore's footballers. The World Cup. Afghanistan. Bad American drivers.

"I'm going to leave you here," the man says as he pulls to the curb on a street with dark stores. Teague spots a lit sign for Kenny's Pub. Maybe somebody in there will help him.

"Oh my God." Kate's eyes dart from Teague's empty bed to the open window. "Ryan!"

Seconds later, he's in the room with her. "Shite. He can't have gotten far."

"I'll call Kiernan." But Kiernan swears he hasn't talked to Teague since yesterday.

They're in the kitchen when Ryan's pager beeps. "It's Marty's number." He scratches his beard. "Why is he calling me on my emergency line? I better find out."

While Ryan calls Marty, she goes back to Teague's room and picks up a sketchbook from the floor. Thumbing through the pages, she stops at a drawing she hadn't seen before.

"I think—" Ryan is at the bedroom door.

"Look." She holds up the drawing. "It's uncanny. Down to the green door and caved in roof."

"No question, it's spot on." Ryan says after she hands him the pad. "It also adds up with what Marty just told me. Teague is in Ballycarrick, asking at Kenny's where he and Fiona live. Let's get over there."

The bartender refused to give Teague Marty's address without calling him first. That's a drag because he just wanted it for the name of their street. He wasn't planning on dropping in for a visit. Now Marty's on his way over. Luckily, the bartender let it spill that the Quinn dairy is on Big Rock Road. Kate told him the Callahan cottage was walking distance from their farm.

"Thanks. I'll wait for him outside." That was a necessary lie. Teague doesn't want to get bogged down with Ryan's relatives. He needs to find Finn. A young guy in a truck gets him part of the way there. The moon is close to full, which helps him avoid stepping into a mother of a ditch filled with water. He walks to the Quinn dairy and keeps going.

It's nine o'clock by the time Kate and Ryan reach Marty's farm in Ballycarrick. The late hour adds to her worry. Marty comes outside to tell them Teague wasn't at Kenny's when he went to pick him up.

"I'm sorry for all the trouble we've caused you," Kate says.

"It's no bother, dear. The boy's determined. Let's just hope—"

"You've been grand, Marty," Ryan interrupts. "I'm sure we'll find him."

"I'll ring your pager again if he turns up here or back at Kenny's."

Ryan puts the key in the ignition but doesn't turn it.

"What are you thinking?"

"You told Teague about the Callahan cottage?"

"Yes, in a general way. But why would he go there, alone and in the dark?"

"I don't know. But like Marty said, he's keen on something. I think we're better off walking there. Keep the element of surprise."

Teague pauses in front of each boarded-up cottage to check for any signs of activity. They're all made of stacked stones and it's too dark to see the color of their shutters or the condition of their roofs, so the drawing he did isn't any help. At the end of Big Rock Road, he comes to a graveyard and sits down on a rock wall to rest. This might not be a great place to hang out for long, but he's tired and his stitches are pulling on his stomach again.

Before long, his doubts gain the upper hand. This whole thing was a dumb idea. There's been one car since he got dropped off on this road. It's going to take him forever to get a ride back home. He's trying to muster the energy to start back when he hears footsteps and sees the silhouette of a large man coming towards him. "Hello?" he ventures.

The figure doesn't answer as he approaches Teague still sitting on the wall. A hand grabs his collar. "What in God's name are you doing here?"

Teague is tongue-tied but relieved it's Finn and not an angry ghost.

Finn turns around as if to check the road.

"There's nobody else with me."

He shakes his head. "All right. Come along. We've got some talking to do."

They walk back to one of the cottages he passed. As they get close to the building, or what's left of it, he makes out a green door and the half-gone roof. Yup, it's the one he drew. The door scrapes against the floor as Finn pushes it open. Inside there are embers burning in a big fireplace and a sleeping bag spread on the floor. A backpack, cans, a pile of wood, newspapers. Finn puts a log on the fire and drags two knee-high stools in front of it. He sits on one, and nods at the other. "I'm not going to ask how you found me. Just tell me why you're here."

"I . . . I was afraid Rafferty would arrest you. They already got Liam."

"I know that. And it's for his own good." He leans back on the stool and frowns. "There's nothing to the story Rafferty is telling about me."

Teague is relieved to hear it. "You didn't poison that guy?"

"I was just helping a friend. I can explain it. But you and I have other business—"

A sound outside stops him. A light shines in the broken window.

"Teague? Are you in there?" Kate.

"Come around to the front."

Kate recognizes Finn's voice and freezes. Ryan takes her hand and points his flashlight toward the front of the cottage. When they reach it, Finn is holding open the door.

"Teague, are you all right?" She rushes past Finn and leans down to hug him.

"Yeah, I'm good." He disentangles his arms from hers and frowns.

"You're good?" She's about to tell him how worried she was when she feels Finn's eyes on her. "We can talk about this later." She turns around. "What's going on here?"

"Kate, why don't you sit down next to your boy," he says. "I've got something to say to both of you."

Even though she's tempted to grab Teague and get the hell out of there, her need to know wins out. Finn goes to the fireplace and puts his hand on the chimney. His jowls and shoulders slacken. Her throat is tight and dry; she coughs to open her windpipe. Finn is half turned away, staring into the fire, running a hand through his hair. She identifies the heat she feels in her cheeks as anger. He turns in her direction. Their eyes meet.

"I'm everything you accused me of at Samhain. Worst of all, I'm the father who deserted you and lied to your face."

Kate gasps. Even though she hadn't ruled it out, hearing him say it out loud knocks the wind out of her. She grabs her side and leans forward. When she sees concern on his face, she takes it as another blow. How dare he care about her now?

"Please, keep going," she hears herself say. She keeps her eyes on the dirt floor.

"Twenty-five years ago, I saw the horrors in Belfast, and I sent them guns. Ma's brother, Finn Mitchell was a true hero who served twenty years for his part in the London bombing campaign. He died on his way home, and they buried him at sea. Should I go on?"

"Yes," Kate says in a steely voice.

"My IRA brothers in New York gave me the news of his passing, and I took Finn's identity to escape going to trial. If they'd convicted me, I would have been put away for ten years."

A reflex takes Kate back to the day Mom told her the man standing in front of her now had been shot dead. Running to her room. Gran holding her on the bunk bed . . . My poor Katy Bird. Only to find out it was all over a lie.

"I'm not sorry about shipping the guns. But I regret the terrible harm I did to my family, to you."

Feeling protective, she puts her hand on Teague's knee. As she meets Finn's gaze, Kate feels a hot current run up and down her spine. Her effort to keep him from reaching her is faltering.

"You're my daughter, and I'm ashamed that I denied the truth when you confronted me with it. It was disgraceful of me. I won't ask your forgiveness, but I want you to know how much I regret my cowardice. After that night, I ran because I couldn't face you, at least not yet."

He turns to Teague. "Lad, when I saw you laying bloody on the ground, I knew my secret had to come out. I'm sorry you had to be the last victim of a feud that should never have started."

Teague's jaw is dropped open. He puts his palms on the top of his head. "You brought me my pendant."

Finn looks taken aback. "It was the least I could do. Maybe it helped you pull through."

Addressing Ryan, who's moved behind Kate, he says, "I shouldn't have said what I did at the council meeting about the work you do. The truth is, Liam wouldn't have pulled that trigger if he'd been on his medication. He let paranoia get the best of him. Because of it, we almost lost Teague."

We? Kate cranes her neck to meet Ryan's eyes. He squeezes her shoulder.

"You're a good lad, Teague, almost a man. I'm impressed you found me here. And grateful. I don't deserve forgiveness from either of you. There's a lot more I could say. I know you have questions. I hope you'll give me a chance to answer them."

"What are you going to do now?" Ryan asks.

"I need to face my friends and neighbors and tell them the truth about who I am. In a way, you've given me a gift. I don't have to pretend anymore."

"Will you still be a Druid?" Teague asks.

"Of course. That's who I am now. It's the best part of me."

Ryan clears his throat. "What about Rafferty's accusations?"

"It's shite he's peddling. Conor Rafferty takes favors from a certain developer who doesn't appreciate my civic actions and would like to get me out of his hair, if he had any." Finn smiles as if to himself. "The man who died was an old friend to me. He suffered the black dog—you know what I mean. I was at his farm that afternoon to try and help him find another way out of his troubles, one believer to another. But he couldn't climb out the hole he'd dug for himself. I told his wife I'd keep her man's secret, since there's still a lot of shame attached to it. If it comes to it, I'll tell whoever needs to hear the truth. Hopefully she'll back me up."

Kate stands and crosses her arms. "We need to go. Are you staying? I mean, here in Ballycarrick?"

"Just a bit longer. I'd appreciate you not letting Rafferty know my whereabouts."

"We have no reason to turn you in," Ryan says.

"I hope you'll talk to me again," Finn says, looking at Kate. "There's a lot more to say."

"Yes, there is. Let me think about it."

"Fair play."

# 2002

Kate can't bring herself to think of him as Jack, and certainly not as *Dad*. And that's before she learns he's been charged with the Sligo murder and is now in custody.

To make matters worse, Rafferty lets it leak that Finn isn't the man the people of Ballymore think he is. He's Jack Callahan, an American who stuck his nose in the Troubles and got caught, then deserted his family in New York and took up with the Ballymore divorcée who goes by Morgan O'Shea. The man's daughter is the very same Dr. Jones who's been trying to hoodwink them into being part of her and Dr. Quinn's lunatic study. Most insulting, this Callahan fellow, whose mother was Ellen Mitchell, pretended to be his own uncle, Finn Mitchell, the true IRA hero. He even appropriated the Mitchell family farm to live in sin with Morgan O'Shea and carry out their pagan activities.

When Ryan fills her in on this scuttlebutt, Kate asks if it isn't time for her and Teague to get on a plane and never return to this place where she's become notorious by association—both past and present. She apologizes for the collateral damage she's done to the clinic, saying, "This can't help the study."

Ryan takes a long time to answer, then says, "It depends on what happens next."

"What do mean?"

"People love gossip; you and your father have brought us a trove. But, as Marty said, this has turned into a fight in the family, and there's a lot to be said for self-disclosure when you're trying to get people to spill all their secrets."

"If Teague and I can help by being your sacrificial lambs, maybe it won't be a complete loss."

Even if she wanted to hide from her new-found notoriety, the news is everywhere and constant. Apparently, the dead Druid's wife is sticking to her story, lending credence to Rafferty's case against Finn. And now Rafferty has called her to say that Finn, or Jack, as she supposes she'll have to start calling him, is out on bail, with his murder trial set for January.

With the study still in limbo, Kate has spent the last three weeks at home with Teague. She's watched him finish six paintings and, in a herculean push, they completed his homeschooling for the semester.

One evening, she's sitting on the sofa engrossed in a new journal while he's stretched out on the floor flipping TV channels. After watching a few minutes of *Dr. Who*, he mutes the sound and sits up to look at her with a pained expression on his face. "Are you ever going to talk to him again?" She knows who he's talking about.

"I'm not sure."

"Why not?"

"Oh, Teague. For one thing, we don't know if he had anything to do with the poisoning. If it comes down to his word against the man's wife, well, he's an admitted liar on a grand scale. Even without the murder charge, and I do hope he's innocent, it's hard for me to get over what he did to our family, to me. I didn't realize how angry I was until he said he was sorry."

He rolls onto his back and stares at the ceiling.

"It's okay if you don't feel the same way." His forehead wrinkles. "We have different relationships with him. You've known and bonded with Finn as your Druid teacher. He's still the same man to you, only now he's Jack. And I understand it's a huge deal having him as a grandfather."

Now he's on his side, elbow bent, with his head resting on one hand. "Yeah, it is."

"What I'm trying to say is you have every right to get to know him—if and when it's safe."

His expression seems to be spelling out equal parts confusion and impatience.

"It's different for me. If I engage with him, I lose the father I used to love all over again because that man is truly gone. If he's alive, standing in front of me, I must forgive and accept this new person. A Druid on top of everything else." She allows a grin, which Teague returns.

"When can I see him?"

"I want you to wait until the murder case is settled." She doesn't say *only if he's acquitted* but that's her intention.

He juts out his lower lip and flops onto his back.

"Teague?"

"All right." He restores the sound to *Dr. Who.*

Kate feels a twinge in her chest. Eventually she's going to have to talk with her father. First, she'd like to know whether he's got blood on his hands.

With the TV grating on her nerves, she retreats to her room, where, curled on the bed, her mother's voice breaks through the din in her head . . . *Jack, why can't you leave Katy out of it?* Dressed in her Sunday best, she had watched and listened to them from the top of the stairs. The fear in Mom's voice. Dad's flushed cheeks. *For Christ's sake, Maureen, it's all on the up and up.* Alarmed that Mom was about to make her miss a rare chance to go with Dad to the old neighborhood, she hurried down and stood her ground next to him. I want to go. *Dad says I can help him and Shane sell raffle tickets.*

And that's what she did, oblivious to the reason for her mother's concern. Now, with the missing piece of Dad's gunrunning filled in, she understands why her mother might not have thought it a good idea to involve a child in an event meant to raise money for guns intended for an ongoing hot war.

But it's no longer just indecision about when and if to talk to her father that's got her by the throat. What is she supposed do about Mom? She imagines picking up the phone. *Mom, I called to tell you Dad isn't dead. He faked it all. He's over here in Ireland with Teague and me and . . .* Her head feels like it might explode. She may well end up having to make that call but she's in no way ready to do it. Not yet. Then again, maybe Mom should be allowed to live in peace, without having this bombshell dropped on her. Of course, by keeping Dad's secret, Kate would also protect herself from the fallout sure to come at her if she's the one who breaks the news to Mom. If she waits too long and Mom finds out, God help her. Either way, Mom will make her choose sides. That's the way it's always been.

# 2002

Five nights later, Ryan appears unexpectedly at their front door.

"What a nice surprise," she says as she lets him in.

"I bring fish and chips—and news."

Teague doesn't need to be called from his room. He's there in seconds. "What's the news?"

"Let him sit. Here, I'll take that," Kate says. She carries the bag into the kitchen and returns with a tray of plates piled with food, and utensils. She puts it down on the sofa table, grabs the back of the chair, and studies Ryan's face. Surely if the news was terrible, he'd look glum. Then again, he's capable of pulling off a neutral expression in any situation.

"It appears the widow's conscience has prodded her memory and she's changed her story to back up Finn's. She admits he went to their farm at her request to try and talk her husband out of taking his own life. As we know, Finn was not successful. Suicide is still considered a mortal sin by many Catholics, so she let the gardai' come to their own conclusions. In the end she couldn't go through with the lie if it meant Finn going to jail. And she has no idea where her husband got the yew needles."

Kate lets out a long sigh.

"I knew he didn't do it," Teague says.

"I wasn't sure, but I am relieved," she says.

"I knew you'd both be," Ryan says as he turns from Teague to her.

"Isn't it strange that Rafferty didn't feel the need to let me know himself that his big murder case just fell apart?" she says sarcastically. "Wait. It wasn't in the paper today. How did you hear all this?"

"The receptionist at the Sligo guard station is an old school friend of Niamh's. She called to tell me."

"Of course." Kate says and shakes her head.

Another surprise arrives in Friday's *Ballymore News.* An open letter from Finn Mitchell, aka Jack Callahan. He makes a public confession of his false identity and apologizes for abusing his friends' and neighbors' trust. He goes on to explain what he did and why. As part of his mea culpa, he throws his support behind the Ballymore Family Study, writing:

> Friends, you won't offend me if you look the other way
> when we pass on the street. But I do sincerely hope you might
> come to the same sad conclusion I've reached that hiding from
> the truth does none of us any good. In fact, our secrets can kill
> the people we love. I say let Ryan and Kate finish their study
> and let's give our young ones the help they need to heal. I, for
> one, want to spend whatever time I've got left making peace
> with my daughter and grandson.

Despite his notoriety, Finn's changed stance on the study appears to have gotten the ball rolling in their favor. Other fierce critics, including Eamon O'Malley, follow his lead and contact Jim Lynch to let him know they no longer oppose it. The council members hold a heated private debate . . . and since nothing stays private in Ballymore for very long, they soon hear . . . in which one holdout argues against the study's resumption, because Finn's, now Jack's, change of heart, shouldn't influence their decision about the study, since he's really a Yank. The majority come around.

Lynch invites Ryan back to the chamber to give him the news personally, saying their green light is contingent on there being no more data leaks. The funding agencies in Dublin and Washington release the rest of the grant money, which will allow the clinic to staff up and expand the number of interviews and therapy services. Kate can begin taking DNA samples. It's an unequivocally positive development in a time when it's been difficult to find good news in all the bad.

She's in her office, having just heard from Ryan that phase two of the study has been green lit. It's the work she's been looking forward to doing since she arrived six months ago. But all she can seem to do is sit at her desk, unable to find the energy to open a file, or make a simple to-do list. So unlike her.

If only she could lose the sense of dread that's chased her since the night her father made his confession in the decrepit family cottage. She's been walking around encased in a bubble, removed from real life. It's not an altogether unfamiliar feeling. But she hasn't felt it this intensely since she was the sad little girl who spent years waiting for her father to come home to her. Knowing he never would.

From her purse, she pulls out the letter she received from him yesterday, asking her to meet him alone. He promises to hold off on seeing Teague until she lets him know it's all right. How grand of him, she thinks, as she drops the letter on her desk and pounds it with her balled fist. As her eyes well and a fallen tear blurs the blue ink, she lets out a loud *No*. She has no more tears left for this man. She used them all up long ago. Why should she forgive him? She's lived this long and done okay without a father. A conversation among competing parts of herself ensues.

*What are you talking about? You're a mess.*

*Granted. But is that any reason to let him back in to do more damage?*

*Maybe consider what it might be like to live without this hole in your heart? Unless that's the scarier scenario?*

*No, thank you.*

She puts the letter back in her purse and numbly hits the button on the stack of electronics under her desk to turn on her computer. As its hum builds to a roar and the monitor alights, she waits for the quickened heartbeat and rush of blood to her forehead these rote steps usually elicit. The cursor on the screen is blinking as if calling her name but she can't find the will to move her hand to the keyboard. Her throat tightens as a wave of apathy takes possession of her, creating more distance from the work that has always been her salvation. Jesus, who is she without it? She's never felt so out of control, and she hates the feeling.

# 2002

Teague steps out of Kate's car at the gate to the grove and leans back in the window. "Jack says he'll give me a ride home after dinner."

"Okay. See you later, sweetheart."

After a relentless series of requests from Teague, Kate ran out of excuses and gave him permission to see his grandfather. In the same call with her father, she agreed to see him herself. Teague would go first.

The two of them are hiking up a hill to see a yew that Jack says is the oldest tree in the county. Teague has never been in such a dense forest. It's a lot more work—pushing branches out of your face, slogging through underbrush—but as he does it, he feels less like he's a visitor, more a part of the place. It's cold out but he's working up a sweat as he goes.

At a soggy dip one of his boots gets stuck in the mud—oh right, he doesn't mind wearing shoes now—and it's sinking like he's in quicksand.

"You okay there, lad?" Jack asks looking back.

"Not really."

"Here, hold on to my arm," Jack says, as Teague yanks his foot from the stuck boot and grabs Jack's coat just in time. "Atta boy." He balances on one foot until Jack retrieves the boot.

As Jack waits for him to get it back on, Teague decides this is as good a time as any to ask a question that's been on his mind since he found out they're related. He takes a deep breath and spits it out. "Um, what should I call you now?"

Jack does a double-take and turns away, making Teague sorry he brought it up. "Never mind."

"No. I'm glad you asked. You see, when I was a lad, it was hard not having a father, and I didn't dare wish for a grandpa. Now I'm an old man, but no has ever called me that. I'd be happy for you to be the first."

"Okay. I will."

As they pick up the hike, Teague watches where his grandpa puts his boots and matches his steps.

By the look of it, this tree should be in a sci-fi movie. It's as wide as a semi. The trunk looks like it's made of ten or twenty smaller trees banded together.

Grandpa is winded as he lowers his butt onto a log. Teague sits next to him and cranes his neck as he leans back. The crown of the yew is so thick only small streaks of light break through.

"We're lucky we still have this one. It's the last of a grove that used to stand here."

"How does it grow so many trunks?"

"That's one of its mysteries. Yews have been known to live five thousand years. This one could be that old. When the original trunk reaches a ripe old age, it decays inside, and a new one grows in its place. It's constantly sprouting new trunks and branches. Some reach up for sun, but others go down into the soil and link up with their brethren underground." He breaks off a spiky sprig from a low-hanging branch and puts it under his nose, then hands it to Teague. It smells like a whole forest.

"The yew reminds us that death is an illusion."

Shit, why did he have to say that? Teague stands up and runs his hand over the bark, following its spiral around the giant trunk. When he closes his eyes, he hears a female voice. She welcomes him by name and lets him know she understands his hurt.

"Grandpa, I think you might be wrong about that. I know people who died and they're still dead."

He looks at him and nods. "You're right, Teague. They're no longer who they were, and they're not with us. We miss them. But, in the Druids' way of thinking, death is just a temporary stop before we return in a new life. We believe when our soul is reborn in a new body, it tends to go back to the clan they came from to keep working on things left undone."

Teague straddles the log facing him, waiting for his brain to catch up with what he just heard. Grandpa puts a hand on his shoulder. "You've got a lot of time ahead of you to think about that sort of thing."

"Yeah.' He debates asking the other question that's been on his mind. Shit, he may as well go for it. "Do you think it's weird how Kate and I showed up here?"

Grandpa tilts his head to the side and scrunches his face, making Teague think he doesn't understand the question. So, he elaborates. "I know Ballymore used to have a lot of schizophrenics and some of their kids and grandkids have it. And that's why Kate got her job at the clinic. But then we find out Gran and Michael got run out of this town. And you turn up here. How does stuff like this happen?"

"I know what you're asking, Teague. We can look at nature for an answer. Take the wolf. In forests here and around the world, men killed them off because they didn't want them preying on their sheep and cattle. But for hundreds and thousands of years before that, wolves lived in these forests, where they killed game to survive, and they knew where to find the roots that were their medicines. Pups learned the best feeding grounds and the places to make their dens. Every generation that came along would use the same paths and the same dens. You following me?"

"Yeah."

"Where this gets interesting is after a century or more goes by with no wolves living in a particular forest and they're reintroduced with the help of scientists, like the fellow from the university in Galway who explained this to me. Mind you, *these* wolves never lived in that forest, so they couldn't have learned anything about it from their mammas or pappas. When the scientists tracked them, they saw the wolves were using the same paths to hunt and the same dens to have their pups as their ancestors had used before them."

"Maybe those were just the best paths and dens around."

"You have a sharp mind. But the land changes too much over a hundred years for it to be that simple."

"How *did* the wolves know where to go?"

"If you ask a Druid, he'll tell you that creature gets information from the land, because the soil holds memories made from the skin and bones left behind by his ancestors."

"You mean like the DNA from their cells?"

"Could be that. Or another link we can't see or measure. At least not yet."

"Wow." Teague stands up. "Like the voices I heard coming from the rocks around the old church."

Grandpa tilts his chin up and laughs. "You heard them?"

Teague nods.

"I remember the same thing happened to me the first time I went into the square."

"Yeah. Those voices are crazy."

"Losing everything will do that to a man or a woman."

"I guess." Teague goes back to the stump and thinks about Gran. How he wishes he could tell her everything that's happened to him since he got to Ireland.

Grandpa is watching him. "Who are you missing, Teague?"

"Gran."

"My mother was a fierce lady. It meant a lot to me to make the trip back here that she could never make herself."

"She used to talk about stuff you did when you were a kid and how proud she was when you became a cop. She called you, *my boy*."

Grandpa's eyes get misty. Two birds talking to each other is the only sound for a while.

"Are you hungry?"

"Yeah."

Grandpa puts one hand on his knee, the other on the log, and pushes himself up. The way back is mostly uphill, so it's harder. As the sun goes down, rain turns to sleet and slides off Teague's jacket onto his jeans. He's soaking wet and shivering.

They're halfway there when Grandpa runs out of breath. He leans against a tree with a hand resting on his ribs. Teague sits on a rock a few feet away. He never thought about not having a grandpa, but now that he has one, he'll miss him when he's gone. Which sucks, but that's the price you pay for having one. Grandpa breathes easier and Teague relaxes.

"You've come here at a perfect time. You know how I know that?"

"How?"

"The rocks and trees in this part of the world don't talk to just anyone who comes along. They're calling you to what need to know."

"You mean this place brought us here without our realizing it?"

"That's my opinion. When a family has unfinished business in a place, it's going to pull them back. That's why I'm here, too. Though I'm sad to say I never did settle my father's business."

"You mean about the tip-off that got the rebel executed?"

"How did you know about that son?"

"Sean Mitchell told us."

He shakes his head. "If people repeat a lie often enough it becomes the truth."

As soon as he stops talking, a gust of wind comes up out of nowhere and moves in a circle, picking up leaves and debris as it turns into a funnel cone, spinning faster and faster, making a loud hum. Teague's arms and legs tingle like they did at his first ceremony. The funnel is twirling and skipping around like a tiny tornado.

The light in Grandpa's eyes shines through the cone.

"We call that a faerie eddie," Grandpa yells over the hum. "I think our good folk are happy about the two of us being here together."

Flashes of green and white light spark like fireworks inside the funnel. "Show-offs."

"That they are."

The wind slows and the leaves drop on the ground. Grandpa winks at Teague.

"That was pretty cool," Teague says.

"The best thing, son, is this land will always be here for you."

# 2002

It's not yet noon and there's just a single, middle-aged man at the bar, chatting with Kenny, when Kate enters. She carries her beer to the same booth she and Ryan occupied two months ago. She can hardly believe how much has happened since that night. She catches her breath when her father enters and grows more nervous watching him exchange pleasantries with Kenny, before bringing a cup of coffee to her booth.

After awkward greetings, he asks if she wants to hear the details of his escape from New York. At first, she finds the question offensive, almost boastful. Until she realizes she does want to know how he pulled the whole damn thing off.

"All right, then. Only two cops, Shane and our precinct captain, knew I didn't die that night. A crooked medical examiner did the dummy paperwork. Then the Provos helped me get over here."

"Provos?"

"That's what they called the IRA during the Troubles. The longshoreman who talked . . . that happened after I was gone. I felt terrible about Shane taking the rap for it on top of the smuggling. More likely the order came from over here to protect their East Coast dealers. The feds knew it was me who ran the operation. The US Attorney suspected the robbery story was a load of crap, but they couldn't prove it. There were still a lot of guns coming through, so they made Shane an example."

As bizarre and interesting as these details are, Kate realizes they're nowhere near the top of the list of things she wants to hear from her father after twenty-five years of thinking he was dead. Still, she lets him catch her up on his legal problems. As Rafferty predicted, nobody in Ireland or the Southern District of New York has any interest in dredging up the gunrunning case. She's relieved to hear it.

"Do you regret being a cop?" It feels like a safer question than others she's waiting to ask him.

"No, I don't. Young men want to be warriors, and the police force is as good a place as any to train a boy for it. If it's done right. But that was never all it was for me. I joined to help my neighbors. I felt useful when I took a perp off the street or had a serious talk with a man who was taking out his sorrows on his wife. Like I told you, to this day I feel no shame over what I did for the people of Northern Ireland. Now I'm helping my neighbors in a different way. Of course, with my secret out, it could be that nobody will want to see my face again in Ballymore." His eyes become dull.

"It's going to take time." It hits her after she says the words aloud that she needs to give herself the same permission. Forgiveness is not a simple up or down proposition. It takes as long as it takes. With the pressure off, her chest expands.

As for the Druid sitting across from her, she'll have to take him at his word. He's found his true calling. Who is she, an avowed atheist, to judge anyone's religion?

"As you know, I've made a few enemies."

"Not too long ago, you saw me as one of your enemies."

"Well, I changed my mind about your study and I'm glad it's back on." His eyes wander. When he meets hers again, he says, "I'm a changed man, Katy."

Changed from what, she wonders, since she's not sure she ever knew this man. She nods and lets it go. The clawing in her stomach is a reminder that the hardest part of this conversation is still ahead. She waits for his cough to subside before she makes her first attempt to steer them there.

"Did Mom know?"

His face contracts like he's swallowed bleach. Guilt is written all over it.

"The way I saw it, and still do, your mother suffered enough because of me. She doesn't need any more grief on my account." He presses his lips together. "I'll leave it to you to decide how much you want to tell her."

Blood rushes to her head. This is exactly what she was afraid he would do. It takes all her focus to form the words. "No, Dad. It can't be up to me."

His mouth opens but he doesn't speak. She falters and swallows hard.

They sit in tense silence. She's been going back and forth about this since he confessed to her. She's still torn but clearer about who needs to act first. And it's not her.

"I need your word that you'll tell Mom everything. Soon."

He turns toward the empty bar, leaving her to examine his familiar profile, now softened with age. "I've been writing letters to each of you in my head since the day I left. Nothing felt right or enough. I ended up thinking you were better off not hearing from me." He shakes his head. "You're right. It's not fair to ask you to tell your mother. I'll write to her before the New Year. I promise."

Relief washes over her. She stretches her legs and points her toes.

"How is Maureen?"

He catches her off guard. "Mom is . . . the same. I think she's a lot happier than she was back then. She never remarried. Stayed in nursing, in fact she just retired, moved in with Aunt Connie, who's also on her own now."

"Hmmm. Maureen and Connie in one house. They were always tighter than a nun's gee . . . if you'll excuse the local expression." He looks sheepish.

She's embarrassed. But she's heard worse.

"Why aren't you asking about Meghan?"

"Shane got word to me after Ma wrote him about her overdose. Shane was Meghan's godfather, and he knew I worried about her the most. That little girl needed more than we could give her. Even at thirteen, I saw it, but I didn't know what to do."

"Doctors weren't much help then either."

"It's a blessing you kept Teague close after . . . He's an extraordinary lad." He cracks a smile. "And I'll have you know I came to that opinion before I knew

278

he was my grandson."

"Did you tell Gran before you left New York?"

"Not directly, although not much got past her. I put the pendant where she'd find it."

Kate's leg has fallen asleep. She rubs her thigh to get the circulation going. The next move is his. Maybe he knows that. He's got the heels of his palms covering his eyes. When he drops them and leans forward, tears are welling up. He bites his lip. "I've missed. . . everything. I never wanted to leave you kids. Either way, I knew I wouldn't be there to see you grow up." The color drains from his face and his pupils dilate. He looks haunted. "I was selfish. At least you could have visited me in prison. I just couldn't face it."

His breathing has a staccato start-and-stop quality to it. He seems frail, vulnerable.

"I know saying *I'm sorry* isn't worth piss." He grunts. Pain takes ownership of his face. He seems to be waiting for her to say something.

Her throat is closing, she can barely swallow. After several awkward seconds, she pushes the words out. "For the longest time, I didn't believe you were dead. And then I just wanted to be with you wherever you were."

"My poor Katy." His palms are flat on the table. "When you were little, you saw only the good in me. Your love was pure, I could hardly stand the guilt. I was a terrible father." He rests his forehead on his raised fists.

She's thankful for the pause as she scrambles to find her feelings. She feels unfairly pushed to make it right for him. He speaks before she's ready to hear anymore from him.

"I hope you believe how much I regret hurting you."

Does she believe him? It might not matter. Maybe certain things aren't forgivable no matter how much time passes. Her chest hollows out. Never have words seemed so inadequate. She's torn but not ready to let him in. She turns to the wall and lets her mind drift far away. His hacking cough jars her back. He reaches for a handkerchief, wipes his mouth, and tilts his head to the side. His eyes widen, and his upper lip curls into a smile. "You still do it."

"Do what?"

"The rocking."

She freezes.

"You used to do it when you were upset or thinking hard. Your mother pointed it out to me once when we were all watching TV, then I noticed it on my own. You always had such a big brain."

Damn. The bastard. Tears fall, and she can't stop them. His features fade until she sees only a backlit silhouette of his head and chest. Stripped of distractions, she understands the hold he's always had on her as if she's reading a surreal clinical profile of herself. His murky sorrow and thinly veiled anger were the blinking red lights that let her know he wouldn't be staying long. His volatile moods shaped her to serve him. She became his photonegative, not a separate person. She cultivated her willpower for the sole purpose of keeping him close. Later, that push and pull became the schema for how she was with men. The blinking red light became her type. The way she held on to her missing father was to attach herself to a man who was certain to leave her. Now she's looking at a phantom of the knife-wielding man who made the first cut and left the rest of the job to her.

"When you stood there in front of your followers and denied you were my father, it broke me. Then, for a short time, it felt good to be that furious at you, even if I was directing my anger at an old guy named Finn, who wasn't even you. How crazy is that?"

"It's not so crazy."

"When Liam took that shot at Teague . . . nothing else mattered. Which helped me back away from you and forget about the accusation I might have just made to a stranger. After he pulled through, and you came clean, I was gutted. I didn't know who I was anymore."

"I swear to God, I didn't recognize you the first time we came face to face at the council meeting. I thought you were a pushy New Yorker sticking your nose in our business. It was only when you rattled off names and held up my pendant that I realized who you were. I knew I was busted, and I acted like a pathetic coward. My only excuse is that I had lived so long with this lie, I came to believe it. I don't blame you for not forgiving me." His face collapses as if he's just now facing the possibility that she won't.

She sits back in the booth and widens her gaze. She's seeing double. Two lamps on the table. Two of his eyes, nose, and mouth. If she doesn't speak, he'll disappear. The threat of losing him again removes her last bit of armor. "Even if I wanted to walk away from you right now, I doubt I could pull it off. Finding you, having this conversation . . . I've spent too much of my life dreaming of this moment to deny it. I don't understand why I'm here and or how this happened. But I can't undo it. I don't want to." She's shaking, trying not to cry. She wipes her cheek and forces herself to look at him. His jaw muscles twitch as his face softens and a smile returns. She closes her eyes.

"Thank you for that, Katy."

She hates feeling soothed by the familiarity of his voice but there it is. "How did you acquire this accent?"

"I suppose I always had Ma's voice in my head. Since Finn spent all that time in an English prison, people figured my—or I should say, his—accent when he came back would be a strange brew. The brogue came to me gradually."

He covers her hands with his. The hairs on the back of her neck stand up. She widens her view and it's as if before this moment she'd only seen a weak facsimile of Kenny's Pub. The walls, illuminated by individual lamps at each table, aren't dull white, they're yellow. The lettering on a wooden sign hanging from the ceiling over the cash register reads Founded 1906. A stocky bartender, maybe Kenny, wipes down the counter, scans the room, and talks out of the side of his mouth to a customer on the other side of the bar. Dad's eyes, which she's remembered as hazel, are, in fact, moss green.

"God knows I don't deserve anybody's forgiveness. I tried to be a good Catholic. But I was a phony. I haven't had a drink in . . ." he has to think, "fifteen years. It was the devil's way into me. Any good I've done in my life is because I've found my way home. Where I fit. You coming here, bringing Teague, it mends a broken chain."

"Oh, Dad."

His face brightens and exudes gratitude. Her anger melts the rest of the way.

"I'll never be able to make up for the time we lost. But I plan to spend as much of what I've got left with you and Teague as you'll allow." He takes her hands again. "I hope you come back to the grove for a proper ceremony. We have one on each full moon."

Dad looks thoughtful. His eyes brighten. "The strangest thing happened when I met Teague the first time. My own second sight started coming back, which surprised me. It usually wanes as you age. The boy has a special gift."

"Yes, I'm discovering that, too." She catches herself. It's the first time she's ever spoken or thought of Teague's *gift* without the attendant worries and qualifications. She supposes she's acquired more than enough evidence to see it for the extrasensory, one could even say magical, ability that it is.

"I had to grow old before I understood how it's meant to be used. Seeing what's coming is all well and good. It can help or be hurtful. But the real purpose is to help people reconnect with the land, which means connecting with our dead. It's the surest way to heal what ails us. I don't know if it can happen any other way."

He seems lost in thought, and it dawns on Kate that her father just articulated the same idea that Gran had tried to explain to her on the day she left for med school. In Kate's way of thinking, it comes down to a belief that our ancestors are more than data points to us. They're allies for the living. She catches her breath as she realizes it's also the missing piece she needs to embrace before the people of Ballymore will trust her and get fully on board with the study. As she puts these two things together, she has a keen sense that the peacemaking going on between her and her father is also reaching Ellen Callahan, who, in turn, is helping remove the debris impeding their reconnection. And in that moment, the idea of living ancestors becomes a tangible reality for her. A weight lifts from chest and she takes a deep, slow breath.

Her father makes eye contact and smiles. "I hope you and Teague can accept Morgan, and Liam, as kin. There's no reason for the Callahan and O'Shea clans to hate each other. Not anymore."

"Teague is more than ready. I'll try to catch up as fast as I can."

"Thank you, Katy.

He covers her hands with his. Neither of them speaks.

# 2002

"Hmmm. That's delicious, dear." Morgan licks the spoon after tasting Sophie's homemade cranberry applesauce. "Kate and Teague helped," Sophie says, referring to the apple peeling and cranberry stewing they did the day before.

Ryan, Teague, Sophie, and Kate are at Ballymore grove to celebrate Midwinter Eve with Dad, Morgan, and Liam, who came home from treatment a week ago.

Apparently, this ancient holiday marks the winter solstice, the shortest day of the year—a day Kate has never taken note of other than to complain about having to walk home from school or work in the dark.

"Can you carry this to the table, Sophie?" Kate asks. The bowl is supersized and tipping with fruit.

Sophie looks askance. "I'm a goalie, remember?"

"Of course." She follows Sophie into the dining room, where Dad is explaining to Teague and Ryan how he and Liam converted an old horse cart into the dining room table that's about to hold their feast.

Liam, who's standing apart in the living room, takes a few steps closer. "It was my idea to add a brake, so dinner won't go flying across the room."

Sophie puts her bowl on the table.

"See if you can turn the wheel, Soph," Ryan says.

She gives it a push, but nothing moves. "Good job, Liam," she says with a coy smile.

Liam smirks and heads out the front door.

Kate and Ryan exchange a look. Yesterday at the office, he passed on the news that Rafferty closed the hacking case after Liam admitted doing it—alone, he claimed. The gardai' confiscated his computers but declined to prosecute because he didn't post any hacked patient information on the internet. From Ryan's point of view, the bigger revelation was Liam's admission that he never possessed the master file that would have enabled him to correlate patient names and diagnoses. That part had been a bluff. A very successful one, Kate pointed out.

As she walks back to the kitchen to help Morgan, it occurs to her that if Liam hadn't done the hack, and Teague hadn't become a Druid, it's doubtful she and her father would ever have found each other. It's almost enough to believe it was all destined. Gran would appreciate that.

Morgan has a pork roast in the oven and several side dishes in process.

"Thank you for having us here," Kate makes a point of saying to Morgan before dinner gets underway. They've never had more than a brief exchange alone. "You've been through a lot these past months. I mean, with everything that happened."

"You, too, Kate. Your father told me who he was a long time ago—before we committed to a life together. We married in a Druid ceremony, here in the grove. We didn't need anything else to make our bond real."

She feels sheepish as she bounces between her loyalties to Mom and now, Morgan, her father's Druid wife.

"I'm just glad you two found each other before it's too late," Morgan says to her. The sad cast of Morgan's face makes it clear she's braced for more loss to come, but Kate doesn't want to think about that while she's still processing having a living, breathing father.

"I have plenty of O'Shea kin living nearby. It's been hard for him all these years, not being able to connect with any Callahans. When we got together, he and I were the only ones who knew we came from these warring clans."

"I only learned about the accusation against my grandfather Michael after we came here."

Morgan purses her lips. "It's weighed on your father his whole life. After the truth came out about his identity last month, he reached out to some Callahans who'd moved away a generation back. One of his cousins is coming tonight."

"Oh, that's great." She notices potatoes floating in a pot of water. "Shall I drain these and put them in a bowl?"

"Thank you, dear."

Morgan leans over to open the stove door and her platinum hair catches the late afternoon sun through the skylight. When she stands and gives her a quick smile, Kate notices the crow's feet around Morgan's eyes and mouth. She's a beautiful woman, aging gracefully. The union between her and Dad appears solid. Kate thinks of her mother living the single life she always wanted with Aunt Connie. Thank goodness for second chances.

Teague shivers as he steps out the front door into the frigid night without a jacket. He wants to catch up with Liam before dinner and he forgot where he put it. He's not looking forward to talking to him but it's just going to get worse between them if they don't get it over with. At the bottom of the hill, the ice-covered branches of the oak glisten in the moonlight. He takes a guess and heads to the barn.

Liam is leaning on the cow pen. He turns and looks over his shoulder when the door opens.

"Hey," Teague says.

"You following me?"

"Yeah."

He rolls his eyes and leans back against the pen. Teague gets closer until they're two arms' lengths apart. "What do you want?"

"I just want to talk."

Liam gives him one of his smirks and shrugs.

"They said I had to tell the truth at the tribunal."

Liam huffs. "Did ya think they were going to ship you back to New York?"

"Whatever. I did what I did, and you had to spend a month in therapy, which I bet sucked. But now you're home. Isn't that better than being in jail right now?"

"If I don't mind being the most famous mental case in the county, yeah it's grand."

"Maybe you shouldn't have shot me if you didn't want to be famous."

Liam gives off a strange laugh. "I wasn't aiming at you, eejit."

"You were trying to kill my aunt?"

"Wrong again."

Teague freezes. It had never occurred to him. "Finn?"

"Never mind. I'm glad I didn't kill anybody, okay?"

"Yeah, but why?"

"He pissed me off and I wasn't thinking right."

Teague can't help staring.

"What? He's not my real father, but he rags on me worse than if he was. You being here like his new pet just made things worse."

Since he's never had a brother or sister, Teague has never felt the kind of jealousy coming at him from Liam. He considers pointing out that Finn rags on Liam because he cares about him, but that would sound too much like therapy. Instead, he looks for common ground. "My scumbag father's in prison. Where's yours?"

Liam's eyes pop open. "He's in Cork with his new family."

Teague shrugs. "I don't care if I ever see mine again but it's shitty knowing where he is."

Liam turns his back to him and neither of them talk for a while. A big brown cow moves closer to the front of the stall like she's waiting for Liam to feed her. Teague rubs his arms to warm them and tries to keep his teeth from chattering. He doesn't know if he's fixed anything, but he feels better after spilling what he'd been saving up to say about the tribunal.

When Liam turns around there's a sort of smile on his face. "I guess we're even now. You want to go back?"

"Yeah, I'm fucking freezing."

"Are you two going to join us or will you have your own party in here?"

Dad sticks his head in the kitchen. "We've got Duncan here."

Morgan squeezes her hand before they go to the dining room. Kate squelches a gasp when she lays eyes on Duncan Callahan because he looks just like Dad as a younger man.

Duncan kisses her cheek. "Hello, Cousin Kate. If it's okay with you, I'll dispense with the first and second, once-removed business. It makes no difference, does it?"

"Not to me."

"You've got a slew more of us down in Kerry."

Dad is animated as he tells them that Duncan manages a fine hotel in Killarney.

"I see plenty of Americans coming through. But you and Teague are the first of my own Yank kin I've met."

Dad leads everyone to the living room. He and Morgan occupy the center of the sofa, Teague flanking Dad, and Liam beside Morgan. Ryan and Kate take chairs on either side of the wood stove, with Sophie on Ryan's lap. Duncan picks the seat catty-corner to Teague.

When Dad closes his eyes and takes a long breath, the energy in the room changes. A comfortable silence takes over. After a bit, he opens his eyes and moves his line of sight around the room, pausing on each of them. "I'd be remiss if I didn't offer thanks to our ancestors for bringing us together. We recognize winter as a time of the year when the feminine reigns. My mother's ally was Brigid, a saint, and the Celtic goddess of poetry, also the smith's forge, and healing. Each of Brigid's aspects has come into play to bring you here: Katy's iron strength; the second sight born again in Teague, and Ryan's healing skills. For these gifts, and for our collective health and well-being, please join me in offering thanks."

They bow their heads. Dad's prayer is a chant. There's music in his voice, and the promise of secrets yet to be revealed.

Blessed Brigid of the poets,

I call to you.

Blessed Brigid of the forge,

Creator, transformer,

Who shapes raw material into form and function,
I call to you.
Brigid of the healing well,
Brigid of the healing cloak and the healing word,
I call to you.
Brigid of many welcomes,
Be with me wherever I go,
Accept this offering I give you
And may you prevail.

"Amen. Thank you, Jack," says Duncan. A chorus of amens follows.

"Duncan's grandfather, Colm, was my uncle," Dad says to the group. "A brother to my father, Michael."

"Granddad Colm passed away just last year," Duncan says.

"I'm sorry to have missed knowing him." Dad's eyes wander to the fire in the stove.

Morgan puts her hand on his knee. "What a pity."

"Jack, there's something I need to tell you about Granddad Colm." Duncan's face, jolly since he arrived, has turned somber. "I'd like to get it out of the way if you don't mind."

"Do what you have to do, son," Dad says.

"I was the youngest of five and quite close to Granddad Colm. In the end, he told me what he did as a young man; he called it a shameful deed. He confessed it to the priest at his last rites, and then shared it with me."

Sophie slides off Ryan's lap onto the floor in front of Duncan's chair as if to secure a choice spot. No one else moves as Duncan swallows and stares at his hands, which form a steeple on his lap. "He said it wasn't Michael who gave up Rory O'Shea to the Brits. It was him. He told an RIC named Killian Mitchell where Rory was hiding, and they agreed to say it was Michael who'd tipped him off. Colm admitted he had no good reason for doing it, other than sore feelings between him and his older brother."

Teague whips his head to Kate, and they share a look of recognition. Yes, that Killian Mitchell.

Dad's eyes widen. He falls back on the sofa. Morgan covers his hand with hers. Kate processes the fact that this is the same story Marty told Ryan and her—with Michael painted as the villain.

Ryan makes eye contact with her and shakes his head. To Teague, who appears confused, she whispers, "I'll tell you later." He frowns.

Duncan looks around as if he's seeking permission to go on. Dad picks up his head and nods.

"Colm knew he made a terrible mistake after the rumor forced Michael, and the whole family, to leave Ballymore. Then later, when the O'Shea allies took revenge on Michael in New York."

Dad looks straight ahead and squints as if he can't or doesn't want to see what's in front of him. Poor Duncan. Kate wishes she could think of an appropriate thing to say.

"I need air." Dad gets up and puts his hand on Duncan's shoulder. He leaves it there for a few seconds before he walks out of the room. The front door opens and closes.

Sophie stands and looks at Ryan. "What happened?"

"A misunderstanding long ago between two brothers, which led to a tragedy."

"Oh." Confusion is written on Sophie's face as she falls against Ryan and hides her face in his chest.

"Jack will be okay," Morgan says to Duncan. "You've given him a gift." She stands. "Dinner will be up in a half-hour. Liam, why don't you get your fiddle and play a tune or two. Teague, your drum is in the music closet."

It's midnight when Ryan pulls the car to the curb in front of their flat. Sophie is fast asleep in the back seat.

Teague tumbles out. "See you at group, Ryan."

"Aye. You know we're not meeting this week. It'll be next Wednesday after the New Year."

"Okay, cool."

He turns to her. "Quite a day."

"Another one." She lets out a sigh. "Does this heartbreak ever end? It's like secrets are a major food group here."

"I won't argue with you there." The engine is still running. He cranks up the heat on the dashboard.

"Your father . . ." he begins, then stops. "I'm just curious. Was he a religious man when you were a child?"

"Well. He went to church every Sunday and made confession on Fridays. He would give up drinking for Lent, which, as you know, doesn't add up to much."

Ryan nods.

"While he was reciting that prayer tonight, I remembered him taking me along to go to Latin Mass on Sundays. I would lay down on the pew with my head on his leg and space out. I felt freed from having to follow what was being spoken or sung. It was as if we shared a private space, which felt, well, magical."

"It's good to find those nice memories along with the rest."

"Thanks for coming tonight." Kate grabs the door handle.

"Hang on. You know I closed the clinic for the holidays?"

"Yeah. I got the memo, boss."

He chuckles. "The interns are on their academic break. No one wants to go to therapy at this time of year, anyway. What do you think of getting away for a few days to Achill Island?"

"Are you asking if Teague and I might want to visit whatever island you just said the name of?"

"I'm suggesting you and I do that."

"Well then, yes. I'd love to."

"Wonderful. Bring your rain gear. There's a hurricane in the forecast."

"Oh. That sounds perfect. Goodnight, Ryan." She goes in and leans against the back of the door thinking how lacking in game playing he is. Does she have any hope of matching him?

# 2002

The drive takes them through Connemara and north along the Mayo coast. She's lost count of the number of ancient castles, abbeys, sacred wells, and fairy forts they've passed about which Ryan shares reams of history. He parks on the nonexistent shoulder of a road next to a pasture of incurious sheep.

"I can't believe I found it."

She scans the horizon, looking for a landmark. "Found what?"

"Come. I'll show you."

He separates two strands of a barbed-wire fence, and she slides through. They walk toward a hillside. "There, beside the ash trees."

She sees a graceful stand of tall trees, but little else to distinguish this pasture from any of the others they've passed since turning inland. There's a small herd of sheep in the distance. Intersecting stone walls in the near distance and a line of small, spare trees Ryan identifies as hawthorns, which, he says, with a matter-of-fact tone, are a favorite of fairies.

After hiking up the easy rise, they're in the center of a small circle of upright stones. Three standing close together reach her shoulders, another four are waist high or shorter. Each is one to two arm's lengths wide and six inches thick. A miniature Stonehenge. Or it was, once. Ryan looks serene as his gaze

291

circles the stones and returns to her. "This one dates from the Bronze Age. I like the fact that it's off the beaten track."

"You've been here before?"

"A few times." He rests his hand on a tall stone. "When I stand in this circle, I get the sense I'm being infused with a certain vigor that I don't feel anywhere else." He smiles and shrugs. "I can't explain it."

She takes two steps toward him and covers his hand with hers. "I'm glad you brought me here."

He pulls her closer. Their lips touch, draw back, meet again. The kiss emits a gentle charge, strong enough to punch through her last pockets of resistance. As she tilts her head back, she perceives a glint of hunger in his eyes that flicks a switch in her. They kiss again and allow their tongues to mingle. On the walk back down the hill, they hold hands. The anticipation animates her like a medley of corny love songs, the kind she never seeks out but delights in when they come on the radio.

They pass a half dozen more picturesque towns, spread like gems on a string along the southeastern corner of County Mayo. Their destination is the seaside village of Mulranny, where they'll spend the next two nights in an nineteenth-century manor house overlooking Clew Bay, the Atlantic looming beyond.

They're escorted to a palatial room with its own fireplace and a massive satin-covered bed next to two red-velvet-draped windows offering an ocean view subdued by an ominous sky. The clouds are striated in a way that makes her think of cardiac muscle tissue, crisscrossed by elongated fibers and painted on a spectrum of black to purple. As the sky gets ready to deliver a hurricane that will keep them indoors for much of the next forty-eight hours, dark clouds are interrupted by streaks of gold, orange, and pink.

She twirls and takes in a 360-degree view of the room, which is palatial. "You've left the farm, Ryan Quinn."

His eyes ping-pong from wall to wall until his face is a map of embarrassed pleasure.

"The Irish don't know how to do luxury without pretending we're Brits."

She grabs his hand and falls backward on the bed. "I, for one, love it."

He falls beside her. "I'll try to cope."

One kiss leads to another. For the first time, there's nothing separating their bodies. Her curves slide under his bulk. She rolls on top, and his hands roam beneath her sweater, over her stomach, into her jeans. She catches her breath and finds his eyes, where she's caressed by his transparent affection. Never one to delay her own or her partner's gratification, she assumes they'll keep going. She's surprised when he moves up against the headboard.

"Are you hungry?"

She laughs. "Do I need to answer that?"

Their hands and eyes continue a dance of seduction. Who knew foreplay had room for a complete beginning, middle, and end? It seems like they've just begun.

He locates the dining room menu in the top drawer of the bedside table and studies it. "Let's change and go downstairs for dinner. The night is long."

She's wearing the cocktail dress she brought from home and hasn't had an occasion to put on until now. Ryan's in a sports jacket over crisp shirt and dark trousers. They agree a tie would be over the top. It's already a novelty to see him wearing anything other than jeans. There are three other tables seated, out of twenty something, when they enter the dining room. The maître d' blames the weather. A gust of wind rattles the floor-to-ceiling windows, which face the ocean, now shrouded in darkness, as they sit.

Ryan orders the shepherd's pie. She goes for the hake. The waiter suggests a bottle of French Burgundy.

"You're shivering."

"Blame it on a little black dress in the dead of an Irish winter."

He takes off his jacket and drapes it on her bare shoulders.

"You have no idea how beautiful you are, do you?"

She blows air out of her cheeks and purses her lips. "Don't do that."

"Do what?"

"Women don't like to be lied to on this subject. The flattery intoxicates us at first, but then we doubt your sincerity."

He puts his palms the air and spreads his fingers. "Whoa. You've been saving that for a poor bloke. Feel better?"

"No." Her throat tightens. She can't believe she's ruining this. Her jaw locks in an unattractive clench, she knows since it's the expression that greets her in the bathroom mirror most mornings. "My face has character, I know that."

He shakes his head. "It's too bad you can't see what I see."

"And what is that?"

"At the risk of having you go off on me again, the real you." He tilts his head as if asking for permission. Since she can't come up with an objection that won't sound sour, she manages a half smile.

"When a woman opens to a man, as I dare say you're doing with me, her face changes. It's an intoxicating thing to behold, and I'm afraid a mirror is useless to capture it."

She stares, floored at the number of surprises this man has stored up for her. "Then I'll just take your word for it." An afterthought, "Thank you."

Flames from the burning logs reward them with warmth and dramatic shadows as they start to peel off their clothes. There's an ease to his movements, apparent when he closes the screen on the crackling fire and unbuttons his shirt. The word *substantial* comes to mind as he stands naked by the bed, extending his hand. She's accustomed to thinner, more metrosexual, vainer men. The shiver running up her torso is a sure tell that she's liking the change as she studies his fullness, the hair on his chest, his muscled biceps, giving equal attention to each hill and valley.

His eyes shine as he takes in her nakedness. She straightens her spine and feels lithe, regal, and, well, beautiful, in his gaze. He takes her hand and falls back on the bed, pulling her onto him, and they land chest to chest. Their eyes meet and they shift to that other heavenly state, where touch is the sole language that matters.

She relishes being able to apply the sexual arts she's mastered with all the wrong men in the wrong places, with this lovely man, in this beautiful place. The thrilling moment when he stops holding back and the soft edges of his cheeks sharpen. When he pulls her butt against his groin and covers her neck and breasts with kisses. She loves the way desire reads on his face as pain as much as pleasure. She delights in playing the sadist who uses her tongue to tease raw desire out as far as it can be stretched before he enters her with a slow glide that gains force as she loses awareness of anything other than the places where their bodies and spirits fuse.

When she opens her eyes, sun is sneaking through the curtains, making an accordion pattern on the bedspread. To her surprise, he's sitting against the headboard. A silver tray with a gleaming coffee pot, Irish bread, butter and jam, orange slices, and berries on the bedside table.

"You've been watching me." She reaches out and touches his stomach.

"I would never have pegged you for such a sound sleeper," he says.

"It must have been that trip to the gym we took before bed."

"No doubt."

She moves next to him. He pours her a cup of coffee.

"Just milk?"

"Right." She grabs a naked slice of bread and takes a bite. "Hmm. That's good."

She chews and catches his eye. "I'm glad we waited."

He guffaws. "Come on. You think I had a choice?'

"What do you mean?"

"You had a No Trespassing sign around your neck since you stepped off the train. I had to work hard just to get you to accept a dinner invitation. And that was just a courtesy."

"Oh, really?"

"I mean, back then."

She brushes his groin as she reaches for blueberries. "I did promise my friend, Joanne, that I'd live like a nun for a year. And now, I've broken my vow." As soon as she says it, Archie comes to mind, and she wishes she hadn't.

He pulls her down on top of him and kisses her. The ease of it all amazes her.

"You know why it happened, don't you?"

"Why what happened?

"Why you opened up to me in these last few weeks?"

"If you think you know, do tell."

"I'll go out on a limb and say you've never been available to anybody before now. And that would never have changed until you took care of your unfinished business with your father. You're a daddy's girl, through and through. I'm just the lucky bloke who was standing closest to you after you let go of him."

She hates to admit he's a little bit right. But if she wants this relationship to be any different from the others, maybe she better do just that. "Okay. I plead guilty. But you know it's not that simple."

"It never is. Hopefully we'll have a long time ahead of us to sort out the details."

"I can't wait."

His hand moves up her thigh. "Meanwhile, it looks like I won the lottery."

She dips in for another kiss.

# Epilogue

## New York City
*June 2013*

Their group fills a large circular table at a fancy Italian restaurant in Murray Hill, Kate's old neighborhood. Two waiters take the order for their group, which includes just about everyone Teague cares about in the world. Kate and Ryan, Joanne and Roger, and Sung. Kate clinks her glass with a fork and picks up the *Village Voice*. Oh, no, she's going to read it.

"Quiet, please, you've got to hear this."

Jesus, everyone in the restaurant is watching them.

"The tonal range of Teague Callahan's wildlife and landscape paintings is breathtakingly real. His works are almost sculptural in their density but retain a resplendent glow. The soft, cool atmosphere he creates with his use of blues allows his creatures to recede into a dreamy haze."

"Sounds right to me." That's Joanne, Kate's friend who's been putting him up in Brooklyn for the last three years.

"Wait, one more sentence . . ."

*Oh, no.*

"This is my favorite part . . . 'His work provokes questions of the metaphysical and hints at the sublime, challenging preconceptions of our

297

existence within nature and in relationship to all God's creatures.'"

Ryan, who's sitting next to him, puts his arm on Teague's shoulder. "Savor it, mate." He holds up his glass of champagne and says to the table. "Here's to a long career as a painter of the sublime and anything else he feckin wants."

"Here, here!" "Mazel tov!" "Absolutely!" Glasses clink around the table.

"Thanks, guys. But it's just the Art Students League. No big deal."

"Oh, Teague." Kate is worrying about his self-esteem. "This critic says your work is extraordinary."

"Yeah. It's a good review. I'm happy about it. But—"

Sung nudges his knee and gives him a *what's up* look. She helps him climb out of the not-so-great place he just fell into. Sung is calm ninety-nine percent of the time. The one percent he knows about is the time he saw her lose her cool when a kid was taunting a homeless guy. She's just finished med school. Her people are from Korea, which is a whole other story. She and Teague are best friends, though he'd like it to be more. Joanne says he needs to show her how he feels. Tell her she looks pretty, which should be easy since she's beautiful . . . except it isn't. Roger says he could just come out and ask Sung if he can kiss her. Teague is still working on a plan.

"It is maybe too much wonderful all at once?" Sung asks him.

"Yeah. Like that."

She squeezes his leg, and he forgets about whatever was bothering him a minute ago.

It's been crazy all week after his senior show opened. The first night they had a reception just for his paintings. He was already tripping when this lady who looked kind of familiar came over to talk to him.

"Teague, you've matured as an artist!"

"Ms. Lacey? Oh wow! It's really you." She looked the same, just as pretty, not as skinny.

"I'm on the Art Students League mailing list. I saw your name on the announcement and I had to come. By the way, my last name is Reilly, now."

He had to think fast to sort that out. Of course, she married somebody besides the guy who died in the car crash. He almost told her how he'd predicted the accident, but he was so happy to see her, he let it go. "Oh, that's great," he said, or close to it. "Do you still teach in Rivervale?"

"No. The school district cut art from the budget a few years ago. For the time being I'm a wife and mother and painting when I have the time."

She asked if she could hug him, and he said sure.

Kate and Joanne are laughing on their side of the table. Ryan asks Roger what he thinks of Edward Snowden, and whether he thinks the NSA spying on phone calls of regular Americans is a problem. Ryan isn't sure but Roger says it's a big problem. Probably because he's a lawyer who fights about who owns ideas and how to go after people when they steal yours. He and Joanne did that for Kate by taking her old dickhead boss to court. Kate won and the dickhead was forced to give her credit for the experiment he stole and pay her a bunch of money, enough to cover his tuition for four years at the Art Students League. There was sex in it, too, but Kate never wanted to talk about that.

She and Ryan are here for a conference, where she's delivering a keynote. He hasn't seen them since last summer, when he went home to Ballymore. Too bad they couldn't bring his little sister and brother, Tara and Mikey, who stayed home with Uncle Marty and Aunt Fiona.

*Oh, no.* He can't believe she did it. A waiter is coming toward their table carrying a cake with lit candles. His birthday is coming up and Kate decided they ought to make tonight a double celebration. Ryan has already passed Teague a birthday card with a nice check to cover his summer expenses. Nobody said as much, but he's guessing it's the last one of those he'll get now that he's graduating. What do artists do for a living before they're famous? He'll have to wash dishes or pick up trash if he wants to stay in New York. The cake has *Happy 25* written in blue letters on chocolate icing.

"No singing or I'm out of here!"

Kate puts on a pouty face. "Okay, sweetheart, if you insist. We'll just watch you blow out the candles. Don't forget to make a wish."

"All right." He closes his eyes, and they show up like they've been waiting for a table out on the sidewalk. Grandpa Jack standing between Gran and Michael. Paddy Mitchell in his apron. Even Mom, looking young and healthy. Hey guys, my wish is that you'll stick close by me from here on because things are going to get harder when I need to figure out how to make a living and still do my art. They smile like they understand . . . and fade away. He blows out the candles, and everyone claps and cheers.

They're standing, putting on jackets, about to leave. Kate comes over and gives him a hug. "I'm proud of you. How are you doing with all the hoopla?"

"Mostly okay. You know."

"Yeah, I do. It's all very exciting. Don't forget, the session starts at eleven, in the ballroom of the Midtown Sheraton, which is on Seventh at Fifty-Third Street. They'll have you and Sung on the VIP guest list."

They're the only normal people in a ballroom filled with a couple thousand neuro-whatevers, and it's as warm as an armpit in here. God, he hopes the humongous chandeliers hanging over their heads are better attached than they look.

There aren't too many people in the world who could get him to spend an hour in a place like this. Okay, he's a teensy bit invested in Kate's speech. He's one of her orchid kids. Not the only one. More like her private poster boy. A guy has finished introducing her, here she goes.

"As the researchers among you know, when an experiment delivers a surprising result, you become Dr. Henry Walton Jones, aka Indiana Jones, beholding the Ark of the Covenant. You're afraid to look too closely, lest you be turned to dust . . . along with your findings and grant funds."

She gets a bunch of laughs.

"That's how Dr. Ryan Quinn and I felt about our attempt to replicate the findings of the Swedish researchers, but with a very different test population made up of older, you might say cynical, preteens and adolescents. We wondered whether those Swedish toddlers were more susceptible to the hugs and kind words of their caretakers. Surely our tough-skinned teenagers wouldn't fall for it. I'm pleased to report that those fears were ungrounded. It turns out there's no expiration date on love and kindness. Or, in the parlance of our social science colleagues, social supports."

Kate takes a drink of water. He was in that test population. Along with Kiernan, who took over his father's cement business and is still a buddy. The twins, even Liam, did interviews and gave their DNA. Liam is still a weird dude because no amount of meds can change who someone is underneath. In the end, all the interviews and DNA tests went into the hopper anonymously, but it was cool to know they were in there together.

"Dr. Quinn's original research, begun in 2003 and published two years later, found that the second-, third-, and fourth-generation offspring of our high-density schizophrenia population in Ballymore showed significant spikes in other conditions not previously linked to schizophrenia, including autism, depression, attention, and conduct disorders. We can no longer keep these disorders in their own lanes. When we decided to find out how our test population would fare going forward, we added a robust treatment and prevention program, run out of Dr. Quinn's Ballymore Mental Health Clinic. Essentially, we were attempting to watch the interaction of nature and nurture in real time."

Ryan is sitting at the end of their row, and he looks happy, even though he's wearing a suit and tie, which he hates. Before this, Teague has seen Ryan dressed up like that just two times: first, on the day he and Kate got married, and then at Grandpa's funeral. That was amazing . . . hundreds of people came to pay their respects, even the parish priest.

"As you know, our team tracked two test populations. Our 'dandelions' had the longer, standard version of the serotonin transporter gene. The ones we call orchids had the risk-conferring version of the same gene. I want to call your attention to our five-year follow-up results. Testing these young people for affect, physical health, and school performance, and taking into account the stability of the households in which they lived, we saw the dandelions in our group fare within a range of satisfactory to good no matter who raised them. Also, as expected, the sensitive orchids who were raised in unstable families performed poorly on most measures. The result we'd been most anticipating did not disappoint. The orchid children who spent their early or middle teen years in stable, supportive families outperformed not only the orchids who'd lived in unstable homes, which we would expect, but also the dandelions who had had the benefit of supportive homes . . . by a full twenty-four percent!"

Kate gets a big round of applause for her finale. She calls Ryan to the stage for the question-and-answer period. Phew. Glad that's over. Sung squeezes his hand.

Back when Kate first told him about her orchid child theory, Teague was skeptical. For one thing, he had no idea what it was like to live in a stable family. He sure hadn't grown up in one. Even after Kate and Ryan had Tara and Mikey and they all lived together, with Sophie on weekends, it took a while to sink in that things would stay that way. People talking instead of yelling at each other. Parents showing up after school when they were supposed to. Rules that stayed the same. Adults not doing Jekyll-and-Hyde shit from one day to the next. No police knocking at the door. He wouldn't have believed it if he didn't live it.

His voices hardly ever come around anymore. If he keeps his stress level down and stays away from weed, he can get by without medication. Kate freaked out at first when he told her he quit for good. In fact, she got on a plane and came to New York to try and talk him out of it. Like he told her, and she eventually accepted, he is lucky he got treated early for schizophrenia and they headed off the worst of it. Just to make sure, she made him promise to keep seeing a shrink in New York.

Lots of people have it much harder. They need to stay on meds forever. Hopefully, the brainiacs in this room will come up with better drugs.

He's lucky in another way. No matter what any critic says about his art, painting is his best medicine.

Last night after he got home, he looked up the word *sublime*. He'd skipped over it when he first read the review because he thought it was one of those churchy words that don't mean anything. It turns out, *sublime* has two meanings.

In chemistry, a material is sublimed when it skips the transition to liquid and goes directly from solid to gas. Like ice turning into vapor. The other meaning is even better. A person gets sublimed when he experiences something so awesome enough it skips thought and goes directly to spirit. He wishes Grandpa was around to hear that and then he remembers . . . he is there.

# NOTES ON THE SCIENCE IN ORCHID CHILD

The study of schizophrenia families depicted in this novel was an actual joint Irish American study conducted with a 50 million dollar grant from the NIMH, in the County of Roscommon (renamed Ballymore herein), during the period 1996 to 2003. Titled The Irish Study of High-Density Schizophrenia Families, among its notable findings was the discovery of the first genetic marker (the dysbindin gene, thought to play a role in information processing in the brain) identified as conferring susceptibility to schizophrenia. Another key finding was the wide number of related disorders in the schizophrenia spectrum carried by effected relatives in subsequent generations.

Other neuroscience research and treatment modalities presented in the novel, including neuro-epigenetics, early intervention for psychosis, and the Orchid Child hypothesis, were also coming to the forefront during the period depicted and have since gained wide currency.

# AUTHOR ACKNOWLEDGEMENTS

In traditional Irish storytelling, a story never ends. The one telling it is expected to add their part and make the tale taller, funnier, and more relevant to whoever is listening. This bit of lore emboldened me to pick up the broken threads of my Irish grandparents' story and conjure the missing pieces of their lives. It then seemed only right to send their fictional descendants back across the Atlantic to deal with the family's unfinished business, both real and imagined. During the decade I spent writing *Orchid Child*, the guiding voice in my head belonged to my paternal grandmother, Ellen Mitchell Costello. I didn't know her in life, but she was always there for me when I needed her. Go in peace, dear Ellen.

Among the living, I'm grateful to my dear friend, Michele Voska, who applied her ninja psychotherapist mind and helped me dig deeper to find this shapeshifting story. I thank Bill Nichols for his very real support, and I owe much to Martha and Gerry Jarocki, who always believed in me, no matter what or who I was mucking around with.

While writing and rewriting this novel's last five or so drafts, I relied on the unwavering support of my Fishtrap writers cadre: Laura Pritchett, Beth McMurray, Maggie Bendickson, Adam Sowards, Janet Buttenwieser, and Jackie Haskins. Early readers who helped me keep the faith include Judith Kirkman Scherer, Carol Piasente, Amy Harren, and Carol Crevier.

Along the way, I got great assists from ace editors Margaret Diehl and Nicole Cunningham. More help came from Joanna Scott, who advised me to read Todorov's *The Fantastic*, which gave me permission to write it weird and let my readers decide.

I thank the goddess for Mindie Burgoyne who took me on her Thin Places Tour—ten days in West Ireland that changed my life and made this novel better and stranger. Two key allies I found there were Con Connor, who showed me his Druid school, and Eilish Feeley, genealogist extraordinaire, who tracked down my long-lost Costello kin and allowed me to complete a journey I began two decades ago.

To my agent, Laura Strachan, thank you for standing by this novel.

Lastly, Abby Macenka, of Between the Lines Publishing, and the Mindbuck Media team, Jessie Glenn, Ivory Fields, and Rae Anderson, you have my undying respect and appreciation for being consummate professionals as you sweated the small stuff to get *Orchid Child* out into the world.

This book would not exist in any form without my sons, Brendan, and Devin, who are my motivation for everything.

Victoria Costello is a writer and teacher of memoir and fiction. She lives in Ashland, Oregon. See her work at www.victoriacostelloauthor.com

CPSIA information can be obtained
at www.ICGtesting.com
Printed in the USA
BVHW042022050323
659610BV00004B/22